Books in This Series

The Kate Morgan Series

Simon Says… Hide, Book 1

Simon Says… Jump, Book 2

Simon Says… Ride, Book 3

Simon Says… Scream, Book 4

Simon Says… Run, Book 5

Simon Says… Walk, Book 6

Simon Says… Forgive, Book 7

Simon Says… Swim, Book 8

Simon Says… Die, Book 9

Simon Says… Think, Book 10

Dale Mayer

SIMON SAYS...
DIE

A KATE MORGAN NOVEL

SIMON SAYS... DIE (KATE MORGAN, BOOK 9)
Beverly Dale Mayer
Valley Publishing Ltd.

ISBN-13: 978-1-778863-71-4
Print Edition

About This Book

Detective Kate Morgan arrives at a broken-down house, supposedly the site of a suspicious death, only to receive a screaming warning from Simon *not* to enter the building. Turns out, she had been given the wrong address but does find a dead body at the corrected address.

As Kate sorts out whether she has a Black Widow on her most recent case, Simon tries to help a homeless man, who ends up in the morgue—now one of Kate's newest files because that poor man's body had been found in the broken-down house. That's nothing compared to what else she finds on the premises.

Kate's investigations into these deaths confirms the two properties have connections, including linking Simon to the haunted history of the broken-down house.

When yet another homeless man is found dead at the broken-down house, Kate struggles to sort out the different threads, before the next man is killed—and this one might not be so homeless …

Sign up to be notified of all Dale's releases here!
https://geni.us/DaleNews

CHAPTER 1

First Week of December

KATE MORGAN HAD fast become quite accustomed to counterbalancing work with some free time on the *Running Mate.* They'd been spending more and more time out on Simon's newest purchase, even if just for a couple hours here and there, plus a long weekend or two. It was a perk of the relationship that she was more than happy to enjoy.

As she walked into the bullpen, feeling content, happy, and settled somehow, the others chimed in with a chorus of greetings.

She laughed. "I made it through a whole three days in a row without any witching hour calls this time."

"Yes, but even *one* day on *that* boat," Lilliana said, with an eye roll, "talk about lucky."

"Yeah, you're right about that," Kate agreed. "Talk about lucky, and I don't feel guilty about it at all."

"Good," Lilliana replied. "That's the way to do it. Besides, with a dreamboat like Simon, you should be enjoying yourself."

Having never heard her say anything remotely like that about him before, Kate just laughed.

Meanwhile Rodney looked over at her from his desk and asked, "So, are you recovered?"

"Sure, as recovered as we ever have a chance to get, with more murder cases coming in daily. I've still got some belated reports to finalize, but it's all good."

"Great. We just got a call."

"What kind of a call?" she asked, taking off her coat. "Are we going out?"

"We sure are. Some kids were playing around in an abandoned house, and they say they found a body."

"Did any adult confirm?"

"No, they phoned us first," he replied, with a bright smile. "We're getting the public trained in some ways."

She rolled her eyes at that. "Bet the kids went back."

He laughed. "I won't bet on that because, when it comes to kids, you can never tell, except that all too frequently they're up to no good."

"Ha, good thing I don't have any."

"Oh, but you will," he presumed, with a laugh. "This thing with you and Simon? That's likely to get *hella-serious* real fast."

She stared at him in shock. "Even if it does get *hella-serious real fast*," she replied, "that has nothing to do with having kids."

He just nodded and didn't say anything.

As they got into the vehicle, she asked, "Did they say anything about the body?"

"Yeah. It was dead."

She groaned, rolled her eyes at his sick joke, and added, "I gather you're doing fine."

"I am," he said, with a nod. "Life's okay. And now we have a little wiggle room at work. It seems like some of the crime wave has eased back a bit, so … it's okay."

"Except for this one."

"Yeah, but we get these things every once in a while. It's probably a junkie."

"Maybe," she agreed, "at least then it's likely to be a fairly open-and-shut case."

They walked up to what was once a beautiful house, at least in her day, but now she looked like a grande dame in distress. Kate stopped outside, checked with Rodney on the address.

He confirmed, "Yeah, this is the place." He frowned, as he looked around. "It's a pretty high-end area for a junkie to die in."

"I'm surprised the neighbors haven't complained about this house."

"It's probably caught up in all legal craziness, city rules, or estate issues, whatever," he noted.

Her phone rang just then. She looked down and frowned. "It's Simon."

"Go ahead and take it. I hate to disturb young love. Go on."

She glared at him.

"Take it. Take it. You'll be fussing the whole time if you don't. He probably just wants to tell you how much he misses you," he teased, with an eye roll.

She answered the phone, with a panicked screaming Simon on the other end.

"I don't know where you are or what you're up to, but don't go in that house!"

She froze, looked over at Rodney, who was already walking toward the front door. "Rodney, come back," she yelled. "Wait. Come here."

He turned, frowned, and stepped back toward her. "What's the matter?"

She held up the phone, putting Simon on Speaker. "Simon, say that again."

"Do not go into that house," he roared. "I don't know anything about it, but, all I can tell you is that, if you go into the house, the outcome will not be good."

"When you say *not good*, what do you mean?" she asked cautiously.

"Going inside that house means you'll die."

CHAPTER 2

KATE STARED AT Rodney, a question in her gaze. She turned and looked back at the house, then leaned forward to speak to Simon on the phone. "Are you sure?"

Exasperation filled his tone but also vestiges of panic. "Yes, damn it, I'm sure. And, before you ask, no, I don't know how, and I certainly don't know why. Just get the hell out of there fast, please," he pleaded.

Kate agreed and immediately turned in the direction of their car, while Simon ended the call. She couldn't even believe her feet were following Simon's instructions without any reasonable explanation. Yet how could she not? How could she ignore it when he was so obviously panicked?

She sat once again in the car, eyeing the area, the rich neighborhood, and this monstrous old house. Still looking around and feeling the unsettling pull, she asked Rodney, "Who called in the body?"

Rodney checked his phone and repeated what she already knew. "We had an anonymous tip about the body from a youngster on a pay phone or some burner phone or whatever. Then a black-and-white came to check it out and confirmed a body was in there."

She nodded slowly and asked suspiciously, "Where is that black-and-white now?"

Rodney looked around and started to swear.

"Exactly," Kate replied. "Nobody's here, and we would have walked right into that house, and there may or may not be a body at all in this one. But right now," she stated, searching for anything at all, "I'm much more concerned about where the cop is who supposedly came and checked it out."

"Are you thinking that they didn't even come and that it was a prank call?"

"It would be on record that they came," she noted. "At least I would think so. I'm not sure how that part of our reporting system works," she admitted in exasperation. "I need to sort that out a little bit more."

Just then Rodney's phone rang, and it was Reese, the department's analyst. "Hey, apparently you've got the wrong address."

Rodney turned toward Kate, his eyebrows shooting up.

Kate winced, holding her breath, trying not to go berserk. "How the hell did that happen?"

"I guess the cop who entered the info on the welfare check was pretty shaken up by what he saw, and he got it wrong."

"So, what is the correct address?" Rodney asked, and Kate wrote it down and recognized that it was the same house number but a couple streets over. "So, he's absolutely sure about that address now?"

"Yes, apparently the coroner is on his way over, and other black-and-whites are there." After a moment, apparently sensing tension in their voices, Reese followed up by asking, "Is there a problem?"

"Not necessarily." Kate spoke slowly, as she tried to sort this out. "We'll be there in a minute."

Rodney ended the call and frowned at her, sitting in

their still-parked car. "What the hell?"

"I don't know what to say." Kate got out and took several photos of the neighborhood and the wrong house, then settled into the vehicle once again. With a glance at Rodney, she muttered, "Let's go." She tried hard not to make her tone as brisk as she wanted it to be. However, she felt a complete sense of something gone wrong.

He punched the correct address into the GPS and drove them there, as he glanced at her several times. Yet she didn't look back at him. "You want to explain to me what just went on?" he finally asked.

"How the hell would I know?" she replied. "We were sent to the wrong house, and then Simon calls us in a panic." She pinched the bridge of her nose. "I don't know anything, except what Simon told me. *If we went in that house ... we would die.*"

"What the hell?" he muttered. "And Reese confirmed it was the wrong address. So is Simon picking up something from the wrong house or from the correct one?"

"The first one, but who knows what it was."

"Then not our business."

She glared at Rodney. "That depends. What if somebody else goes into that house? Will they die? And, if we have Simon's warnings, are we responsible to report them?"

"Ah, shit," Rodney muttered. "You're right. ... I suppose it's an easy mistake to make with this house to that one."

"Maybe," she muttered, "but it's not a mistake that we're used to. When was the last time we went to the wrong address for a dead body?"

He snorted. "Never."

"Exactly. Plus, with a highly unusual mistake like that,

we should have been corrected long before we got here."

"It's not as if we were early getting there either," Rodney pointed out. "We had been doing interviews for other cases."

"Precisely."

"It's all kind of …"

She gave him a wry look and added, "It's all wrong, so let's just leave it there."

He shook his head. "Yeah, because it does seem to be *all* wrong."

Rodney pulled into the correct neighborhood, and very quickly they knew they were in the right place because black-and-whites were everywhere. Even the coroner's vehicle had just pulled up to the front yard of the mega-mansion. She watched as Dr. Smidge got out near her.

Rodney groaned. "*Great*, my favorite person."

She grinned at her partner because Rodney was right. Smidge was not the easiest person to talk to. "He's a piece of work."

"But he sure talks to you."

"He talks to you too," she replied. "You've just got a problem with him."

"Why would anybody want to deal with dead bodies all day?"

She raised an eyebrow at that question. "Do you know how many people would say the same thing about us, asking why we would want to deal with all these violent crimes day in and day out?"

He shrugged. "Makes more sense than Smidge's job."

She laughed. "Honestly, I think I could probably do that job."

Rodney stared at her in horror and then winced. "Yeah, you probably could. Something is very abnormal about you too."

"I'll take that as a compliment," she muttered, as she ducked under the yellow tape, nodding at the police officer as she held up her badge to identify herself. Catching one officer off to the side, who looked a little green around the gills, she walked over to him and asked him point-blank, "Are you the responding officer?"

He winced and nodded. "Is it that obvious?" he asked.

She knew he was pretty shaken up from whatever he'd seen, and she gave him a nod. "So, you're the one who gave us the wrong address?"

He nodded again. "Yeah, sorry about that. ... I was busy upchucking into the bushes. It's pretty ugly in there."

"Got it, thanks for the heads-up. Now, the wrong address you did give us, have you ever been there before?"

He looked at her and shrugged. "I have no idea. I didn't even think to check the address online. Is there a problem?"

"Not necessarily," she stated, not giving him any more information than that. She turned and followed another cop, who took her to the crime scene in the residence's home office. Once inside, she almost bumped into Smidge, who turned and glared at her, ready to rip whoever had gotten so close to him.

She smiled as she looked at him expectantly, as if meeting someone pleasant and sharing casual chitchat. "Fancy meeting you here."

He glared at her. "There are better places to meet."

"Yeah, apparently *we* have a problem," she pointed out, with a shrug. "We both prefer to be here."

He let out a whooping laugh that made everybody turn to them. "Yeah, we're both sick, aren't we?"

"Sometimes you've got to wonder," she conceded, with a

nod to the dead body. "So, this one is straightforward? Or is there such a thing?"

"I don't think there is such a thing," Rodney snorted, coming up behind her.

Smidge indicated the body, then frowned. "Single gunshot to the head."

She wandered closer. "Not suicide," she muttered.

Rodney frowned at her. "Don't you want to wait for that call?"

"No, I do not," she replied, with a nod.

Smidge eyed her, a smile playing at the corner of his lips. "Why not, Detective?"

"He would have to be left-handed," she pointed out, "but his pen's resting on the right-hand side of the notepad."

Rodney looked from the victim to the notepad and swore. "I didn't even see that, but maybe the killer switched the notepad."

"I don't think so. Look. You can see that the pad is pressed down slightly where his arm is." Then she walked over to see the writing on the notepad and nodded. "The suicide note doesn't read as if written freely. It doesn't read true."

Rodney came up behind her, read it, and asked, "What part doesn't seem true?" He then read it out loud. *"Honey, I'm sorry. I can't do this anymore."*

"Yeah, sure," Kate said, glancing from the body to the people standing beside her. "But short of, *honey*—whoever that is—having some idea of what it is he can't do anymore, and providing that answer for us, there must be more to it," she determined in a clipped tone. "And really, if you were leaving a suicide note, wouldn't you say why or at least tell everyone you love them one last time or something?" She shook her head. "It doesn't ring true to me."

Rodney shrugged. "I think you're making too much out of this one."

"She is right about one thing," Smidge added, with a snort. "Our victim is right-handed, and he definitely wasn't shot in a way that is consistent with his pulling the trigger, even though it's been made to look that way."

"So, first things first," Kate added, with a nod to Rodney. "Let's check out life insurance plans."

Smidge gave a bark of laughter. "When did you become so cynical?" Then he grinned at the detectives. "Forget I asked that."

"Yeah, working on this job," she muttered, as she gave him a knowing expression, "that would have been the first thought in your head too."

"Yep," Smidge confirmed, "but we've been wrong before."

"Yeah, so find me anything you can," she replied, turning to Rodney and giving him a calculated expression of misery. "We'll go find the wife." She turned, and Rodney followed her out of the room.

Rodney sighed. "I don't get it. How is it that the two of you get along so well?"

"And here I expected you to say that we were two peas in a pod." Kate chuckled because her and Smidge's every interaction was riddled with jabs and whatnots.

"In a way, you are," Rodney pointed out, "but it's freaky because he's definitely not easy to get along with."

From behind them, they heard Smidge's booming voice, as he called out, "I heard that."

Rodney stopped, rolled his eyes upward, and muttered, "Of course you did." Picking up the pace, he moved forward rapidly, obviously hoping that Smidge hadn't heard that last bit either.

Kate laughed as she stepped into the kitchen. "Comments like that will not help, you know?"

Rodney shrugged. "It's as if the guy's got ears in the back of his head."

"He probably does," she agreed, with a chuckle, "considering the fact that he often wears earplugs and is in his own world."

"And yet he's frequently *not* in his own world. It would be a lot easier if he were."

She shook her head. "He's not that hard to get along with, Rodney."

"You're the only person on the planet who would say that," he muttered. "Everybody else believes the opposite."

"Maybe it's time to change your belief then," she countered, as she entered the dining room and found the wife standing beside the table, looking shell-shocked and staring out the window. "Mrs., ah …" Kate paused, looking down at her notepad, "Mulhouse?"

The woman turned to her and nodded. "Yes, I'm Amie Mulhouse."

"I'm sorry to meet you under these circumstances," Kate began, introducing herself and Rodney. "May we sit down and make you a little more comfortable, while we ask you a few questions?"

"Why would you need to ask me anything?" she replied, trying hard to hold back her tears. "Isn't it self-explanatory? For whatever reason he decided that life was too difficult, apparently too difficult to even explain why it was too difficult," she shared, looking at Kate with an exhausted gaze.

Just enough bitterness filled her tone to make Kate consider her closely. "I'm sorry. I know this is not an easy time."

"No, you don't know," Amie declared, turning on her, some fury spilling out. "This is a betrayal in the worst way possible."

"In what way?"

"What do you mean, *in what way*?" Amie repeated, staring at Kate in shock. "My husband just offed himself and didn't give a crap about telling me why or what was so horrible or so hard that he couldn't even begin to deal with it. So, you tell me, Detective. Is it supposed to be easy on me, or I am allowed to feel some betrayal?"

"I'm sure a lot of surviving family members feel that way," Kate explained, "but I'm not sure that your husband's death was a suicide. We are waiting for the coroner to get back to us on that."

Amie stared at them in shock. "What?"

Kate just stared back, not giving an inch, as Amie's gaze went from Kate to Rodney, then back again.

"Are you serious? He left a note. I saw it and assume you did too."

Kate shrugged. "That is just one piece of evidence. Notes can be forged, and who's to say it's even his writing?"

"I told you that I saw it," Amie stated. "It's Robert's writing."

"When did you last see your husband alive?"

Amie stared at her. "I can't believe you're not treating this as a suicide," she replied, an almost hysterical edge to her tone.

"I didn't say we aren't. However, we're keeping our minds open, until we hear back from the coroner."

Rodney walked over to Mrs. Mulhouse, gently pulled out a dining room chair, and helped her sit down. "Just let us do our job, and then we'll all know for sure." And, with that, Rodney asked several questions to which Amie responded readily.

Yet whenever Kate brought up something, Amie clammed up and glared at her—a reaction that Kate found very interesting.

She didn't generally get the hate so specifically directed her way, but having brought up the fact that it may not have been a suicide was apparently enough for Amie to rule Kate out as being a nice person. Rodney was not tainted in that way, and, since he obviously had a better line of communication with Amie, Kate quickly headed back into the home office, where the body was located.

Smidge looked up at her and asked, "How is she?"

"Not quite the way I would expect."

He nodded. "Yeah, that was my take too."

"Was she here when you arrived?"

He nodded again. "She was kneeling on the floor beside our victim, and I had something to say to the cop who didn't secure the scene."

"What was she doing?" Kate asked instantly.

"Just sitting here, bawling her eyes out."

Kate lowered her voice and asked, "But was she really, or was it just for appearances?"

"That's for you to tell me," he replied. "I don't understand women at the best of times, so it's hard for me to pinpoint what she was up to. Still, I was skeptical of it."

Kate nodded. "Yeah, she already made me suspicious because she's incredibly feisty and defensive over having to answer *my* questions, but it seems she'll talk to Rodney just fine."

Smidge snorted at that. "At least she'll talk to one of

you."

"Which is always why it's a good idea to come in twos," Kate noted, with a knowing smile in his direction. "Who knows what goes through anybody's mind at these times?"

"And we never really know how we'll react until something happens," he pointed out.

She nodded. "I'll go through this office, unless you want me out of the way."

He looked around. "Yeah, I need you out of the way."

"Good enough," Kate said. "Any problem with my going up to the bedroom?"

"I haven't been up there yet, so go ahead. Our focus will be here on the crime scene."

"Right," she muttered, and she quickly walked upstairs to check out the master bedroom. Once there, she made a cursory check in one of the night tables, which interestingly enough was loaded with condoms. She wondered how many married couples still used condoms as a method of birth control or whether Mr. Mulhouse kept them for other encounters.

Kate moved to look over on Amie's side and found birth control pills. In the bathroom, she found various sex toys in one of the cabinets. Making notes, but not seeing anything terribly unusual at this point, Kate continued her search, wondering what had been going on in the dead man's head, even as she felt a steady nudge in the back of her own mind that this wasn't a suicide. Just no way. Sure, somebody could have rearranged things at the scene afterward. Regardless, she would try to keep an open mind.

Once she was done searching the upstairs, she went back downstairs and walked over to Smidge and, in a low tone, asked if he had a time of death for her.

He checked his watch, then spoke. "It's ten in the morning now, and, judging by the state of the body, I would say probably between three and six this morning." Smidge added, "Of course I'll provide something more precise when I get back to the office."

"Good enough." Kate returned to the kitchen, where Rodney was in a very solicitous mood, making tea for Amie. When Kate entered the adjoining dining room, Amie stiffened and glared at her. Noting the belligerence, for whatever particular reason, Kate asked, "Amie, where were you between three and six this morning?"

She frowned at her in astonishment. "Here … asleep."

"And your husband, when did you last see him alive?"

"Last night," she replied, stifling a sob. "We both went to bed around … I would say around eleven o'clock. I read for a little bit, and he went straight to sleep."

Kate nodded. "Do you have any idea why he would do something like this?"

"Yet you already told me that it wasn't a suicide."

"No, I didn't," Kate corrected. "We must cover all avenues."

"No, my God, no. … I don't know of any reason," she muttered. "I thought we were happily married."

"Just because he took his own life, or may have," Rodney interjected, "it doesn't mean he didn't love you."

She stared at him. "How is that love?" she asked bitterly, and a sob escaped her. "How is doing something like this to anybody *love*?"

He didn't know what to say to that, and Kate quickly asked Amie a few more questions. "Did you have anybody over last night? Was anybody here who could confirm what you're saying?"

"Of course not." Amie stared at Kate as if she were quite stupid.

That attitude was starting to really grate on her.

"The two of us, we were asleep," Amie declared, raising both hands.

"So, after you got up, then what?"

"What do you mean, *then what*? I got up. I had a shower, got dressed, and came downstairs."

"Were you surprised that your husband wasn't there in bed with you?"

"No, he always gets up ahead of me," she stated, turning to Rodney. "I tend to be a get-up-and-go kind of person, more or less. He, on the other hand, needs a little more time, and that's why he likes to get up early and have a cup of coffee on his own." Glaring at Kate and sounding defensive, Amie added, "That's not unusual, you know?"

"Of course not," Kate agreed, with a nod. "Whatever makes a marriage work, makes a marriage work." Amie seemed to relax slightly at that, but then Kate blew it with her next question. "Do you have any reason to suspect that he might be having an affair or trouble at work or anything that would give you some indication that he would do this?"

Amie stared at her. "Did you say, *affair*?" she asked, with wide eyes and an ominous tone.

Kate sighed. "I'm trying to figure out why he would have done this, and I would really appreciate it if you could bear with me a few more minutes. Then I'll be out of your hair."

Amie rolled her eyes at her. "I don't have an answer for what he did. No one wants to understand why he's done this more than me, I can assure you."

"So, you don't know if he had a recent medical diagnosis

or anything of that nature that may have been too much for him to handle?"

"Not that I know of."

"And you don't know if he was having an affair or some dalliance of that nature?"

"God no, nothing of the sort."

"Did he get fired, or was he struggling at work? Anything?"

And that *anything* part set off Amie again. Kate listened to Amie ramble on about how their marriage was perfect, how she had no idea what was going on, and how dare Kate imply that anything was wrong.

With a headshake, Kate turned and headed back into the home office, where Smidge gave her a hint of a smile.

"I hear you're as sensitive as always with the bereaved."

She snorted. "Apparently I'm not sensitive at all. Not sure why people can't just answer a question," she muttered, shaking her head.

He burst out laughing. "You don't think it has anything to do with the way you asked her?"

"I'm sure it does," she conceded, staring at him, "but the facts remain. We have a dead man, and nobody is prepared to discuss how that happened or why."

Smidge nodded and looked down at the body that even now was loaded onto a gurney. "I can only give you the little bit I have," he shared, as he lowered his voice. "As you pointed out, he didn't commit suicide, unless somebody tampered with evidence here … and that is always possible."

She nodded. "I was considering that, but I forgot to ask about security, damn it."

"There is security. I already checked, but nobody was in or out in the wee hours of the morning."

She frowned at him and nodded slowly. "Was it shut off at all?" He shook his head. She lowered her voice and asked, "What about earlier?"

He frowned at her. "I only checked the relevant time period."

"Fine," she replied. "I'll grab the security tapes and go through it all."

"You're thinking somebody else came in earlier?"

"I'm not sure what to think at this point," she admitted, "but ... it's a little off."

"Yeah, you're not kidding," Smidge muttered, "but I trust that you'll figure it out."

She laughed. "As well as can be, anyway." Heading back into the dining room, Kate found Amie sobbing quietly. Looking over at Rodney, Kate shared, "We'll need to get the security camera footage."

Amie was startled, then nodded. "I don't have much to do with the system. The tapes are in his office."

Kate nodded. "Fine. I'll collect them to review back at the office." And, with that, she quickly left again, not wanting to be very close to Amie, yet not exactly sure why. All the potential reasons why weren't the easiest for Kate to consider in her head either.

With the security camera videos collected, she rejoined Rodney and motioned to him. "Time to head back to the office, *huh*?"

He nodded, then looked over at Amie Mulhouse. "Your friend should be here in a few minutes."

She continued to sob and nodded. "Thank you." She eyed him a little desperately. "You've been very kind." Then her gaze fell on Kate, and she stiffened. "At least the police department has somebody who's nice."

Kate gave her a flat smile. "I'm focused on investigating your husband's death," she murmured, and, with that, the two of them left.

As soon as they got outside, Rodney noted, "She didn't like you much, did she?"

"Yeah, you're not kidding." Kate shrugged.

"Of course you did imply that her husband was murdered and having an affair, so that didn't help."

"I'm not here to help killers get away with their crimes," she stated. "I'm here to figure out exactly what's going on."

"Do you really think he was murdered?"

"Yeah, at this very moment, I sure do," she declared, "or did you not get that memo?"

"Does Smidge agree with you?"

"Yep, he does, unless somebody tampered with the evidence at the scene," she clarified. "Then that would be a whole different story. His forensics team is on it, and I will follow up with that and the security footage."

"You probably could have checked the security there."

"Smidge already did, and nobody was in or out during the wee hours of the morning."

"So, Mulhouse really did commit suicide."

She frowned at him. "That is not a deduction I'm prepared to make based simply on the fact that the security wasn't accessed in that time period."

He shook his head. "You don't really think Amie did it, do you?"

Kate groaned. "Could you keep the bleeding-heart sympathy for other cases?" She then glanced at him in exasperation. "Not one where we potentially have a murder by somebody who would have been in the house at those hours, and, according to her, she was the only one in the house."

His lips snapped shut, and he got behind the wheel of the car. "That doesn't mean she had anything to do with it," he replied stiffly.

She groaned again. "Look. Call her on your free time. Do whatever you want, but please keep personal feelings out of the case."

He winced. "I sounded a little defensive, didn't I?"

"*Ya think?*" she asked, with a sigh. "I'm not accusing her of anything, but I really don't want to fight you and Amie every step of the way through this investigation."

"Ouch." He shook his head.

"Yeah, how do you think I feel?" Kate muttered, and, with that, he remained silent until they got to the office. Once there, she pulled in all the statements and reports available so far from the various officers who had been on the scene. She would return to revisit the home as soon as she got more information from Smidge. However, right now, she didn't have a whole lot. Just as she finished typing up her notes from her initial interview with Amie, Smidge phoned.

"You want to come down?"

"On my way," she replied, as she looked over at Rodney, who was busy talking with Lilliana. Kate hesitated for a moment, then shrugged and announced, "I'm heading down to the morgue."

They both ignored her, as the morgue was not the place for them, if they had any other option. As for Kate, she didn't mind. Knowledge could be found in that morgue, plus a sense of serenity and peace. So, needing answers, Kate knew that would be the place to find them.

She also understood that most of the team had a problem with Smidge, and it didn't help that Smidge had a problem with all of them too. That generally included her as well, yet she and Smidge had managed to forge an understanding. As long as she got along with him, or anyone really, she was more than prepared to bend over backward to make happen whatever Smidge needed, particularly if he would also make happen whatever she needed as well.

CHAPTER 3

SIMON HADN'T HEARD back from Kate after his panicked phone call earlier this morning. That didn't tell him a whole lot and made him uncomfortable. She didn't even call to ask him what his warning was all about either. That worried him most of all. Finally deciding that he needed to check on her, he sent her a text. **Are you okay?**

He got a thumbs-up emoji and a response. **On a new case.**

He smiled at that, not that it was anything worth smiling about. However, if ever anything could distract Kate, it was a new case. He sent her his own thumbs-up, happy that he'd gotten an answer from her at least and confirmation that she was okay.

He still didn't understand what the hell that warning from this morning had been all about. He wasn't at all sure that he even wanted to delve into it, but something *wrong* was going on in whatever house that was, but he didn't know what exactly. He couldn't tell whether it was a man-made danger or something completely different. He just knew that something was off.

Turning his attention back to his own job and his own work, he walked up to see Danny, a suicide survivor, working beside Joe, one of Simon's foremen, as the two unloaded lumber. Simon watched them, smiled, and then nodded. Danny had been a decent addition to the crew. As long as Joe could keep an eye on Danny, which Simon had to give Joe credit for, Danny seemed to be settling more into the reality of life. Then again, maybe it was just wishful thinking on Simon's part, but the last thing he wanted was a suicide on his plate, and something had been just so inherently good about this kid that it would be a damn shame if they couldn't get Danny to deal with his issues.

Simon knew Danny went to therapy because Simon was paying for it. Danny didn't know about that part, but, should it ever come up, Simon would be totally okay to tell Danny. Simon didn't believe he had any real need to keep these secrets, since secrets caused all these problems in the first place. Which brought him back to the warning for Kate this morning. Wishing he had answers now, yet he would wait, as they would surely discuss this later, when she got home.

Generally, whenever he got these psychic warnings, it had something to do with her and the cases she was involved in. Even if he tried to send out messages into the ether that he wasn't interested in being a psychic, that he refused to deal with all the woo-woo stuff, these telepathic messages bypassed any barriers or blocks or security systems he thought he had in place in his mind. Acknowledging this made him feel as if he had absolutely no control over any of it, which he didn't.

Just then Joe called out, "Hey, are you okay?"

Simon turned to face his property manager, who had seen Simon freeze on the way over to join them. Simon nodded. "Yeah, sorry, just a lot on my mind."

"Some days are worse than others apparently," Joe teased, with a big grin.

Simon nodded and addressed the two of them, "How are things today?"

Danny grinned at him. "They're just fine." He looked over at Joe and added, "I'll head back over to the guys."

"You do that," Joe replied, as Danny took off.

"How is he handling things?" Simon asked Joe.

"He's doing really well," Joe stated, a note of affection in his tone.

"Sounds as if you two are hitting it off."

"We are, and it's nice to see a kid who gets it. He's had some tough times, but he's pulling through, and we've got to give him credit for that."

"Absolutely. The last thing we want is a downward slide. Slides are … deadly."

"They are, indeed." Joe nodded. "That's all right. I'm keeping an eye on him."

"Good. Any problems with the project?"

"You mean, outside of the usual?" Joe gave Simon an eye roll. "We got shorted on our lumber today. The back-ordered roofing tiles still haven't come. Two of our guys didn't show up today, so we'll be a little shorthanded."

"Tradesmen?"

"No, in this case, general labor."

"It would be worse if our plumbers or electricians were absent, I guess." Simon groaned. "Yet we have a shortage of laborers overall as it is."

"True," Joe agreed, even with a smile, "but it's part of the deal in the construction industry. Still, we're holding steady overall. So it's all good." After going over a few other details, Joe waved him away. "Go on, go off, do something else," he suggested. "We're fine here."

Simon laughed. "I'm glad to hear that, since I don't

want anything to hold back this project."

"We're on target, as much as we can be when we're talking about another six months," he clarified. "However, right now, we're moving along in the right direction. So go do something else, and, for God's sake, get that look off your face."

"What look is that?" Simon asked his friend curiously, even as he started to walk away.

"The one that says that you can't figure out something going on in your world."

Simon turned to him and frowned.

Joe replied in a low tone, so no one else could hear. "You never really talk about it, but I know that you get these *feelings*."

"Yeah, I do," Simon admitted. "And you're right. I generally don't talk about it."

"And I'm not asking you to. I just know, from that expression on your face, that something is brewing."

Simon winced. "I was hoping it wasn't noticeable."

"Maybe to somebody who doesn't know you as well as I do," Joe pointed out, with a grin. "Yet we've been working together for a lot of years. When shit happens, it's generally something I hear about, even if you don't tell me. And I've been hearing an awful lot of it lately."

And, with that, Simon nodded and headed to his usual coffee shop, where he picked up a coffee and walked to his next rehab project site. Joe was right though. Something was definitely coming down. The problem was, Simon had absolutely no way to know what it was among all the possible shit going around, and that thought had him on edge. In time, he noticed he had taken the wrong route.

Groaning, he turned and changed his route to the block

that took him down and around to his project. As he approached, he heard shouting on the scaffolding. He looked up to see several of his men arguing. He let out a roaring whistle that stopped them all in their tracks.

Embarrassed, the men winced. "Now you're in for it," one of the workers yelled at the other. "That's the boss."

His foreman for this project rushed over to see him. "Hey, I know it sounds bad, but it's not as bad as it seems."

"If you say so." Simon glared up at the scaffold. "Fifty feet up is not the place for an argument."

"No, it sure as hell isn't," his foreman agreed. "Permission to fire one of them?"

"Why?" Simon asked, turning to face him.

"Because he keeps riling everybody up, just causing shit for no reason."

"Such as?" Simon asked, eyeing his foreman closer. "We are so short-staffed that he's got to be making real headaches for us to get rid of him."

"Yeah, he's already making real headaches," his foreman declared.

Simon sighed and then nodded. "Get rid of him then. Better we have people who know what *getting along* means than having to deal with this shit." He stared up at the scaffold, even now coming down to ground level.

"Done," Steven declared, as he walked over to the two guys on the scaffold. He pivoted to add, "And everything else is fine here, by the way."

"Are you sure?" Simon asked.

"Yeah, I'm sure," he confirmed, then shrugged. "I just need to get rid of a troublemaker."

The conversation with the terminated employee was short and swift, and the guy was removed rather quickly from the property. Simon watched the efficiency with which his foreman dealt with it.

When he rejoined Simon, a sense of satisfaction on his face, Simon noted, "You've been wanting to do that for a while, haven't you?"

"Sure have," he agreed, "but we're shorthanded, and that's why I kept him. Yet, if anybody caused us trouble, it was always him."

"What trouble though … and why? I don't understand that whole mentality."

"No, you and I don't. … I get that the guy's got some issues and that he's struggling with them, but that isn't our problem. I can't have that disobedience in the crew, especially up on the scaffolding."

"No, we sure as hell can't," Simon concurred, staring at Steven. "You never did tell me what trouble he causes."

He faced Simon and winced. "Trouble that makes people worry … as in threats, subtle little digs behind the back, saying that a strap might get cut one day, or he'll ensure that somebody doesn't come back down from being up top."

"Lord Jesus, we don't need that shit in our workplace."

"Exactly, and most of the time all these other guys are good. We've worked with them for quite a while, and I don't have any problems with them." Steven paused. "Then this guy comes along, and all of a sudden trust becomes a problem." With that, he launched into a rundown of all the rehab problems of the day.

Simon groaned. "It would be nice if, one time, we had a rundown of all the *successes* of the day."

"*Right,*" Steven murmured. "The nature of the business means that we generally have more problems, more scheduling conflicts, more supply issues, and, of course, more inspectors."

Simon listened to the litany of issues, as he nodded at times and asked the occasional question. Just when he was about finished and could walk away, his phone rang. He checked his cell phone screen and held up his hand. "Hang on. I'll be back in a minute." He stepped off to the side and answered the realtor's call. "What the hell are you doing calling me right now?" he asked in exasperation.

"I have another building for you," Ariel replied in a preemptory tone.

He hesitated. "I'm pretty full up at the moment."

"I'm sure you are," she agreed, "but it's one that's been on your list for a while."

"How would you know?" he asked, a sarcastic and lethal edge to his comment.

"Look," she began. "We don't always get along … but I do know the buildings you're looking for and the ones that you work on."

"Maybe," he conceded, "but it's very bold of you to assume to know what I'm after."

She laughed. "I could say something coy about you being male and what you're all after," she quipped, "but, in your case, you're a bit of an enigma."

"Why? Just because I keep turning you down for anything beyond business?" he asked in a mocking tone.

She snorted. "Okay, fine. I guess I deserved that. I thought maybe we could have a relationship beyond business, my bad."

"I told you repeatedly that I'm already in a relationship and that I don't cheat," he stated calmly. "Now, if you've got something to say to me about a legitimate business matter, then speak away."

"The Paragon building."

That made his eyebrows go up. She was right. It was on his list. "What's going on with it?" he asked.

"The original owner has passed away."

"I know," he stated, "but it's been caught up in a court case between the two brothers and is still pending investigation. Isn't that right?"

"One of the parties was killed in a car accident and left no issue behind, resulting in the remaining share of the building going to the last remaining brother in the court case."

Simon pondered that. "Are we sure the other brother's death was an accident? Was something done to knock off the family member?"

"Wow," she muttered, then laughed. "I guess that's always something that the cops would look at. I'm surprised to hear you consider it in that way."

"I'm not investing my time and money only to find out down the road that the last standing sibling doesn't have full legal rights to the property."

"It was a head-on car collision and has been listed as an accident, with absolutely no sign of anyone else's involvement. Therefore, not any connection or anything to do with the remaining heir."

"At least that you know of," Simon pointed out in a qualifying tone.

"Exactly, but regardless, it will be up for sale. He wants it settled smoothly, cleanly, and as fast as possible."

"And for as much money as possible, I'm sure," Simon added in a dry tone.

"I don't even think the biggest offer is necessarily an issue with him. I think it's more about his feeling incredibly guilty over the court case with his brother and wanting to find a way to get past it."

"Interesting," Simon murmured. "What figures are we talking about?" Simon was definitely surprised to hear the beginning price.

She added, "From your silence, I guess you weren't expecting that."

"I'll take a look at it," he replied.

"At least you're interested."

"Depends," he noted. "Are you planning to set up a bidding war?"

"I know, if I do, that you're out."

"Exactly. I won't do business that way."

"Yet you do realize that a lot of the world doesn't have a choice."

"That's a problem for the rest of the world," he pointed out. "I'm only prepared to do business one way. If you don't want to deal with it, that's fine."

"Hey, that's okay," she replied. "I didn't say I wasn't prepared to."

"No, but you were checking it out."

"Hey, you've got to understand that I'm representing the seller."

"You can't represent both of us," he stated, with an inward smile. "I'm sure that's an issue for you."

"It certainly makes my life more difficult, but we can run it through somebody else in my company."

"I have my own realtor," he reminded her, "which you are aware of too."

She sighed. "Every time I turn around and try to make things easy, you just get belligerent."

"Oh, this wasn't belligerence," he muttered. "Trust me

that you do not want to see me getting belligerent."

"Nope, I sure don't," she agreed, with half a laugh. "Anyway, if you decide you want to see it, let me know, and I can show it to you anytime."

"Why? Is it locked up?" he asked.

She hesitated and then asked, "You really don't want anybody around when you go in, do you?"

"No, I sure don't," he declared, finality in his tone. "So find out if I can go in on my own. Otherwise we'll talk another time." And, with that, he deliberately ended the call. This realtor knew perfectly well that he only went into buildings alone, and still she always played these games, thinking he would change his mind one day and would take her with him, but that wouldn't happen.

She phoned him right back and said, "You know perfectly well you can go in or I wouldn't have called you."

He smiled. "Today?"

"Ooh, you are eager," she purred.

"No, not particularly," he clarified, realizing his own eagerness and tempering it. "I'm already plenty busy, but I do happen to be in the neighborhood." He pivoted, looking around. "As a matter of fact, I'm one block away."

"I can't even get there in that time."

"Which is a good thing," he shared, "since you know how I feel about that."

"Fine, fine. I'll arrange for it to be opened for you."

"What you really mean is that the derelict building has absolutely no security, and I can walk in as I wish, but now you'll give me permission." Silence came, and then she gave a snort, and he knew he was right.

"You're a real headache."

"Good," he stated. "So is that a yes then?"

"Yes, that's a yes," she muttered, "and get back to me whether you want it or not."

"And if I don't?"

"Believe me," she replied in a casual tone, "that I'll have it on the market so damn fast it'll make your head spin."

"So, you're not putting it on the market right now?" he asked, wondering just what she was up to.

"No, but that's only if you want it. I told the seller that I had somebody potentially interested. So he's willing to give you a chance at it first."

"Not at auction?"

"No, I told you that," she snapped. Without giving him any goodbye, she ended the call.

He smiled, turning in the direction of the Paragon building, picking up his pace.

CHAPTER 4

KATE WALKED INTO Smidge's office, finding him talking on the phone. He disconnected when he saw her and motioned her into the back room. "What have you got for me?" she asked, mildly curious.

"Don't expect it every time," he replied briskly, "but I figured we would start the process pretty quickly with one thing."

"GSR?"

He looked at her, then smiled. "I think you should come into my field."

"*Nah*," she said, "somebody's got to do my job."

"They do at that," Smidge muttered. "Anyway, there is no GSR on his hands, so he wasn't holding the gun when it was fired. There you have it. You were right about it not being suicide."

"Unless the victim wore gloves."

"Which he was not wearing when I showed up."

Kate nodded. "So somebody didn't even put the gun in his hand when it was fired to make it look as if he was holding it?" she asked, shaking her head. "Yet maybe they did it *afterward*, but not at the proper time when it would have done them some good."

Smidge frowned. "So, you're looking for somebody who potentially isn't all that aware of gun residue and who doesn't know we can figure it out? Given all the cop shows these days," he noted, "that surprises me."

"It doesn't really surprise me that our killer is some novice," she muttered, "but I'm grateful nonetheless because we want some tools that every criminal doesn't have."

He snorted. "Good luck with that. It seems as if the criminals are aware of all these details and are too far ahead of us."

"Yeah, but we're catching up, slowly but surely."

He gave her a smirk. "*You* might be, but it seems as if my morgue is just getting fuller every day."

"Yeah," she agreed in sorrow because he was right. "Population density really adds to our crime rate, and the cities are blowing up around us. Then the pandemic didn't help."

"No," he muttered, "it really didn't, did it?" He crossed his hands on his desk and studied her.

She waited, but, when he didn't divulge anything further, she began, "So, it is not lost on me that normally you don't call me over, unless you have something more than GSR. So I assume you've got something you didn't want to tell me on the phone."

"Normally I don't call you over. That's true." He hesitated, then added, "Yet something is odd, and I didn't want to talk with the wife right there at the crime scene either."

"Such as?"

"When I arrived, she was on the floor, leaning over the body, going through his pockets. I lit into the cop, and his response was that she just wanted a few minutes to say goodbye before everyone got there, as she wouldn't be allowed anywhere near him."

"And he bought that, did he?" Kate pointed out.

"To him, it looked to be a suicide." He shrugged.

"I don't give a shit if it seemed to be a suicide or not," she snapped, making a note to talk with that cop—a talk he would *not* enjoy.

Smidge nodded. "You and me both. Anyway, you need to take a look at that. The home security cameras should have been on at the time, but I didn't see what she was going through his pockets for."

"Yet she *was* going through his pockets?"

He nodded. "As near as I could tell."

"Wait. Why the hell did he have pockets?" she asked, staring at him. "Was he dressed, or was he in pajamas?"

He frowned at her and then shook his head. "He was fully dressed." He motioned at the sheet-covered table. "Of course he's not now."

She walked over to the table and asked, "May I?" Smidge nodded. She flipped back the sheet and took a closer look at the victim. Unfortunately he couldn't answer the questions clamoring in her head. She turned and asked Smidge, "Did you go through his pockets?"

"I did, and I didn't find anything."

"But that could be because she found it first."

He nodded. "That is exactly what my concern is."

"Damn it." She sighed, frowning at him. "Okay, tell me *exactly* what she was doing when you got there."

He shrugged and gave her as much of a rundown as he could. "Remember that I was only there for a brief second, and the next thing I know, she was up, bawling her eyes out, and gone. The search happened right before me, so that was a switch I wasn't expecting at all."

"*Right,*" Kate murmured. "So, guess who gets to go back and have another interview with the lovely widow? Won't she enjoy that?"

"Yeah, from the sounds of it, she didn't think much of you," Smidge noted, with a glimmer of a smile.

"Nope, she sure didn't, and I won't be taking Rodney with me this time either."

The coroner frowned at her and then nodded with a knowing look. "She definitely has that female thing going on, doesn't she?"

"She sure does," Kate agreed absentmindedly, as she studied Amie's husband's body. "Was there any jewelry, tattoos, anything like that?"

Smidge shook his head. "Not yet, but obviously I haven't done a full check of the body."

She didn't say anything for a moment, then nodded. "Okay, keep me in the loop. I'll go back and have a talk with her right now."

"What was all that about you guys being at the wrong address this morning?"

She turned to him and nodded slowly. "*You* were given the right address, weren't you?"

"Yeah, I was," he confirmed, with a shrug. "We got there within minutes. I was quite surprised you weren't there already, and then I heard you were directed to another address."

"Yeah, I was trying to get there," she muttered, "but we were given an address a few blocks away."

"I wonder why," he muttered.

"According to the officer who found the body, he was just so rattled by what he saw that he gave the wrong address," she replied. "It was the right number but the wrong street."

He frowned at her. "The crime scene was at 438 Creswell."

"The house I was sent to was at 438 Farwell."

"Was anything at the house?"

"It was an abandoned house, but we never stepped inside," she replied. "So, in a way, it wasn't a surprise to be called there."

Smidge shook his head, shuffling through the papers on his desk. "What was the address again?"

"At 438 Creswell is where we picked up the victim, yet at 438 Farwell was where I was initially told to go."

He now turned to his computer at a hurried pace. "That is a very interesting address."

"Why is that?" she asked, waiting as he clicked through his computer.

"Because that address has become notorious, since several murders happened there."

She stared at him and slowly sank down in his visitor's chair, as the memory of Simon's frantic voice rang in her ears. *Get the hell out of there fast, please.* "How long ago was this?"

"Oh, quite a while ago," Smidge shared, looking up the file on his screen. "Ten years maybe. Hang on, and I'll take a look." Moments later he gave her a date.

She nodded slowly. "That's interesting."

"Why? Did something happen while you were there?"

She winced. "In theory, no, and yet, in theory, yes."

"What the hell does that mean?"

"Simon."

"Ooh, Simon's involved, is he?" Smidge rubbed his hands together gleefully. "I have to admit, as a man of science, I find everything Simon has to say completely dubious and definitely something that everyone should back off from," he shared, raising his hands in apology. "Yet I still find myself absolutely fascinated by that element of the unknown."

She stared at him in shock. "I didn't realize you understood very much about him."

"I don't have nearly enough insights into it," he noted, staring at her, "but I can appreciate the mystery. What did he say about that house?"

"We were walking up to the house, when he called me in a panic and told me not to go into whatever house I was at. He was literally screaming into the phone about it."

Smidge nodded. "Why?"

"He told me that, if I went into that house, I would die. The only explanation he could give later was strong, ugly death energy. Whatever the hell that means. But to give him credit, we didn't go in as we were at the wrong location so maybe there was someone inside… I have no way to know." Smidge stared at her, dumbfounded. She gave him a wry smile and added, "Welcome to my world."

Long after she left the morgue, she was still wondering about Simon's message earlier this morning. She couldn't forget that warning, yet she hadn't had a chance to even discuss it with him, and that was becoming more of an issue too.

She checked her watch. It was late, and her workday was over. However, for her, particularly after hearing and seeing what Smidge had shared, wishing he had mentioned something earlier, she was already driving back to Amie's house.

As she walked up to the front door and rang the doorbell, the door swung open by a man. Kate looked at the stranger. "Hi. Who are you?"

"I'm Nate." Then he looked annoyed for a moment and scowled at her. "Who are you?"

"What is your relationship to Amie?"

"Well, if I have a chance," he replied, then took a deep breath, "now that her husband is dead and gone, I'm hoping to marry her." Kate nodded and pulled out her badge. He flushed. "I guess that was the wrong thing to say," he muttered. "Obviously she's pretty stressed out and upset right now. I'm just here to comfort her."

"Comfort her while trying to take over her husband's place, when his body's barely cold?"

"I didn't mean it in that way," he protested, "and I certainly didn't have anything to do with it. They'd been unhappy for a while, so I guess in a way I'm not surprised."

"Why do you say that?" she asked, eyeing him curiously. "How unhappy are we talking?"

He shrugged. "They were talking about going to a counselor, and her husband had mentioned a couple times that he wanted out."

"And yet, if she's got you, I'm sure she wanted out too."

"Yes, but divorce isn't that easy," he muttered.

"Or that convenient," she noted.

He frowned and added, "I think you need to talk to her."

"Oh, don't worry. That's why I'm here," she replied in a dry tone, as she stared at him. "I'll need your name, contact information, and where were you this morning between three and six a.m."

He stared at her in shock. "Good God, the man committed suicide. Jesus," he swore and then looked back at her. "What the hell has that got to do with me?"

"Just answer the question," she stated patiently and gave

him a look.

"I was home."

"How long has your relationship with Amie been going on?"

He again flushed and shrugged.

Just then Amie appeared at the door and stepped out, glaring at Kate. "Why are you here?"

Kate smiled sweetly. "Hi. Amie. So glad to see you. I need you to come with me and talk to me at the station."

"Oh, I don't think so," she snapped. "I'll talk to that partner of yours, but I won't be talking to you."

"You will be," Kate declared, with a hard smile, "particularly now that I realize you couldn't wait for your husband to die."

"It doesn't matter if I wanted him dead or not," she snapped. "I didn't kill him."

"Interesting," Kate noted. "Of course no life insurance or anything is waiting for you, is there?"

Amie's gaze widened. "You can't think I had anything to do with this."

"Why not? And, while we're at it, considering that we know you were caught in the process of searching his pockets, while he was dead on the carpet, I want to know what you removed."

Amie's face went red and then pale white. "Do I need a lawyer?"

"Maybe," Kate replied. "So far you haven't answered my questions."

"Where's your partner?" she asked, barely in a whisper, and then her voice got stronger, angrier. "You obviously don't like me."

"I don't know you enough to decide yet. As for my partner, he may be a little more influenced by the wiles of a woman," she shared calmly. "I, however, do not have any such problem. So, answer my questions now, or shall I issue a warrant instead?"

"I need my lawyer with me."

"Call him now," Kate said, "and then we'll talk about interfering with our investigation of a dead body, obstruction of justice, and anything else I can come up with between now and then."

Immediately the boyfriend raised a hand, moving closer to Amie. "Whoa, whoa, whoa, come on. She wouldn't have done anything wrong."

"Says you," Kate noted, gesturing at the two of them, standing in each other's arms. "That doesn't change the fact that, when the coroner came in to see the body, Amie had already convinced the police officer that she needed to be alone with her husband. However, instead of actually bawling her eyes out or praying for his soul," Kate shared in a dry tone, "Amie was busy going through his pockets."

Nate turned to face Amie.

She stood straighter and declared, "You make it sound so terrible. All I was doing was checking to ensure he didn't have anything incriminating on him."

Even her boyfriend gasped at that.

"Why would you do that?" Kate asked. "If he had supposedly committed suicide, what could he possibly have on him that was incriminating? Come to think of it, why would you even care? You've already got your next partner lined up, or at least lined up to keep you company while this all plays out. Then whatever happens at the end of our investigation, who knows?"

Nate stared at Kate in shock and then back at Amie.

"Tell her that it's not like that."

"She doesn't want to hear anything," Amie snapped, glaring at Kate.

"I want to know what you took from his pockets, and I want it back."

"It's not yours," she snapped.

"Guess what? It's not yours either, not until it's released from evidence by the court. If we find that your husband did commit suicide, and you have absolutely no culpability in this case," she stated, "then we will release everything back to you. However, in the meantime, that's not happening. So, either I'm taking you down to the station right now and you can call your lawyer when you get there, or you can answer my questions here, give me whatever you decided you needed to steal from his cold dead body, and we will talk further." Kate gave Amie a hard glare all the while.

Amie stiffened and then slowly sagged. "I didn't have anything to do with his death."

Kate just waited.

Then the boyfriend spoke up. "I know you didn't. It's so terrible." He plastered her to his chest and comforted her.

"*Terrible*, yeah. Apparently your husband finding out his wife was having an affair may have been just *terrible*," Kate muttered, with an eye roll.

"As if you're so high and mighty and perfect, I suppose," Amie snapped.

Her boyfriend shook his head. "Hey, hey, hey, none of that. Let's just get through this."

"Yeah, that would be good," Amie replied, shooting daggers at Kate with her gaze. "Her partner is a nice guy, but she on the other hand ..."

Kate gave her a wolfish smile. "Exactly, and, from now

on, you'll be dealing with me," she announced, with a nod and a bigger grin. "I don't let women influence how I work."

"Maybe you should. You might not be such a bitch."

"We can talk about who's a bitch after we discuss what you stole from your husband's pockets. Best we get back to the matter at hand. The insults can wait."

"I didn't steal anything. Everything that was my husband's ... is now mine."

"Oh, is it?" Kate asked, with a knowing smile. "I guess that depends on how the will is made out, whether there are other beneficiaries or any heir apparent."

Amie hesitated. "Fine, I'll get it for you."

Kate motioned at the boyfriend. "You didn't tell me if you were alone at your home at that hour?"

"Yes, I was alone," he replied, then he looked uncertainly back to where Amie had disappeared. "She's not usually like this."

"That's because she's been caught doing something completely wrong and illegal," Kate explained. "So now the question is whether she will fess up and tell the truth or if she'll continue to be difficult."

He winced and nodded in understanding.

"She's not exactly a grieving wife," Kate pointed out, "which makes this all very suspicious."

"Yet he committed suicide, so I don't understand what the problem is."

"But did he kill himself?" she asked, looking at him. "How do you know that?"

He stared at her in shock. "Of course he did," he sputtered, as he blinked, looking around as if for Amie, then turned back to Kate. "Didn't he?" His voice was a harsh whisper but low, almost as if the awareness had suddenly hit him that his married girlfriend might not be quite so innocent.

Kate shook her head slowly. "No, he did not. This is a murder investigation."

SIMON WALKED CLOSER to stare up at the building for sale. The Paragon was definitely on his wish list, but that didn't mean his buying it would ever happen. His decision always included price, condition, and how the cost analysis came out, but he could already feel his heart beating with excitement as he got closer and closer. The Paragon was one of the old majestic originals in the downtown Vancouver area, and it needed a lot of work. Too many people would just drop the building, but that wasn't Simon's style.

It would happen in some cases, even for him, but, if he could make the original structure stand as firm and tall and elegant as it had been in its day, then that was his preference. However, in this case, he wasn't so sure that was even doable.

As he walked closer, his heart pounded faster and faster. He hesitated, then looked around, wondering just what was going on. As he took another step, a voice slammed in his head.

Are you sure?

He froze, slowly looked around to see if somebody on the street may be talking to him. Unfortunately, in this crazy woo-woo world that he lived in, sometimes he got a little confused between actual voices and those in his head. But right now? No, he was alone. He pondered that, as he stared up at the Paragon building. Walking to the front entrance, he pushed on the door, and it opened easily. It wasn't locked and probably hadn't been in a very long time, which also meant that the place could be full of vagabonds and any number of other things that he may not want to see, but that was part and parcel of the work he did.

Sometimes it seemed as if these old buildings were crying out to Simon for help, crying out for somebody to care and for something other than the bottom line to be a determining factor in their restoration.

He stared at the open entrance and sniffed the air cautiously. He found no smell of death or decay, only that of a musty, old, neglected building. He was happy to take a step inside. As he did so, that voice spoke up again.

Are you sure?

He frowned, looked around, and asked, "Why not?"

He found himself hoping for some answer that would make sense, but nothing came. He walked in slowly, studying the building, which would have been absolutely stunning in its day. However, not so much at this point in time. Its heyday was over, and the building was very much worse for wear, and sad in a way that Simon couldn't really explain. Yet he'd seen it time and time again with these older buildings.

While these age-old structures had been loved when in their prime, nobody had put in the money to fix them up, as they slowly collapsed downward from the inside out. All too often, once that decline started, people abandoned ship, and then the complete neglect began, making the erosion even worse.

Simon wandered the main floor. The place wasn't condemned, at least not according to any signs posted, but he would check with the city to see if that was in process. He wouldn't put it past the realtor to make that happen, to squeeze a sale through before Simon could be notified of the city's intent to condemn, but he hadn't been at this work for this long without having some idea of what realtors were likely to do. Some were honest, but all too often they were all about their paycheck and much less concerned about anybody else's money.

Still on the main floor, Simon noticed all the windows were broken, and the back walkway appeared to be in even worse shape than he expected. Frowning, he considered that this building would need a serious gutting to get it viable again. It's not that the rehab wasn't doable, and he'd done plenty of serious guts in his time, but it broke his heart to see this past grandeur left in such ruin.

Once again it just reminded him that so many people were completely driven by money and nothing else, and this building was a prime example. When he got a text from the nagging real estate agent, he looked down at her question and snorted. She had always been pushy, and, as much as she may understand some of what made him tick and the things that he liked, she really didn't understand who he was at his core.

Still, the decision to seriously gut a new acquisition or not depended on where his money was allocated, where his budget was for the upcoming project, how many overruns he had on any current rehabs, and the future economy in the construction business. Of course the real estate market had also gone completely chaotic, and sales prices had been driven way up. He hadn't bought into that whole scenario, preferring instead to focus on the projects he was working on. But then prices had started to drop to a point where many people were now panicked and trying to sell, to get out, which didn't make for a particularly stable market either, as far as property sales went.

Again, not something he would get into right now. His decisions to buy rehab properties were complex. When he bought projects that worked for him, he would do it for a lot of reasons, definitely based on the cost analysis but also that emotional factor, which he couldn't always pinpoint or recreate exactly. Yet he would know whether a building was one he could work with or the soul of the building was gone and he couldn't bring it back, no way, no how.

As he wandered the huge space, he could almost see the finished rehab, with loft apartments on the upper floors and complex commercial requirements filling out the first floor in front of him. It was as if seeing a movie, slowly creating from his imagination, incorporated into the specific building before him.

He hadn't really ever thought anything of his particular process and just figured it was part of his creative ability to visualize. Still, Simon knew that, if anybody else saw what he could see right now, they would think he was beyond weird. He already had more-than-enough people thinking that, so making sure that nobody ever saw him in this process was a priority. Right now, the building was singing to him, as if a serenade of days gone by playing gently in his head.

As he continued his wandering throughout the building, sometimes it roared into a crescendo and then crashed into a faint voice, a whisper almost. He called out, "I know. I hear you but no promises."

With that, the noises gently eased back, letting him know that, whatever made the songs around him, they were here, watching and waiting and … listening. He understood that too, but, just because he was here, it didn't mean that this building was his or that he could promise to provide what the soul of this building was looking for, which seemed to be everything, eternity even.

With half a smile on his face, he headed up to the second floor.

CHAPTER 5

KATE WALKED INTO the station, still pissed.

Rodney looked up, frowned, and asked, "What's your problem?"

"Your little girlfriend," she replied in a sarcastic tone.

He stared at her. "What are you talking about?"

"Amie Mulhouse," she stated, glaring at him. "That little witch was searching her husband's body when Smidge walked in."

Rodney shook his head. "What do you mean by *searching*?"

"Yeah, that's the question. Smidge caught sight of her but didn't say anything to us at the time because Amie was there. He went through the security video and confirmed that she removed something from her husband's pockets."

Rodney frowned at her in shock. "Maybe it was just innocent."

"Maybe it was, so I went over there—after finding out that it was definitely murder, with no GSR on our victim's hands, so he did not fire or hold the gun that killed him."

"Ah, shit," Rodney muttered, staring at her.

"So, I went back to speak to Amie, and who opened the door but her boyfriend." Rodney blinked several times as she nodded. "Apparently they were just waiting for the right time to tell her husband."

Rodney closed his eyes and pinched the bridge of his nose. "Fuck."

"Yeah, fuck is right … literally." He rolled his eyes at that. "And this," she added, as she dropped a little notebook in front of him, "is what she supposedly took out of her husband's pocket."

"Supposedly?"

"I don't believe anything she's said so far, so I'm not sure I believe this now. Plus we have missing pages."

As he flipped through the notebook it fell open right where the pages had been ripped out. "Well, crap. Surely she doesn't think that'll fool us."

"Probably not, but, without being able to see on the videotape what she took, or what she did with those pages, it's a problem." Kate walked over to her desk, sat down at her computer, and quickly brought up the video from Amie's house.

"Do you really think she killed him?" Rodney asked, looking at her. "I swear to God, I thought she was innocent."

"No, your gonads thought she was innocent," Kate clarified absentmindedly, "and believe me that she had an awful lot to say about me being there and not you."

"Yeah, sorry," he said sheepishly. "It just seemed as if you were being really hard on her."

"I *was* being really hard on her," she confirmed, with a huff.

Lilliana joined them and asked, "What's going on?" Rodney filled her in, leaving nothing out. "Jesus, Rodney."

"I know, but hopefully it's nothing," he muttered. "So now you're making me doubt my own senses."

"Or maybe tell your senses not to make decisions based on your gonads," Kate repeated. When he glared at her, she shrugged. "I'm still stinging from that last little visit with the woman who had been busily rummaging through her dead husband's pockets, while her beloved boyfriend waited in the wings. Her husband wasn't even cold yet when the boyfriend stepped right into her bed, literally the dead guy's bed."

"Jesus," Lilliana muttered, "that's cold."

"Yeah, it really is, and it also says an awful lot about who Amie is, and the new boyfriend didn't like hearing it either."

At that, Rodney turned to her. "I bet he doesn't believe Amie did anything wrong though."

"Of course not, any more than *you* do." With the security video loaded, she quickly sped up to the time period where Smidge walked in and saw Amie rummaging through the pockets of her dead husband and pulling out the little black book. Amie flipped it open, smiled, then ripped out several pages, tucking both the pages and the notebook into her pocket. Kate called Rodney over and replayed this section.

As soon as he saw it, he swore. "God damn it, that's cold," He stared at the screen for a minute and then looked down.

"Yeah, so now we'll bring her in and find out what happened to those pages."

"She probably burned them," Lilliana guessed. "I would have."

"Maybe," Kate acknowledged, "but, if it were me, I would have taken a picture of them first."

Then Lilliana laughed, a big grin spreading across her face. "That sounds about right ... because you're a bitch."

"Damn right I am." Kate picked up her phone and ordered Amie Mulhouse in for questioning the next morning and suggested she bring her attorney with her. She looked over at Rodney as soon as that was done and asked, "So, partner, will you be there?"

He snorted. "Yeah, I'll be there because that shit she pulled, that isn't happening … not on my watch."

"*Not on your watch*?" Kate repeated, with a headshake. "How about just not happening at all?"

"Yeah, fine, whatever," he conceded, raising his hand. "So, how did you know?"

She frowned at him. "Smidge told me. Didn't I say that earlier?"

He groaned. "Of course he did."

"It's probably in the report that he just sent out as well. He's still working on the case, but the first thing he did was check for GSR. Apparently he tried that at the house but was out of one of the chemicals he needed and has been raking a tech over the coals for not restocking his medical bag."

"Oh, I'm sure that tech is loving his job right now," Rodney muttered, still staring at her.

"Probably not, but he'll likely never make that mistake again, will he?"

Lilliana studied Kate. "You really do get along with old Smidge, don't you?"

"They're two bloody peas in a pod," Rodney snapped, and Kate glared at him. "Sorry. Yeah, I'm just pissed at myself."

"Go be pissed somewhere else." As Rodney and Lilliana both turned to walk away, Kate stopped them, and they turned to look at her expectantly. "Smidge did ask why the hell we took so long to get there."

Rodney shook his head. "Oh, great, and I'm sure we're in trouble for that with him too."

"I told him about the address mix-up. When I mentioned the wrong address, he got this really weird look in his eye, went back to his computer, and I'll be looking into it more right now," she muttered. "Smidge mentioned a tie to a fairly famous case from years ago at that wrong address."

"What famous case?" Lilliana asked.

"A pretty famous murder of a family."

Rodney stared at her. "Oh, shit."

Kate nodded. "Yeah, *oh shit* is right." She frowned at Lilliana's glazed look. "The Feldspar house."

Lilliana stared at her, as if everything clicked over in her brain. "What? *The* Feldspar house?"

"Yes," Kate said. "Apparently we stumbled into something else."

"Yeah, but not just us though," Rodney stated, looking at Kate. "Simon too."

Lilliana looked back and forth between the two of them.

Kate sighed. "I'm not looking forward to going home and sorting that one out." She grabbed her purse, her wallet, and her keys. "Yet I can't wait to see our lovely little actress Amie tomorrow morning."

And, with that, Kate turned and walked out.

SIMON WALKED UP to the second floor of the Paragon building, carefully checking out the amount of rot on the floorboards as he went. No doubt that most of this building would require a 100 percent tear-down job. The plumbing and electrical were old, but the infrastructure appeared to be solid. He would get one of his engineers to take a look just to confirm. Simon had a good eye but still needed the occasional expert to make serious assessments because not being correct in this estimation period could potentially severely set back Simon, at least regarding his building rehab program.

As he climbed the stairs, an eerie sense of emptiness encompassed Simon, yet the building no longer felt abandoned. Something else was going on here that he just couldn't put his finger on. Moving cautiously, keeping himself on what looked to be solid floorboards, he wondered how the Paragon could have fallen to this level of disrepair without anybody classifying it as unsafe and condemning it for mandatory demolition—unless nobody had come through the property in the last God-only-knew how many years. That surprised him a little because love for this building had been here back in the day. So who had let it fall into such bleak disrepair?

He stopped at the landing at the top of the stairs on the second floor and just stood here, looking around. One of the most incredible things about this place was the view. He walked over to one of the windows, many of which were still solid and still intact on this floor, which surprised him, as he stared down at the city below. It was a pretty stunning sight, and, with that view, he thought he could make profitable apartments here, providing he could get the property at a cheap-enough sale price. He was sure the seller probably felt that the listing price already was cheap enough, but Simon was certain, once he did his cost analysis, the price would have to come down quite a bit more before he would put in a bid.

Even if the Paragon had been one of the properties he had long had his eye on, still a level of trepidation filled him, not wanting to take it on unless it was something he could manage, and, for him, that meant not losing money. It was one thing to take a bit of a loss, but another thing entirely to take a complete dive.

He continued to wander, then moved up another floor and then another. By the time he'd done a complete check on the place, he felt a little better about it. Obviously more inspections were needed to make a clean and whole assessment, but it felt right. It felt good. Honestly, it felt … He smiled at the word ringing in his ears. It felt *special*, and that was pretty much all he needed.

As he moved back downstairs and used the far set of stairs, he smelled something that made his stomach churn. Not so much death, just decay. Moving cautiously, he headed down to the next floor and, in the stairwell at the bottom, was a crumpled heap of clothing. He stopped, stared, and moved cautiously toward it. When sounds came from the heap, Simon realized somebody was sleeping off something, but he wasn't sure whether they needed help or not. Moving slowly, he carefully nudged the pile of clothing with his boot. "Hey, are you okay?"

A man with bleary eyes lifted his head. "Just sleeping, man. Just sleeping." He yawned, rolled over, and curled up some more.

"You know this building is being sold, right?"

He just waved him off. "It won't happen for a while. I just need to get some sleep."

"Are you sure that's all you need? Shelters are nearby, if you need a place to spend the night."

The homeless man snorted and said, "Take a hike."

Simon just smiled because a guy needed a certain amount of attitude to live that homeless life. He added, "Just don't get into any trouble in here."

"What trouble?" the other guy asked, shifting around.

"I don't want to see anything bad happen to you."

The guy studied him for a long moment. "Been a long

time since I heard that from anybody."

Simon nodded. "We're not all assholes."

He snorted. "Yeah, you are." The man shuffled a little farther away, as if more wary of Simon's presence now and clearly not used to anyone being concerned about his welfare.

Simon crouched beside him. "Do you need a meal?"

The other guy shook his head. "No, I'm good."

Simon sighed, then stood. "Okay, but, just so you know, realtors and inspectors will be coming through this place in a while. You might want to find a better place to sleep."

"They're really selling it?" A note of shock filled his tone, and then he added, "What about the ghosts?"

Simon turned to him and asked, "What ghosts?"

"Lots of ghosts are here," he muttered. "Just so you guys know, if you want to buy it, she's haunted. I don't mind the ghosts, but I'm pretty sure lots of people would."

Simon half smiled at that because some wanted ghosts on their property, and some didn't. "Where are the ghosts coming from?"

"Don't know," he muttered, as he yawned. "I really need sleep, man."

"Got it," Simon said. "Just one more question. How often do the ghosts come out?"

He squinted up at him. "Every night. I see them every night."

"You *see* them?"

"Yeah, and I know what you're thinking. Nobody ever listens to me when I tell them that I can hear ghosts or that I can see them, but they're always around."

"Anyone in particular?" Simon asked.

The homeless man stared at him in surprise. "You believe me?"

"Sure. Why not?"

The guy just groaned at him. "I'm not joking."

"I'm glad to hear that," Simon replied. "So, what kind of ghosts are they?"

"The dead kind," he stated, frowning at Simon as if he were a little more bizarre and abnormal than he'd first thought, and it definitely made the homeless guy nervous.

Simon nodded, then stepped back out of his space a little. "That's fine. If they come around when I'm here, I'll have a talk with them and see if I can get them to move on."

"Yeah, you could try that," the homeless man muttered, with an eye roll. "Like that'll happen."

"Why? You don't think they'll move if I ask?"

"No, I don't think they'll move. Why would they want to move? It's a nice place. It's their place."

Simon smiled. He always checked up on the people living on the streets, just to see if they were hungry or needed a blanket or a shelter for the night or whatever. Yet he had also learned long ago to talk to the local homeless population about the goings-on in the immediate neighborhood before buying a property. They always had some inside scoop that he factored into his decision-making process. "Sure, but the place will go through some major changes, so it won't be comfortable for them any longer." The homeless guy stared up at him, and Simon nodded. "Anyway, have a good sleep." Then he turned and started to walk away.

The other guy called out, "When are all these changes happening?"

"Soon, but you probably have a while yet."

"Damn good thing. I'm not kidding. I need to sleep."

Simon laughed. "Then go back to sleep. You should be

just fine for now."

And, with that, he headed back down to the street, a broad smile on his face. The thought of the building being haunted didn't bother him in the least. If anything, he was the one more likely to enjoy the haunting, providing the ghosts weren't causing trouble. He had certainly heard of buildings where the ghosts caused mischief, but, so far, he'd been surprised, given his abilities, that in almost every building with signs of paranormal activities, the ghosts had mostly left, once Simon had moved in with his rehab crew. He figured they were happy to see Simon save each of those buildings.

He would expect that to happen here too. He just didn't know if the ghosts had any particular reason for hanging around the Paragon. And of course had no idea how long they'd been there. In theory it could have nothing to do with the building at all. He used to worry that he would find dead bodies in these empty buildings on his radar, and he had found a couple, usually homeless transients. Older buildings tended to collect homeless people, and sometimes they died from overdoses or just old age. Most of them didn't live to be very old, their lifespans definitely cut short by their lifestyle.

Still, Simon wasn't worried about any ghosts in the Paragon. Maybe he should be. Maybe that would make his decision a lot easier, but honestly, what he'd found and seen with Kate was more than enough to keep his psyche thankful to just deal with the woo-woo stuff that he ran into on a regular basis.

As he walked back out into the sunshine, he stopped and took a deep breath but still felt that weird sense in the background behind him. He turned and saw what seemed to be a flutter of movement to his side. A spirit. He nodded. "I am buying her," he called out, "so you might want to leave sooner rather than later."

And, with that, wearing a big smile, he turned and headed home.

CHAPTER 6

KATE WALKED UP the front steps to Simon's building, where he resided in the penthouse apartment, wondering if she should have phoned ahead of time. She was just so damn tired that it seemed almost impossible to keep her brain flowing properly at the moment. As she got to the front door, the doorman, Harry, opened it for her and smiled. "Hey, Kate."

She lifted a hand in acknowledgment. "Is he home?"

"He is, indeed. Is he expecting you?"

"I don't think so," she said, yawning, "I should have called him, but I didn't."

"Do you want me to let him know you're on the way up?"

She shrugged. "If it's part of your mandate, feel free. Otherwise he'll find out in a few seconds." She walked over to the special penthouse elevator, stepped in, and pushed the button to get to the topmost apartment. As soon as the door opened, Simon stood there, waiting for her. She smiled at him. "There is something to be said for having somebody waiting for me with a happy welcome on their face."

He nodded. "There is, indeed," he replied gently. "Tough day?"

"It shouldn't have been, but, yeah, in some ways it was. How about you?"

"It was okay. I looked at a new building today."

She sighed. "Don't you have enough projects on your plate?"

"I do." He nodded in agreement, "but this one's been on my wish list for a while. Besides, it has ghosts," he added, with a laugh. She frowned at him, startled, because he didn't often joke about such things.

He shrugged. "Whether I like it or not … it is what it is. According to a homeless guy I came across sleeping inside, ghosts are in this one."

"Interesting," she murmured, as she walked in, kicked off her boots, and collapsed on the couch. A glass of wine was held out to her, and she groaned with appreciation. "I wonder if I come here for you or for all the things that come with you?" A moment of silence came, and she grinned at him. "Just kidding." She caught him smiling too.

"I'm sure you're not kidding because in your mind that really would be a question you would ask yourself," he declared, amusement in his gaze. "Most people wouldn't broach such things out loud."

"It's much better to bring those things out into the light," she muttered, as she collapsed a little deeper into the couch. "Otherwise they're just lying about everything."

"It's not that they're lying, but they're choosing not to look too closely."

She stared at him over the rim of her glass. "Isn't that lying by avoidance?"

"No, it's simply avoiding the subject," he stated, with a chuckle. "Something else I don't ever see you doing."

"Not that I'm trying to bring up something that's unpleasant," she began in a tired tone, "but it just occurred to me, as you handed me the glass of wine, how damn nice it is to know that I get a warm welcome, and with it comes a glass of wine."

"I understand that. I really do. I'm just not sure that everybody would."

"Maybe I wouldn't say it to everybody," she suggested, with a shrug. "Maybe I would just not worry about it and keep it to myself. … However, in your case, I really don't want there to be anything that isn't open and honest between us."

He laughed. "And some people would say that's going beyond open and honest."

"Probably," she admitted. "As you know, I don't do the whole relationship thing very well."

"I think you do it marvelously," he declared, as he sat down beside her and tugged her to lean against his shoulder.

"You're quite cold," he noted in concern, as he shifted and took the glass from her hand, tucking her right half onto his lap. "How come?"

"I forgot to take a jacket with me today," she mumbled, as she nuzzled against his chest and smiled at the furnace underneath her ear. "I wasn't even really thinking about it when I was out walking around during the day, but the nighttime weather is definitely turning colder. Hard to believe it's almost Christmastime."

"It is, indeed. Do you have a jacket?" he asked.

"I do have a jacket," she said, "and the cold outside has made me a little cold inside." Then she laughed. "Which makes total sense, doesn't it?"

"It absolutely does," he agreed, "but why do I think that also means you didn't eat today?"

She looked over at him, shifting so she could look up to see his gaze, and half smiled. "I did eat, just don't ask me what or when because I don't remember."

He groaned. "Which really means that you probably didn't eat very much."

She shrugged. "Why do I have to eat very much, as long as I'm eating? … Isn't that enough?"

"Not necessarily," he replied. "If you're not eating sufficiently for your needs, then you'll be even colder."

"That's not fair. I get food down, so why does everybody have to panic about the amount?"

"Because you work in a high-stress field, where you need that energy at a moment's notice."

"Yeah, well … I haven't done any running or even my workouts lately," she muttered. "I feel so out of shape these days." Then she yawned again and curled up deeper against his chest, feeling his warmth seep into her soul. "Just *thinking* of coming up with some energy to do what I need to do right now is beyond me."

"What do you need to do?" he asked curiously, as he cuddled her close. She murmured an answer, but barely legible. He tilted her head back and kissed her. "You're not even talking clearly. Are you that tired?"

She nodded. "Just let me close my eyes for five minutes." And, with that, she soon fell asleep.

When she woke up, she was in the same position. Pushing back, she lifted up bleary eyes to stare around. "Did I really fall asleep?"

He smiled and nodded. "You really did."

"Christ," she muttered, as she collapsed back down again. "Sorry."

"Don't be sorry," he said. "I'm sad to see you so overworked."

"I don't even know what it was about today," she admitted, as she shifted. "I shouldn't be this overworked and this tired, but apparently I am anyway." She got up, walked to the bathroom, and quickly used the facilities. As she came back, he remained seated on the couch. She asked, "I don't suppose you ordered food while I was sleeping, did you?"

He burst out laughing. "As a matter of fact, I did." Just then the doorbell rang, and he got up and walked over to see Harry, holding out his food. "Hey, Harry, thanks so much." With a nod from the doorman, the elevator took him back down to his post.

Simon carried the food delivery into the kitchen and asked her, "How did you know I did that?"

"I didn't," she confessed, "but I was really hoping you did because, all of a sudden, I'm starving."

"It goes along with being cold and exhausted. You've also been on some crazy cases without too much of a break, and all of that will have an impact."

"Maybe." She yawned again. "But what was this about ghosts?"

He laughed at her. "Yeah, we were talking about that before you crashed."

She nodded and slumped down on a dining room chair. She felt his concern and waved it off. "I'm fine. ... I just need to wake up."

"*Uh-huh*, you don't look fine."

She half smiled as she looked up at him. "But I don't look *terrible*, and the nap left me more on the groggy side than I expected," she shared. "Other than that, I'm feeling pretty good."

"If you say so," he muttered, but she could sense the caring in his gaze.

She smiled. "I didn't really think I would like being

fussed over."

"You're getting there," he noted. "You're still quite a way from letting anybody actually *fuss*, but it's nice to see you not fight it as much."

She shrugged. "I think you wore me down. Besides, it's kind of nice."

"You still aren't ready to move in here with me?" When she stared at him in shock, he burst out laughing. "No, I'm not pushing."

"Oh, God," she mumbled, "that is definitely not on my horizon." She watched the wince come over his face and rushed to say, "At least not right now."

"Don't mind me. I brought it up in the spur of the moment. I didn't really mean to discuss that now."

"But you did mean to," she noted. "I'm just not … I'm not there yet."

"I got that," he replied, with a nod, "and, as always, your honesty is appreciated."

She saw his shoulders slumping, as if she had let him down in some terrible way, and she knew she had. The trouble was, she hadn't even really gotten comfortable living in her own skin. So the thought of being in a partnership and living with him was scary shit, and she just wasn't there yet. "Maybe I'll get there soon," she added, "I'm just …"

"I know." He held up his hand in peace. "We'll park this discussion for now. You're just not there yet."

She nodded. "I'm really not, but I feel bad now."

"Don't," he murmured, with a wave of his hand. "Again, I shouldn't have brought it up."

"Sure you should, if that's something you want." She frowned and added, "I don't even know what that would be like."

"Just more of this," he noted. "It's not as if it would be stressful."

"And yet"—she looked around his penthouse—"it certainly would be a jump up in my lifestyle, but not in a way I'm comfortable with."

"I know. You prefer to visit but not necessarily live here."

She winced. "It's a really nice place," she admitted.

"And you do like what you can have from it, but I get it. You're not a person to be swayed by the things that I can offer."

"No … I'm really not, and, for some reason, that makes me feel terrible."

He burst out laughing. "You are very much *you*, and I don't want you to change," he declared, still chuckling.

She glared at him, not sure what she had missed, or if it was something not important and if she should just walk past it. However, sometimes people mentioned things that she didn't quite understand, and it always made her feel as if she was missing out on something major.

He leaned over, kissed her hard, and announced, "Food, let's get food."

"What kind is it?"

"Chinese. I was looking for vegetables."

"Egg rolls?" she asked, as she bounded over to the bag.

"Yes, egg rolls, all kinds of stuff." He brought out six containers, and she stared in surprise.

"Wow, were you hungry?"

"I'm hungry, but I also know, if you crashed as you did, that you were also hungry." He quickly dished up two plates and served them on the dining room table.

As they sat here eating, she eyed him curiously. "Tell me

about the ghosts."

He chuckled. "I should have known that would be the part you would remember."

"Hey, I didn't get the rest of the story, so I'm not exactly sure what part of it was for real or not."

"I'm not sure if it's real either." He quickly told her about the property that he was looking at.

When he gave her the address, she thought for a moment and nodded. "That's been empty for a long time now."

"It has," he agreed. "That's one of the reasons I'm looking at doing something with it." When he mentioned the listing price, she stared at him in shock. He shrugged. "We're not settled on a price yet, so I'm hoping to get it for quite a bit less than that, but that's their current asking price."

"Jesus," she muttered, "not in a million lifetimes would I earn that much money."

"No, it's not exactly money anybody earns," he replied, with a chuckle. "It's one of those investments where you hope that you get your money back and that you don't kill yourself in the process."

She shook her head. "I would kill myself in the process, but you apparently do pretty well with your rehab projects."

"Sometimes," he stated, with a smile.

"Have you ever lost big money on one?"

"No, not big money, and the ones that I would say I've lost money on are pretty close to making the money back to cover the cost. Yet, at the moment, they just won't make much of a profit," he explained. "Those are the ones that I tend to operate more as rentals, so on a longer-term return."

She nodded and stared down at her food. He was talking figures so astronomical to her that it just didn't compute.

"Don't worry about the purchase price," he added. "A

ton of money will then go into the rehab as well."

"That's the thing," she said, putting down her fork and staring at her empty plate. "Not only are you putting out money to buy these properties, but, with the condition they're in and the amount of work they need, that's just about the same money all over again."

"If not more," he added.

She shook her head. "This homeless guy told you there were ghosts, *huh*?"

"Yeah, and they came out at night. More or less every night," he shared, pondering that. "I don't remember exactly how he phrased it, but I definitely got the impression that he had seen them on a regular basis."

"Sure, but is this guy on drugs, and just what kind of ghosts are we talking about? For all you know, it could be smugglers using the place or thieves using it as a hot spot to meet up and exchange stolen goods."

He looked at her in fascination. "I say *ghosts*, and all you think about is *criminal activity*."

She shrugged. "Why wouldn't I? When you consider it, most of these places are being utilized for something along that line, particularly when they are as abandoned and as unloved as that one."

"Maybe that's what it is, and not ghosts after all," he conceded, with a shrug. "I won't really know until I go back there one night and take a closer look." She stared at him, but he nodded. "Of course I'll go. I just don't know when."

"Sure," she muttered, still feeling dazed. "I can't imagine."

"What about your case?"

"Yeah, I'm not so sure about it," she muttered, "but we need to talk about the Feldspar."

"The Feldspar," he repeated, staring at her. "I know lots of properties, but that one isn't ringing a bell."

"That's the house you told me to not enter today, or at least related to that property," she pointed out, as she leaned forward to study his face. "You want to explain that one?"

He looked at her and sagged back, as if his energy drained from him in an instant. "No, I really don't."

NO WAY KATE would let that go, even if Simon wanted her to, because she really did deserve some explanation. He just didn't have a whole lot of explanation to give.

"Look. I don't really know what that warning was all about. All I can tell you is that I felt an absolute panic this morning, and it had to do with you, and I knew that you were heading somewhere dangerous."

She nodded. "We didn't see any danger outside the house. Then we didn't have any reason to go into the building within a few minutes of your call because we'd been sent to the wrong address by mistake."

He stared at her in surprise. "Really?"

She nodded. "That has never happened to me before," she shared. "So we got back into the vehicle and headed to the correct address, but now I'm quite concerned about the property you told me not to enter, the Feldspar house."

"Did you look it up afterward or something?"

"I was talking to Smidge," she began, trying to make it casual, "and he knew the property because of some famous murder history to it."

"Of course." Simon groaned. "It could never be anything happy or nice."

She laughed. "I haven't had a chance to look it up yet,

but the press called it the Feldspar murders at the time."

He sat back, picked up his glass of wine, and twirled it around, trying hard to get his brain to figure out what was looping back and forth in his mind, staying just out of reach. Then it hit him and hit him hard. "Oh, that's right," he said, sitting up straighter. "Three generations were shot. Maybe the brain-damaged sister was supposed to be killed. Then, yes, three generations were supposed to be murdered." She stared at him. "It's just coming back to me now. You didn't look it up yet?"

"No, I planned to do that tonight. I just never got there, what with the current case I am working on."

"You should do some research into it," he suggested, as he stared off in the distance. "Now that I recall, it's unsolved."

"I don't know about unsolved," she replied cautiously. "Just because the media didn't hear about it doesn't mean it hasn't been solved."

He gave her a wry look. "The way the media works these days, it means exactly that." He watched her concede the point. "Anyway, if you do find out something interesting," he suggested, taking a moment to collect himself, "I know the world would appreciate an update."

"I don't know about how I would get any update, since you're the one who told me not to go in the house," she stated crossly.

"For some reason that's upsetting to you."

"It's not upsetting me," she clarified, raising her hand in protest. "It's just that, at the time, I felt stupid listening to you blindly."

"Don't, please," he replied, raising a brow, "because I only had a few minutes to get you on the phone and to tell you that your life was in danger."

"And yet it was fine," she pointed out.

"Sure, because you listened to me and left," he stated, staring at her in growing frustration. "If I'm telling you to get out of a place, it means we have a problem."

"I know," she muttered, showing her palms in surrender. "Anyway, I may go back there tomorrow." He stared at her and swallowed hard, and she nodded. "I know you don't want me to, but ... if something is going on there, I should find out. I have to go there."

"You mean, something along the ghost line?"

"Oh, I wasn't thinking it was a ghost sending me out of the house, but rather some real-life horror," she murmured.

"And that could be," Simon noted. "Let's hope I don't get the same sense of panic."

"Hopefully whatever happened there at the time of your warning won't continue to be a problem tomorrow."

He shrugged. "I don't think so. I certainly can't imagine that it *wouldn't* still be dangerous. If you think about it, already so much could be going on in that place that, just from an energetic standpoint, it'll be a nightmare."

"Yes, but I'm not concerned about the problems of energetic ghosts. I'm concerned about some neighbor kid entering the place and getting blown up or whatever," she pointed out. Then she laughed. "I'm much less worried about *energetic ghosts*. You do know how bizarre that sounds?"

"I know."

"Anyway, why don't we completely change the topic? I was wondering ... how do you feel about going out on the boat this weekend?"

"That's a great idea. I am definitely ready to step back

for a few days. Shall we plan to leave on Friday and maybe spend the weekend out there?"

She pondered that. "The only thing would be if work becomes an issue."

He frowned, but her work would always be an issue. Still, he nodded, yet his frustration remained evident on his face. "We'll just have to work around that, but let's try. If we can't get out of the harbor because you get called in on a case, then that's just the way it is."

"It's a problem, isn't it?" she asked softly.

"No, it's not. It's only a problem if we make it one, and, like you ... I really want to get back out on the *Running Mate.*" He sighed. "I'll arrange food for the weekend, and, if nothing else, we can stay on her in the harbor."

"That would be lovely," she said warmly. Then she looked back at the remaining food on the counter and asked, "I don't suppose I could have seconds, *huh?*"

CHAPTER 7

K ATE WALKED INTO the office the next morning to find Rodney at his desk, glaring at his computer. "What's got you upset so early in the day?"

He frowned at her. "I did some research on Amie, the grieving wife," he said, with an eye roll. "I figured I had better try to redeem myself."

"Hey, it's an age-old issue," she murmured. "Nobody'll blame you."

"I blame myself for not seeing what was right in front of me."

"I'm not sure you would necessarily see anything either," she pointed out. "A beautiful woman caught up in grief is what we *should* see, until we find out differently."

"Sure, but just like the officer in charge at the crime scene, I allowed her to distract me." He frowned. "That is something I struggle with, and what I'm chastising myself for."

"Okay, so what did you come up with?"

"She was married twice before our victim," he shared.

"She's pretty young for that," Kate murmured.

"She is."

"Why do I feel you haven't told me the punchline yet?"

He snorted. "Yeah, that's because it's you. I swear to God, you and Simon are more alike than you and Smidge.

Come to think of it, you are getting more psychic than Simon is."

She glared at him. "Jesus, Rodney. Don't start pissing me off this early in the morning," she muttered.

He chuckled. "Both of Amie's former husbands died," he stated abruptly.

She froze in the act of pouring coffee, then turned slowly to face him. "Died in what way?"

He shook his head. "One was suicide, and the other was shot during a B&E."

"Was anybody ever caught for that one?"

He shook his head. "No, it's still unsolved."

She poured her coffee, then walked back over and sat down beside him. "So, what do you think of our Amie now?"

"Now I think we have to consider that she might very well be a black widow," he declared, staring at the computer screen in disgust. "Something that never even occurred to me when I was there."

"I don't think that possibility occurred to any of us."

"Oh, it occurred to you," he pointed out, turning to Kate. "It was obvious to you, and it's why Amie got so pissed off. You saw right through her."

"Maybe I saw right through the act she was putting on in the moment. Plus, she wasn't answering questions, which also pissed me off," Kate admitted, with a shrug, "but the idea that Amie already had multiple dead husbands was not on my radar. I wonder if the boyfriend knows. If he doesn't, I think we should probably tell him."

"Why?" Rodney asked.

"So he doesn't end up becoming dead husband number four," she explained, with a huff. "It's one thing when somebody kills one or two husbands. Generally they space them out so that it's not quite so easy to get caught. Amie also could have changed provinces and could have done all kinds of things to mitigate her chances of getting caught. So why would she kill her three husbands so fast?"

"Probably because she already had a boyfriend each time," Rodney guessed. "I mean, the latest boyfriend, Nate, was literally there waiting in the wings."

"I know, and that just pisses me off too," she replied. "Doesn't anybody respect the sanctity of marriage anymore? Does nobody keep their promises?"

He smiled as he looked at her. "That's your dinosaur side coming out."

She glared at him. "The world would be a better place if we had more dinosaurs then," she snapped. "And this changes the tenor of our talk with that woman," she murmured. "Hopefully she'll show up this morning."

He nodded. "Yeah, I hope she does too. I came in a little early to get some research done before we talked to her. Sure glad I did."

"Yeah, good call, but honestly, I'm not sure it's a good idea for you to even be in there."

He narrowed his gaze and stared at her for a minute. "Believe me that I'm over it."

"You might be, but it'll be a distraction if Amie thinks she can coerce you into her point of view in all this. We can't afford that little act of hers at this point, not when she clearly led us astray."

He contemplated Kate for a long moment. "I would like to be there."

She frowned and then shrugged. "Fine," she conceded, but then came back with a warning. "However, if I don't like what's happening, I'm kicking you out."

"Christ," he replied, "you know a lot can be said about the methodology behind your delivery."

"Most of it isn't that great," she admitted, "and I've heard that before. Yet it does tend to make for less in the way of issues. If I need somebody in there … I'll bring in Lilliana."

Lilliana had just walked in behind her. "Ooh, what do you need me for?" she asked in an excited tone.

Kate quickly explained, adding the new information that Rodney had just dug up. Lilliana looked from Rodney to Kate and then rubbed her hands together in glee. "I'm really looking forward to seeing this gal in action. We haven't had a black widow before."

"We don't yet know for certain that she's 100 percent duplicitous in this case," Kate pointed out, frowning, "but she's not very cooperative, and I really don't like how she went after Rodney the way she did."

"Hey, she wasn't that bad," Rodney protested.

"No, you're right, but you're equally to blame." She got up and walked over and got another cup of coffee, leaving him sputtering in place.

Lilliana laughed. "I tend to believe Kate on this. If she says that's what happened, that's probably what happened." Lilliana patted Rodney on the shoulder. "Occasionally we all get completely blindsided by the people who walk in through those doors, and we don't want to believe anything bad about them."

"Yeah, don't remind me. But Kate's right in the sense that, in the moment, I didn't want to hear or even consider the possibility of anything being wrong with this woman. Thankfully I wasn't there all that long, so it's not as if she had me under her claws too long, right?"

Kate snorted. "She had you long enough. I went back there yesterday to talk to her all on my own, just so you weren't there."

"I know"—he glared at her—"because you didn't trust me."

"More that I didn't trust her nature around you," she clarified in a different tone. "Obviously she has that effect on men and knows it, but it won't work on me, and it won't work on Lilliana, so that alone makes it that much better for her and I to do the interview."

"Do you really want me to come?" Lilliana asked her.

Kate had no reason to say yes, but her instincts were telling her that she might need Lilliana. "I'll say yes, but I don't really know why."

Lilliana raised one eyebrow. "Unless you think that she'll be difficult to deal with."

"No, I think she'll just cry foul, and I won't have someone to back me up, so your coming would be good," Kate murmured.

"Oh, in that case, I'm definitely coming," Lilliana stated, with a big smile. "Bring on the bitches."

Kate laughed. "Amie will be ... as sweet as pie when she sees you and then turn into an absolute cat when she sees me."

"Good, the cat will at least be more honest, and maybe we can get answers. Now, let's go over what it is that we need to know."

Kate explained about the latest husband's supposed suicide and how no GSR was found on his hands.

"So, it wasn't a suicide then. Not if he was shot and didn't hold the gun. That's definitely not a suicide," Lilliana said.

Kate nodded. "I told Amie yesterday that there was no way he killed himself. I also told the boyfriend," she added, with half a smile. "He looked a little shell-shocked."

"Yeah, but that doesn't mean the newest boyfriend is at all prepared to see Amie for who she really is."

"I'm not sure that *she* necessarily killed her husband either, *any* of them," Kate pointed out. "We don't have enough information to make any solid judgment at this point."

"Good enough," Lilliana replied. "Let me know when she's here, and I'll come in with you." And, with that, Lilliana returned to her desk.

About twenty minutes later, with everybody cleaning up paperwork and researching as much as they could before the interview, Kate got a call saying that Amie Mulhouse had arrived. Kate looked over at Lilliana and smiled. "Showtime."

Lilliana bounced up, a big smile on her face. She was very fashionable and all dolled up all the time, with lipstick, eyeshadow, the works. She had on more makeup today than Kate would most likely ever need. Lilliana wore it well, and that was the difference between the two of them. Even on a good day, Kate didn't look put together because it just didn't matter to her. She was clean, and she was dressed, and she looked professional, and that's all that mattered in her world. Maybe it was a type of armor for her.

As they walked into the interview room, Amie looked up, and her gaze immediately narrowed as she assessed Lilliana's presence. Kate just laughed, then sat down across from her and greeted Amie in a sweet voice. "Lilliana is here to help me with the questioning."

"Of course, as if you'll need help to further antagonize me," Ami stated. "Considering I had absolutely nothing to do with any of this, obviously you'll need somebody here to point out your mistakes." She gave a conciliatory wink to Lilliana.

"Yeah, sure," Kate quipped, completely ignoring her. "Now, let's go over the details."

"What details?" Amie asked, as if Kate were out of her mind. "My husband committed suicide. That's it."

"Sure, says you."

"What do you mean by that?'"

"We've already told you it was a murder," Kate stated bluntly and then stared her down. "So you can keep putting the words out there that don't apply, but it doesn't change the fact that this was a murder through and through. Now we'll need to know a whole lot more about you and your husband."

"I don't have to give you any details," she declared, glaring at Kate. "You're just harassing me, and I haven't done anything wrong. As it is, I'm still trying to deal with my loss."

"I'm sure dealing with your loss is a whole lot easier with your boyfriend around," Kate noted, with a mock smile. "Plus, you don't have your attorney with you, no matter what you said yesterday. So don't give me that nonsense about being sorry that your husband's gone because I don't see sorrow anywhere in this equation. And that just gives me all the more reason to check out why you're so damn happy about his death."

"I'm not happy." Amie gasped in horror. "How can you be so heartless and cruel?" With that, she turned to look at Lilliana. "Can't you do the questioning?"

Lilliana replied, "It's Kate's case. I'm just here to ensure things flow smoothly."

"Obviously it won't flow smoothly," Amie snapped. "This woman is a menace, and she's making all kinds of accusations with absolutely nothing to back them up."

"Yeah, and what accusations have I made so far?" Kate asked.

"I mean, you're making it sound as if I had something to do with my husband's death."

"Somebody did," Kate pointed out, "and I certainly haven't in any way implied it was *you*. So it's interesting you started there. All I asked for was some details, and you go straight there. So, since you brought it up, let's go back over your alibi."

"I told you that I was in bed, asleep."

"When did you last see your husband?"

"I told you, when we went to bed."

"And that was what time approximately?"

"Approximately eleven," she said, nodding. "We did have a disagreement before we went to bed," she added, raising a hand to Kate as if she were about to jump on. "Of course that's something else I have to live with now too."

Kate completely ignored the fake tears flowing from Amie across the table. "Whatever. Now let's discuss the fact that your husband was fully dressed."

"Of course he was fully dressed," she spat. "He was already up."

"Not everybody gets up at that hour of the morning and dresses fully for the day, not when it's three or four o'clock in the morning."

"Sometimes he gets up to go to work," she explained, with a shrug. "I mean, he wasn't exactly the kind of guy who stays in bed, if you know what I mean."

"Interesting," Kate murmured and didn't say anything more.

"What do you mean, *interesting*?" Amie asked.

"Obviously there was nothing keeping him in bed," Kate replied smoothly.

Amie gasped. "Did you just say that?"

"I'm allowed to say anything I want to say when it comes to trying to get answers," Kate shared, "and, so far, you've told me that your husband got up at four o'clock in the morning because he's not the kind to stay in bed. So, based on your response, I'm left to conclude that obviously nothing was in bed to keep him there. Now, do you have anything else to add to that?"

"No, I don't, but he was in the habit of getting up early anyway," she declared, glaring at Kate. "And not because we didn't have a good sex life."

"Okay, that's a good topic to segue into, thank you. So, what was your sex life like?" she asked, with a grin.

Amie sat back and stared at her. "I don't have to answer that question."

"No, you don't have to answer that question, but, by not answering, you're basically telling me that your sex life sucked. ... Did you two even sleep in the same bedroom?"

"Of course we did," Amie cried out. "We didn't have any marital problems."

Kate chuckled. "I wonder if your boyfriend, Nate, would appreciate that comment."

Amie flushed. "He has written more into our relationship than is there," she stated stiffly.

"Oh, I see, so you haven't been sleeping with Nate?"

Amie stared at her. "My husband and I had an open arrangement."

"Ah, an open arrangement. … Okay, and can I assume your boyfriend will confirm that?"

She nodded. "I'm sure he will." She lifted her chin and glared. "You don't have to be quite so judgmental."

"I'm not judgmental at all. I couldn't care less what you do in your free time," Kate said, with the wave of her hand, "unless it ends up with somebody murdered."

Amie swallowed several times and then tried to mask the fear that still remained in her facial expression. "I had nothing to do with his death."

Kate nodded. "So, the last time you saw him was eleven o'clock the prior evening, and then the next time you saw him was?"

"When I walked into his office and found him dead," she muttered, shuddering. "Blood was everywhere."

Now it seemed as if real tears came from her eyes. "Being shot tends to do that," Kate noted.

Amie glared at her. "I really don't like you."

"I understand that," Kate replied, "and I'm not really bothered, by the way." She looked over at Lilliana. "Do you have any questions to ask her?"

Lilliana nodded. "Mrs. Mulhouse, obviously this is tough for you. Nobody ever expects somebody to be murdered and then to deal with the scene you were exposed to, but I do have to ask some questions."

"Sure."

"So, if you guys were sleeping together, did he not wake you when he got up? In my case, as soon as somebody gets out of bed, I'm immediately awake."

Amie shook her head. "No, I'm a heavy sleeper, and I don't usually wake up at that hour. He gets up at odd hours.

Sometimes he doesn't sleep very well, and he just gets up and gets to work."

"And there were no marital problems that you knew of?"

She sighed. "Obviously things weren't great. Otherwise I wouldn't have been looking elsewhere."

"Yet you mentioned that your marriage was open, so then it wouldn't matter if you were looking elsewhere or not."

Amie just glared at Kate, but Amie wouldn't elaborate.

"So, when did the boyfriend come in on the scene?" Lilliana asked.

"My boyfriend, as you call him, his name is Nate, and he has absolutely nothing to do with this."

Kate interrupted, "Good, I'm glad to hear that, but I'll need to hear that from him in the meantime."

Amie glared at Kate. "I've known him for years."

"And when did he become someone you did more than just *know*?" Kate asked, glaring back at Amie.

"Do you really need to air out all the dirty laundry, or are you just taking some sick pleasure in all this?"

Kate shrugged. "I don't think any pleasure can be had when I'm standing over your husband's dead body," she stated. "I've already been to the morgue and heard no gunshot residue was found on his hands, and I looked at the damage the bullet did to his body in great detail. Believe me that I get no pleasure in any of that." She took a moment and added, "My job is to ensure that the asshole who did this pays for it, and that's what I'm doing."

Amie swallowed hard and nodded. "I want that too."

Something in her tone almost made Kate believe her. She studied her for a long moment. "Did your husband own a gun?"

"Not that I know of," she said, as her eyes squinted and her forehead creased.

"Do you own a gun?"

"No, I don't own a gun," she replied.

"Okay, let me rephrase that. Do you *have* a gun?"

Amie looked at her in horror. "So that would mean that now you think I have an illegal gun?"

"I'm just asking a question," Kate said, trying to hang on to her patience, but absolutely nothing coming out of this woman's mouth made Kate feel any better. "Amie, this is difficult for you, but you have to bear with me and get through these questions if you want to get rid of me. So do you *have* a gun?"

Amie shook her head. "I do not."

"How were you doing financially?"

"Fine. He handled all the finances."

"Was there life insurance?"

Amie choked at that and said, "I don't know."

Kate snorted.

"I really don't," Amie repeated, gritting her teeth now. "As far as I know, there wasn't any insurance policy."

"Interesting," Kate murmured. "I'll check into it."

"You can just do that? You can just turn around and check into it that?"

"Absolutely I can. Insurance is a common motive for killing spouses," she pointed out, with a knowing smile in Amie's direction.

Amie glared at her. "You must really love your job. All you do is torment people."

"Apparently," Kate agreed cheerfully, "but do you know what else I take pleasure in? I solve cases, and I put people behind bars. Especially those who kill people for profit or for any other reason," she shared, with a shrug. "Everybody is entitled to a full measure of life, and no one deserves for it to be cut short by somebody full of greed."

Amie snapped her mouth shut, then muttered, "That's not me."

"Good, then it won't matter what we find."

"It doesn't matter if you find anything. Nothing will come back to me."

"Interesting wording. That brings us back to the fact that you took a notebook from his body while he was dead, his blood all over his home office floor."

She stared at Kate. "I gave you that notebook, and it has nothing to do with anything."

"And yet it was important enough that you felt you had to take it from your husband's still warm and bleeding body."

Lilliana glanced over at Kate, reminding her that she hadn't shared that little bit of detail. Kate nodded and Lilliana winced. "Do you have an explanation for that?" Lilliana asked. "That sounds cold, even to me."

"I needed that book because it has some incriminating evidence."

"About your partners, about your open lifestyle, about what?" Lilliana asked.

"Exactly," Amie said, followed by a sigh. "I know you wouldn't believe me, so I took the notebook."

Kate added, "And yet it was *his*."

"Yes, but it's also got some of my partners identified in there," she muttered.

Kate continued. "Okay, so that's interesting. You took the notebook, and you lied about taking the notebook, and then you took pages out of the notebook."

"I did not," Amie snapped.

Kate quickly brought up the security video on her laptop and turned it so that Amie could watch herself on the recording. She gasped as she stared. "He has a video camera in his office?"

Kate studied Amie. "Oh, that's interesting. It seems as if that is more of a shock than anything to you."

"Do you want video cameras in your house?" Amie asked, staring at her. Then she turned, her face twisted, as if feeling sick inside, while she watched the evidence of her tearing pages out of the book. "Fine, I ripped out pages from the book. What do I care?"

"I don't know that you care at all," Kate pointed out. "So far, you've lied every step of the way. So, at this point in time … I don't believe anything coming out of your mouth."

Amie glared at her. "You can't convict me because I lied," she declared, with a sneer.

"That depends on if you lied and if your husband died as a consequence of it."

Amie stared at her in shock. "I had nothing to do with my husband's death."

"And yet you wanted him dead."

"No, I didn't," she snapped. "I didn't want anything to do with that. I loved him." Then she stopped and raised a hand in protest. "In my own way I loved him … and I admit I probably was a shitty wife, but that's not the issue here."

"You're wrong there. It's definitely an issue," Kate declared. "So now that we've discussed that, let's go to the next topic."

Amie groaned. "What more could you possibly ask me about?"

Kate opened up her file and smiled as she began, "Besides the fact that we want those missing pages back ... how about dead husbands number one and two?"

EVEN AFTER WORKING with Kate for months—and maybe because of the other events that had happened, particularly his own personal experiences that had so unnerved Simon— he found that he was a lot more compassionate, a lot more caring, and in many ways a lot more worried about other people. On that note, he headed first to the Paragon building that was for sale, wondering if the homeless guy was still there, hoping to coerce him out for a meal and to ensure he was really doing okay.

As he got there, the realtor was inside with another client. She looked at him in delight, while he shrugged and shared, "A homeless guy was here yesterday. I just wanted to see if he's okay."

She rolled her eyes, as if she didn't believe him.

He slipped inside, past the other potential buyer, who he smiled at and tilted his head. "Walk carefully in here. It's a bit of a death trap." Then he kept on going, knowing that the realtor would be pissed off to no end at his comment. Yet it was true. The Paragon *was* a bit of a death trap, and he wasn't too worried about the realtor's reaction, since she was bound to give him shit about something anyway.

As he walked over to where the homeless guy had been sleeping, Simon was relieved to find no sign of him. Even his bedroll and all his personal belongings appeared to be gone. With a smile Simon nodded, then looked around at the place and whispered, "Good choice."

He exited the building, ignoring the realtor and her client, then headed to his favorite coffee shop to pick up a cup of coffee, one of several for the day. As he did so, he saw the homeless guy, sitting off to the side. Simon walked over and asked him, "Hey, you vacated the building, did you?"

Bleary-eyed, he looked up at him and nodded.

"Have you eaten?" Simon asked.

"No, man, I haven't eaten in a while. If you're feeling generous, I could really use a coffee."

Simon handed over his own coffee. "How about food?"

He looked up at him hopefully. "Are you serious?"

"I'm serious. Obviously I don't know for how long I'll be serious, but, right now in this moment, if you want a meal, I'm happy to supply you with one."

"Yes, please."

Simon headed back into the café, grabbed another coffee for himself, and came back out with a couple breakfast sandwiches for the homeless guy. He handed them over and gave him a cheerful smile. "Have a good day." And, with that, he turned and headed off.

The homeless guy called out, "Thank you."

Simon lifted a hand but didn't slow down, until he heard the homeless guy's next words.

"They approve of you, you know?"

Simon stopped, turned to him, and asked, "Who approves of me?"

"The ghosts. They told me that you could buy the place."

"Ah? Is that right?" he replied, studying him. "You talk to them often?"

"Don't have much choice when they keep me awake at night," he muttered. "I've asked them to not be quite so noisy, and they've asked me to not be quite so irritating," he shared, with a laugh. "Neither one of us really got what we wanted."

Simon didn't know what to say to that, so he just nodded. "That doesn't mean I'll buy the place."

"You should, man. You should. It's a good place, and it's got a good vibe."

Simon agreed with that, yet, if it was full of ghosts, that would add an element of complexity that he wasn't sure he really wanted to encounter while rehabbing that building.

"They just want somebody who would care about the place, about them," the homeless man explained, as Simon continued to walk away.

"I'm sure somebody will buy it, and somebody will care."

"It needs to be you," he called out.

In exasperation, Simon turned again. "Why?"

"Because they said it needs to be you."

"Then the owners need to drop the price," Simon stated, with a smile, "because that building needs a lot of work. It's not very safe the way it is."

The homeless guy nodded. "Yeah, that's true. It's one of the reasons I sleep there."

Simon frowned at him. "Why? You got a death wish or something?"

"No, not at all, but I also know that nobody else will go in there. Between the ghosts and the fact that the building itself is such a disaster," the homeless guy explained, "nobody else will go in there and hassle me."

"Good point," Simon noted, with a smile, "and not bad logic."

"I figured the stairwell is one of the safest places because, if the building comes down, that is one of those locations where I would have a little bit of coverage."

"I wouldn't count on that," Simon noted, as he thought about it. "Why don't you just find another abandoned building that won't come down around your ears?"

"Yeah, that might be an idea to consider too," he replied, "but the Paragon still needs to be your building. The ghosts said so."

"Then they'll need to find a way to facilitate that." With a laugh, Simon lifted a hand, leaving once more.

"What's your name?" the homeless guy asked.

Simon gave him a smile. "Simon."

"I'll tell them to ensure Simon buys it then," he stated, with a nod. "It really should be yours."

"What's your name?" Simon asked, eyeing him closely.

"Shawn," he murmured, "at least that's my street name."

"It's still the name that you go by," Simon declared, "unless you're changing it."

"*Nah*, no point in changing it," he murmured. "Nobody remembers my real name."

"What was your birth name?" Simon asked.

"Jack Ludwig."

Simon smiled at him, then reached out to shake his hand. "I'll remember both names, Shawn. Have a good day." And with that, Simon was off to start his workday.

CHAPTER 8

KATE STOPPED AT Reese's desk and asked, "Can you pull all the files relating to the deaths of the two prior husbands of Amie Mulhouse? I'll need all the available details surrounding those deaths."

"Two husbands?"

"A third one just passed, supposedly a suicide, but it wasn't," she added, with a nod.

Reese's eyebrows shot up, and she nodded. "I'll have that for you soon."

Kate returned to her desk to find Lilliana standing off to the side, talking to Rodney.

Lilliana looked up and muttered, "Amie's really a piece of work."

"Yeah, a piece of work she is," Kate confirmed, "but how much of her story did you believe?"

"Not a lot," she admitted, "although I'm not sure she killed him—her latest husband, that is. Definitely a hint of reality or truthfulness to her statements in there."

At that, Kate nodded. "I know, but definitely something more is going on, and she's not what you would call a cooperative witness."

"No, and you sure got her goat." Lilliana laughed. "I could see how much she really hoped this guy would be in there." She nudged Rodney's chair.

"Oh, yeah, Amie would have led him all over the place," Kate noted.

"Only if I allowed it," Rodney replied stiffly, glaring at her. "And obviously now I would not."

"Good to know," Kate said in a teasing voice. "But, if she's cleared for murder on this one, don't ask her out, considering you could end up as dead husband number four."

"Besides, she already has at least one boyfriend lined up," Lilliana pointed out.

"Exactly," Kate agreed, "but I do feel somebody needs to warn Nate though."

Lilliana shook her head. "Chances are Nate's too far gone to believe anything we say."

Rodney looked over at Kate and asked her, "You really think Amie had something to do with all these deaths?"

"I'm not sure what to believe yet," she clarified, "but what I can tell you is that she's a very uncooperative witness and that she's lied since the first moment we arrived at her place. She also protested her innocence in the previous deaths of husbands number one and two." She looked over at Lilliana. "How is your workload?"

"It's holding," she replied, "and, of course, the minute I say that, things will blow up."

"I know, right?"

"Why? Do you need help?" Lilliana asked her.

"It's not so much that I need help," Kate acknowledged, "but I'm just thinking about opening an investigation into the deaths of her other husbands."

Lilliana warned her of the obvious, though it wasn't as if she didn't know. "That's pretty serious if you do."

"I know, but how can I not at least take a look at them?

Once I get those files …"

"Is Reese pulling them for you?" Lilliana asked.

"She is."

Just then a shout came from the other side of the bull-pen, as Colby had heard part of that.

Kate walked over to his doorway and asked him in amusement, "Did that shout have something to do with me?"

He grinned at her. "Maybe. What trouble are you into this time?"

"Me?" She glared. "Why am I always in trouble?"

"I don't know," he said. "I've been asking myself that since you started here."

"It's this latest case," she muttered and then quickly explained why she brought Lilliana in on it.

"That's a good call," Colby noted, "but you can't be too hard on Rodney. That guy is a soft touch."

"How does anybody stay a soft touch in this business?" she wondered out loud.

Colby laughed. "We don't have much in the way of innocence anymore," he admitted, "but let's give us a little bit of credit when we do feel empathy. Keep me informed if anything else happens." And he took a moment to stare her directly in the eye. "You really think she's good for the husband?"

"I don't know whether she's good for any of her husbands or not, but she's definitely a liar and a cheat."

"Which will never be good in your book," Colby stated. "Got it."

She shrugged. "I'm not a prude or anything, but she had a boyfriend lined up and already in the house when I got there to ask some questions."

"Yeah, definitely suspicious, isn't it?"

"Not my favorite people, for sure," she murmured. "Yet again, that's just the way of the world, isn't it?"

"Doesn't have to be," he pointed out, "and don't take any of that as being the way *all* of the world functions."

"Are you sure?" she asked, with a wry look in his direction. "It sure seems as if a lot of the world is exactly that shitty."

"Yes, but it doesn't have to stay that way," he muttered. "Anyway, keep me informed." He waved her off. His phone rang just then, so it was a good time to leave anyway.

As she walked out, the others looked at her with raised eyebrows. She shrugged. "Just wants to be kept informed."

At that, Lilliana laughed. "*Of course.* You do know that if it was any of us though—"

"Any of us what?" Kate looked to Lilliana for clarity.

"We would all be in shit for something," she replied smoothly.

"I'm always in shit," Rodney declared, and he glared at Kate.

"Like hell you guys are," Kate argued, staring from one to the other.

"Where the hell is that coming from?" Rodney asked, sounding offended. "And here I thought we were just starting to get along."

"We are," Kate noted. "It's been good. Let's keep it that way. And, Rodney ... you just need to stay away from the female suspects."

He snorted. "Do you want me to question the boyfriend before he has a chance to be primed by her?"

"Amie was heading somewhere else right now," Lilliana said.

"That doesn't mean Amie didn't phone Nate," Kate added, "so let's call him right now." Then Kate quickly called the boyfriend. When he answered, he was cautious. "Have you spoken to Amie this morning?" she asked bluntly. When he hesitated, she knew the next words out of his mouth wouldn't be the truth. "And of course if we check and find out you're lying …"

"We spoke earlier for just a moment. She told me that she wanted to see me later this afternoon, but she had an appointment first. She sounded pretty frantic, and, more to the point … she also told me not to talk to you."

"Amie doesn't have the right to decide that," Kate replied smoothly. "I get that she's not very happy with me right now because we're looking into the cases of her previous dead husbands as well." When only shocked silence came on the other end, she asked, "Oh, did you not know that this is her third dead husband?"

"Jesus. What?"

"Yes," Kate replied, with a hint of sorrow. "So, before you get too involved with this woman, you might want to take another look at whether you're prepared to risk becoming dead husband number four."

"That's not fair. She's really sweet."

"I'm sure she is, especially toward the men in her life, the same way I'm sure that every one of the men who married her would have said the exact same thing."

More shock came on the other end. "You're serious, aren't you?"

"I don't know if she had anything to do with any of her husbands' deaths," Kate clarified, "but I do know that, when you get this many dead husbands around a single woman, we definitely have an issue. So, what you do with Amie is up to you, but I would really hate to find myself standing over your body next."

She asked him a few more questions and then disconnected, leaving him to stew, but getting him to promise that he would call Kate if he thought of anything that was pertinent to the case. Then Kate pulled out the file that Reese had compiled on the previous dead husbands and sat down to read it. In the meantime, Lilliana left, and Owen arrived. Andy was still out on extended medical leave and had yet to be replaced, although there was still talk about doing just that. Rodney got up soon and left, with Kate sitting here, still reading.

When Rodney came back after lunch, he frowned at her. "You haven't even moved."

"Fascinating reading," she muttered, with a mock smile, "but unfortunately, in both prior deaths, the files are a little on the thin side."

"So, what took you so long to read them then?" he joked.

"Reading between the lines as much as anything."

"What do you mean?"

"There were a lot of accusations with the suicide death of her first husband, but nothing ever came of it. The family was pretty irate, as they were damn sure he would never have committed suicide."

"Interesting," Rodney murmured.

"Yeah, *interesting* is right." Kate continued writing down notes, names, addresses, and questions that she wanted to ask.

Rodney watched her work, then asked, "So, are you really-ly pissed at me?"

Surprised, she lifted her head and gave it a shake. "No,

not at all. Why?" He frowned, and she realized she had to put his mind at ease. "I figured you weren't the best person to come into that Amie interview with me. She's uncooperative enough without being distracted by thinking she could play up to you."

"But still … maybe it would have worked out better if she could have. We might have gotten something out of her."

"I don't think so. She probably would have just ended up hating you at the end of the day, but this way she gets to remember the nice cop," Kate added, with a laugh.

"It doesn't bother you that you're not seen as a nice cop?"

"No," she declared. "I would just as soon *not* be the nice cop. I find it much easier for me."

"But you're not that much of a bitch."

She looked at him and then laughed. "Glad to hear it," she replied, with a grin on her face. "But when it comes to these assholes out there, I really would rather be the bitch. That may not make a whole lot of sense to you nice guys, but I really don't want any of these jerks taking advantage of their supposed spouses."

"And yet Amie's not overly happy with Robert's death, and nothing indicates she did the deed either," he reminded her.

"I know," she admitted, then added, "but what are the chances that she hasn't had anything to do with all three of them?"

SIMON STARED UP at the Paragon building for the second morning in a row, as he found himself automatically walking toward it, which was driving him nuts. Even from a block away it towered majestically, even though it was dwarfed by other new high-rises. Still, something about this one building gave it presence. Simon gave a happy sigh as he realized that it was possible that this building could be his. As he turned around the corner heading up the block, he groaned when he saw Ariel, the irritatingly pushy real estate agent, standing outside the entrance.

She saw him and beamed. "Look at that," she crowed. "I knew you would be back."

"Maybe. What's that got to do with you?"

She glared at him. "You would get along better in this business if you were nicer." She fluffed at her hair, as he backed up a few steps and shook his head.

"Business and being nice don't necessarily have to go together."

She groaned. "In your case I've never known you to be anything other than prickly."

"That's not true," he stated in a firm tone. "I've done several deals with you, and clearly I don't have to be your best friend for that to happen."

She shook her head. "It would be easier if you used me exclusively as your realtor."

"As you already know, I don't use anybody exclusively," he declared, "and I have my own realtor."

"One I've hardly dealt with," she snapped, "so your real-tor could be just me."

"Could be, but why would I do that?" he asked, eyeing her curiously. "What's in that for me?"

"Why not?" she retorted, raising her hands. "I make life easy for people."

He half smiled. "There really isn't any way to make life

easy in my world," he stated. "It's a very busy and chaotic space."

"Sure, and that's why you need somebody to keep an eye on these properties for you."

"So, you're telling me that you don't already do that?"

She flushed. "Of course, but I could do so much more."

He just gave her a nonplussed look. "What are you doing here?"

"I could ask you the same thing," she replied slyly. "As it is, maybe I'm waiting for a client."

He shook his head. "Nope, you're not."

She stared at him. "How would you know?"

He laughed. "Nobody else wants this place."

"You don't know that," she replied, giving him a crafty look. "You don't know anything about the interest I have generated for this place. Of course, if I were your exclusive realtor, then I could potentially help you with that."

"Would that not also cross some lines of ethics in your world?"

She shook her head. "No, of course not. I would ensure it was all aboveboard. Obviously that's important to you."

He sighed. "It *should* be important to you too."

"I didn't say it wasn't," she protested. "Don't go putting words in my mouth."

He shook his head at that. "Yet you appear to be putting words in my mouth. I'm not ready to deal exclusively with one realtor, which I have told you multiple times, so stop hassling me about it."

"Okay, fine," she muttered. "I'm not hassling you, but I won't bring it up again."

He snorted at that. "Until next time."

"Maybe." She shrugged. "You can't fault a girl for trying."

"I also don't understand the pressure to be exclusive."

"I could be there to make it happen for you."

He didn't say anything to that and just stared at her with a wry look in his gaze.

She sighed. "It's really not wrong in this world to have somebody on your side," she added.

"I don't need a full-time realtor, and I already have my chosen realtor."

"But you don't know what all I could do for you," she repeated, with a smile. "So, don't dismiss me just because you don't know what I can do yet."

He motioned at the Paragon building, behind them. "So, will you tell me how many people you have interested in it?"

"I can't really do that," she said, "but other people are interested, and I can say with surety that it's got prospects."

"Maybe, but not at the current asking price," he stated. "It's a drop-down for most people."

"But not for you," she replied shrewdly. "I've seen you buy properties similar to this one before. To everybody else they're dumps and teardowns, but, to you, something was there that you kept going after."

Not liking that she had intuited as much as she had, he shrugged. "Sometimes it's still not worth it."

"Of course it's not," she agreed, "and you have to do a cost analysis. I understand that, but once you do that …"

He nodded in agreement. "If I get that far on this property, I'll get back to you."

"You better hurry up," she warned, "because there is other interest."

"If I lose it, I lose it." Obviously the realtor was not happy with that response, so Simon stepped around the now-scowling realtor and moved on into the building.

"You can't just walk in and out all the time," she said in exasperation.

"Why not?" he asked, turning to look at her. "The homeless certainly are."

She frowned at him. "I did ask that guy to leave yesterday."

"Did you talk to him?"

"For a few minutes. He seems to have a mental illness problem."

"I would say that a lot of our homeless have that problem," he stated gently, "but that doesn't make them any less of a person."

"Of course not," she snapped, "but I do wish they could be helped elsewhere and not have them squatting in abandoned buildings."

"He wanted the peace and quiet, and this building was haunted and kept most people out."

She frowned. "You don't believe that, do you?"

"Doesn't matter whether I do or not, yet I bet a lot of your *interested people* would consider it."

She wasn't happy hearing that either. "I'm sure I could dissuade most of them, particularly knowing that this guy is not all there mentally. Still, I wouldn't want that to stop a sale."

"No, of course not." He chuckled. "That doesn't mean that it won't. Not everybody wants to get involved with ghosts."

"You do?" she challenged.

"Didn't say I do. Didn't say I don't." He gave her a beaming smile. "What I can tell you is that ghosts won't make a difference in my decision." Almost a whisper of relief crossed her face, and he nodded. "But I'm not yet ready to make the decision as to whether I want it or not."

"That's why you're back for the third time then, *huh?*" she asked, beaming at him. "You think I haven't noticed?"

"I'm sure you *have* noticed, since it would be typical of you to keep track of my movements."

"Hey, you make it sound as if I'm some stalker or something," she protested. "I'm just keeping an eye on my client's property."

"Yeah? And I'm sure he wants to know whether I'm interested or not?"

"Sure, of course he does," she stated, then frowned. "I mean, he's anxious to sell … but he needs to get a good price for it."

"They'll get the price that I'm willing to pay, and it won't be anything you can push me on either."

"I know, which is both irritating and much easier on me."

"In what way?" he asked, turning to face her.

She shrugged. "I just tell them that I've worked with you in the past and that this is the best price they'll get and that you won't budge." She took a moment, then went on. "They generally give me quite a bit of grief about it, but then eventually believe me."

"Also it's pretty easy to look at my history of purchases," he pointed out, "and to realize that I can't change my system just because of them."

"I think eventually they get around to understanding that it's your price or no price."

"Exactly," he replied, "and I do take on buildings that a lot of other people won't."

"But you've lost a lot too," she pointed out, "and, when you look at the history, I could have helped you get those all along."

He laughed. "If you're representing the seller, I'm not interested in working with you."

"You know the laws have changed, right? I can't represent both sides."

"I also know that you would just get somebody else in your office to handle one side or the other," he clarified. "So don't even try to tell me that you're not involved in both." She frowned and he nodded. "I know the new law was intended to change the inherent unfairness in the real estate market, but I highly doubt it's changed anything at all," he muttered. "Are you coming or leaving?" he asked her, as he turned to look at the entrance, which seemed to be calling to him, "because I'm going in for a look."

"But you were just here yesterday," she protested. "What on earth could there possibly still be for you to look at for another round?"

He laughed. "That's why I buy buildings, and you don't."

"It's also why I sell buildings," she snapped right back at him, "and you don't."

"Yeah … if I would have been in your business, I would probably end up broke."

"How on earth would you end up broke?" she asked, startled.

He shrugged. "Because I would buy mostly whatever I wanted, and you can bet I would be stacking up my inventory pretty damn fast." And, with that, he closed the front door in her face and walked into the building. When she didn't open it behind him, he felt the tension inside him relaxing.

Sparring with a realtor was never at the top of his list of things to do for fun, but, in many ways, it was a necessary evil.

In theory, he could have approached the last remaining Paragon owner privately, as Simon had approached the family who owned this very building a couple years back. However, at that time, it was all caught up in a dying owner and a pair of not-too-cooperative heirs, so Simon had walked away. Obviously the slate had changed now. The old man he'd talked to had also passed on, and now the sole heir was looking at what he had for options. The longer the Paragon sat empty, the fewer options the seller had, and Simon wasn't in any rush.

Did he want the building? Yes, though he still hadn't made a definitive decision yet. Even as he had that thought, a voice inside, *his* voice, told him that he already knew what he would do and called him a liar, laughing at him. Of course that was also correct, but Simon wasn't at the point of making a solid decision that would end up being a viable choice. He would eventually. He just wasn't there yet.

Sometimes it took him a long time to get there, and sometimes he lost out because of it, but he took that as a sign of the property not being for him. He was okay with that too. Somedays it just seemed as if life offered more lemons than lemonade, and he would often take that as a sign as well.

As he stepped deeper into the bowels of the building, he felt that same sense of agelessness about her. He studied the walls, trying to see through the structure, knowing that one of his engineers would have to walk through and take a closer look. He made a mental note to get his guys on that. The Paragon's interior was absolutely gone and was something he had to look past in order to get to the next stage of what he was doing, and he would eventually. He could get there, but something about this old building kept calling him, and it had absolutely nothing to do with the value of the real estate. It had everything to do with the ghosts, but he just didn't know why.

He felt a shiver slide across his arms, raising the hairs along his arms and the back of his neck.

CHAPTER 9

KATE HAD GONE through both of the previous case histories on Amie's first and second dead husbands and had written down a series of notes for herself. The first husband committed suicide two years into the marriage. The second husband was killed on their honeymoon. There had been a break-in, and, as the reports had stated, he'd fought with the intruder and had been shot and killed in the struggle.

Nobody was ever questioned on the murder at the time, and no one had ever been caught or convicted since. This had also occurred in the Philippines. She didn't want to say that things were a whole lot more casual over there, but, in truth, things were a whole lot more casual over there.

She frowned as she went through the bits and pieces of both dead husbands' files, finding family members of the two husbands. With that list in hand, she picked up the phone and contacted Jimmy, the brother of Amie's first husband, John. When she identified who she was, silence came on the other end. He had clearly not seen this coming.

"Why are you calling me after all this time?"

She frowned. "I get that five years later is a long time for a grieving family, but it's not necessarily a long time for investigations into these cases."

"If you say so," he replied, "but all it does is bring up all that pain again."

"I'm sorry for that," she murmured.

"What possible reason could you have for bringing this up again now?"

She hesitated, then dove in. "Because Amie's third husband just passed away."

"Third?" he asked in shock. "She's already been married twice after my brother?"

"Yes, and her second husband was murdered on their honeymoon in the Philippines."

Another long silence ensued, and then he said, "Jesus, either she's got the devil's own misfortune or …"

"Exactly," Kate agreed, "and I'm just doing a check into the events of the first two deaths in case she possibly helped them along the way. Hence, my investigation."

"Good," he declared brutally. "I never liked that bitch. I told my brother that he shouldn't marry her and that absolutely no way he would ever be happy with her."

"Why was that?"

"Because he loved education, and he loved people who pursued education. It was really important to him, and then suddenly he married somebody just the opposite? Education had absolutely nothing to do with her world. I asked him what they even had in common, and he just laughed. I told him it didn't matter how good she was in bed because, at some point in time, he would want someone he could converse with. I didn't like the bitch from the get-go, but he was *in love*. He was madly in love with her, and I couldn't talk him out of it. Then two years later, he was dead, after being so unhappy, so miserable that he committed suicide," he shared bitterly.

"Never *ever* in a million years would I have thought that

my brother would do that. He was a guy who loved life, and he was absolutely full of life," His voice broke as he spoke, and Kate felt sorry for him as he went on. "The whole thing remains completely incomprehensible to me." Then he stopped, and his tone took on an odd note, as he asked, "Hang on a minute. Are you thinking that John didn't commit suicide?"

"At this point I'm just inquiring into the circumstances around his death," she clarified. "I know that the investigation was concluded and that the cause of death was determined to be suicide."

"Sure, he swallowed a bunch of pills and ended up in the morgue," Jimmy confirmed, "but what if he didn't knowingly take those pills?"

"And that is always something we have to look at. The police report stated he was quite depressed beforehand. Do you know anything about that?"

"If he was, he didn't tell me about it. That was *Amie's* version of events," he stated bitterly. "She would never talk to us afterward either, saying that it was way too painful. She didn't want anything to do with us and couldn't even tell us about his last days. Those two years of his life were lost to us," he added. "After they got married, it seemed as if it didn't take very long before we had no contact with him. She completely isolated John, and, the next thing we know, we're getting a phone call, saying that he'd committed suicide. *Yes, it's absolutely horrific, but, sorry, he's gone.*"

So much bitterness filled Jimmy's tone that it was easy to see how he still felt the pain of his loss. "I am sorry," Kate replied, "and I'm not trying to stir up anything untoward. I'm just trying to find some way to get to the truth. My job is to investigate the death of her third husband, and I felt as if we needed to take a hard look at everything."

"Yes, of course, of course, and thank you for that," he added hurriedly. "I'm sorry. I'm not trying to be bitter, but it's really hard when you lose somebody who you love, and you can't understand the circumstances. It would be absolutely godawful to find out that John had been murdered," he admitted, his voice rising. "But, in a sick way, it would also be a hell of a lot better because then we would know that he didn't choose to walk away from us."

"Would he, if he was terribly unhappy, have contacted you?"

"I would have thought so, yes," he stated. "At any point in time, up until John married her, we were close. All of us were close. But, with that marriage to Amie … everything broke apart, and John just wasn't there for us anymore. He wasn't there for any of us—or against us either, really. With any phone calls we made, he was either too busy, or he didn't answer them himself and never called back. So I don't know what it was."

"That's not normal behavior."

"We wondered if Amie was trying to separate him from us, to isolate him, you know? He was all about her and hadn't been terribly impressed that we were not fans of Amie's. Plus, their marriage happened very, very quickly. Far too quickly from my point of view, and he didn't get enough time to really know who she was inside. We weren't terribly supportive," he shared, with a groan, "and believe me that we paid for that dearly. We never got another chance to talk to him. Next thing we knew, John was just gone, with no warning, Amie telling us how he supposedly committed suicide because he was so unhappy and depressed."

Jimmy continued. "I *can* imagine that he was unhappy

because, honest to God, nothing good was between them. And," he said in frustration, "yes, opposites attract sometimes. I get it. We've talked about it among ourselves many, many times since, but it was all just so wrong."

"Wrong in what way?" Kate asked.

"Amie and my brother were so *not* the same people that you would ever in a million years think they would be happy long-term, and the family was right because obviously he wasn't happy. Not if he committed suicide and certainly not if he was murdered," he snapped. "Jesus, I can't believe you called me, and now I won't stop thinking about this."

"I'm not here to stir up anything," she reminded him, "and yet I realize that making these phone calls will do just that. But I'm not doing my due diligence by this latest husband or by your brother if I don't take another look at all this."

"Honestly, Detective, I'm grateful that you're looking into it," Jimmy muttered, "and I'm sorry. I'm obviously allowing my emotions to get the better of me, and that's not fair either. Please do a thorough check, look into every angle, and, when you come to a conclusion, let us know. I just want the truth. That's all."

"I will," she promised, "and I guess I need to ask if there were any other friends who your brother hung out with? Anybody who he might have talked with, anybody online maybe? Did he belong to any support groups or anything?"

"None that I know of," he replied, after a minute. "Again, that would have all been in the time period when we had almost no contact with him. It was hard enough to know that his life was going on without us, but to know that he was so unhappy that he didn't even come home when he obviously needed somebody? ... Talk about a challenging time."

"What about your family? Are your parents still alive?"

"My mother is. My father died last year," Jimmy shared. "Also a very difficult time on the heels of losing John. My father was never the same afterward."

She winced at that. "Yes, of course. I'm sorry."

"Not your fault," he murmured. "Anyway, if you have any other questions, just get a hold of me, and I'll do my best to share whatever I might know. Just be aware that we had almost nothing to do with him in the last two years of his life, once he married that bitch. You can imagine that reality has tormented us terribly. You would think, with our family so close before that, if your brother is down and out, his family is the one place he should turn to." Jimmy ended the call soon after that.

Kate made notes of her telephone conversation with Jimmy about his brother John. But the longer Kate stared at that data, she had to wonder if anything Amie said was true or if it was all a fabrication of Amie's. Something in all this related mess didn't ring true, but Kate had yet to find absolutely anything in this latest case, the death of Robert Mulhouse, Amie's third husband. Was it anything other than murder, maybe not even involving Amie? Just something else for Kate to unravel.

She sat for a long moment, tapping her phone. Then taking a cleansing breath, she picked up her phone and contacted Susan, the sister of Amie's second dead husband, Daniel, currently living in San Diego. When she reached the sister and explained what she was calling about, Susan was soon crying.

"Dear God," Susan muttered in between sobs. "I sure hope somebody will look into this, though I don't even know what you could possibly do about it since it didn't even happen here in the States. We've been completely tormented over the fact that nobody seemed to give a crap about Daniel's murder."

"I'm sorry," Kate replied, wincing at the impassioned plea in the sister's voice. "And you're right. I'll have a very limited influence in the investigation. I can request the files, but it won't necessarily help."

"So, why are you calling?" Susan asked, suddenly curious. "I mean, if you can't have the investigation reopened or do anything from a distance because it happened in a separate country, what is it that you're hoping to do?"

"I'm looking into the circumstances of Daniel's marriage," she replied.

"Why?"

Kate respected Susan's bluntness, especially when it came to the people she interviewed. "Because the third husband of your ex-sister-in-law, Amie, just died."

"Third husband? Wait. When was the second marriage?"

"Your brother was Amie's second marriage. She was married once before she married your brother," Kate explained. "So, apparently you didn't know that?"

"No, we didn't know that. I bet Daniel didn't know that either," she declared, sounding puzzled. "Why would she have kept that from us?"

"Because her first husband committed suicide," Kate shared, "and I'm sure a certain amount of that she didn't want to explain."

Susan gasped. "Oh God, that would be horrible."

"Yes, I'm sure it was."

"So, what about this third husband? Amie obviously moved on." An odd tone filled the sister's words. "Somehow, it doesn't seem as if it's been all that long, but maybe that's not fair. I don't know."

"Two years have passed, I believe. Two and a half, I guess."

"Yes, so how long was she married this time?" she asked.

Kate hesitated, and then, knowing it would cause quite a ruckus, she replied, "Two years."

Shocked silence came on the other end. "What? So, six months after my brother's death she married someone else?" The pain was evident in her tone. "That's all Daniel meant to her?"

"I don't know about that," Kate replied. "All I can tell you is that Amie's been married for another couple years, and this time her third husband supposedly committed suicide."

"Why do you say, *supposedly?*"

"We're treating it as a murder."

"Good God." Another shocked silence filled the other end that went on for a while. "Detective, I feel as if you're not telling me an awful lot."

"I'm not at liberty to tell you much, at least not at this time," she admitted. "I'm sorry about that, but it's just part of the work I do. Until we have confirmed details, we won't release them to the public."

"No, no, of course not," Susan murmured. "Christ, if Amie had nothing to do with it, I can't think of anybody unluckier in love than her. However, if she did have something to do with my brother's murder," she snapped, "I hope she rots in hell." She choked up before adding, "Look. I need a few minutes to even contemplate what you've just told me and to get ahold of myself. So, if you have any other questions, could you call me back at another time?"

"I can do that," Kate said, "but I do need to ask a few questions right now, specifically regarding how Daniel felt about the marriage, how you felt about Amie, and things like that."

"There wasn't anything to feel. It seemed as if she separated him from us very quickly, before the engagement even," Susan shared. "We really hoped she wasn't the kind of person who would isolate Daniel from his family, but ... no doubt that's what she did."

"So, they broke off all contact?"

"I think it probably would have just gotten worse, but Daniel didn't make it very far into the marriage, did he? He didn't even survive his honeymoon after all," she stated bluntly.

"If he hadn't been murdered, how do you think it would have ended up down the road?"

"I don't know for sure, but I can tell you that my other brother was already heartbroken by the fact that Daniel was avoiding us, or at least not wanting to spend time with the family anymore, mostly because he was spending that time with Amie."

"Right."

"Is that similar to what happened in Amie's other marriages?"

"Certainly in the first marriage, but I haven't had a chance to connect with the family members of the third husband yet."

"I wonder if she just isolated them all," Susan murmured. "A lot of insecure women do that regardless, and it makes them feel as if maybe they're more loved if they can get rid of the family members. Thus the husband isn't spreading that love and attention among too many people."

That was an astute observation on Susan's part. With a deep sigh, Kate asked, "You didn't have a whole lot of time to spend with Amie, so do you know what she was like as a person? Can you tell me something about her?"

"I thought she was bitchy," Susan declared, "not my kind of person. I did ask Daniel at one point in time what he saw in her, and he told me that she was the only one who ever loved him, and I felt that was extremely telling."

Kate sat back and frowned. "Did Daniel have a lot of friends prior to this?"

"No, he was a loner where girls were concerned. He was absolutely shocked when he hooked up with Amie."

"Right," Kate muttered, as she stared down at her notes. "So, Daniel was probably overjoyed then at having a relationship and having somebody who loved him."

"Exactly," Susan agreed. "My mother and I … we just seemed to cease to exist, even though we had been there for Daniel all this time."

No bitterness filled his sister's tone, and Kate had to wonder why that was. "You seem to be fairly calm about this whole scenario."

"It's not even so much that I'm calm," she explained, "but, when you love somebody as deeply as I loved my brother, you just realize that you can't change some things. You just hope that they're happy, wherever they are." She spoke with that same calmness in her tone, and that was unnerving for Kate. "And, in this instance, I really hope Daniel enjoyed his life before it ended too quickly. Also, if you find out that Amie had anything to do with it," Susan shared, "I hope you nail her ass to the wall. Now I really need to get off the phone." With a click she disconnected, leaving Kate to stare down at her notes.

When Lilliana walked back into the bullpen, Kate asked her, "I guess a case from another country means we don't have any access to the files, right?"

"We can send a request," Lilliana suggested, "but it generally won't be fast or necessarily easy to get. A lot of time they'll eventually give us a copy of their investigation file, but it'll be very incomplete, and you'll be left staring at it, wondering how it was even a completed case."

Kate nodded. "I was thinking that, but the least we can do is try."

"Why? Has it got to do with this recent murder?"

"Yes," Kate said. "Amie's second husband was murdered … in the Philippines."

"Ah." At that, Lilliana winced. "The Philippines, now that's the wild, wild west when it comes to murder."

"Apparently you can hire it done pretty easily there?"

She nodded. "You can absolutely hire it done."

"Amie had contacts there too. That's why they honeymooned there, to see her family—supposedly."

"Jesus. So, she's from the Philippines?"

"She is, but she's a Canadian citizen now."

"Right, so you request the file, and we'll see what you get, but I wouldn't count on getting any information that'll be helpful."

"Right," she murmured. She picked up the phone and spoke to Reese. "Can you get that Philippines file on Amie's dead second husband?"

"Sure, no problem. Just may take a while to receive it."

"Understood. Plus, do you have time to dig up any family for Robert Mulhouse and ask them about his marriage to Amie?"

"I'll see what I can find."

"Thanks." Kate ended the call, then stared down at her handwritten notes in front of her. "Three husbands," she murmured, without looking up. "All three dead."

"Life insurance?" Lilliana asked.

"No idea for now, but that's next. I've got Reese on it because, as soon as life insurance is involved …"

"I know. Our suspicions go way up, and, in this case, she's already got a boyfriend on tap, all lined up to be husband number four."

"Which is also sketchy."

"More than just sketchy," Lilliana stated. "I would suspect the boyfriend needs to be taking a serious second look, but I don't really have any reason to say it that specifically at this point."

"Sure you do," Kate countered, with a bright smile. "You just don't want to imply that he's in danger until you have something concrete."

Lilliana shrugged at that.

"Would you?" Kate asked her.

"No, I sure wouldn't," Lilliana responded, "but whenever you solve whatever is going on, I highly suggest you give him a heads-up."

"I know," Kate muttered. "I made him aware of the other husbands, as well as their shortened lives, so he's not entirely clueless, though he appears completely smitten. So my warning may have fallen on deaf ears. This case won't be the fastest to close, I'm afraid."

"Did the tapes get you anything?"

"Forensics has them," she shared, "and I saw a little bit that Smidge had found, and we've pulled the security tapes for the full night, as well as security tapes from the neighborhood, because we found no other signs of anybody entering or leaving the house. We also still have to find out where the gun came from and if they got the gun and matched the bullets to it. More so, I want to know if Amie even knows how to use it."

"When it comes to guns, all it requires is point and shoot," Lilliana murmured, looking over at her.

Kate grumbled, "Yet, according to what we have on file, Amie doesn't have any experience with them."

"Again, essentially nothing there would rule her out." Lilliana took a moment and then added, "Sounds to me as if your wifey is guilty."

"Maybe, maybe not. I don't know yet," Kate muttered.

"Where was the boyfriend at the time of the hubby's death?"

"Nate says he was at home alone."

"So, we don't have a confirmation on that either?"

"Nope," Kate replied, then something clicked. "You think he might have killed the husband in order to free up the wife?"

"It's hard to say with what little we have right now," Lilliana stated, "but I wouldn't be so quick to release him from the suspect pool."

"Oh, I haven't released *anyone* yet," Kate declared, with a grim smile. "I'm just getting started."

SIMON'S MORNING HAD been a complete crap show, and, as his afternoon wore on, Simon realized he needed to shift today's mood. When things went bad, if he didn't soon interrupt that momentum, it seemed to stay on course, getting even worse. That was not how he wanted the rest of his day to go.

He called out to Joe, "I'm heading to get coffee, and I'll work at the café for a bit." Joe raised a hand in recognition of his words but didn't respond. Like Simon, Joe was fully invested in keeping things on track, plus dealing with supply issues, which were now becoming even bigger problems, through no fault of their own. Life just happened and, with the pandemic, became a whole lot worse. Now they had this constant issue in the world of supplies, and no matter what Simon tried to do about it, things just didn't seem to get any better. That was frustrating in itself, but they were dealing with it in creative ways, and that's what counted.

As Simon walked to the coffee shop, he looked around, remembering the doctor who had frequented this location. Sadly the man chose to end his own life rather than face the consequences of his actions, but that didn't stop Simon from casually glancing around, expecting to see him—his ghost really. The fact that he hadn't seen his spirit was a good thing.

As he walked into the coffee shop, he placed his order and then waited for his coffee to be made. Taking it with him, he sat at one of the outside tables. As he spent a few minutes sitting here, he became aware of an odd feeling catching his attention. He looked around, not seeing anything. Yet, when a man spoke, his voice scratchy and sounding half sick, Simon turned, not surprised to see the homeless man, Shawn. Simon nodded. "Hey there. Bad day?"

"Bad life," Shawn admitted.

Simon pointed to the other chair at his table and motioned for him to sit. "What's up?"

Shawn asked, "Any chance of some food?"

Simon nodded, then caught the attention of one of the

waitresses, cleaning up tables nearby. She came right back with a couple sandwiches and a coffee.

When placed in front of Shawn, he looked at it appreciatively. "Thanks, I really need that."

Simon didn't say anything, just waited while Shawn scarfed down the food.

With a full stomach he sat back, closed his eyes, then released a groan, as if he were in pain. "I don't remember the last time I've felt this shitty."

"Are you sick, or what's going on?"

"No idea," he muttered. "Just one of those times where you feel as if everything's wrong, and nobody gives a crap."

"Yeah, I've had a time or two like that myself."

Shawn studied Simon, and, as if seeing something in his gaze, Shawn nodded. "You have seen some shit, haven't you?"

Simon's lips twisted. "Yeah, I've definitely seen some shit," he agreed.

"Look. I can't keep hassling you for food, but ... I really appreciate the fact that you came through when I needed it," Shawn said. "It's hard to keep food down right now."

At that comment, Simon studied him a little more closely. Shawn appeared pale, but not as if he would collapse or anything. "Do you need to go to the hospital and get checked out?" Simon asked.

Shawn shook his head several times. "*Nah*, hospitals and I don't get along."

"I can imagine," Simon replied, without judgment, "especially when tolerance and patience goes out the window after you've been there a time or two."

Shawn nodded slowly. "I didn't really expect to live this long as it is," he shared, staring off in the distance.

That's not exactly what Simon had expected to hear, so he just waited.

"A lot of people told me that I would be dead a couple years back." He glanced at Simon, then shrugged. Seeing the question on Simon's face, Shawn added, "I got this heart thing going on."

"Sorry, man," Simon said, genuinely feeling sorry for the guy.

"I'm not. Life hasn't exactly been an easy thing to get through," Shawn noted, with a smile. "So I can't be at all upset to leave it. Yet I do want you to get that building."

Simon laughed at that. "If I can make it happen, I'll do it. However, I don't think you or I can do anything about it."

"Maybe," he muttered, "but the ghosts really want you to have it."

"That concerns me a little to even consider that they're bothered about it."

"They're bothered because of what happened," he noted, leaning in.

"What happened?" Simon asked him.

"Talk to the ghosts," Shawn suggested. "I know you can. They already told me that you can, so you should ask them yourself."

"Maybe."

Shawn sat here for a long moment just sipping his coffee, while Simon worked. Finally Shawn broke his silence. "Do you know anything about the Feldspar house?"

Since that was the name of the house that Kate had gone to and that Simon had been so adamant that she not enter, the comment was surprising in the least. "I've heard about it." Simon frowned, thinking about the mention of the murders of the century. "I don't know all the details." Shawn didn't say anything, just nodded his head. "I gather you do?" Simon asked.

"Not necessarily," Shawn replied, "but the ghosts at Paragon? They know. ... They say the Feldspar house and the Paragon are connected."

"In what way?" he asked, truly wanting to get this right.

Shawn frowned. as if sorting through the question. "I don't know. I don't really know what the deal is. The ghosts don't talk to me in that much detail. *You* should talk to them."

"But they brought up Feldspar house with you?"

"Yeah, they sure did," he muttered, and then he yawned. "Man, I've got to get me some sleep."

"You not sleeping either?"

"I was totally okay to sleep in the Paragon building, but then you told me about all the realtors coming, and you were right. ... They did come, bloodsuckers every one of them," he muttered. "I just couldn't take all that negative energy, so I left."

"I'm not sure we'll see too many more of them now," Simon noted, eyeing Shawn closely. "Yet I can't say that for sure."

The homeless guy pondered that, as he slowly swirled the last of the coffee in his cup. "Yeah, not sure I want to take the chance."

"Why? Do the ghosts get really angry when people enter the building?"

"Oh, they get angry all right," Shawn agreed, looking up at him. "If you don't get that building ... they'll get really angry. You don't want them angry."

"I still don't understand why they want me to have the

Paragon though."

At that, Shawn shook his head. "They just do, and it's got to do with that Feldspar house."

Simon stared at him. "That makes no sense."

"It doesn't matter," Shawn replied. "All I can tell you is that they're connected." And then he frowned and looked over at Simon and asked, "Do you know somebody named Kate?" When Simon stiffened and glared at him, Shawn nodded, surely seeing his expression and the tension coming off Simon in waves. "She's needed somehow too." With that, Shawn got up, yawned, and muttered, "I need to get some sleep. ... I'll see you later. Thanks for the food and the coffee, man."

And, with that, Shawn walked away, leaving Simon staring after him.

CHAPTER 10

K ATE SLOWLY LOWERED the wineglass in her hand and stared at Simon. "Wow. Did you really just say that this homeless guy gave you some psychic warning about the Feldspar case?"

"I'm not sure it's the Feldspar case as much as the Feldspar *house*," he noted, with a thoughtful expression. "Somehow it's connected to the Paragon property I'm looking to buy. Remember how I initially found Shawn sleeping in the Paragon stairwell?"

"Yeah, you found some homeless guy camping in there," she noted, eyeing Simon strangely and then staring far off. "And he gave you my name?"

"I know. I get it. It's weird, and it makes no sense."

"Yeah, you're right about that," she declared. "Weird, makes no sense, and yet how did it come up that the Feldspar murders were even connected?"

"Shawn asked me out of the blue if I knew anything about the Feldspar place itself, and then he told me it was connected to that Paragon property that I am currently interested in."

She stared at him and asked, "What's the address of the property you're looking at?" When he gave it to her, she typed it into her Notes on her phone, but then shrugged. "I don't really know what I'm supposed to do with that information, but at least I have it."

"Maybe nothing," Simon muttered in exasperation. "What was I supposed to do, not tell you?"

She stared around the living room. "Sometimes I wonder if I'm not better off without any of your information."

"That may be true, and I can certainly keep it to myself, if you prefer."

She gave him a wry look. "Would you really?"

"No, not if I thought it would do some good, which I can't tell you because I just don't know. You would be the one to know."

"Right," she murmured, "and I get that. I really do, and I'm not blaming you in any way."

"*Gee, thanks,*" he quipped in a heavily sarcastic tone. When she glared at him, he asked, "What do you want from me?"

She sighed. "Wouldn't it be nice if a ghost would tell you that *Hey, X, Y, and Z happened, and here is the murderer?*"

"Yeah, wouldn't it?" he snapped. "So far that hasn't happened, but, rest assured, you'll be the first to know when it does."

She closed her eyes and pinched the bridge of her nose. "We're both frustrated by this turn of events, so let's not fight. I didn't come here for that. I just don't know how to react sometimes, when you tell me these things."

"How about just take note of the information without judgment?"

She winced and nodded. "Wouldn't that be nice?"

"Yeah, wouldn't it?" he muttered. Then he got up, grabbed the wine bottle, and quickly refilled his glass. She watched as he walked over and topped hers up as well.

"I'm sorry," she said, "It's ... it's just so frustrating."

"*Yeah?*"

But no give was in his tone. She knew that it had to be *more* frustrating for him, yet she never quite remembered that part, not before she opened her mouth and blasted him for something. She groaned. "So, I'm not sure of the rules to this relationship." When he glared at her, she raised her hands in frustration. "Now you look as if you're really pissed."

"I am, so don't say shit like that. Our relationship is what we make it, and, if we screw it up, we screw it up all on our own and not because of some stupid unwritten rules."

She smiled at that. "Now that makes more sense to me that anything else tonight," she admitted.

"Then don't go saying shit like that."

"Shit like what?" she asked, staring at him. "I'm really *not* trying to pick a fight here."

"Good," he growled, "because, for somebody who's not trying, you're doing a hell of a good job."

She sat back and stared at him. "Want to go for a walk then?" He glanced at her, and she saw the instinctive no starting to form, and she just shrugged. "I just thought it might change things up, take us out of it a little bit, so we aren't stuck in the same energy." At her use of the word *energy*, his gaze narrowed, and she raised both hands in frustration. "I don't know what to call it. I just thought, if we changed the scenario, maybe we can get ourselves out of this fight faster."

He blinked several times and then nodded. "Actually, that's a good idea."

She got up and walked to the door. "Come on then. Let's go." Together the two of them went down the elevator, waved at Harry, and stepped outside.

She stopped on the walkway, took several slow deep breaths, and whispered, "I hadn't realized just how much I needed some fresh air." When he frowned at her, she shrugged. "I've been on the phone a ton today, instead of running around. With everything so rushed, I just have no time anymore."

"I'm not sure there ever was enough time," he muttered. "Time is one of those things that we take for granted, until all of a sudden we don't have it anymore."

"I would agree with that," she said, with a nod. "It's just sad because you try to do everything right, but you still end up screwing up."

"If that's a comment in reference to our relationship," he stated, with half a laugh, "you haven't screwed up."

She stared up at him. "Seriously? I feel as if I've done nothing but screw up."

"No, not at all," he muttered, "and I don't want you ever thinking that."

"What do you want me thinking, Simon?"

"Nothing about relationships is easy, and my particular *gift* doesn't help either," he began, "but I certainly don't judge you for what you consider screwups. They're not really screwups. We just have to adjust, the same as everybody else. It would be absolutely lovely if I had some rule book on how to handle my *ability*, but I don't."

"What about your grandmother? How did she cope?" Kate asked.

He shook his head. "Her relationship experiences were even worse."

"In what way?"

"She encountered a lot of hardship in maintaining relationships in her world. Most of the time, as I recall it, she was alone, and that was very hard on her."

"The more I hear about some of this stuff, the more I realize that it's not so much a gift but almost a curse."

He laughed. "Pretty sure I've mentioned that before."

"Maybe I just wasn't listening." She groaned, reached out her hand, and he quickly laced his fingers with hers. "Sometimes it's a bit much, so I back off, trying to find some semblance of balance—almost refuting everything you say or wanting to refute it but not knowing how. So it just becomes something I dismiss. At least that's my initial gut reaction."

He didn't say anything at first, and they just continued to walk. "I guess one suggestion would be to double-check what happened regarding that Feldspar case."

"I've had the files pulled," she shared. "I just haven't had even a minute to look at it."

"Are you still looking at that recent suicide-turned-murder?"

"It's definitely a murder case," she muttered, "and what makes me even angrier is that it involves a greedy wife."

"I don't have any answers for you on that case," he admitted, "but it seems to me as if greed runs everything."

"And how sad is that?"

He looked over at her and smiled. "Very sad, but not *our* sad."

Surprised and yet half understanding what he said, she nodded. "I guess that's one cheerful point in our favor, isn't it?"

"We don't get very many of them," he noted, "so let's take what we can get. Honestly, we have a lot of good things in our lives. ... Both of us just need to remember that."

"I agree," she muttered. "You just threw me when you

connected your building with my current case *and* with me."

"And yet," he pointed out, "*I* didn't do it. Shawn did, the homeless man who sees and talks to ghosts."

"Right, so maybe we should talk to him," she muttered, staring off into the distance.

"We could," he replied, understanding what she was getting to. "As I understand it, he's not long for this world. He wasn't expected to make it this long." When she frowned at him, Simon shrugged and added, "He's got a heart condition of some kind."

"Ah, it can't be very easy living on the streets if you've got some health condition too."

"I'm not sure being on the street is easy at any point in time, but he didn't ask for any help to get off the streets. He just asked for food, and he sat there in front of me and ate it."

She smiled at Simon. "Of course you gave him food. A lot of people wouldn't have."

"Maybe, but I am not a lot of people."

Sensing something in his tone, she turned and looked at him closely. "I didn't mean any insult by that either."

He let out a heavy sigh and replied, "I know you didn't." They continued to walk along the harbor, and he took a deep breath, soaking in the fresh air. "Are we still on for the weekend?"

She nodded. "Yes, no major panic is happening right now. Obviously I'm still dealing with this case, but nothing's broken at the moment." She took a minute, looking at the far-off lights. "As much as I could hope that something will break my case wide open, it won't be that easy to get to the bottom of what's going on here."

"How come?"

"Because I'm waiting for forensics," she muttered. "That just adds to the frustration."

"Of course." He didn't say anything for a while. As they crossed the street, he asked her, "How about dinner out tonight?"

She smiled at him. "That might be a good idea."

He steered them to a small restaurant nearby and said, "I've never been in here. Shall we try it?"

She nodded. "I'm game." As they stepped inside, she looked around. "I should have known. Is this another Italian place?"

"It is, but more from the Sicilian area, so not Mama's brand."

"No, not Mama's." Kate laughed at the misery in his tone. "Have you been back to see them in person?"

"Several times," he replied.

"How is the family?"

"Holding on, but still pretty upset and grieving in many ways. They keep asking about you."

"We could also have gone there," she noted, "except, if we're walking, I guess we don't really have a whole lot of choices."

He chuckled. "If we just keep doing what we're doing, we'll get back there eventually."

"You order in all the time," she added, "so that makes a huge difference to them."

"It does, and it's one of the reasons why I do it because it does make a difference, trying to keep everybody in business, but I can't do it all."

"No, you certainly can't, and you shouldn't feel as if you have to." He gave her an odd look, and she shrugged. "I know you help a lot of people, more that you don't tell me about, a lot of people who nobody knows about," she shared. "And that's all right. You don't have to tell anyone, but you also can't save everybody in this world, Simon. Everyone has their own problems, and not all problems can be fixed."

"*Hmm.* Is this a good thing to remind you of down the road too?"

She winced. "Probably not."

He laughed. "You know there are worse things than to go to our grave knowing that we tried to help, even if we didn't succeed every time," he noted.

"Maybe, but I would still rather go to my grave successful at helping rather than a failure."

"It's not a failure if you are trying," he reminded her.

"No, it's not, but it sure doesn't feel much like success either."

"So, how will you change that?"

"Tomorrow I'll dig into the Feldspar family murders," she muttered, "and I still have to research the Paragon building and talk to your homeless guy."

"What about Amie, who may or may not have killed her husband?"

"Yeah, I'm letting something rattle around at the back of my brain on that one," she muttered. "I'm not sure that it'll be quite so easy or open-and-shut by any means."

"Probably not," he muttered, turning to face her. "Did anybody else want her husband dead?"

"I don't know," she admitted, thinking over the details. "The boyfriend maybe, but Amie and her husband were already talking divorce—according to Amie."

"Right, so that doesn't mean the husband would say the same."

She chuckled at that. "Not sure that the husbands ever

say anything when it comes to this shit."

"In your cases they can't. They're dead." When she glared at him, he just smiled. "Come on. Don't shoot the messenger, please. Let's eat." And, with that, he quickly took a table at the far end of the restaurant.

She sat down and smiled, as she looked around. The place was great, and the ambiance was perfect. "It's nice in here, and I really like the decor. It has a very old Italian look to it, almost like that district in Vancouver."

"It does, doesn't it?"

They were served quickly, and the place wasn't terribly busy, so it gave them even more privacy, as they continued to talk and just unwind a bit. When their dinner was in front of them, she smiled at him. "This really was a good idea."

He nodded. "It was. We need to get out and about for our own good a little more."

She sighed. "Then maybe we won't be quite so touchy." When he snorted at that, she grinned and admitted, "And, yeah, I'm usually the touchy one."

"No, it's both of us, and we just have to remember that."

In the back of her mind, she was already thinking about Feldspar and what it would mean in terms of her other case. It's not that she didn't have time for another case, but she wouldn't be given any leeway to open it up. The one thing her department didn't do was cold cases. They had a whole separate division for that, but she didn't really want to bring them in. How could she possibly tell them that her clues came from a homeless man who spoke with ghosts, a reluctant psychic, and then the ghosts themselves? That thought alone gave her goose bumps.

As she scooped up a slice of pizza, she asked Simon, "Did Shawn happen to share what the Paragon ghosts said about it?"

Simon shook his head. "Just something about being connected to the Feldspar family."

"Family," she repeated. "That's pretty open-ended."

"It's *too* open-ended," Simon declared, "but hopefully it does give you something."

"It does, just not very much right now."

CHAPTER 11

T HE NEXT MORNING, Kate walked into the office twenty minutes early, sat down, and pulled the file for the Feldspar case. As she dove into the material she had, Reese walked in and handed her the rest of what she had collected.

"Feldspar is a pretty fascinating case," Reese stated, "and unsolved the entire time. Cold Cases looked at it a couple times but never really found anything new that they could do with it."

"Good enough," she muttered absentmindedly.

At that, Reese stared at her. "You have something new, don't you?"

Kate flushed and nodded. "Maybe."

Reese's gaze glinted with excitement. "This is a really famous one."

"What does that mean?"

"It could really cement your name if you solved it. Feldspar is one of those unsolvable cases."

"Ha. I'm not so sure that solving it will be all that easy."

"If it were easy," Reese replied, "somebody would have done it already. Anyway, if you need anything else, let me know." And she turned and walked out.

While Kate was making notes, the front desk called her. "We've got a man here to see you."

"Who is it?" she asked, as she got up. When she heard

the name, Kate stared at the phone. "Interesting. I'm coming." She walked out to the reception area and, sure enough, found Amie's boyfriend. Nate looked up in relief when he saw her. She motioned him to one of the interview rooms, where they could privately talk.

As he sat down nervously, Nate looked around the room. "Am I in trouble?"

"No, but I presume you want to talk, and privacy is a little hard to get around here. This is just the easiest place for that."

"Oh." Nate accepted her word and relaxed a bit.

"So, what's going on?" she asked.

"I've been a complete wreck since we last talked."

"Why is that?" she asked curiously.

He hesitated but then asked, "Do you think Amie did it?"

"I don't know," Kate admitted. "What I can tell you is that her husband did not commit suicide. He was murdered. You don't have an alibi, and neither does she. According to her, she was sound asleep."

He nodded. "That's what she told me too, and I don't have any reason to disbelieve her."

"But now you're wondering."

"It's not that I'm wondering," he clarified, yet winced as some odd expression crossed his face. "Hell yeah, I'm wondering. I don't want to be dead husband number four."

"Good thinking," she replied. "So give us a little bit of time to figure it out and be available for any questioning for now."

"Is that it?"

"Do you have anything more to offer?"

"Not really, but I think she's been threatened a couple

times."

"Threatened?" she repeated, staring at him.

He nodded. "She hasn't really talked to me about it, so I don't know how bad it is. She's not been very open when it comes to her personal life."

"Does that secretiveness concern you?"

"It should, shouldn't it?" he asked, looking at her. "I thought we were close enough because we were talking marriage."

"*Were?*"

He winced. "I have to admit to being a little worried about going down that pathway, especially now."

Privately Kate thought it was very wise of him to be a little worried, but she didn't want to set him off into making drastic changes in his life, not when she couldn't confirm any details of Amie's life or the untimely deaths of her three husbands. "What about any friends of hers or family? Do you ever see any other people around Amie?"

He shook his head. "No, I really don't. It's just been her."

"What about her husband's friends?"

"I don't know any," he replied, dropping his head in his hands. "Honestly, I feel shitty about the affair now, but I didn't have anything to do with him dying."

"So, how did you meet Amie?" she asked curiously.

"At her work. We work together."

"Ah, and did she tell you that she was married?"

"Not at the beginning ... no, she didn't," Nate shared. "I was pretty upset when she finally told me, and then she explained that her marriage was done and that she was figuring out how to leave him and all that stuff, and I believed her. I still believe her," he added quickly. "Yet, when you bring up other dead husbands, it's hard to separate fact from fiction."

"I'm glad to hear you're at least thinking about it," Kate told him. "I don't yet know for sure what Amie may or may not have done, but obviously we don't want to walk into a room and find you as the next victim either."

"No, God, no. … I told my sister." When Kate stared at him, he shrugged. "We're really close, so I told her about Amie's husband."

"That he was murdered?"

"I didn't realize you were sure it was murder at that point, but I told her that he committed suicide."

"What did she say?"

"Her instinctive thought was that it didn't surprise her."

"Why is that?"

"Because obviously he was unhappy, and, if he had found out about me, that would have made him even more so."

When Nate glanced at her, she saw tears in his eyes.

"God, if it wasn't suicide, and it was murder, that changes things."

"It changes a lot of things," Kate confirmed, "but what was the concern when you thought it was a suicide?"

"I was afraid that I was responsible."

"Ah, you mean that he'd found out about your affair and decided to take his life instead of facing a divorce and the truth about his wife?"

"Yes," he agreed, raising both hands in frustration. "It sounds godawful when you say it that way." She just stared at him, and he nodded. "I know. I get it now. Having an affair *was* godawful. Somehow, someway along the line here, I took a wrong turn and lost sight of that, at least according to my sister. She's not very happy with me."

"You can see her point, I presume?"

"Yes, of course I can," he muttered in frustration. "Especially now, but the thing is, I love Amie."

"Good. Amie needs to be loved too," Kate noted, "but let's hope she's not killing her husbands in order to make way for the next love in her life." When Nate swallowed hard at that, Kate added, "Have you seen Amie do anything strange or act in any way unusual, guilty even, or anything suspicious? Have you ever even asked her about her past?"

"No, I never did," he said, raising his head a bit, then dropping it again. "I didn't consider her past, which is even more stupid of me because everybody has a past."

Kate didn't know what to say to that, but it was true. Everybody did have a past. Then she took this opportunity to ask him several more questions. "Did Amie ever get any strange phone calls?"

"Just the threatening one that she said was a bit of a concern."

"And you believed her?"

"Sure, of course I believed her." Then he stared down at the table again. "That makes me feel even stupider because my instinctive response is, *Of course I believed her*, but then maybe I shouldn't. ... I shouldn't because she had hidden things before, such as being married in the first place. Should I question everything she's ever said or says now?"

"It certainly would be a good idea to question anything you have doubts about. You should ensure that everything happening in your world with her is up-front, particularly under these circumstances."

"She told me that she had nothing to do with her husband's death and that, although she wanted out of the marriage, she would never have killed him," he murmured.

"Did she say anything else?"

"No, just that it would be completely stupid of her to do that."

"I can't argue with that because it certainly looks suspicious as hell for her three husbands to all die on her."

"God." Nate stared off into the distance. "It just makes me sick."

"Did you ever meet the husband?"

He winced and shook his head. "No, and that makes me feel like an ass too."

"Why?" she asked. "Seems to me having an affair would make you avoid him."

He just stared and muttered, "He shouldn't be considered a nobody. He shouldn't be buried now because somebody decided to knock him off. He had a loving wife ... and I don't really know what happened to that relationship. Yet it feels very wrong to think that, just because he's dead and gone ... everything in his life is gone too."

"And yet it is. He's not here anymore, and he's not part of either of your lives anymore, is he?"

"In a way," he clarified, staring at Kate, "he's a big part of our lives ... bigger than ever before, at least for me."

She asked him a few more questions, then brought up the threatening phone call Amie spoke about.

"All I can tell you about the phone call or the threat was that she told me it was made against her. And she did get a weird look in her eyes."

Kate tried to school her expression. In her gut, she felt this Amie bitch was lying. Again. Trying to cast doubt away from her. Kate didn't believe Amie was receiving any threats.

More likely Amie was sending out threats herself. "Did she say anything about who it was from or why she was being threatened?"

"No, she wouldn't say anything." He swore then. "Of course, at the time … I just let it go. I shouldn't have."

"Now you have a chance to talk to her," Kate noted, "because, if she didn't have anything to do with her husband's murder, she could be in danger." He looked at her hopefully, and she shrugged. "I have no way of knowing yet what's going on, so I just want you to look after you. This is a good time for you to think back and to see if you let go of anything else that maybe you shouldn't have."

"Right." He gave a heavy sigh. "That's one of those next issues, isn't it?"

"It sure is," she declared, "and it's never an easy *next issue*, but you must do everything you can to keep you safe. So, if you think of anything or hear anything that worries you or makes you think she might have done something, please contact us."

He nodded, as he stood up. "I should have said something right away. I just didn't want to believe that she could have had something to do with it."

"We still don't know that she did," Kate repeated, looking at him intently. "That's the thing. We still don't have proof of that."

He winced and nodded. "I guess that's good for her, isn't it?"

"If she did it, yes. It's good for her to escape justice, in her mind. If she didn't murder her husband, we don't have any answers to give her about who killed her husband."

"She's pretty adamant that nobody killed him and that this was suicide."

"She can be adamant all she wants," Kate replied, with a gentle smile, "but we have forensic evidence that says she's completely wrong."

"Christ," he muttered. As he walked to the interview room door, he looked back at Kate expectantly. "I don't suppose you have a card, do you?" When she handed him one, he looked down at it and nodded. "Let's hope I don't need to be in touch."

"If you do, call me, no matter what you have to say. Just call me, okay?"

He nodded. "Okay, thanks." With that, he left.

When Kate exited the interview room, Lilliana was there. By the looks of her expression, she had heard everything that was said.

"Do you believe him?" Lilliana asked Kate.

Kate winced. "I'm not sure I believe him, but I do think he's a little freaked out. Now, as to the reason behind that, I'm not entirely certain."

"You mean, outside of the fact that he could just as easily have been coerced into killing Amie's husband, only to find out afterward that she may have already done this a time or two before?"

"Yeah, that's part of it," Kate noted, brushing a strand of unkempt hair from her face. "Also, according to him, Amie's been getting threatening phone calls. Technically only according to Amie though."

"*Hmm*, I wonder about that. I'm not so sure I believe that either."

"Exactly. I'm not convinced of that myself. On the other hand, we don't have anything to prove it one way or another. I'll contact her and see what she has to say."

"She won't like that."

"Nope, she sure won't," Kate said, with a beaming smile, "and that'll just make me even happier."

Lilliana laughed. "You really don't like her, do you?"

"No, I do not," she admitted, frowning. "Yet I don't have any particular reason, outside of my gut, so I promise it won't interfere with my job."

"If it does, the rest of us are always there to pull you back," she pointed out. "In the meantime, go, tiger, go." With that, Lilliana turned and walked off.

She had said what she wanted to share, and Kate wasn't in a position to argue.

ALL THROUGHOUT THE day, a theme repeated in the back of Simon's brain about Shawn, the homeless man, and what Kate had shared last night about her plans for today. Simon sent her several texts already, asking her *not* to show up at the Feldspar house, the house he had warned her about earlier. When he got a phone call, he pulled his cell from his pocket. He checked the Caller ID. It was her. "Kate, where are you?"

She hesitated. "I didn't mean to," she began, a note of humor in her tone. "Yet I find myself standing outside the Feldspar house."

"Jesus," he muttered, his hand slapping his forehead. "Even after all the warnings I sent you?"

"Nobody is around, and I see no signs that anybody is living here," she explained. "I need to look around the exterior of the house and get the lay of the neighborhood. I'm also not sure what the danger is that you're talking about, and it's definitely something I take into consideration, but—"

"But what?" he snapped. "You have absolutely no need

to be there right now." Then he stopped, and his voice cracked as he asked, "Or is there?"

"No, just curiosity," she murmured, "and the fact that it's somehow connected to the Paragon property you and Shawn were talking about. This has all been spinning around in my head, and somehow I need to get it out of my system."

"You don't have enough work on your plate?" he asked in frustration.

"I'm outside the house, not inside, and I'm still considering my next move. But, if it's dangerous for me, then we need to ensure that we mitigate or remove whatever that danger is, so that other people around this neighborhood won't be affected. Children play on the street here, so if you see a bomb or something, tell me so we can take care of it."

He groaned. "And the fact that I'm telling you it's dangerous isn't enough?"

"But is it dangerous *right now*?" she asked. "I assumed when you told me to not go in there a few days ago that potentially a killer was in there, somebody with a gun doing a drug deal or something."

He stopped and stared at his phone in frustration. "I don't know."

"Exactly," she murmured gently. "Just because it was dangerous then doesn't mean it still is today."

He frowned, but he wasn't getting a message either way right now. He thought about lying to her to keep her safe but knew Kate would see through that. "I don't get a warning now," he conceded. "Yet I got such a definite warning before, and it really didn't take much to hear it, loud and clear."

"I get that. I do," she stated, "and I understand you still don't want me to go in there."

"But you'll go anyway, won't you?"

"Yeah," she replied. "I'll walk up to the house and take a look in the windows."

She gave a running narrative to Simon, and, all the while, he heard her footsteps getting closer to something. "You're really walking up to the house?"

"Do you have something you want to tell me?" she asked. "I mean, if you say a bomb or something is inside, that's a different story. If you tell me a murderer is in there, that's a different story too. You told me when I was here before that it was dangerous, and I believed you. I got an odd feeling myself about it back then, but today, right now? There just isn't any strange feeling."

"What do you mean that you had an odd feeling back then?"

She hesitated, then replied, "I didn't argue with you, did I?"

"Ah, so because you didn't argue with me, that means you had an odd feeling?"

"I can't argue about it now," she said, exasperation in her tone. "What I can tell you is that I don't feel anything is wrong here, yet last time I did. I'm just not feeling anything negative in the here and now."

He groaned, then closed his eyes and sent out as much of a probe as he knew to send. When it came back completely blank, his shoulders slumped. "Neither am I."

"Exactly," she said, her tone turning cheerful. "So, I'll just walk through, and, if you get any messages about a problem, you call out for help."

"Meaning that I'm your backup."

"Sure, it's not as if I have anybody else at the moment."

"Why the hell is that?" he snapped. "Why the hell can't

you just get a bomb-sniffing dog or whatever?"

"First, I don't have backup because everybody is busy with their own cases, and the Feldspar house isn't part of anybody's case—not even mine, for that matter. I shouldn't be working a cold case. Which is why, second, I can't call for a bomb-sniffing dog. It's not in the budget to satisfy my every whim. Therefore, *I* am here."

"And … there you are," he grumbled.

"I know you are worried, and yet it should be clear now, right? Isn't that what your woo-woo senses say?"

"I don't know what to say," he stated crossly.

"Is it wrong for me to deal with my curiosity here?" she asked in exasperation. "Now I'm standing by the window, and, so far, I'm not seeing anything dangerous."

"Sure, but that danger could come up from behind and kill you before you have a chance to respond."

"I understand," she muttered.

He heard something on the other end. "What are you doing?"

"I'm just trying to wipe the window a bit. Years of grime have built up on the outside, and it doesn't seem anybody has been here for quite a while."

"Yeah, well, that's what happens to empty buildings after a few months," he stated, mocking her, plain and simple, "and definitely people go through those unoccupied places."

"And you know that people have been through the Feldspar house?" After a moment of silence on the other end, she groaned. "Fine, I'll accept that there may have been traffic through this place."

"There definitely has been traffic, and some of that traffic is very dangerous."

"Any idea which part of it?"

"No," he snapped, "and I really don't like the fact that you're there."

"I get that."

"No, you don't."

"Simon, I'm just walking around to the back now," she shared. "I looked in the front and wasn't a whole lot there to see. Oh, look at that."

"What do you mean? Look at what? Look at what, Kate?" When she didn't respond fast enough, he was frantic, panicking in a big way.

"Back door is open," she muttered.

Simon's panic peaked. "And what? Something is wrong, isn't there?"

"There's a distinctive smell."

Then he groaned because he knew in his gut where this was headed. "Please, no."

"Sorry, but it's a definite yes. I'm walking into the kitchen right now."

"Shouldn't you have a forensics team there? Aren't you contaminating the scene?"

"Not if I'm careful," she said. "I must be sure before I call in a team, shouldn't I?"

And then Simon heard her sigh heavily. "I presume you just found your confirmation?"

"Yeah, I sure did. Looks to be a homeless guy," she whispered in a gutted tone. "I need to call this in."

"Fine," he muttered. "Do that, but I sure as hell wish you weren't there. Do remember that I am just trying to keep you safe."

"I know, and I love you for it," she replied in a cheerful voice, "but I've got to go now." With that, she disconnected.

Yet Simon was much less focused on her hanging up as

the words she had just left him with. In all of their relationship, she'd never once mentioned *love*, and, even now, it was a backhanded compliment, and that was an odd thing for her too. But she had also sounded oddly cheerful. She was the only woman who he knew was made happier by homicide cases.

He got it, and she always respected the poor victims, but she was never happier than when she had a case to work on. When she had multiple cases, she really thrived. This meant she had another case to work on, and he would probably have to get interviewed about the little bit he'd told her.

That wasn't something he wanted to deal with, but then he never wanted to deal with the police. Kate was the exception, and grudgingly he admitted to himself that the team members she worked with were okay as well. Simon had no problems with any of them, something else that surprised him. Yet, so far, they'd all proven to be upstanding and straight shooters, and he appreciated that.

He slowly pocketed his phone, then turned to look around. The whole time he'd been talking, he'd been walking as well, and where had he ended up? Damn it all, he was back at the Paragon, the ghost-filled building. He made a quick trip inside to see if Shawn was here but found no sign of him. As he stepped back outside again, he noted a group of three or four homeless guys nearby. He walked over and asked them about Shawn but didn't get much of a reception.

They just shrugged and stared him down. One of them finally said, "Haven't seen him for a couple days."

"But he's usually right around here, isn't he?" Simon asked.

"Oh, he is. Yet he keeps telling us about the ghosts in

the building," another shared with a laugh.

Simon nodded. "He told me the same thing."

"Well then, you better listen to him because he definitely got something right."

Since they didn't know where Shawn was, Simon headed to the coffee shop, as that's where he'd last seen Shawn yesterday. Simon looked around the whole time he walked there but still saw no sign of him. He bought a coffee and sat outside and waited, thinking this would likely be a better place to run across him.

Still sitting here alone, he then got that ugly feeling at the back of his neck. Pulling out his phone, he quickly texted Kate, asking for an image of the homeless guy.

She phoned him instead. "Why do you want a photo? That's not something we generally do."

"I get that," he replied, "but I can't find Shawn, and now I've got this ugly feeling."

She sucked in her breath. "Oh, crap, hang on a minute."

Within seconds he had a grainy photograph. As he stared at it, his heart sank.

She called him right back. "And?"

"It's Shawn. His birth name is Jack Ludwig."

"Shit," she muttered.

"Yeah, that's a good word for it." Simon stared around. "He normally hangs around this part of town. I spoke to a couple of his friends this morning, and they confirmed that the Paragon was his usual hangout."

"Then what the hell was he doing clear up here, and how did he even get here?"

"I don't know, but I'm sure you'll find out."

"Yeah, damn right I will," she declared. "Forensics is on the way. I've got to go." Then she quickly disconnected.

CHAPTER 12

KATE COULDN'T QUITE believe that this was the same homeless guy who had been speaking to Simon. Of course, with her luck it would be, and that was the last thing she needed right now.

When Smidge arrived, he frowned at her, and she shrugged. He bellowed, "What the hell are you doing here? I told you about the old case from here, didn't I?"

"You did," she confirmed, then she explained about the homeless guy and Simon.

He sighed, his gaze narrowing on her. "More woo-woo stuff, *huh*?"

"Apparently, although I'm not exactly sure any of us like that term."

Smidge shrugged. "Then come up with a better one."

She winced and nodded. "I would if I could."

"Right, so in the meantime, *woo-woo* it is." He looked down at Shawn and began, "Blunt force trauma to the head, but what's he doing here anyway?" He sighed, when he looked around. "This place has got such an ugly history."

"I know," she murmured, "and I'm really not trying to add to it, but, after what Simon told me the other day, I found myself wanting to come back here."

"I'm sure that thrilled him to no end."

"He was pretty livid that I would disregard his warning

and come back anyway."

"Yeah, that makes sense to me," Smidge agreed, without looking her way. "I mean, it's a death wish if you'll ignore Simon. He's already saved your ass a couple times, so going against his suggestions? … You're just putting your ass in a sling. Nobody will have any sympathy for that."

She glared down at him, as he bent over the dead body. "That's one way to put it," she muttered.

"How else should I put it?" Smidge asked, turning to look at her. "Somebody warned you well and truly. Not to mention that Simon's got a good record of telling the truth. You ignored him, and you got yourself into this shit. What else is there to say?"

She groaned. "Fine, if you want to look at it that way, then, yes, it was probably a foolish thing for me to do. I did call Simon when I got here at least," she snapped, "and he did say that, at the moment, he didn't feel any warnings."

"That's interesting. I wonder if it's something that comes and goes."

"Or maybe Shawn just died recently."

"Why do you say that?" Smidge asked, twisting back on his heels to look up at her. "I don't have a time of death yet."

"No, but Simon ran into Shawn at Simon's usual downtown coffee shop yesterday."

"So, somewhere in the last twenty-four hours? That's a good start." He rolled his eyes. "Pretty soon you won't even need me to do my job."

"Ha, that would mean you could retire."

"I don't know what retired coroners do," he muttered. "I still find myself unable to watch the cop TV shows because of all the ways they screw up the process."

"Yeah, but those shows are for entertainment only, not

because they're technically correct."

"Good thing, otherwise everybody in the production world would get fired for the bullshit they promote on their shows."

"Don't you like to fish or something?"

"I do," he said, "and fishing does sound like a good way to retire."

"So, there you go. However, right now you're not retired, and I need some answers."

"So do I," he stated, "and you'll get them when I get them, so leave me alone."

Now she rolled her eyes. "Fine. I'll go search the rest of the house."

"You mean, you haven't yet?"

"No, I haven't. I was sticking by the body."

"Anybody come around?"

"No, but I did hear something," she noted.

At that, Smidge stood and turned to look at her. "Like what?"

She winced. "Nothing of this earthly plane," she shared.

"Ah, noises, things that go *bump* in the night." Smidge nodded. "Yeah, place where mass murders occurred would have lots of those, but then abandoned buildings are at the top of that list anyway."

"Apparently," she muttered. "Anyway, do your thing. I'll go check out the rest of this place." And, with that, she walked away and left Smidge to gather whatever information he could scrounge up. She had done a bit of walking around, while she'd been waiting for forensics to show up, but only in the downstairs portion. Now she wanted to go upstairs.

There had been noises earlier, but she chalked it up to the creaking of an old house—at least that's what she was hoping. She had certainly not seen anybody but wasn't taking any chances at this point either. With an officer beside her, she quickly did a sweep of the rest of the house—the second and third floors. When they confirmed both were empty, after they had searched everywhere, top and bottom, she let the cop go downstairs again.

Now she went over the second floor again, looking for clues of whatever. Something must be here, but that didn't mean it would have anything to do with Shawn's murder, and it certainly didn't mean it was evidence for any other known case, other than confirmation that the Feldspar property had been left abandoned for many, many years. She wondered who currently owned it and what their plan for it was.

In many ways the house was a stunning property, but, with such an ugly history, she wasn't sure how easily it would be to sell. Somebody like Simon would be okay to buy it, and she had to wonder if he hadn't already considered it. After all, he did property rehabs, although this house may not be a big-enough project for him. He generally preferred the larger apartment buildings and complexes, whereas this was definitely a far smaller space.

And yet, as she wandered upstairs, she noted that this home had to be four or five thousand square feet, and that was an astronomical amount of space to her. Even untended for a decade now, it was also quite beautiful.

As she returned to the third floor, she looked around carefully. A few things remained hanging on the walls, and some personal possessions remained, with things left in bedrooms, things that nobody wanted or cared for at this point in time. As she continued to search, she went from bedroom to bedroom and realized that, in many ways, this house had been put into a time capsule of sorts.

No wonder people liked to come in and browse through it. Some bedding and various items remained in the bedrooms. Some of it had been tossed on the floor. Some of it had obviously been stolen, with only the bare mattress remaining, and some of it was still here, just rotting away. The longer some of these things remained here, the worse they got the less likely they were to be stolen.

SIMON WAITED ANXIOUSLY to hear from Kate. When she didn't contact him fast enough, he sent her another text, and he kept it blunt. **Are you alive?**

When his phone rang, and he saw it was Kate, he put his cell to his ear. "That answers that question," he muttered.

"It sure does, and, yes, I'm alive. You already know that I found your homeless guy here in this house, but I'm checking out the rest of the house now that Smidge is here. Anyway, I'm still at the Feldspar house. I don't think I'll make it to your place tonight."

He felt a pang of regret at that. "I suppose that also means our sailing this weekend's off?"

"*Um*, I'm not so sure about that," she said. "I'll check security cams around this area, and I'm waiting for forensics to come and work the kitchen. I've got officers doing a canvass of the neighborhood, starting that right now. So, depending on what information we come up with, I'll need a day of downtime, just to let some of this work away in my mind."

"How about you take off tomorrow night? It'll be Friday, so we can go out for an hour or two tomorrow before dusk and stay out overnight. If we get Saturday off too," he suggested, lost in wishful thinking at this point, "we can stay out on the water."

"I would like that. I would like it a lot, but, for now, I've got to go. I'll talk to you in the morning."

He looked down at his phone, checked the time, and calculated that she would be there for the next few hours. It was close to seven in the evening, and he couldn't believe that the entire day had just ended like that. At least Ariel had turned the lights on when they'd arrived. It was a huge building to walk through with only flashlights.

He wanted to go back to the group of homeless guys who he had talked to earlier, to see when and if anybody had seen Shawn more recently than Simon had, but he also figured Kate might need to do that canvassing of the homeless guys herself, since she had found Shawn.

On a whim he headed downtown and figured that he would stop off at one of his favorite restaurants. As he came back by the Paragon, his stalking realtor stood there, talking impatiently on the phone.

Ariel's eyes lit up when she saw him. "I knew it," she crowed, as she put away her phone. "You just can't stay away."

"The homeless guy I found in the building was murdered today."

Her face fell, and she looked back up at the building. "Dear God, please not here."

Simon shook his head. It was so typical of Ariel to only be concerned about the property value. "No, it wasn't here. His body was found on the other side of town."

Ariel frowned. "That's strange, since most homeless guys stick to a small area they can navigate on foot."

"I know, and I'm not sure how he got from here to

there, but that's for the cops to sort out."

"It's not our problem," she stated, then boosted her smile and gave him a pointed look. "I was talking to another client just now."

"That's nice," Simon muttered, knowing full well Ariel was faking it. "I'm sure once people find out that the homeless guy got murdered, it might change their view of the property."

"He didn't get murdered *here* … so it has nothing to do with the Paragon property," she repeated, "and the sales price is already pretty cheap, so don't try to get the price down."

"If I decide to put in an offer," he stated flat-out, "it won't be full price anyway. The place is a dump, and at least 90 percent of it will have to be completely redone, taken down to the bones," he declared, looking back at the building from the bottom up. "I won't even begin to look at it seriously until after my engineers go through it."

She nodded, as if none of that surprised her, which it didn't, since he'd bought several properties that she had listed before. As he stared at the property looming up behind her, he added, "Besides, if it's such a great deal, how come you haven't sold it yet?"

She glared at him. "You know these old buildings. … Sometimes they go fast, and sometimes they don't."

"You mean, they go fast if it's cheap, but they don't go unless it's dirt cheap," he said, with a smirk, "and this one isn't dirt cheap."

"It is a very good price," she stated, raising her hands in protest.

"No, it's not a very good price, and it sure as hell isn't cheap."

"I suppose you only want it if it's a really cheap price,"

she noted warily.

He gave her a lopsided smile. "Maybe, but looking at the amount of work potentially involved in getting it back in shape, I'm not so sure I want it at all."

"One of the big conglomerates contacted me about it today," she added, with a smug note.

"Good. If you can get that price for it, more power to you." He had injected just enough happiness into his tone for her to step back slightly in order to search his features. He nodded. "Yes, I'm serious. Am I interested in it? Possibly. But at that price? … No way. So, if you can get that price for your owners, that's good for you and them. We also know that they could have sold the Paragon to me years ago, and it would have been a hell of a lot better deal, and they would have made more money on it. As it is now, it's falling down around their shoulders. So, the sooner they can get rid of it, the less the city will be all over them to demolish it."

"Has the city been here?" she asked, startled.

"You can bet I'll make that phone call pretty damn fast, if need be."

She shook her head. "That would be a shitty move."

"It doesn't matter if it's shitty or not," he declared. "The building will fall down all around you, all around them. And the owners will be liable for damages."

She winced. "I'll keep that in mind."

"My engineers will be out soon," he told her, "and I'm not kidding. If I don't end up buying it, whoever does knows perfectly well it'll be on the city's demo list."

"I haven't been down there to talk to them, but I presume that they're fully aware of the condition of the building. I assume so anyway," Ariel muttered. "It's not the first time we've had that happen."

"No, and it won't be the last."

She glared at him and nodded. "If you're interested, don't waste any time." And, with that parting shot, she turned and walked away.

He almost laughed at her grandiose exit, but he had to give her some leeway. It was always tough to sell these old buildings. She did pretty well on them, but mostly because he had purchased so many of them. But this one? Well … this one would have a special place in his heart. He just wasn't entirely sure he needed to take it on. This rehab wouldn't be easy, and it sure as hell wouldn't be fast. But, as he stared up at the old building, he knew it would be a worthwhile endeavor.

CHAPTER 13

KATE ARRIVED AT the downtown building, the Paragon, Shawn's ghost building, not sharing her plans with Simon. She was running on empty as it was, but she was trying to get everything checked on her list before the weekend and her plans for a day off that she rather desperately needed, if she could get it. If things blew up, then sailing with Simon just wasn't happening, and that was a simple fact of life. She'd long given up arguing about it because they needed whatever breaks they could get, and, right about now, she was even more confused about her current case.

The forensics work done on Robert Mulhouse confirmed the supposed suicide was really a murder. Amie Mulhouse requested her husband's body, but that wouldn't happen yet. So she wasn't terribly pleased about it. When she found out that a full autopsy was in progress, she caterwauled pretty heavily.

"He was shot, for God's sake. You don't need to do anything else," she cried out. "Talk about harassment."

Kate didn't quite understand how looking after her husband's death was harassing Amie, but, hey, certain people, particularly people who were potentially murder suspects, weren't exactly the most reasonable, as far as Kate was concerned.

As she waited for the realtor to arrive to open up the

building, she studied the nearby area and saw several homeless guys standing at a corner. She figured they were probably the homeless guys Simon had spoken to earlier. Since she was ten minutes early, she headed off to talk to them first. They stiffened as she approached, and a couple of them gave her sly smiles. She just nodded at them casually and began, "Old Shawn, he hung around here a lot, *huh?*"

They just nodded.

"Don't suppose you heard that he died, *huh?*"

Their eyes widened, but they didn't say anything.

She nodded. "He was found in the Feldspar house on Farwell Street."

At that, the older man wearing a cap shook his head. "Not familiar with the area."

She added, "It's a pretty high-end place."

"No reason for him to be there," noted the other guy. "He stayed here, so why would he be there?"

"That's what I'm trying to figure out," she murmured. "The first problem is how Shawn even got from here to there. Do you know if old Shawn ever worked or helped anybody out?" They just frowned at her, and she continued. "Or maybe he had a friend, somebody in that area?"

"Aren't no friends up there, not for people like us," replied the eldest of the trio. "Any friends any of us had walked away a long time ago."

"Maybe you walked away too," she murmured, staring at him intently.

He nodded. "Maybe we did, at that."

"I don't begrudge you your lifestyle," she stated, "and, if this is where you want to be, I'm totally okay with your being here, just as long as you don't hurt yourself or anybody else." The homeless men almost visibly relaxed, as if realizing she wouldn't roust them from their spot. "I do worry that you won't stay warm enough over the winter and that things will be a little tougher than you expect them to be."

"They always are," one stated.

"And what about Shawn? … Was he happy out here?"

The talkative one shrugged. "Sometimes he tried to get jobs and returned to mainstream life, but it didn't work out so well for him. He had a lot of PTSD to deal with."

She'd heard that about many, many of the homeless. "Was he a military veteran?"

The tallest guy nodded. "Yeah, and it really affected him. He also had some other issues." He made a circling motion around his ear.

She smiled at him. "Yeah, I hear you." Of course many of the guys out here had issues, not necessarily mental ones. However, mental health was a huge factor in the homeless population. "You guys got any idea how Shawn might have gotten from here to there?"

They shook their heads.

She faced the tallest guy again. "What about you? How well did you know him? Would somebody have picked up Shawn and taken him home, maybe for a meal?"

He shrugged. "Could happen to any of us," he muttered, as he looked around, frowning. "Shawn really was a good guy. He didn't break into places or steal. He begged, but everything was handed over willingly," he explained, and a touch of sorrow filled his tone for what had happened to Shawn.

"What about the Feldspar house?" she asked, her gaze going from one to the other, but locking onto the older guy's face. "Do you know anything about that?"

The old guy shook his head. "Don't know no Feldspar

house.”

“That’s where Shawn was killed, or at least where he was found,” she corrected herself.

“Meaning he wasn’t killed there?”

“We don’t know yet.” She looked from one to the other. “I have to admit we are a little stumped as to how he ended up there.”

“Somebody took him there,” the youngest of the three said, with a snort. “Even I can figure out that much.”

She glanced at him, then nodded. “That rings true, but did you see anybody pick him up? Did you see anybody give him a ride somewhere?”

He shook his head. “I haven’t talked to him in a while.”

“Why is that?”

“He wouldn’t let anybody into the Paragon. He was protective of it,” he replied, pointing at the old abandoned building. “He said ghosts were in there.”

“I did hear that he believed ghosts were there,” she noted, turning to look at the Paragon. “Have you guys ever heard or seen any?”

One guy snorted. “We hear and see lots, but it sure as hell isn’t ghosts.”

She gave him a sideways glance. “I don’t suppose you want to elaborate on that?”

“No, I sure don’t,” he snapped and turned his back to her.

She looked over at the older guy, and he shrugged, before adding more.

“Old Shawn was getting a little bit more tetched in the head all the time, but he kept saying ghosts were in the building, and somebody needed to make them happy.”

“Maybe the ghosts killed him to make them happy,” the

youngest guy snapped. "I don't like this talk of ghosts." And, without warning, he booked it away from them. As Kate watched him run, she looked over at the others and asked, "Is that normal for him?"

"Yeah, it sure is," the older guy confirmed. "Too many drugs, so he's also tetched in the head."

She nodded. "If you remember anything else, call me." She handed over her card to the two guys. Then she pulled out a couple bills from her pocket and handed one to each of them. "Otherwise go get yourself a hot meal and a cup of coffee."

The older guy smiled at her. "Didn't think you would be all bad."

"No, I'm not all bad," she said. "I don't move along the homeless. I'm only here about the dead, and right now the dead is your friend Shawn, and I will do my best to find out what happened to him."

Just as she went to walk away, the other guy who had remained fairly quiet so far added, "There was a black truck."

She pivoted and asked, "When and where?"

He hesitated, then looked at the older guy, who just stared at him, almost as if giving him encouragement to continue. "I saw it the other day. Shawn was talking to the driver, and they … they seemed kind of friendly."

"Shawn knew him?"

He nodded at that.

"Did Shawn get in the truck?"

At that, he nodded.

She felt the first vestiges of excitement inside her. "Would you recognize the truck if you saw it again?"

He shook his head. "No, probably not. But it had a dent."

"Okay, where is the dent?"

"Front bumper," he muttered. He looked back at the older guy again, obviously needing the other guy's approval to even talk to her, at least in his own mind. Then he finally said, "It was black and had 289 on the license plate."

"Where on the plate?"

"At the end of it," he said in a low voice, "and the guy was tall."

"How do you know he was tall?"

"Because his head came clear up to the top of the cab. I was just sitting here, thinking about how tall he seemed."

"Was there anything over the bed of the truck? Did it have a tonneau cover or a canopy?"

He shook his head at that. "No, it didn't, but it had those silver hooks sticking out on the edge of the bed for tying down stuff," he muttered. "I don't remember any more, except it was dirty, really dirty. I was thinking it would be a good graffiti truck," he shared, with a small smile.

"And which direction did they go?"

He stared at her blankly, then pointed down the road.

She nodded. "Any idea how long they were standing there, talking?"

He shrugged. "Five, ten minutes, I guess, but it was friendly, like they knew each other, but I don't know how old Shawn knew anybody with a truck like that."

"Because we all have a past that isn't this life," the older guy noted. "We all have history, and maybe Shawn bumped up against a bit of his. That happens from time to time."

"If he did, he didn't seem too upset about it," the other man said, with a surprised look in his buddy's direction. "Most of us turn and walk the other way when we see someone from our past."

The older guy pondered that for a moment and then nodded. "That's true. That's true." He looked over at Kate and pointed. "Your lady is waiting."

At that, Kate spun around to see the realtor standing there, shifting impatiently on the steps to the Paragon building that Kate needed access to. She smiled at the two helpful homeless guys. "Thank you. Remember to get yourself some food." And, with that, she quickly crossed the road to talk to the realtor.

The realtor glared at her as she approached. "Jesus, we all have work to do. You could have been here on time."

"*You* could have been, yes," Kate replied smoothly. "I was talking to the guys across the street, while I waited for you to show up."

"Oh," the realtor's face twisted in a sour expression. "Jesus, the building's empty."

"Whether empty or not isn't the point," Kate explained. "I prefer legal access if I can get it, but, if you don't want legalities in place for your clients, I'll note that in the future."

"Oh, whatever," the realtor huffed.

As she walked into the building, Kate could see why Simon was in love with this place. She sighed as she stood here and stared up at the vast majestic entrance and the openness of the old building.

"What was that sigh for?" the real estate agent asked, but only curiosity seemed to fuel her curiosity, not her previous snarky attitude.

"I imagine this building was really something back in the day," Kate noted.

"Yeah, it sure was."

Kate turned to her and asked, "Where did you find the homeless guy staying?"

She shrugged. "A client told me where he was." She quickly led the way to the stairwell and pointed at the mess on the floor. "This is where he was sleeping."

"Did you talk to him?"

"Only to move the human," she muttered, with a wince. "I'm not generally a person who talks to the homeless."

Kate didn't say anything to that, just stared at the realtor.

"That doesn't make me a bad person," the realtor snapped.

"I didn't say it did," Kate clarified, still eyeing the other woman closely. "I just happen to know that Shawn, the homeless guy in question, has been murdered."

The real estate agent looked sick at that comment. "Jesus. See? That's one of the reasons I don't talk to them," she muttered.

"They have broken lives, lives that they get murdered for," Kate muttered, and she shook her head at that, "and don't even tell me that you don't know what I mean."

"If you mean they live vulnerable lives in society and are, therefore, exposed to a lot more crime, illness, and other unfortunate elements such as inclement weather"—Ariel nodded—"that's quite true. But if you are suggesting that homeless people get murdered more often than other people … I don't think we have statistics to support that theory."

Kate wouldn't waste her time updating this realtor's ignorance on the subject. Kate wandered the area, then put on a pair of gloves and sifted through the garbage left behind in Shawn's usual spot.

Not a whole lot to see. A couple empty food wrappers, a bottle of water with some odd substance in the bottom of it.

Frowning, she tightened the bottle cap and put the bottle in an evidence bag. As she walked around a few other areas, she looked back at the real estate agent and said, "You don't have to stay."

The agent looked around nervously and nodded. "I do need to leave."

"That's fine. Go ahead and go." Kate smiled. "It's not as if I need to lock up when I leave."

"That's quite true." Ariel hesitated and then added, "If you do come up with anything, can you please let me know?"

"Why?" Kate asked, looking back at her.

"So I can tell the owner, of course," she replied in astonishment.

"I'll contact the owner myself."

"Oh, yes, of course." And, with that last uncomfortable move, the realtor made her escape.

As soon as she knew that the woman was gone, Kate turned, looked around at the building, and her thoughts just flew out of her mouth.

"Simon seems to really love you," she shared, "and I can see why, but secrets are here, lots of secrets, and I really want to find out what they are." After that, she did a pretty intensive search of the old building. It was mostly empty, with very little in the way of personal possessions of whoever else had been here. Yet she found glimpses of what this building had been at one point in time—multiple offices on various floors, plus a couple residential units.

She found various items and paperwork lying around, all of which, if she had time and budget money, she wanted forensics to go through. As it was, she carefully went through a lot of the paperwork, trying to get an idea of just what had been going on here and maybe what could have been the connection between this place and the Feldspar house.

As she wandered up and down the various floors of this building, she got a text from Simon, just two words.

Third floor.

She frowned at it and shook her head but headed up there anyway. She stared out one of the windows at the view and found such beauty and a sense of serenity in the city outside that she felt some of her tension easing.

"I hope Simon does buy you," she murmured. "He would do you justice."

And, with that, she walked along the third floor, nothing but offices set up here. At one she stopped because of the papers all over the floor, some of them water damaged. An old desk, scarred and well-worn, remained. She looked inside and found a couple of old business cards.

She smiled as she saw a private detective agency's name on both, but one was more crumpled than the other. She took the crumpled one and pocketed it for future reference and then continued her search. Simon had pointed her to the third floor, and here she was. Yet she just didn't know exactly what she was looking for.

As she entered the last office in the far-right corner, she groaned because this area seemed to have housed a ton of people for a very long time. She found empty food packages, old clothing, towels, and generally a disgusting mess. She walked deeper inside this room, grateful to be wearing gloves, as she saw needles and medicinal bottles in various corners.

She kicked away a pile of papers and uncovered a mangled briefcase, probably stolen in hopes of finding money, cash, or jewels inside. She almost laughed at that because it served them right if they thought they would get one million dollars out of this. Then she dropped down for a closer look at the papers, which appeared to be legal documents.

As she reviewed some of the pages, she saw *Feldspar* listed in the contact info. These were legal documents pertaining to the Feldspar family. Reading that, she got down on her knees and got to work sorting through the pages, not sure what she was looking for, but knowing more than ever that something was here, and she was determined to find it.

THE NEXT DAY, Simon was walking one of his rehabs, with Joe bringing him up to date, when his phone rang in his pocket. He quickly fished it out and groaned when he saw the name. "Ariel, what is your problem?" he snapped into the phone. "If I'm interested in a property, I'm interested when it suits me and not before."

A moment of silence came on the other end. Then, the real estate agent, her tone huffy, replied in a snappish tone, "I thought maybe you would want to know that the seller dropped the price."

He gave half a smile. "Of course they dropped the price, but it still won't make me jump for joy unless it's a major drop." Of course any drop showed that the owner had an interest in selling, and that was important information for Simon. "What did he drop it to?" he asked, keeping it casual, or at least trying to.

She sniffed in that way of hers that was enough to make it sound arrogant but held back enough so Simon really couldn't get pissed off at her, yet at the same time he wanted to.

"They dropped it one hundred grand."

Simon sighed. "So, they're interested in selling, but they're still a long way off from market."

"Why do you think that?" she asked. "It's prime real estate."

"Only if you're prepared to drop it and rebuild," he noted. "And, with the interest rates and the other major building going on downtown right now, I highly doubt that anybody is too interested at present."

"I've certainly had a lot of interest," she declared in a smart tone of voice.

"Good for you," he replied, deliberately not rising to her bait. "You'll probably get more nibbles, until they see the state of the building. I haven't been down to the city offices yet to see if there are any issues with the property. Have you?"

"No, of course not," she said, with a laugh that rang in his ears. "Who has time for that stuff?"

"Anybody who wants to sell it," he murmured, "or who wants to buy it."

"I'm busy. I've got to go." She wasn't having any of it. And she quickly disconnected.

He understood what she meant because really the responsibility fell to the buyer to check with the city to ensure that any problems were found at this point in time, not down the road after you had tied up millions of dollars to purchase a property that would quite likely be nothing but a headache. Simon surely didn't need that.

Joe looked at him intently. "You're after another property?"

Simon shrugged. "It's not that I'm after another property, but a property that's been on my wish list for a very long time is for sale."

Joe frowned. "I won't tell you *not* to buy anything else because obviously that's how I make my living too," he shared, "but we are spread a little thin right now."

"This one needs engineers on it before I get too cozy with the concept of taking it on," he added, with a small smile. "Besides … it also comes with ghosts."

At that, Joe's eyebrows shot up. "Ghosts?"

Simon nodded. "Apparently it's haunted, at least according to a homeless guy who had been living there for quite some time."

"Yeah, homeless guys being what they are," Joe noted, shaking his head, "I wouldn't put too much stock in his words."

"This guy wound up murdered just recently, so I don't know."

"Is he connected to the property?" Joe asked in a careful tone. "You don't need that. Most of my guys aren't superstitious, but I would really hate to see us rehabbing a building guaranteed to cause even more problems. We have enough as it is."

Simon nodded. "We don't need any more. I agree with you there."

"What building is it?"

"The Paragon."

Joe just stared at him for a long moment. "That's been empty for a really long time," he said cautiously. "It could be a pretty-big job."

"No doubt about that. It will definitely be a big job," he confirmed, "and, as you know, that's what we do."

Joe winced. "Yeah, we sure do, but wouldn't it be nice if we had an easy one for a change?" But he was smiling at

Simon. "I do appreciate that we fix up these old buildings and don't just take the easy road and drop them. I know that a lot of people, if not most, would think dropping them was the answer, but …"

"But it isn't always," Simon finished his sentence, with a nod. "Lots of times it isn't the right choice."

Joe replied, "That one could be biting off a lot."

"Oh, it will be for sure, but that doesn't mean I'm not interested though."

"Right, and that's why that bitchy real estate agent's all over you." Joe laughed. "Anybody who's got money for buildings like that? No wonder she's calling you all the time."

"Sometimes I find her irritating. Most of the time actually."

"Sure, but how come that one hundred thousand drop in asking price doesn't interest you?"

"It interests me in the sense that it means the owner is serious about selling, but realistically it's not enough to make a difference."

"Seriously?" Joe asked.

"No, we're talking millions here to buy it and more millions to fix it," Simon pointed out. "I want us well on track before we get to that point. So, the lower I get that selling price, the better for us all. Yet I can't do anything until I check things out at the city, and I haven't had a chance to get down there yet."

"I'm heading down there this afternoon," Joe noted. "Do you want me to pick up something?"

"Yeah, I sure do," Simon said. "How are you at standing in line?"

Joe snorted. "I guess you're paying for my time, so what

do I care?" Simon groaned at that, but Joe just laughed. "It's part of the business, and we don't really have a choice."

"I know, but wouldn't it be nice if we did? Anyway, if you're going anyway, I'll get you a list of the documents I need."

Joe nodded. "Seems as if you're plenty busy yourself these days, without spending hours down there."

"Neither one of us really has time for that," Simon conceded, "but I don't trust too many people to get the right documents."

"Right, and that's not something we can screw up either," Joe agreed, with a nod.

"Why do you need to go down?" Simon asked Joe.

"To check on the paperwork and to ensure all the permits were filed properly for one of our other projects," he stated. "The plumber told me that they were, but I got a weird feeling from him when he said that."

"Ah, yeah, if you feel something is wrong there, please go check," Simon suggested, "although surely you've got those guys on speed dial."

"I do, but, with a lot of illness and staff changes down there," he explained, as if thinking out loud, "I prefer to show up in person, so I can talk to one of the clerks I know. A lot of times I can get more answers from them than the actual inspectors."

"I'm not at all surprised," Simon said, "and you are smart to build those relationships when you get a chance." With that, Simon quickly provided the addresses and lot numbers of a couple properties he needed information on. "I'll need the entire city file on the Paragon building though. I can't even contemplate buying it until I have a whole lot more to go on." He frowned and asked, "The clerks won't tell the realtor if anybody pulls that information, will they?"

"No, but they might inform the owner, yet that's unlikely. If you think you have grounds for a lawsuit, I would say rest easy," Joe added, with a laugh.

Simon shook his head. "I don't think anybody gives a crap about lawsuits when it comes to this stuff."

"It's probably all considered public information and available for anyone who wants to pay to have it pulled."

"There you go," Simon agreed. "Head down to city hall and get me those documents then, because I really need to see all of it."

"Then what will you do?"

He winced. "I'll head back over to the Paragon building and have a look around."

"Didn't you say that homeless guy was murdered there?"

"He was murdered, but not necessarily there. I won't know that until I get there and see if it's been declared a crime scene."

At that, Joe shook his head. "I don't know how you can even handle any of that crap," he muttered. "I don't want anything to do with it."

"And I get that." Simon nodded, and he did. After Joe's brother-in-law's death, Joe was even more sensitive to police matters.

"Better you than me," Joe muttered, with a shrug. "I'll finish up a few things here and then run down to city hall."

"Okay." Simon gave him a nod.

With that task out of his hair, Simon took one final look at the job being done here, then turned and headed out. He picked up a coffee on his way to the Paragon building. Once there, he stopped for a long moment on the street and took a look. As always, it seemed to be completely deserted. He didn't really want the realtor to know he was here yet again. He could do only so much bluffing. Yet, if he continued to be caught on the premises, she would know he was far more interested than he wanted her aware of.

Yet he didn't really have any reason to keep it a secret. If people knew he was interested, a few would take another look just to see what Simon saw in the building. Still, most would walk away, thinking he was nuts. Half the time they thought he was nuts anyway, so that made no difference to him at all. Yet, if he could make this work, he wanted this building.

It was a special building and had tugged at him for a very long time. Thus, if he could make it work, he knew in his heart he would be happy to rehab it. His emotional response to a building was a large part of what he bought anyway, and was the reason a lot of people thought he was nuts. He never talked about the reasonings behind his interest in certain buildings. He kept that to himself, knowing full well that other developers would say he was completely dealing in lunacy, since business and emotions never worked well together. But Simon also knew that, at certain times in life, you had to make decisions based on things besides the bottom line. For him, it was all about saving some of these old buildings and about what they could mean to him and to others.

The street was busy with office workers racing out for a meal, trying to pick up something to go, or quickly eating with friends and then racing back again. That nine-to-five rut that some people flourished in, and that others just detested, was being played out all around Simon. He understood, but he much preferred being his own boss, but that also meant that he took hits personally, when they came, and he certainly had had enough of them to keep him on his toes.

Buildings had a way of deceiving even the most diligent inspection, never knowing when you would open up a wall and find a completely different ball game. You almost had to plan for the absolute worst case in these situations, and Simon could do that, provided it was a building he was prepared to go all in for. He just had to make that decision ahead of time and then be prepared to absorb those bumps when they came, ready to just keep on working from there, trying to make the numbers work. At the end of the day he always strove for everybody to win.

It wasn't even about winning for him. It was the challenge that appealed to him. It was about saving something special, about restoring something to its former glory, something a lot of people didn't agree with. Regardless, most of them did not understand his obsession with restoration, which was okay too.

He thought Kate understood, not that he had explained a whole lot of it to her, but she had an understanding that went far beyond what he'd ever expected from her. He found this interesting side to her personality particularly fascinating. It's not that she accepted anything blindly, but she accepted a lot of things without question and internalized whatever she was working to understand. She was methodical, and he loved that it wasn't blind belief. She seemed to take a pause on a specific issue, until she had a chance to see it from different angles and to work her way through it. He had to appreciate that because so many people didn't give him the benefit of the doubt, instead opting for an all-out thought process, generally leaving him in the dust, not exactly a comfortable place to be.

When he'd first started out at meetings for some financing, he'd been very careful to keep his reasoning for picking various buildings to something that the banking industry would understand, which was literally the bottom line, and only the bottom line. Once he'd managed to keep them out of it, he'd been more than happy. Now he just worked on the buildings that he wanted, knowing he could handle things within the time frames and other parameters required. So far, he didn't have to deal with any more of those people who didn't understand or didn't choose to understand. They were all about themselves, and Simon got that; he really did.

Everybody had to work, and some had their own dramas. Simon just didn't want it to be his drama. When the dramas came his way, that's when things could get ugly.

It was one of the reasons why he deliberately didn't let any realtor know he was interested in any property because all too often they used that as leverage to contact other clients, with a marketing ploy of *Hey, so-and-so is looking at this property. If you want in, you better put in a bid soon.* As expected, it tended to increase interest and to jump the prices. Half the time he wondered if the bidders weren't ringers, with the realtors doing it deliberately, just getting other people to show interest in order to bump up the prices. Personally, Simon wouldn't put it past Ariel to do just that. The seller may have dropped the price on this property, but it was still high enough that Simon wouldn't be dancing to anybody's tune about it, at least not yet. Maybe never if they didn't come to some better terms, assuming his engineers didn't return with a deal breaker.

The building reared up in front of him, as he turned the corner, and he smiled, once again struck with almost a sense of awe at the beauty and majesty of her. He headed to the front step and opened the door, nodding as he realized that the door itself wasn't locked, even if it should have been, even if the real estate agent was supposedly on top of it.

If it were his building, it would definitely be locked, but so many people didn't have that same sense of care, which bothered Simon. Those people determined the property, as is, had no value. Therefore, they wouldn't respect anything about it. Simon felt a certain reverence to every deal he did, but he didn't care whether the sellers had it or not. In fact, it would be better if they didn't just because that made it easier for Simon to secure the deal that he wanted and to close it and move on.

Walking through the main floor of the Paragon building, Simon felt that same familiar sense, almost a possessiveness, that *this is mine* proprietary feeling, as if ownership was a given, as if just the paperwork needed to be done. Yet he knew he could lose this one because that was just the nature of the real estate beast. Either he would pay up or he would walk, and right now neither was of particular interest.

Almost as if Ariel knew where he was, Simon's phone rang again, and it was his lovely stalking realtor.

"Just wanted to let you know that I've got interest from Sancurr Developments," she greeted him, her tone almost swollen in delight.

"Good. Let me know if they make a move." Sancurr was known for dropping anything and everything and putting up new buildings as fast and as cheap as possible, then selling it off and moving on. So *not* Simon's type of thing.

"Wait. ... As far as I know, they *are* making a move, and this is your one warning phone call," she added in exasperation.

"Good for you. Sounds as if you won't have to worry about it sitting on the market for too long."

"If you wanted it, you could have avoided this step."

"As I've told you repeatedly, I'm still not sure I *do* want it. So it'll be interesting to see if Sancurr goes through with it."

"Why? Don't you think they will?" she asked warily.

"Somebody showing interest," he began, then laughed, "is one hell of a long way from putting in an offer—especially on this place."

"Do you even realize that you're not very far from losing the entire thing?" she snapped. "I don't know why I keep trying to help you out."

"*Are* you helping me out? Or are you helping yourself out?"

"It's business," she replied, her tone turning stiff. "God, you're impossible when you're in this mood." With that, she disconnected.

He smiled because she was probably right; he probably was impossible in this mood. But what he definitely wouldn't do was get pushed by her, and she hadn't yet figured that out.

As he walked through the main floor, he headed for the stairwell where Shawn had been the first time Simon had run across him. He felt an odd sense as he got closer and closer. He frowned as he turned around warily, looking to see if he was still alone. Maybe he wasn't, as if somebody else was taking Shawn's spot. As Simon stood here, he closed his eyes, trying to get a handle of what he was sensing, and damn-near jumped when he heard a voice. He turned, and this weird shimmer stood in front of him.

"Oh, no, no, no," he muttered under his breath. "Oh,

hell no." He didn't want to deal with spirits. He didn't want to deal with that kind of stuff. It was bad enough dealing with the psychic crap he already had to deal with, without having to deal with ghosts too. Yet, sure enough, the ghostly spirit stood before him.

When a voice called out to him a second time, he realized just how bad it was. He stared for a long moment and then in a low whisper asked, "Shawn?"

A rumble came, and Simon wasn't sure whether that was a yes or a no, but he definitely got some response. Before he had a chance to even question the spirit, the shimmering ghost, or the shadow … or whatever the hell it was in that space, just disappeared.

CHAPTER 14

THE NEXT MORNING, back at her office, Kate was still waiting to hear from Dr. Smidge on his forensics findings for both cases, Robert Mulhouse and now Shawn. She was getting more and more frustrated as she sat here and did her due diligence on everything, without anything concrete to even go by. That drove her crazy. Yet she knew waiting for forensics was a constant in her world and there was no point in trying to push Smidge because it invariably just turned bad. Pushing someone was not helpful in this line of work, particularly not Smidge, as others had found out, and had forever regretted.

At least waiting for forensics gave her a chance to go into the history of this ghostly Paragon property downtown and the mystery as to how anybody had gotten Shawn to the Feldspar property. She had already made that request of Reese to chase down that license plate to the black truck that took off with Shawn.

Just as she picked up the phone to call her, Reese walked into the bullpen area. Kate caught sight of her and set down the phone. "Great minds and all that."

Reese rolled her eyes. "That just means you're looking for information that I may not even have."

Kate nodded. "Yeah, it sure does. It's the license plate I'm worried about now."

"That's interesting because it was stolen."

"Why does it always have to be stolen?" she complained, staring at Reese in frustration. "Why does no criminal ever use their own vehicle for these things?"

Reese laughed at her. "When you get the answer to that question, you can enlighten the rest of us, but I wouldn't hold my breath on that."

Kate groaned. "Of course not. So stolen from where?"

"Actually stolen just a few blocks away from where Shawn was picked up. The truck was parked behind a business, as the truck's owner raced into the building to pick up something he had left behind. He reported it stolen immediately and was pretty pissed about it."

"Right, I'm sure he is, and now I suspect that it'll turn up sometime very soon, probably clean as a whistle."

"I would think so," Reese agreed, with a smile, "but, in the meantime, I don't think you'll really care about the history of it. Still, I'll fill you in. It belongs to a workman who does a lot of construction downtown. He was literally dropping stuff off and had forgotten to pick up something else, and his truck was stolen right outside this business as he quickly ran inside."

Kate nodded, then reached out a hand for the information in Reese's file. "I'll add it to my report." Then she froze for a moment before asking, "Is there anything on the history of the Paragon property, where Shawn was last seen alive at?"

"I can run some more down," Reese offered cheerfully.

Kate nodded. "So far, nothing has really popped that was unique, different, or of interest, but …"

"But?" Reese asked Kate.

"My gut instincts tell me that we will find it of interest."

Reese laughed. "Yours or Simon's?"

Kate groaned again. "That's the trouble with having Simon around. ... Nobody thinks I have a gut feeling anymore. It's so frustrating."

Reese laughed once more. "No, we just think you have superspecial x-ray vision in your world now."

Kate shook her head and sighed. "All I'm doing is good old-fashioned police work."

"Yeah, we agree with you, but it certainly doesn't hurt to have Simon around."

"Unless we start depending on him," she said in a flinty tone, "and then it'll hurt us a lot. We can't exactly haul him into court, not without expecting to be laughed right out of the courtroom."

"I know," Reese agreed, "but, if we can get any direction from him, we can start digging."

Kate nodded. Reese quickly disappeared, and Kate added the information on the stolen vehicle to her report. It wasn't much, and it wasn't a big help. Yet, when it came to getting convictions in these cases, they had to tie off these bits and pieces constantly, just so they didn't leave any loopholes for somebody to come back on, saying they hadn't checked out everything. She had a hard-enough time with the court as it was because it seemed as if her department did a ton of work, and then these criminals still got off sometimes.

So far, she was grateful that the ones she'd been involved with were going down for a very long time, even though she still had a couple court dates coming up that would make her not sleep well at night, mostly out of fear that they would get off and go terrorize the world again. Not something she looked forward to.

But then, sitting back, gazing at her computer screen

with a photo of the license plate number in front of her, she thought more about that. A stolen car meant preplanning, and that meant somebody needed Shawn out of the way. What could possibly be important enough to take a homeless guy off the streets? Unless of course he knew something that was dangerous, but, if he did, what did he know, and did he understand how dangerous that was?

Did he make the mistake of trying to blackmail somebody about it?

Did he contact someone?

The questions swirled around in her mind, and then she remembered that, of course, Shawn had talked to somebody. He had talked to Simon and to his homeless buddies. Frowning, she glanced around the office, but she was completely alone. Everybody else was off working on cases. She picked up the phone, and, when Simon answered, his voice cheerful and bright, she sighed. "When you talked to Shawn," she began, "did he mention talking to anybody else? Maybe warning anybody else or having any conversations with anybody else?"

"No, I don't think so."

She groaned. "Of course not," she muttered in exasperation.

"Why? What's the angle you're working on?" he asked, curiosity in his tone.

"The only point in killing him," she replied, "is if the killer had a reason to do so."

"Sure," Simon agreed. "Almost every killing has a reason behind it."

"Exactly, but Shawn was pretty harmless," she pointed out. "I mean, most people—and I don't mean this in a bad way—but most people didn't even know Shawn existed."

"That's very true," he replied thoughtfully.

"And, looking at the way this went down, I would say it was premeditated."

"How so?" he asked, his tone sharpening over the phone.

She explained about the stolen vehicle and was again met with silence at first, but then Simon spoke, sounding surprised. "That definitely seems premeditated, doesn't it?"

"Absolutely, and, when it's premeditated, there's a reason. This isn't somebody just stealing a vehicle and going off and killing a homeless guy. The driver stopped, talked to Shawn, and he got in the vehicle with the driver, for whatever reason, and then Shawn didn't come home."

"And, of all the places for Shawn to disappear, it happens to be the property he was most connected to. So the driver knew where to find him."

"Yes, that's true."

"Did you find any connection between the Paragon property and the Feldspar house?"

"My analyst is looking further into it, but I did find something of interest, when I did a walkthrough of your ghost property on the third floor."

"Right, the third floor."

"Yes … where you told me to go."

"I did?" he asked in astonishment.

She froze. "You texted me *third floor.*"

"Well, damn," he muttered. "I'll have to look back on my call history, but I don't remember that."

"I'll just assume that you did it on purpose and that whatever was going on in your world was something that had you so busy that you forgot."

"And it could be that," he muttered, an odd tone in his voice.

"Is everything okay?" she asked.

"Sure. Plus, you'll probably be pissed if I tell you, but you'll also be pissed if I don't," he added, as he took a deep breath. "So this is definitely a no-win situation."

"You better tell me then," she snapped back, "so I can get pissed and get over it."

He burst out laughing. "I really don't know how this works, and I don't have any idea if this is even what I saw, didn't see, or may have seen."

"Whoa, whoa, whoa," she interrupted. "What did you see?"

"I thought *maybe* I heard and saw …" He hesitated for a long moment, then finally the words burst out. "Shawn's ghost."

"Oh, Christ," she whispered, staring at her phone. She looked around the bullpen again to ensure she was alone. "Is that possible?"

"I don't know," he admitted. "I'm not a medium, remember? But it seems awfully fast if it was him."

She racked her brain, trying to figure out the difference between what everybody's woo-woo title was and what they could do. And that was easier than contemplating an average time frame for a dead person to appear as a ghost. This was so not in her wheelhouse. "But didn't Shawn tell you how he could *see* ghosts and even talk to them in your ghost property?"

"That's very true," Simon confirmed. "Yet I didn't necessarily think of Shawn as a medium."

"Right," Kate agreed. "Most people think the homeless are nuts when talking about ghosts—or are on drugs or something."

Simon sighed loudly. "Plus, I wouldn't have thought the

transition from dead man to ghost would happen so quickly. I thought mediums, or whatever they are called, would take messages, somehow communicate with the ghosts, but I don't know if mediums can *see* the ghosts. I am, for sure, no medium, and have no desire to be one," Simon shared.

"Right, okay then." She had to admit that some of this was starting to make a little more sense. "I'm sure that must have been a very strange experience for you," she murmured.

"Yeah, that's one word for it." He groaned.

"I don't suppose Shawn's ghost shared anything helpful, like, *Hey, catch my killer, and his name is so-and-so*, right?"

"No," Simon declared, with a snort. "That would have been nice though, wouldn't it?"

"Any chance that's why he appeared to you?"

"His ghost was at that ghost building."

"Oh, so ..."

Simon asked, "Does that mean Shawn was killed at the Paragon building? ... I don't know."

"He was seen leaving from there, with the driver of the stolen truck."

"Exactly. But we are just talking, since I figured you would be pissed if I didn't tell you about seeing a ghost."

She half laughed. "Wow, do we have a difficult relationship?"

"No, we don't," he argued. "It's just one that we must keep our lines of communication open and our minds adaptable."

"That's a good way to deal with it," she noted, "and I am sorry you're having that kind of a day."

"Yeah, me too, but it sounds as if you're getting somewhere."

"No, not really. I'm still waiting for forensics, and that

always frustrates me to no end. Even with a good relationship with the coroner, he and his staff still have a lot of materials to sift through, and it takes time. As Smidge always says, he will contact me if and when."

"Right, so nothing else on your *not suicide* case?"

"No, not at the moment. Again, still waiting for forensics, and that one is frustrating too because it was a murder, but the wife will deny it until the bitter end."

"Yet, if it were a suicide … she probably doesn't get any money."

"What do you mean?"

"Suicides are generally not part of a valid claim within the insurance system. Therefore, if somebody commits suicide, the spouse or whoever the beneficiary is, whoever is supposed to receive the benefit money, won't get anything."

"Right, and Amie is one greedy bitch who would definitely have confirmed the existence of life insurance."

"Check that out too."

"I'll do it right now." She quickly rang off, phoned to check for any life insurance in the husband's name. Yes, indeed. Now that the husband's death had been classified as a murder, the life insurance proceeds were eligible for a payout.

"Shit," she muttered to herself, as she sat here. That makes no sense, yet in an ugly way it made a lot of sense. She just didn't like the way it was turning out because Kate would end up being the instrument for this hideous woman getting an insurance payout on her dead husband, and that was not good news at all. It's not that Kate had any personal animosity to the wife, other than Amie could be responsible for at least one of her three husbands' deaths. The question was, how could Kate prove Amie was guilty?

KATE WALKED INTO Simon's apartment building a little later to see Harry smiling at her.

"You don't look quite as tired this time," he noted, with a smile, "but you do look frustrated."

"*Ya think?*" She glared, sure daggers darted from her gaze. "The damn criminals are getting smarter all the time."

The smile fell from his face, as he nodded. "But it really all comes down to the same elements," he pointed out, "usually greed."

She groaned. "Yeah, greed is a big one. Love and power are others."

He winced at that. "I don't understand how *love* can turn into something so bad," he murmured.

"Oh, it doesn't generally happen on its own," she noted. "Too often an awful lot of other bits and pieces go with it. Generally somebody loses out on the deal."

He nodded at that. "Power is a bad one, isn't it? Regardless, I'm sure you'll find your killer. I'll buzz you up."

As she walked over to the penthouse elevator, gave Harry a wave, and headed up, her thoughts were centered on his words about how those three concepts corrupted so much in life. The supposed *love* in this life seemed to turn to hate, without any discrimination or motive needed. Yet there was always a reason why it happened, and it was usually something to do with lust, somebody breaking up with somebody, somebody realizing, all of a sudden, that their partner wasn't the same as they thought they were.

All kinds of things can and did happen, like how Amie would get a payout from this, assuming her husband hadn't committed suicide. That was really a challenge. It made Kate feel like a terrible person. By doing her job to the best of her ability, that just gave Amie a big insurance payout. Even if Amie didn't have anything to do with killing her husband, Kate was almost rooting for her to be guilty of something else, so at least Kate could charge Amie with something that would stop this repeating cycle of dead men in her life.

Kate was instinctively blaming Amie without proof yet, and that wasn't fair either. It was also not part of Kate's job, and she typically tried hard to be professional and detached.

Simon took one look at the expression on her face and asked, "Change of plans?"

She blinked at him, not getting where he was coming from. "Change of plans over what?"

He let out a long sigh. "We're supposed to go out on the boat."

She stared at him and then nodded. "You're right. We are."

He winced at that. "So, change of plans?"

She thought about it for a moment, not sure how to proceed. "I'm definitely off for the evening," she stated, "and, unless anything else happens, there's really nothing else I can do for the moment."

"And let me guess. ... That's really eating at you, isn't it?"

"It's not so much that it's eating at me but I have open cases, and people are dying, like Shawn, and I don't know why or how." She shook her head. "It makes no sense, and I just want answers. Yet answers are a little thin on the ground."

He nodded. "Sounds as if we need to go out in the boat."

She finally smiled. "I think that's a great idea. And if I do get called out?"

He shrugged. "Then you get called out, and I return us to shore. … At least let's go find some enjoyment in the rest of this crazy world that we live in."

"Yeah, I can get behind that." She looked around, frowning. "Do I have clothes here for that, or do we need to go back to my place?"

"I wouldn't want to go back to your place if we don't have to," he noted. "It'll just eat into our time. So take a look at what you've got here, see if you've got a change of clothes for the night. I've already ordered a picnic for tonight and tomorrow. We'll pick it up on the way."

She grimaced. "Damn, I'm really sorry. … I forgot what day it was."

"It doesn't matter," he said gently. "You've got a lot on your mind."

"So do you," she noted, mulling over her own carelessness, "but you didn't forget." As she walked into the bedroom, she realized just how much of these relationship things she seemed to continuously louse up. It wasn't a very comfortable feeling. She considered herself beyond competent when it came to most things. However, it seemed she could use a refresher course on this relationship stuff.

She winced at that because a refresher course sounded terrible and made her feel as if she were back in school and not as good as she could be. That was never a good thing.

She decided that whatever she had in Simon's closet would definitely do and quickly packed up a change of clothes, adding several towels. She came out with two full travel bags. "Hopefully this works."

"Let's go now before anybody else decides to interrupt our time off." Then laughing like children playing hooky, the two of them grabbed their bags and hurried downstairs.

Harry was still on the front desk as they raced past him. He called out, "Have a good evening."

Simon lifted a hand, then turned to face Harry, just as they went out the front door. "We'll be down at the boat, if anybody calls. Hopefully nobody will need us, but ..."

"Oh, I know," Harry acknowledged, with a quirky tone. "The chance for time off is a little thin when it comes to her line of work."

Kate winced. "Exactly, and boy, do I need to get out a little more."

"Go, go, go," Harry urged them.

And with that, they quickly raced outside. By the time they had picked up their food for the trip and headed to the docks, she was starting to completely fall in love with the idea of taking off for the weekend.

"Are you on call this weekend?" Simon asked.

"No, but yes," she replied.

"Right, *no, but yes*, in that everybody's dead and gone, and you can't help them anyway ... besides working hard on solving the cases."

"I've just run out of anything I can do with these right now," she admitted, with a shrug. "And, as callous as it may sound, I only have so many hours in a day and only so many hours I can put in, without needing a change or a chance to recharge."

He squeezed her hand and glanced over to her. "I'm actually glad to hear that. Is your department getting any new people in?"

"Supposedly," she muttered, "although we're just finally jelling as a group. So I'm not really too thrilled with the idea of getting anybody else in. Yet we need another person to fill Andy's void."

"I would think so," he agreed, "yet you don't really want anybody else?"

"Not really. We're pretty happy now that we're finally to that point of acceptance."

He pondered that and nodded. "I get that. Obviously an awful lot of things are going on in your world and a lot of cases to handle, but you still need some downtime."

"Which is why I'm here," she noted, then quickly sent Colby a text message that she was out on Simon's boat, if needed. In a surprise move, Colby called her to talk over how far she'd gotten on the one case.

She explained where she was, waiting for forensics, how she still had nothing new in terms of either of her current cases.

Colby replied, "That's definitely *not* how we want the cases to go."

"I know. Do you want me to come back in?"

"No," he stated quickly. "You've done a ton of overtime already, so it would be good to do something different for a while. Then come back rested, with a fresh perspective."

"I know, but I admit to feeling guilty."

"Which is not what you should focus on," he stated firmly. "We're supposed to get new staff, but budget cuts and all that. … The trouble is, we need detectives on board twenty-four hours a day, and we won't ever have the staff to do that. … Check in tomorrow. You may only get tonight, but check in tomorrow."

"Will do," she confirmed, then ended the call. She looked over at Simon and saw him nodding.

"That's fair," he said. "I get it. You're short on staff. These victims' families all need answers, all of them, Shawn too."

"I couldn't find any for him so far," she noted, "and that was one of the things we were looking at today. We're trying to track down family, but I believe they're back east. We haven't got any solid information for him."

"I suspect he lost track of any family when things got difficult for him."

She frowned. "After his military service?"

"Probably. Most people—not most but several—lost somebody. So, they often struggle when the PTSD gets bad. Not everybody can handle the symptoms."

"Particularly him," she reminded Simon.

"Exactly, and it's hard enough when you're just dealing with it yourself, but, when you also have little kids around, and spouses, it can all go off the rails pretty fast."

They soon got to the marina, and Simon got on board to prep the boat. Then he carried all the bags in, while she quickly unhooked the ropes on the mooring. He started the engine, and gently they powered their way out toward the bay.

As soon as they got out far enough, she settled in beside him and watched as they ate up the water. With every passing mile, she felt her insides release stress.

He smiled at her and asked, "Feeling better?"

She nodded. "Surprisingly, yes, and that's not exactly something I expected so soon."

He nodded. "That's one of the reasons why we do this, even if only for tonight or just a few hours. ... Let's get out on the water and remember why we're alive and why it's worth fighting for."

She looked over at him. "Does it seem as if it's a fight for you sometimes?"

He nodded. "You're telling me it doesn't for you?"

"Yeah, it does," she admitted, "and I hate that aspect of it. I'm fighting the bad guys, but the murderers are getting trickier, and I'm fighting liars who never seem to want to give up the truth."

"That's because they can't face the consequences," he noted, "particularly if they're at fault. Most people who do these unimaginable deeds—unless they are psychopaths and take great pride and joy in the devastation they caused—are people with a conscience. Too often they can't accept the reality of what they've done and have to hide it even from themselves."

She pondered that as they moved out to the open water, her face turned up to the wind, loving the tug against her skin, the crisp fresh air almost biting into her cheeks. She laughed as a wave splashed up and over.

He smiled at her. "Not everybody appreciates the water," he noted. "I'm really glad that you do."

She nodded. "I've never really had a chance to before, but this is pretty special, and I'm really grateful you bought this boat."

He eyed her in delight. "Lots of people would have told me that it was a stupid purchase."

"No," she murmured, "not a stupid purchase at all, and one I certainly understand better now that I've been out here." Then she added, "On the other hand, if you didn't bring enough food, I might have to send you back in early."

He burst out laughing. "Why don't you check out the food, and maybe we can get started on that." And that's what they did. By the time she had the food dished out and ready to be eaten, he idled the engine and let the boat gently motor along, as they sat under the canopy with just enough of the breeze to counter the lingering warmth in the air.

"You know, for early December," she noted, "it's surprisingly warm out here."

"I'm surprised you are warm at all," he declared, looking at her. "You're often chilled."

"Maybe," she muttered. "Maybe it's just that feeling of being out here in the fresh air."

"Probably," he said, with a smile. "An awful lot can be said for coming out on the ocean, but most of the time it is colder on the water," he warned.

"I know. You've told me that before, but I'm okay with it. I feel as if I've acclimated fairly quickly to being out here," she murmured. When her phone rang, she hesitated, but he nodded.

"Answer it," he urged. "It'll bother you if you don't, and we both know that clear as day."

She sighed, and it was her analyst. "Reese, don't you go home anytime?"

"Yeah, I'm actually at home. But I just got a call back from one of our messages, trying to locate Shawn's family."

"Oh, good, give me the contact information." And, with that done, she frowned at it and asked Reese, "Do I know that name?"

"Yeah, you sure do," Reese confirmed. "Shawn's father and grandfather were politicians."

"Wow, not what I expected."

"No, and, because of it … I think they've been a little more distant from his world than intended."

"Right, of course, Shawn wouldn't exactly be a boon to anybody in politics, would he?"

Simon looked at her curiously.

"Probably not, but we'll see how much they actually care for him," Kate noted, "because he did deserve to have somebody in his life."

"I'll let you handle that," Reese noted cheerfully. "If you need anything else, *don't* call me."

Easier said than done because, if Kate needed Reese, then she would be called in to help. Just like the rest of them.

SIMON WOKE IN the morning to the sound of Kate talking to somebody outside. He checked his watch, surprised that it was seven. He'd slept like a log, but something about being out on the boat was … He wasn't even sure how to say it, but it was special. He felt a sense of peace, a sense of relaxation that he hadn't expected, and he was absolutely loving it.

He got up, quickly dressed, then headed outside to see her tucked up on the deck, staring out at the ocean around them, her phone at her ear in one hand, a cup of coffee in the other, a blanket wrapped around her shoulders. He ducked back into the cabin to grab himself a coffee from the kitchenette.

He looked around, wondering whether he needed to make any upgrades to his boat or if it was just fine as it was. It was probably fine as is, at least for a while, until he figured out what he was doing. Yet rehab was always in the back of his mind. So, if he needed to renovate it, he certainly could. Money wasn't that tight, certainly not when it came to the one thing he'd bought for himself, which was this boat.

At certain times in life you should do something for yourself, and he almost laughed at that because it seemed as if he was still trying to justify his purchase. That wasn't how he wished to see this acquisition, but maybe it made sense, when reviewing his life to date.

With a cup of coffee in hand, he headed back up to see Kate pocketing her phone. She looked over at him and smiled. "That was Shawn's family."

He stared at her enquiringly. "Oh?"

"Tears, some recriminations, some sadness, and a lot of history on Shawn that basically fits what we know."

"And that is?"

"PTSD, as you suggested. He was traumatized from his military service and ultimately left the family unit because he couldn't deal with the panicked outbursts and the pain that he thought he was inflicting on everybody," she shared, with a far-off look to the side. "He moved west, and they lost track of him. They sent out multiple people to search for him over the years, but nothing ever came of it. Of course now they want to know what happened and how, and I don't have any answers for them at this point in time. Yet I will follow up as soon as I do," she declared smoothly. She stared at the ocean and sipped at her coffee, but he could sense a disquiet in her.

"What's the matter?" he asked.

She shrugged. "It's not so much that anything's the matter, but it's always sad to think that Shawn lost touch with his family and ended up dying alone."

Simon winced at that. "Not a scenario we want for anybody, is it?"

"No, it isn't." She gave him a small smile. "But thank you very much for bringing us out last night. I could never have managed a break on my own."

He laughed. "Oh, you were willing to take the time off … and we needed it."

"We did," she agreed. "I've also just received a text."

He knew exactly what was coming and asked, "Are we

going back in then?"

She winced and nodded. "Yes, if you don't mind terribly. Is it possible?"

"Of course it's possible." He looked around and sighed. "We should think about spending actual holidays out here."

"After last night," she shared, with a smirk on her face, "I think that's a great idea. You're right. We need more time to commune with nature, without everything else interfering."

"And speaking of interference," Simon asked, "why are we going back in?"

She grimaced. "I have another body."

CHAPTER 15

O N THE RETURN trip to land, Kate had told Simon the little bit she knew about her newest case, which wasn't a whole lot. Now here she was, staring at the crime scene address on her phone. She shook her head, got into her car, and drove toward the scene itself, to get an idea of all the problems ahead of her in this one.

Simon hadn't asked too many questions and had basically left this subject alone, as he had just been happy to see her eat breakfast before taking off on the run again. She herself? Well … she somehow knew this case would be a whole lot more than she was expecting. Almost as if he understood that, her phone buzzed with his call. When she parked at the address, she answered. "What's the matter?"

"You tell me. I've had nothing but a feeling of disquiet ever since you left."

"That's probably because of the address I'm at," she began, and then let it hang there.

"Where?" he asked a bit impatiently. "Is it the Feldspar house again?"

"No … your building downtown."

"Shit," he muttered. "I should have come then."

"Why is that?" she asked in an odd tone. "You're not the owner—or are you?"

"No, not yet. Damn."

"It's all right. I'll fill you in whenever I get a chance. Got to go." She disconnected, then walked up to the police officer, waiting at the entrance.

She didn't see any sign of Dr. Smidge. "Has the coroner's office been called?"

The cop nodded. "They're on their way."

She shrugged. "Yeah, everybody's pretty tired at the moment. We've had a lot of cases this week. I'm sure Dr. Smidge will be here in a bit." At that, she heard a call from behind her, and, sure enough, Smidge pulled his bag from the trunk of his car. She walked over to him. He stopped, then glared and asked, "Is this one yours?"

"Since I got called in on it," she said, with a laugh, "and maybe because of the location, I'll say yes."

"Right," he grumbled, with a stern stare. "You don't get any more free passes on this," he declared, shaking a finger at her.

She smirked because she obviously had no control over where people dumped bodies or where people ended up dying, but, as it was, she agreed with him. Enough of this place, enough of these bodies, enough of these deaths.

As she walked up to the building with him, Smidge asked, "What are the details?"

"No clue. I just got here myself." When he frowned at her in amazement, she nodded. "I was out on the boat."

He gave her a deep sigh. "Now, for that, I'm sorry. ... You don't take enough time off as it is."

"I try. It just never seems to work out."

As they walked in, she led the way.

Smidge noted, "It's almost as if you know where you're going."

"*Ya think?*" she quipped, followed by a laugh. "I was

here earlier this week and found some documents that had Feldspar's name on it." At that, he frowned at her. She nodded. "I haven't yet been able to contact the issuing company that supposedly rented an office in this building and both created and had possession of those documents, all of which was some years ago," she explained, without looking back but leading them in.

"That's very suspicious in itself."

She smiled, yet shook her head. "Not really. The company went belly up at least ten years ago, if not more."

"Ah," Smidge muttered, "then that makes sense. This building has been empty for a long time, just from the looks of it." Smidge kept pace with her on the way up.

"Yes," she murmured. "Simon is considering buying it."

"Why would he want this dump?"

"Because he takes these dumps and returns them to their previous glory. It's his saving grace."

"The real question is, did it have any former glory?" he asked.

"Now that's a good question." She smiled, glancing back at him. "Maybe way back when, but it's definitely had a few tough years in the meantime."

"*Ya think*?" Smidge looked around. "We have a ton of abandoned buildings all over Vancouver, but I agree that something is quite special about this one."

"There is," she stated, with a smile. "That's how Simon feels too."

"Good to know," Smidge noted, "but, in order to put a stop to this killer, Simon needs to deal with the entire city, so it doesn't become a dumping ground."

"It depends on who we've got here," she replied, "and it could be a junkie."

"Would they have called you in for a junkie?"

"I sure as hell hope so, for unexplained deaths and unintended deaths."

"Exactly. I keep testing you," he admitted, with a sigh, "and you keep giving me the right answers. You're such a disappointment."

She burst out laughing. "You just want to be seen as a curmudgeon," she pointed out, "but the truth is, you're just a teddy bear."

He shot her a horrified look that had her laughing again. "Don't you dare tell anybody that."

"No, I won't," she said. "You give me timely information, and you might start holding out on me if I did tell everybody."

"I might," he agreed, with a nod, "and, if I ever did, you would know that you deserved it."

She would have laughed at that, but right in front of them was a pile of clothing that had seen better days. She walked closer, then bent down, so she could see the face of the victim, and sighed.

"What?"

"He's possibly related to one of my existing cases," she shared, "but I can't be sure until I get a better look at him. I'm pretty sure this is one of the other homeless guys I spoke to about Shawn, the same one who also gave me a description of the vehicle that had picked up Shawn."

At that, Dr. Smidge turned to her and nodded slowly. "At least they called the right person. Looks as if this is definitely your case."

"Seems so," she murmured, "and now all I need is for the best doctor in the city to give me the forensics on this guy."

He sighed. "In that case, get the hell out of my way." And, with that, he got down to work.

She walked around the immediate area, then waited in the hallway, while forensics collected evidence. She knew they would find a lot here, what with the homeless traffic this building seemed to have. So fingerprints, boot and shoe prints would likely be found. Forensics would expect that and more.

This place had been abandoned for a long-enough time period that it would be full of forensics, and, in all likelihood, none of it would do her any good. Just knowing the time and resources that would be spent getting through all that miscellaneous and unrelated data made her wince.

While Smidge was still working, she left the building, searching for the other homeless guys she had seen and had spoken to earlier. Yet she saw no sign of anyone. She waited until a little later in the afternoon, when the body had been removed, to see if any of the other homeless guys had come back to the area. Outside of a few curiosity seekers, people she had seen earlier in the day, the surrounding area was still basically empty.

The local homeless community had all gotten the message to stay away now, with a second homeless person dead so soon. So nobody would be around the ghost building at all. She couldn't blame them for it. It was tough enough to see one of your friends get put down, but it was something else to lose two of them in the same week.

As she walked back up to the front of the Paragon building, she watched as the police officers canvassing the neighborhood just started to filter back here. She waited for them, but they all basically shook their heads.

"Nobody saw anything."

She nodded. "The trouble is, with a deserted building, people expect to see it empty, and they expect to see homeless people gathered around it," she noted. "Therefore, the neighbors don't really see anything beyond that." As she turned to go back in, she stopped when she saw Simon approaching. He raised an eyebrow. She shared, "It was another one of the local homeless guys," she shared, "one of the two I spoke with about Shawn's death." When he stared at her wordlessly, she nodded. "Yes, you would not be wrong in thinking it could be connected."

"Wow." He stared up at the building. "Somebody is using her as a dumping ground, but why?"

"That's a very important part of it because he was dumped here, *not* at Feldspar."

He nodded. "And that could be for any number of reasons."

"It could be," she agreed, "but this won't be an easy one because nobody saw anything. Once again we have no cameras, no security, and, short of any of his friends being warned off or saying anything, I don't expect much will come up for us to go on."

"I suppose I can't go in, can I?"

"No, not only are you not the owner but the forensic team is still in there."

He snorted at that, giving her a headshake. "Nobody will help your case with the forensics in that place. They'll find way too much stuff, as too much time has passed, and way too many people have gone through the Paragon."

She nodded. "I know that, but we've still got to process it."

"Okay, I'll leave you to it." Yet he lingered, looked back, and added, "It's such a shame. It's almost as if she's there waiting for me to help out."

"Maybe she is," Kate replied, "and maybe somebody is sending a message."

He frowned at her and asked, "What possible message could that be?"

She stared at him for a long moment. "We use all manner of people for info gathering, including the homeless. They are like waitstaff at hotels and restaurants, where people don't see them and thus talk about all manner of stuff in front of them. So, if this homeless man's death is a message, you can bet I will figure it out eventually." This time as she looked around, she caught sight of one of the other homeless guys who she had spoken to earlier. "I'll be right back."

With that, she dashed across the street. When the homeless guy wearing the cap saw her, he froze, as if a deer in the headlights. She called out, "Hey, I just want to talk to you. You remember how we spoke before, right?"

He nodded. "Yeah, and now Frankie's dead."

She winced. "How do you know that?"

"Because I saw him being taken away," he muttered.

"Did you see him in there?" When he hesitated, she added, "Please don't lie about it. Just tell me the truth, so we can find Frankie's killer and can clear you."

"*Clear me?*" he asked in a shocked, gutted tone. "I didn't have nothing to do with it."

"That's why I need to clear you," she stated smoothly. "Look. I get it. You were probably there with him at the same time."

He nodded. "He had something to tell me, and it was really eating at him."

"Any idea who else he might have told?"

He shrugged. "I don't know, but he needed to make

some money."

"Right, so what are the chances that he might have known who picked up Shawn?"

The older guy stared at her in shock, then slowly nodded. "He was always a little cagey about that. He kept saying that just because the guy picked him up, it didn't mean the driver of that truck had something to do with Shawn's death."

"We don't know for sure, but that vehicle was stolen." When the older guy frowned at her, she nodded. "Now two of your friends are gone. Please don't make any mistakes and be extra careful out here."

He frowned at her, as if she what she'd said was ludicrous. "Nobody's after me. I haven't done nothing."

"You think either of your buddies did something wrong? Something worth getting killed over?"

He hesitated and then shrugged. "I don't know."

"Right," she agreed, "and, because we don't know, let's just not have any more accidents, okay?"

"Are you really thinking it was an accident?"

"Hell no. Shawn and Frankie were murdered, and, for once, there is no doubt about it."

The older man swallowed hard and sighed. "We see the world in a very different way, but we expect to get that kind of response from a lot of other places, other people—angry punks, shop owners, people who want us to just disappear— but to be murdered specifically? That doesn't make any sense. Not unless some punk kid was on a mission to take out the homeless."

"Do you think it was some punk kid?" When he shrugged, she shook her head. "I don't either. So, if you know anything … even if it seems insignificant, please tell me, so I can put a stop to this before anybody else dies. The last thing I want is to come into one of these buildings and find out you were the next one."

"Shit no, that's not what I want either," he muttered, as he stared off into the distance.

"Is there a reason anybody would expect you to know anything?"

He swallowed, then shook his head. "I don't think so."

"Would Frankie or Shawn have mentioned anything about you to the wrong people?"

He stared at her. "I don't know anything."

"Good," she replied. "If you don't know anything, maybe the killer believes that too." Not that she believed it. Most of the time these murderers would kill just on an off chance of silencing a potential witness.

"It doesn't make any sense why they would have killed Shawn anyway," the older man shared, "or why he went up to that truck or why he was dumped at that house across town."

"Maybe not," Kate conceded, "but, once I figure it out, it will make sense, at least to the person behind this."

He sighed. "Does it always end up making sense?" he asked, with a hopeful note.

She hesitated. "Sometimes the motives and the reasons behind it all only make sense to the killer. But, once you realize how it makes sense to them and how their minds work"—she shrugged—"it's not always something easy for us to accept."

"I guess that's your way of saying *no*."

She laughed. "It's *not* my way of saying no. It's my way of saying how it will make sense to the killer, just not necessarily in a way that we can understand."

He pondered that. "Kind of like our problems too, *huh?*"

"Yeah," she agreed. "Not everybody understands or accepts that homeless people have problems." She smiled at him in sorrow. "I'm sure lots of people think you're just lazy and don't want to hold down a job."

"Yeah, we get that a lot," he noted.

"Anybody in particular hassling you?"

"No," he stated, with a vehement nod. "We generally just move on, rather than get into any confrontation."

He was right to consider that, but she had no idea if he really did that in practice.

"Too many times confrontations end up really ugly." He stared back at the Paragon building, and then his shoulders slumped. "I think Frankie mentioned something about recognizing the guy."

"The guy who picked up Shawn?"

He nodded. "Frankie didn't recognize the truck, or at least I don't think he did, but I do think he recognized the driver."

"And yet you didn't?"

"Frankie, he knew the guy."

"How?"

"From a different time," he explained.

"So, Frankie told you that he knew the guy who picked up Shawn, and now Frankie's dead?" she asked, as she turned to look back at the front of the building, where Simon stood, waiting patiently.

"What about him?" asked the homeless guy, staring at Simon oddly. "Maybe he did it."

"No, he was looking to purchase the building."

"Maybe he did it to drop the value," he suggested, with a shrug. "It's nothing that hasn't been done before."

She winced at the thought. "Maybe, but I highly doubt that's his problem."

"Maybe, but he's here a lot."

"Again he's trying to purchase the property," she murmured, not sure why she felt she needed to defend him. "He is just looking out for the property."

"Maybe," the older guy muttered, and then he groaned. "When Frankie told me that he recognized the driver, I didn't even think to warn Frankie about it."

"Of course not. Why would you?" she asked. "You didn't know the driver would be a problem."

"No, I didn't, but I should have. I should have looked out for Frankie. He wasn't the most brilliant of people."

"Would he have likely said something he shouldn't have to the guy?"

"Oh, yeah, particularly if it got him some money," the older guy stated, nodding his head to stress his point. "Out of all of us … Frankie's the one who had the biggest trouble with alcohol and drugs. Shawn was pretty clean most of the time, and he didn't do drugs, but Frankie?" The homeless guy just shrugged.

Kate frowned at this new information.

"Let's just say that, once Frankie got a little booze in him, it was really hard to get him to back off again."

"Of course," she replied in understanding. "That makes it pretty hard to help him."

"Sure does," the older guy muttered, "even if he wanted the help."

"*Did* he want the help?"

"Most of the time, yeah," the guy noted, staring off in the distance. "Yet, once he got into the booze again, not so much. In a way, this is not that surprising," he pointed out.

"I worried I could lose any one of them on a daily basis." He stared around the street, shaking his head. "But I really didn't expect to lose Frankie anytime soon, and not so soon after Shawn."

"Shawn was a good guy?"

"Shawn was a good guy," he confirmed, turning to face her. "I mean, he didn't have any money, but he would always protect the newbies and tried to offer them some advice. Sometimes he would get the crap kicked out of him for his trouble, but he would always try again. He would always try to send them back home again, if he could, if they had family, if they had anybody who cared at all. He was real big on making sure you didn't waste an opportunity to go home, if that was a possibility at all."

"So, Shawn was a great guy."

"Yeah. I can't imagine what his family would say, if they even know about him."

"They do know," she confirmed. "I spoke to them this morning."

He looked at her and nodded. "I'm glad that he will be at rest now at least."

"Do you want to come into the station and give me a formal statement?"

"Hell no. Homeless guys don't seek out the cops. You may be okay, but what about the others there? Will they roust us out of here now that they are more aware of us?"

"How about going to a shelter for a while? Just until we catch this killer. I can recommend a couple, give you a ride there. Or do you have another place you can stay?"

"I'll take care of it." He turned to look at the Paragon, then sighed and sank onto the ground. "Shawn and now Frankie. It's such a waste, but Frankie just didn't have the same awareness of the value of life. … Now he never will." Moments later, he slowly got up, then turned and walked away.

She watched him leave, seeing the age in his footsteps and the shock and the sadness in the slump of his shoulders. Colder now, she walked back over to Simon. He raised an eyebrow, as she shook her head. "Not necessarily anything new to say," she shared, "but he did figure that Frankie was in there." She motioned with her head toward the Paragon building. "Frankie also knew the guy who had picked up Shawn."

"Well, shit."

"Yeah, I told this guy to be extra careful, just in case somebody thought he might know something too."

Simon nodded at that, as he stared off in the distance. "He's likely to be next."

"I told him that too, but he kept telling me how he doesn't know anything. I suspect he'll just disappear into the woodwork for a while."

Simon nodded. "And yet, if anybody even suspects that he might know something, we both know what is likely to happen to him."

"Exactly," she noted, with sorrow, "but I can't really do much about it. If he doesn't want to come in and talk to me, which he definitely does not," she stated, with half a smile, "I can't do much, except warn him to keep him safe."

"Do you think he'll be okay?" Simon asked, still staring in the direction that he'd disappeared.

"Hell no. If he changes locations, maybe. I highly doubt that Frankie knew anything, or at least not very much, but he might very well have recognized the driver who picked up Shawn, and that's probably what got them both killed."

"It would only have gotten him killed if he'd had seen something and then had told somebody something," Simon noted.

"And that's the problem," she murmured. "Frankie absolutely shared something, and now he won't be talking to anybody anymore."

SIMON WALKED INTO the Paragon building, Kate at his side. He knew he wouldn't be allowed very far, but he wanted to talk to her without any prying eyes. He bent his head toward her and asked, "Do you want me to go talk to him?" He nudged his head toward the front door that had just closed behind them.

"What good will that do?" she asked him cautiously.

He gave her a smile. "I do know lots of these guys."

She pondered that and then shrugged. "Feel free to talk to him, but, if you get any information, bring it to me."

"Of course," he agreed, with that cheerful smile.

She frowned at him. "Why would you want to talk to him?"

He looked at her for a long moment, wondering if he could tell her the truth. As her gaze narrowed, he realized he wouldn't be given an option. It would always be the truth or nothing with Kate. "Because I feel half responsible for these guys."

She shook her head. "Why the hell would you feel responsible for the homeless?"

He gestured with his arms to the building standing tall around them. "Because of her."

Kate pinched the bridge of her nose. "Is this one of those things that I have to really stretch to believe?"

He snorted. "Knowing what I deal with daily—and nightly—you shouldn't have to stretch to believe anything," he replied. "I get why you might, but it shouldn't have to be that way."

"Yeah, I agree," she grumbled, as she stared at him. "So how is it that you feel guilty?"

"Because they were staying here in this building, and I kind of put them on the street."

She shook her head. "Or is it because you talked to Shawn, and he told you about the Feldspar house?"

He pondered that and sighed. "I don't know. Yet I'm pretty sure Shawn in his spirit form was talking to me, or trying to. So, if a restless spirit out there is connected to me, then I want to help him cross." When her jaw dropped at that, he winced and added, "I get it. That's probably a little more woo-woo information than you wanted to know."

She glanced around to ensure they were alone, thankful to see that they were. She sighed.

"I've been doing a little bit of research into it."

She swallowed hard as she stared at him. "What possible research is there to look into?"

He gave her a wry look. "It's probably better if we discussed this at another time."

She didn't know what to say obviously, so just nodded for now. "I'm not sure I can make *that* compute. ... The idea of spirits needing help crossing over and all that?" She shook her head in exasperation. "It's really not part of my world."

"Neither were psychic messages or warnings that you're in danger, or a lot of other such things, for that matter," he pointed out. "You've come a long way."

She shot him a look. "I didn't necessarily *mean* to come a long way."

"No, of course not." He looked around and noted, "At least the realtor's gone."

"This place is not locked up, and she certainly doesn't need to be here. She's not the owner either."

"No, not unless she's been designated as the agent in charge, or has legal authority to handle this mess right here."

"I need to talk to the actual owner," Kate stated.

"I can get that information for you." Simon pulled out his phone. When she frowned at him, he shrugged. "Just part of my regular research when I look at purchasing a building."

She seemed to accept that at his word, but Simon knew it was more about taking in the information and walking away, so she didn't have to deal with the rest of it right now. He smiled at her. "We'll get through this, you know?"

She pulled out her phone and quickly took down the information on the Paragon's owner. "Does this affect your wish to purchase the property in any way?" she asked curiously.

He shook his head. "No, it doesn't affect me at all."

"It's already been suggested that the property price would drop now that we've have two murders connected to the place."

"And that means what? That I'll be *more* interested?" he asked, with a note of amusement. "Or that I may have had something to do with it in order to make the property price drop?"

She shrugged. "I'm sure you do have enemies out there. Somebody always wants to stir up trouble."

"If you say so," he replied, as he looked around. "However, no, it doesn't affect anything about it. I probably wouldn't buy it until I hit the price point that I want anyway. While these murders could help it get down there faster, I still wouldn't dive into the purchase without having it at the price and the terms that I want. So, no, it really isn't an issue." She nodded and didn't say anything more. He looked at her curiously. "Surely you don't think that?"

"No, of course not." She gave him a smile. "If you wanted the damn building bad enough, you would pay whatever you had to, and I can't imagine you particularly caring about the price point by then."

"Oh, I care about the money," he clarified, as he took in the building around him, his hands on his hips. "Yet I care a lot more about the building itself. It just doesn't always get me what I want."

"No, of course not, and you seem to have this big wish list of buildings, much like this one." She pointed at the walls. "You clearly saw something that I initially didn't. At first glance I just saw an old dump, but now it's growing on me, when I try to see what you see."

"I see something majestic and aging, but nobody else is willing to put in the time, money, or effort to helping her age gracefully or to give her the extra life she so rightly deserves."

"Most people would think that she doesn't deserve any extra life," she noted, eyeing him curiously.

"I know, and I get that makes me strange and a complete oddball to other developers," he admitted, "but there's plenty of room for all of us in this world." With a smile, he added, "And now I've got to head out and get some work done."

"And here I thought we would head back to the boat."

He froze in his tracks, then turned to face her, his eyebrows lifting in potential delight. "Do you think you'll make it?"

"Once I've done what I need to do here," she replied, with a smile, "I'll head back to the office, but, hey, I have to get sleep sometime."

"Then by all means come back to the boat," he offered. "I'll pick up some supplies, and we'll spend the night there."

"Did you ever find out if we're allowed to do that?" she asked. "I mean, is sleeping in the marina even an option?"

"I'm sure it is for a night or two," he replied, "but, if it bothers you that much, I can take a closer look at the rules and regulations."

"Yes, please. For all I know, we're supposed to pay for moorage or something."

He snorted at that. "Oh, I pay for moorage," he stated. "Don't you worry about that. … I pay *a lot* for moorage."

She frowned. "Oh, right. I hadn't even considered that you have to pay to keep your boat there anyway, don't you?"

"I sure do," he agreed cheerfully, "and you can bet I didn't get any discount."

"No, but you did get to pick your spot, right?"

"Yeah, I sure did, but why does that make a difference?"

"I don't know. Does it? Is that something people fight over?"

He laughed. "I suppose, but rest assured, I chose our moorage location based on what was available at the time, so no one was harmed by my choice. Though you would be surprised at how people respond when you take something that they consider to be theirs."

"Oh, I doubt I would be surprised at all. That seems to be one of the biggest problems these days, people thinking they have the right to take whatever they want, leaving everyone else behind."

He stared at her, then nodded. "Regardless, I'll see you

back at the boat tonight."

"It could be late," she warned.

"Good," he said, giving her a look. "Then we can sit out-side and enjoy the evening, with a glass of wine and a bite to eat, relaxing before we crash for the night."

She smiled as she whispered, "I would like that."

And, with that, he waved goodbye, then quickly headed outside. At the front steps, he stopped, turned to look back at the old building. "It's all right, sweetheart. We're working on it. I know it doesn't seem to be all right just now, but I'll get to the point that you want me to. It'll just take a little bit. Unfortunately it'll take longer now, while the police do their job."

Kate might not think that her department ever inter-fered, but in no way could Simon avoid shutdowns and delays when the police were involved. It was one of the reasons everybody absolutely hated finding something amiss on a jobsite because the police would shut things down. It all meant money, time, and effort wasted, as they waited in the wings for the cops to do whatever they needed before they could release them back to work again.

All too often, that took far longer than it ought to, but Simon was still responsible for keeping his people on the payroll, for keeping them employed. While waiting for the police to do their thing was inconvenient, expensive, and frustrating, Simon could hardly blame them for doing what they needed to do. He certainly had developed a lot more understanding since Kate had come into his life, but it was still hard at times.

Sometimes he just wanted to yell at the cops to get their jobs done so he could get back to work, but that was not the answer, particularly not if Kate was involved. He knew for a fact that her back would go up, and she would take ten times longer, just to prove that she could.

He laughed at that. Power plays were a part of life, and, although she would only do it if necessary to make the point, everybody would use them at one time or another. He understood and respected that. At least for him, it was less disruptive having the police shut down a particular project when involved in a crime scene. Simon never worked on just one rehab at a time. And, with the constant shortage of workers all over, Simon would just allocate his workers elsewhere in the interim.

He whistled as he headed in the same direction where the last remaining member of the homeless trio went. Simon had barely turned a corner when he saw the older guy standing there, as if waiting for him.

The older guy nodded, yet eyed him resentfully. "I figured it was you. I've seen you over there a couple times, and, for all I know, you are part of the murders."

"Considering two of your buddies have gone down in a very ugly way, you shouldn't be thinking that at all."

"How do I know that it wasn't you?" he asked, looking around nervously.

"I don't kill anybody to get what I want," he stated. "I'm the one who fixes buildings around here."

The older guy studied him. "You're the one looking at buying the place?" he asked, with a nod toward the Paragon property around the corner.

The homeless guy certainly didn't have any problem understanding which property he meant, and Simon nodded. "Yes."

And, with that, the homeless man tilted his head and frowned at Simon, as if he were crazy or something.

Simon could understand his confusion, as lots of people struggled with the idea, and this guy had more reasons than most to not understand Simon's motives.

The guy asked Simon, "But why?"

"Because I want to bring the building back to its former glory, yet in a new way."

"In other words, you want to drop it and put up some multibillion-dollar project. Then sell it, make your money back, and head off into the sunset, so you can retire in the Caribbean?"

Simon laughed. "No, that's not my style at all, and I'm not moving anywhere." He looked around and whispered, "You need to be careful."

"Yeah, why is that?" Suspicion once again filled the older man's tone.

"Because two of your friends have died," he replied carefully, "and we don't want anything happening to you. So what can I do to help you out right now?"

CHAPTER 16

W HEN SHE GOT back to the office, Kate had a lot on her mind. Not the least of which was why two homeless guys were targeted and killed in a matter of days. She was pretty sure Frankie's death had been because he had opened his mouth—and Shawn had probably opened his mouth as well—but what was the connection between Shawn and the Feldspar house? Why were those Feldspar papers found in the Paragon building on the third floor? It frustrated Kate to no end that Frankie and Shawn knew something that she didn't know. *Yet.*

She walked to her desk, then printed out the images she had taken of that paperwork, before she'd handed it over to forensics. With printouts in hand, she sat down and pondered them.

Lilliana walked in a little bit later, looking a little worse for wear. When Kate spotted her, Lilliana shrugged. "Just had a messy confrontation with somebody whose kid died," she explained.

Kate immediately understood and nodded. "I'm sorry. It's never easy when a child is involved."

"No, it sure isn't, particularly when I have a nasty suspicion that she's behind her child's death."

Kate raised an eyebrow. "That makes it even worse. You got any proof?"

"Oh, yeah, we'll have lots of proof when I get all the forensics in," she stated, sitting down with a *thump*. "It's a slam dunk, but I've got a lot to work on." She frowned at Kate. "How are you doing?"

"A dead homeless guy was found in the Paragon building, where the first dead homeless guy used to hang out. Not in the Feldspar house, where the first body was found," she added cautiously. "Yet he and his buddy were known to frequent the Paragon."

Lilliana frowned at that. "So, somebody is killing homeless guys?"

"Maybe, except both homeless guys seem able to ID the driver of a stolen vehicle that the first homeless guy got in and was the last time he was seen alive."

"Ah, crap, so he probably got killed for it."

"I suspect both homeless guys shared something that got them both killed for it."

Lilliana nodded. "Somebody is trying to cut the threads that tie them together, just to keep things quiet."

"And most of these homeless guys don't have too much fight to put up, so they're definitely vulnerable members of society," she murmured, "and that just pisses me off."

"Why? You want them to kill off other people?" Lilliana teased, giving her a smirk. "The thing is, this shit pisses off *all* of us," she declared, emphasizing *all*, "and it doesn't matter if they're homeless or not."

Kate groaned. "It just seems these assholes always pick the weakest to attack."

"Of course. That way they don't have to worry about having too much pushback. Imagine them trying to attack somebody who's fit and strong and capable of fighting back? The assholes might get hurt," Lilliana noted in a sarcastic tone.

"I know," Kate muttered. "In that same building, the Paragon, I found some old papers from a company that used to run the place."

"Run the place into the ground is more like it," Lilliana said. "So, you found something, but that doesn't mean the papers were left there. Maybe somebody else came to see the company, found out they were out of business, saw that the building was in complete disarray, and, in a fury, just dumped all those documents. Or else maybe a briefcase was stolen, and its contents were found there."

Kate frowned. "But, if stolen from that company, why would they take it back to where their office once was?"

"Maybe the documents were always there, and the homeless guys staying there wondered what the papers were about? Maybe your homeless guys knew the company from way back or something, and so they wondered what the related paperwork was all about," she suggested, yet with an odd note in her tone. "Were the papers important?"

Kate headed to the coffeepot and then, as she returned with her cup, answered Lilliana. "I'm just looking at it now," she shared. "I turned the originals into forensics, but took a bunch of photos for myself first."

"Smart," Lilliana agreed, raising the coffee cup in her hand. "You never know when you'll get it back from them, and that's only half the problem. We're always waiting on stuff, which will always be the problem because we have more crimes than we have crime fighters for," she noted, with a knowing smile.

"It's constantly an irritant, isn't it?"

"It sure is." With that, Lilliana started in on her own cases.

Kate wondered if she should offer to help Lilliana, but honestly Kate had more than enough to do on her own. She turned back to the case in front of her, studying the paperwork. And, with that, she brought up the company name on the internet. She'd already checked earlier but hadn't been very invested, just because it was a defunct company from years ago. However, now that they had the Feldspar paperwork, issued from the Paragon building years ago, then somehow returned to the Paragon, plus a murder at the same site, that changed things, maybe in a good way.

She always had to toss out a wide net of conjecture, hoping to catch something. Yet all too often nothing was there, and they had to make a case another way, if they could. That was always the challenge, and her greatest nightmare was that some asshole would wind up as only a person of interest listed in a cold case file because she couldn't find what she needed to put them behind bars for their crimes.

Other people had nightmares too, maybe about their kids dying or car crashes or even falling from a cliff while hiking. However, in her case, it involved not being able to put away criminals. Until she brought a case to a conclusion, something constantly nudged at the back of her mind, driving her to dig into every lead, to seek out new avenues when she wasn't making progress. It all made her quite mad, and maybe that was what drove her so hard to work so diligently.

She persevered not only to determine whoever was behind all this, but also to prove her case. She didn't want to spend her entire life going crazy over one unsolved case. Her missing brother's cold case notwithstanding, maybe Kate pushed so hard on these other cases because she couldn't make headway on her own sibling's case.

While researching the history of the businesses that had long ago operated in the Paragon building, she felt an impatience nudging at her. She really needed a report on the forensic evidence found in the building in relation to Frankie's death. She kept looking at her phone, wondering if she should call to ask about it, but the more she pressured Smidge, the more he would get pissed off at her. That would put her in the doghouse, a place she didn't want to be.

She quickly found the former address of that now-defunct accounting company—which had prepared the taxes for the Feldspar family—plus some other details, including the identity of the business owner, Jet Mahoney. He had since died, but his wife, Daisy Mahoney, was still alive, yet retired. Kate quickly sent her cell phone photos of the paperwork and copies of the tax documents to the printer.

As she got up to collect them, Lilliana had picked up the copies and was sorting through them. She brought Kate's copies to her, and Lilliana kept the rest, retreating to her desk.

"Thanks." Kate picked up her phone and quickly dialed the number for Daisy Mahoney. When she heard a woman's voice on the other end, Kate identified herself and asked if she was speaking with Daisy Mahoney.

"Yes, that's me," the woman confirmed, with a little bit of a wobble in her voice. "Goodness me," Daisy said, almost in a panic. "What could the police possibly want with me?"

Kate explained, "It's quite possibly nothing, but your husband owned and maintained an office in the Paragon building. Is that correct?"

"Oh my, my, my," she replied softly. "Yes, but that was many, many years ago, dear."

"And that was your business, correct?"

"Technically speaking it was my husband's business, but I worked there, yes. But why? What has this got to do with anything?"

"We found some income tax forms left in the building."

"No, no," Daisy argued. "We removed everything when we closed down. Those were highly sensitive financial and IRS documents," she noted in a panic. "We removed everything."

"I was just in the Paragon building myself a few days ago, and I found these documents," she explained almost apologetically to the older woman.

"I don't understand how that is possible."

"I don't know at this time either," Kate replied, "but the documents were prepared by your husband for Albert and Mandy Feldspar."

"Oh my, Albert and Mandy Feldspar," she repeated, with sorrow evident in her tone. "Yes, yes, yes, they were murdered in their home, right?"

"Yes," Kate confirmed, "which is one of the reasons why I'm bringing this up."

"Why on earth would you?" she asked, her voice almost faint. "Bring it up?"

"Because we had a recent murder in the Paragon building. Unfortunately that death led me to these Feldspar documents, which I found on the third floor of the Paragon."

"Why on earth?" she asked.

Kate realized just how confusing this probably was. Using a soothing tone, Kate continued. "I'm trying to figure out if your business had any connection to this Feldspar family, other than preparing their taxes and whatnot."

"My husband had a close connection, beyond keeping

their books," Daisy began. "Albert was a friend of my husband's."

"And your husband passed away a few years ago?"

"Yes, three years now. … It's been a very lonely three years."

"I'm sure it has, and the Feldspars were murdered at least ten years ago," she added, pulling on her memory.

"Yes, it was so devastating. But back to the papers you found, the only way those income tax documents would have come back to the Paragon would be if they were taken from the Feldspars, from their own house," she shared in a confused tone. "Back then, we provided paper copies of everything to our clients. It was just part of the service that we offered." She sighed. "But the Feldspars were pretty fanatic about security and privacy and didn't want us to mail them, so those we delivered."

"Were there ever any irregularities in their income taxes?" Kate asked curiously.

"Irregularities? What do you mean by that?"

"Just asking for due diligence, ma'am. Were there any reasons to be suspicious about their trying to hide anything in their income tax forms?"

"Oh my, no. However, I'm not an accountant. I was a file clerk and answered the phone and greeted clients for my husband."

Kate made note of that, then went on. "We're trying to find out anything that would reveal some motive for the Feldspar murders from a decade ago."

"But why now?" Daisy asked again.

Kate drew in a deep breath, before she responded. "We have had two deaths this week, both homeless men, one of whom was found in the Paragon building—which led me to the Feldspar tax documents in the third floor of that space. However, the first dead body this week was found at the Feldspar house. That victim found there was a homeless man who inhabited the empty Paragon building a lot too. Both these men knew each other. Since homeless, they don't generally have fixed addresses. Yet they have locations where they're known to frequent. Thus, we have another link between the Feldspar address and the Paragon building downtown, and I'm wondering if the Feldspar deaths are also connected to the more recent deaths of these two homeless men."

Daisy gasped and kept right on gasping.

Kate winced and realized that she probably should have visited Daisy instead of calling her. "May I come talk to you about this in person?" Kate asked hurriedly. Daisy seemed to be in shock, as she gave no answer on the other end. "Will that be all right?"

"Yes, yes, of course," Daisy replied. "When would you come though?"

"When would you want me to come?"

"Now please. I just can't even imagine how this is connected," she murmured.

"That's fine. I'll be there in …" Kate checked the address and realized it was probably a fifteen-minute drive. "Give me twenty minutes, maybe half an hour, and I'll be right over." With that she disconnected, snatched her bag, and headed out.

As she got closer to the address, she observed the well-to-do area, suggesting that the Mahoneys' business had most likely done well but wasn't in the uber-rich classification. Maybe they retired, shutting it down instead of selling it. That certainly meant a big difference in their bottom line.

As Kate walked up to the front door, it opened, and there stood a tiny birdlike woman, not even five feet tall. Kate smiled gently and held up her ID. "Hello, Daisy. I'm Kate. I'm the one you were just speaking with."

"Yes, yes, come in." Daisy led Kate into the house.

Kate looked around curiously, aware that it had that familiar old-person smell, as if no fresh air flowed through the premises. She followed the older woman into the kitchen, and Daisy motioned to a kitchen chair, where they both got settled.

Once Daisy was seated, Kate began, "I'm sorry. Obviously my call was a shock for you this morning."

"Oh, yes, it absolutely was," she replied, now more animated. She tapped a box in front of her. "It's even more of an upset because we knew the family. As I mentioned before, my husband, Jet, and Albert Feldspar were quite good friends. Jet was really shocked and so upset when the Feldspar murders happened, and he didn't really ever get over it."

Kate winced at that. "I'm sorry. That makes this even harder, doesn't it?"

"Yes, but, if we could finally get answers, that's all Jet ever really wanted ... right up to my husband's last day on this earth," she murmured. "Yet it just wasn't meant to be. It seemed as if you guys weren't getting anywhere."

"I'm not sure that we're getting anywhere now either," Kate admitted, "and that's not what you want to hear. However, now we have two recent deaths which seem to be connected back to the Feldspars deaths. ... So it's something I need to take a look at. I would absolutely love to find the killer of the two homeless men who died this week, plus also to close that old murder case and bring closure to the

Feldspar family and to all their friends out there who have been waiting for answers, just like you."

Daisy nodded. "It was so hard at the time. Jet just kept screaming and yelling, walking around at night, saying something like, *Why did they do it? Why?*"

"Meaning, why did whoever it was kill them?"

"I always thought that, at first," Daisy clarified, with a glint in her gaze. "But then one time Jet asked out loud, *How could they?*"

Kate stared at her for a long moment. "Did Jet explain that?"

"No, he wouldn't explain it at all."

"Okay. Do you have any idea what that was all about?"

"I didn't at the time, but it's something I've thought about a lot since then. Of course now that you've brought up their income taxes, it's definitely something on my mind."

"Even if Albert had cheated on his taxes," Kate suggested, easing into the topic gently, "it wouldn't necessarily have been something that would get him killed, I don't imagine."

"No, and I don't think it was so much about his taxes as much as other documents. He was trying to set up a shell company for something, and he and my husband had an ongoing argument over it. I didn't really understand what the shell company concept was all about back then, but Jet told me that it was bad news. When Jet got angry ..." She flushed. "I didn't really pressure him because he got very difficult."

"Of course," Kate replied. "So, the Feldspars were setting up a shell company?"

"That's what they wanted, yes, and they wanted my husband to help them, but he didn't want to."

"Because of what they were trying to do?"

"I believe so, yes. I don't know that for a fact, but I think it was because the Feldspars wanted to move money into that shell company, just so they didn't have to pay taxes on it."

"And, of course, if Jet were an ethical accountant …"

"I agree. Jet, as an ethical accountant, wouldn't have anything to do with it, and I think that is where the problem was."

Kate pondered that, her mind racing. "The documents I found didn't really mention anything about a shell company. And I've not checked with any remaining Feldspar family members."

"A son and a daughter both survived the attack on the parents—well, if you can call it surviving when the daughter suffered a serious brain injury. Albert's sister was supposedly there at the time of the other murders too, but I don't think she has ever been seen again. I believe Albert's mother was killed as well. Quite a few family members were involved in the attack, and they all may have been living in the one house. Well, not Albert's sister. If I remember correctly, she may have lived nearby but was otherwise always at Albert's house."

"And what happened with the injured daughter?"

"Poor thing. She was so badly injured. … She will need lifetime care, as in some special facility maybe. I don't know. I might be getting that a little confused."

Kate nodded. "I can check on that. I don't suppose the siblings had any wealthy family or other connections to rely on at the time?"

"I don't think so," Daisy replied, "but definitely a lot of care and love and attention was extended to the surviving family members by their neighbors and friends because what the Feldspar siblings were going through was so horrific." Daisy shuddered visibly, then went on. "The kids were so young to lose their parents, their grandmother, their aunt. The son was just fourteen, I believe, with his sister maybe eighteen. I seem to recall that the kids got help of some kind, but again I'm not privy to the details of that."

"Surely your husband would have known something, being so close with Albert?"

"My husband might have helped them out, as a chunk of money disappeared from our savings account at one point in time, and we had quite the brawl about it."

"You think he might have done something to help them?"

"I think so, yes."

"Would he have done that because he cared or … because he felt guilty?"

Daisy stared at Kate for a long moment, trying to understand the insinuation. "I wondered if you would imply my husband might have had something to do with it."

"I'm not implying anything," Kate clarified gently, "but, until I really understand exactly what's been going on, I don't know who could be involved in anything. So I certainly don't know that Jet would have killed this Feldspar family."

"That's good because he didn't," Daisy declared flatly, "and he's not here to defend himself now anyway."

"Exactly," Kate noted, "so just talk to me. Tell me what you do know, and maybe I can solve these Feldspar murders, as well as my two murdered homeless guys."

In the back of Kate's mind, she wasn't exactly letting Amie and her not-suicidal husband off the hook at the moment either. However, she would march forward on this somehow connected side trip. She brought out her small notepad and looked at Daisy in the hopes that something was here. "Let's go over the details again. The Feldspars were interested in a shell company, and your husband refused. Would he have referred them to another accountant?"

"He did," Daisy stated in a clear tone. "Jet had split with an old business partner because my husband *was* extremely moral and ethical, and his partner was much less so. Let's call him *fluid*, if you will. After parting ways, Jet's former partner set up his own accounting business, and, every once in a while, when clients came to my husband with requests that he wasn't comfortable with, he would send them over to this friend."

"Who is this friend?"

"Jackson, Darrian Jackson."

Kate sat back, frowning at Daisy. "Why do I know that name?"

Daisy shrugged. "No idea, but I'm sure you probably have case files on him." She hesitated and then whispered, "He's *slippery*."

"Okay, good enough." Kate wrote down the name, then continued to ask Daisy questions. "Did you have anything to do with the Feldspars or other clients yourself?"

"No, I didn't. My husband clearly told me that it was *his* business, and I just worked for him," she stated, with half a smile. "Honestly, I wasn't in it for the work. I was in it so that we would have retirement money. We had already raised the kids, and I was back to helping him at work, rather than being at home, where I'd gotten so bored. So, I was helping my husband," she stated, with a nod, "but it was very much *his* business."

Kate wasn't so sure she believed that, but, as she contemplated the mind-set of the time and the age of the woman before her, it was quite possible. At that point in time, men were much more dominant than they are now, especially when it came to men and women working in businesses. "Did you ever resent that?" Kate asked out of the blue.

"No, not at all," Daisy shared, with a smile. "I didn't even particularly want to work. I was looking forward to when we both retired. So, if he had told me to stay at home, I would have in a heartbeat. I was bored at home, but I could have found other things to do. I didn't particularly enjoy what his accounting work involved, but it wasn't necessarily anything that I wanted to continue with either."

"Did Jet know that's how you felt?"

"Sure, and I think that's also part of why he kept me out of a lot of it."

"Did he keep secrets from you?"

She nodded and tapped the box in front of her. "He kept *a lot* of secrets from me," she declared. "Secrets that, even now, I find hard to fathom."

"Such as?"

Daisy swallowed, looked down at the box again, and stated, "When I first opened this … I opened Pandora's box."

Kate frowned. "But, if these secrets are bothering you, maybe it's time for them to be exposed. If you shed a little light on them, it makes them not quite so scary."

Daisy looked up, and a host of tears filled her eyes, but she shook her head. "But then I'd have to deal with them," she pointed out. "As long as I keep this box closed, I can forget about what he did."

"Maybe," Kate said, "but maybe we're all better off

knowing exactly what Jet did. And, even though he's not here to defend himself, maybe we can make peace with it, one way or another."

Hesitating for only a moment, Daisy then opened the box and pushed it over to Kate.

She lifted up a picture of a man, standing with his arms wrapped around a young woman, holding twin babies. "Oh, look at that," she murmured. "How lovely. Is this a picture of Jet?"

"Yeah, it is," Daisy said bluntly, "except that's not me."

Kate frowned at her.

"Jet had a second family," Daisy shared, her voice getting strong, filling with anger. "A second family I didn't know about until after he died. The only reason I ever found out was because *that woman* contacted me, saying she had heard about his death and had heard how I was his wife. When I explained to her that what she'd heard was correct, she added, "But I'm his wife too.""

"Ah, hell," Kate muttered, as she sat back and stared at Daisy.

Daisy nodded. "It explains all the late nights he worked and all the supposed business trips he took."

"It also might explain why he may have done something he shouldn't have—if he needed money to support two families—plus why he may have had secrets, just to keep you from finding out," Kate suggested, with a nod.

"Yes, and, in his mind, it was his job to support us, so he was busy supporting both his families. Yet, because I was working at the business myself and because I was Jet's *legal* wife," she explained, "I inherited his estate. Whereas this other woman, who wasn't his legal wife—but didn't know that—didn't inherit anything."

"Good Lord," Kate whispered, "I bet that was a shock to her."

"It was a pretty rough shock for her, as you can imagine. She had children too, those twins in the picture," she added. "Imagining my Jet, the old fool, running around with a young wife and his children from her? It wasn't a fun time."

"And yet you still protect his image and his name?"

"A part of that, I think, is just habit," she conceded, as she stared down at the box and shook her head. "It still doesn't mean he had anything to do with anything illegal. I don't even know why I'm telling you about this, since it's not pertinent."

"Maybe you're telling me because it's important to get it off your chest and to know that you loved him—before finding out this, I suppose. I'm not sure what you feel about him right now, but he had to know that, once something happened to him, it would all come out."

"In a funny way I think he was happy to know that it would all come out. It had been wearing on him, and his heart was starting to give him trouble, and he just couldn't easily keep up the pretenses."

"I'm not surprised," Kate said. "How old was he when he died?"

"Sixty-seven."

"He still lived a long time, especially considering he was living a double life. I'm sure the stress must have been pretty rough and had taken a toll on him to some degree."

"I'm sure it did," Daisy agreed, "but then I never got the retirement that I waited and worked for either. We never had the money, or so he told me, and now I know why."

"Is that the chunk of missing money from your savings account that you mentioned earlier?"

"That was one particular lump that went missing right after the Feldspars died," she clarified. "I always figured it went to the surviving siblings, but maybe it didn't. Maybe I have no idea what really happened, and maybe it went to this woman and her children. Who knows."

"Do you begrudge her that?"

"No, I don't begrudge her anything. I should be totally angry at him," she stated, "though somehow I still feel angry at her."

Kate could understand being angry, since it was obviously a shock and a very confusing scenario for Daisy after decades of marriage. Kate was confused as well, since she didn't know how or if any of this could possibly apply to her current murder cases or how Shawn's and Frankie's deaths could possibly be connected to the Feldspar murders from a decade ago. Shaking her head, Kate asked, "Do you think Jet would have done something illegal or something on that edge of legality to support his two families?"

"I would have always said no. Then I look down at this box, knowing he absolutely loved those kids with her, which I can see in his face. So, in his mind, maybe he felt compelled to do something which he normally wouldn't have. I don't know," she muttered, with a headshake. "He's been gone three years now, and I'm still completely confused over the whole thing." After that, Daisy took a deep breath and shook her head. "I feel such a sense of betrayal and … abandonment in a way. He lived with me and presented us as a happy couple, but then he didn't really live with me honestly, did he?"

Kate sighed. "No, he didn't, and I'm sorry for that. Words are so inadequate right now."

"Exactly, for you, for me, and, of course, for him, who

managed to pass away without facing any of us," she stated.

"Did you have any other contact with the other … family?" Thankfully Kate caught herself before she said *wife*, which would have been sure to rile up Daisy.

"Only after the funeral notice had been posted in the paper, when she realized no inheritance was coming for her because she wasn't Jet's legal wife."

Kate nodded. "Has she remarried? Do you know how she's been doing since then?"

"No, I haven't had any contact with her," Daisy muttered, staring down at the box. "A part of me says I probably should have helped, that I probably should have shared. And I did consider it at the time, but then I decided to hell with that idea," she declared. "I mean, she was the second wife, the one who broke up my family. Yet I realize that she was just as much of a dupe as I was," she muttered, "or more. So, I'm still pretty messed up over it all."

"And your children?"

She hesitated before responding. "They're both dead. A car accident last year on their way to the interior for a fishing trip."

"Oh, no. That must be any parents' worst nightmare, losing their children. I am so sorry," Kate said.

"Me too," Daisy murmured, as she stared out the window. "They did find out, of course, and it was one of the hardest things to watch them realize that their father had done such a thing to them too. I don't even know whether my husband understood just how much pain he was inflicting on us, or he just got so sucked up into the second-family scenario that he didn't see any other way out."

"Chances are it's the latter," Kate noted, trying to ease Daisy's mind. "I've seen more than a few cases where people make a selfish decision and then lie to conceal the decision. Yet, once you lie … the lying just never stops."

Daisy nodded. "And the reality is that I won't be around too much longer myself."

Kate studied Daisy, noting her skin was thin, translucent almost. Kate could see the veins underneath, wondering whether Daisy was dealing with a specific health issue or nothing more than just age.

Daisy shrugged and sat back. "I don't really care at this point," she murmured, "with my kids gone and how things with my husband went. I don't even want to see him in the afterlife because I'm afraid I'll get so angry that I'll want to kill him all over again."

It was all Kate could do to hold back a smile because, of course, in the afterlife, she wasn't at all sure that death was something Daisy could inflict on Jet. "I'm sure that anger has been eating away at you."

"It sure has," she muttered, as she dropped her head to her hands, yet still staring at the box. "It's just one of those things, where you are left to go through life, asking yourself how you could possibly have missed all the signs, wondering what you could have done differently, so you didn't wind up feeling like such an idiot at the end of the day."

"I'm sure this other woman doesn't feel very good about herself either."

Daisy rummaged through the box, then handed Kate a piece of paper. "This was her address back then, though I don't know if you need or even want to contact her. I don't know if Jet spoke about work more with her than he did with me, but you could give it a try. I was there in the same office with Jet, but I didn't really have that much to do with his business." She took a moment and added cautiously,

"But a connection is there."

"A connection? In what way?" Kate asked.

Daisy pointed at the dreaded box, at the piece of paper with the second wife's address on it. "The Feldspars were *her* family."

"Ah, hell." Kate moaned, not sure why she always heard the most important tidbits at the end of her interviews.

"Yeah, so maybe that's how it started. Maybe Jet went over to see whether she was doing okay, or ... I don't know. She's the niece. I believe she's the niece." She frowned at that. "She's quite a few years younger than he was."

Kate didn't say anything. The woman in the picture looked to be quite a bit younger, but photos were deceptive. "I don't suppose you have a phone number for her."

"No, not now anyway," she shared. "But, if you look in the box, I think you'll find the number I used in the past."

"Good enough," Kate murmured. "Between that and the address, it should give me a start."

Daisy closed the box and pushed it toward her again. "Take it with you." Seeing the surprised expression on Kate's face, Daisy added, "I'm not long for this world, and, with my kids gone, I don't really care to see that box ever again."

"When you're gone from this world, what will you do with your estate?" Kate asked.

Daisy flushed. "Is it wrong of me to have it all for myself?"

"Not at all," Kate replied. "It's from your husband."

"I don't know if *she* needs it now, though she probably needed it back then. I'm sure she should be fine by now. Yet I don't know," Daisy muttered. "Maybe I'll just leave it all to charity."

Kate didn't want to get into that discussion, so she just

nodded. "Hopefully you'll have time to figure it out, just please do something on paper to make it legal and not just leave it as a mess for someone else to deal with."

Daisy gave a bark of laughter. "I wasn't an accountant's assistant for nothing," she stated. "Paperwork is part of my world, and it's one of the reasons I don't want to keep any of that." She pointed to the box that Kate had her hand on. "Such bad memories."

"I'm sorry. I'm sure you're very confused over it all."

"Confused and devastated," she declared. "That's the story of my life. You think you know somebody, somebody you married, somebody you lived decades with, someone you had children with, someone you worked with even. You loved him, and you told everybody how much you loved him, and then you find out his secrets, and you just really hate him. … In a way, my death would be a saving grace."

"Maybe, but it will also be the end of your chance to forgive and to forget," Kate pointed out. "So maybe find a moment or two for some time in a quiet space and see if you can find some peace in your own soul before your time comes. For all you know, you'll go *upstairs*, and he'll have gone *downstairs*."

At that, Daisy started to laugh and laugh. "Lord, I hope so because, if I'm going *downstairs* too, you can bet I'll definitely be looking for him." With that, Daisy stood and said in a pleasant tone, "Take the box with you, dear. I don't have any other information for you, but that other woman might."

"Can you give me her name?"

Daisy sighed. "Rosemary, Rosemary Mahoney."

Kate nodded, and, with the box under her arm, she thanked Daisy and quickly escaped. As soon as Kate got into her vehicle, she phoned Reese. "Find out everything you can on a Rosemary Feldspar, will you?"

"From the Feldspar house?"

"Yeah, apparently she's the niece and unknowingly ended up being a clandestine second wife to Mr. Jet Mahoney. I've just spoken with Daisy Mahoney, his widow, his legal wife." Kate looked down at the box in her lap. "She gave me a box with some information and photos and other materials. I'm bringing it back to the office right now, but her husband died three years ago, with his secret still in him. He left behind two families and was secretly married to both women."

"Oh, what an ass," Reese declared. "That's messed up."

"Yeah, and, not only that, he was best friends with the Feldspars from the infamous Feldspar house, and Daisy believes her hubby took a chunk of money out of their savings to give to the Feldspar siblings, who survived that attack. So probably through that interaction, Jet met and started the relationship with the niece Rosemary. He was apparently good friends with the whole family. Though, if that were the case, I don't know how Rosemary wouldn't have known that Jet was already married."

"Yeah, exactly. If he were good friends with the family, you would think that Rosemary would have definitely known."

"So, maybe he convinced Rosemary that his first marriage was over or something. I don't know. And, with both women and their children living in town, how the hell did they not end up meeting each other? I mean, Rosemary's twins are a lot younger than Daisy and Jet's kids would have been, plus Daisy lost her kids last year. All I can tell you is that, according to Daisy, she didn't know anything about his second family, not until Jet passed away. Rosemary supposedly reached out, after finding out Jet had died and had left behind a wife who wasn't her, only to find out that she wouldn't inherit anything because he was already legally married to somebody else."

"Oh boy," Reese muttered. "I'm on it, and hopefully I'll have something for you by the time you get back to the office."

As she disconnected, Kate whispered, "I hope so too." A weird sense overcame her that sometimes came to pass when they were just starting to catch a break in a case. It was such a great feeling, the excitement of knowing that something was about to burst wide open, or at least she hoped so. And this time, maybe, just maybe, she could solve both of these damn cases.

She laughed as she headed back to the station. She felt sad and sorry for Daisy but wasn't at all sure how to feel about Rosemary at this point. Jet, the accountant, was definitely in the middle of things. He'd been a busy guy. No wonder he died of a heart attack.

Keeping one wife happy was hard enough, but keeping two? That had to be an easy ticket on a one-way street. And, with that thought, she headed back to her office.

SIMON WAITED UNTIL the forensics team was done in the Paragon building before he walked back inside. He was due to head home soon, picking up a few groceries on his way, getting to the boat in time to meet Kate. Yet he wanted to visit the Paragon building, and that was nagging him badly. How stupid to even think that he could talk to Shawn's ghost? Yet the more he dealt with this woo-woo craziness, the more he wondered how much more could be possible.

Was it his imagination that Shawn had called out to him, or was it something completely different?

Could it have been another homeless guy, having fun at Simon's expense?

That and other thoughts ran in his mind, but he had no answers. Not yet anyway. It was so hard to get any clarity, even when he knew these strange voices were constantly talking to him. As he headed back into the huge building, the nagging realtor, Ariel, called him.

"Did I hear what I just heard correctly?" she cried out.

"You mean that a murder victim was found in your listing?" She groaned, which amused him. "Yes," he confirmed, with a surprising note of humor in his tone.

"I suppose you think that's funny," she snapped.

"I don't think anything is funny about murder," he declared, glaring at his phone. "And, if you just called me to insult me, I will end this call right now."

"No, no, no," she interrupted. "I didn't mean it that way."

"Yes, you did," he snapped, all traces of his good humor gone. "I'm not enjoying this conversation at all, and I really don't have time for it. If you have a legit reason for calling, tell me what it is. Otherwise I'm gone."

"No, I just ..." She took a deep breath and let it out in a noisy exhale.

"You just heard the news that the building itself was crawling with forensic technicians?"

"Is it still?" she asked.

"No, now that they've gone, I'm stepping inside to see what condition it's in."

"Oh God," she muttered. "I should be down there."

When she hesitated, he understood her intent because he would want the same. He offered, "I can send you photos, if you want."

"Would you mind?"

"Of course I don't mind," he replied irritably, "but let's be clear. It's *your* listing, not mine."

"Trust me," she said. "The owners are quite perturbed about it all."

"Of course they are. Their building up for sale is now a murder scene. The victim was also a friend of the other homeless guy, who was murdered and dumped somewhere else, yet also used to hang around this building."

"Why the Paragon?" she cried out.

He sighed. "It's huge and unlocked, which makes for easy access. The police have somehow connected the Paragon building to the Feldspar house."

"Feldspar, Feldspar, Feldspar. Oh my God, the Feldspar murders?" she screamed.

He winced at her volume and held the phone away from his ears as much as he could, waiting for her shrieking to subside. "Yes, you could say that, but I don't know in what context."

"Oh my God, I'll never sell that property."

He snorted. "Spoken as a true realtor."

"Hey, it's not that easy to sell these old buildings as it is," she muttered.

"I understand that. I buy them all the time, remember?"

She snorted into the phone. "It would be a hell of a lot easier if you would just buy them outright at the asking price."

"For you and the sellers, yeah." The note of amusement had returned in his tone, as he wandered through the building. "It looks as if the crime scene folks are done in here at least."

"I don't understand why they took so long," she muttered, with a hint of frustration.

So she knew all along. Figures. "All I can tell you is that they don't appear to be here now."

"That's something to be grateful for," she murmured, completely unaware that she had been caught lying to Simon … again. "Did they do any damage? Man, I wonder if the seller could charge the city for that?"

"I wouldn't try it," he stated, with a chuckle. "The city is well within protocols to do whatever they need to do to investigate a crime."

"Sure, but that doesn't mean they get to damage buildings."

"I'm pretty sure they would have a solid case against those charges, particularly about how much damage anybody could inflict on this already damaged place. Not to mention how dangerous the building itself seems to be," he noted, his tone deepening, as he surveyed the growing darkness around him. "And it's getting dark in here because I don't have any lights on."

"The building has power," she told him.

He walked over to a light switch and flicked it on, nodding. "That's interesting. There is power."

"Oh, good. We need lights to take clients around, so they turned the power back on."

"That makes sense. It'll also bring in more homeless because now they have lights too."

"*Great,*" she muttered, "but, if the cops or the squatters didn't damage anything, I don't have to go down there right now. I'll absolutely make a trip in the morning, but it would be great if I don't have to come right at the moment. I really don't have the time. I'm swamped."

"No, it looks fine so far, other than the fingerprint dust all over the third-floor office where the body was found," he told her. "I'm walking up to the other floors."

"There shouldn't be any disturbances on the other floors, should there? That wouldn't make any sense."

"I don't know what makes sense at this point in time," he said. "There's definitely been activity on all these floors, but how much of it is criminal and how much of it is related to this particular crime, I can't say."

"God," she muttered, "sometimes I think I need to change jobs."

"Now, if you don't need anything else from me," he quipped, "I want to get back to what I was doing."

"And what is that?" she asked. "Why exactly are you even there?"

"I'm doing a cost analysis."

"Oh," she said, perking up, her tone turning sly. "Tell me more."

"No, I won't tell you more," he stated. "Now that this place is directly related to a couple murders, I'll also have to consider that."

"No, you do not," she declared, "not at all. You don't need to reconsider based on that. You and I both know that it doesn't change a single thing."

"Yeah, says you," he snapped, with a wry look around. "But now it'll have that reputation, won't it? Just like the Feldspar house, which is still empty, by the way."

"God, I hope it's not still empty," she complained. "That would be a tough sell too."

"I'm sure, and it most definitely is empty. I just don't

know whether it's empty because the heirs didn't want to sell it or because nobody could sell it."

"Nobody could sell it," she stated, her voice distracted. "I'm just bringing it up on my screen now. It hasn't been for sale for years. They did try way back when, but didn't get any bites."

"Even with the murders, I wonder why though," he muttered. "I mean, a massive property comes with perks. Someone who could afford it could surely move past the fact that there were murders onsite. Murders happen somewhere every day."

"But, better than the Feldspar house, the Paragon building is a different story. It's an empty building downtown with lots of different spaces, and the dead guy was homeless," she added, gearing up for the pitch again, "and that's not news."

"It should be news," Simon replied, trying for a mild tone, but her callous wording and attitude was starting to piss him off. "The homeless are still people. Those two murders this week were still someone's father, brother, son, uncle."

"I know that," she declared, "but it's not as if some woman was enticed there, raped, and then murdered. It was some guy who was sleeping probably, and maybe someone just shot him because he saw something."

"Maybe," Simon conceded, "but have you ever seen anybody hanging around here?"

"No, I haven't—well, except for that one time," she clarified. "It's not exactly a place I want to spend any time at."

"No, downtown can get pretty rough."

"Yeah, rough and then rougher," she stated, "and that corner can get especially rough."

He wondered how she knew so much about it but decided not to ask. As he returned to the third floor, he looked around, having that weird sensation again. "Did you ever see any of the homeless guys in here?" he asked her.

"I shooed one away once when I was in there. He wasn't too friendly."

"No, most of the time they aren't. Most of the time they just want to be left alone."

"They shouldn't be on other people's property then," she stated in exasperation. "What am I supposed to do? I've got clients, and I need to be looking after the properties too."

"*Uh-huh*, that's your theory at least."

"And it's a good one," she said. "It's not as if I don't visit my listings."

"*Sure.* Yet these abandoned buildings attract the homeless, who should *not* be considered as unimportant. These people have lives that are just as important as everybody else's." He then quickly disconnected before he went into a full-on rant with Ariel. Plus, he felt that weird foreboding, as the hairs on the back of his neck raised. He slowly turned in a circle, staring in all corners. "Hello, anybody here?"

Getting no answer, he continued to turn in a slow circle, not sure whether he was looking for something human or something a whole lot less than human. Even the thought of encountering a spirit was something he had to shut his mind to. He didn't want to even consider it, yet it was hard not to.

Hearing a voice behind him, he spun around, but nothing was there. Frowning, he called out, "If you want something, you can talk to me."

He thought he heard another voice, and yet he couldn't see anything. Frustrated, he walked several steps forward, still looking for whatever source was causing him such unease. As he got to the hallway, a door slammed hard nearby. He froze and then called out, "Yeah, I heard this place was haunted.

I'm not sure what you ghosts want around here, but, if I can do something to help, let me know."

A weird almost inaudible laughter came in response.

He winced, realizing that the ghosts had their own issues, and not a whole lot Simon could do about it. A good part of their issues would be the reason why they were still here in the first place.

He called out again and added, "I don't know why you're here, but you might want to leave before things turn ugly." Again more weird laughter came. Frowning, he realized that, for them, things had already gotten ugly. Yet, for whatever reason, they were still tied to this place. Wincing, he turned, gave the area a long, slow look and called out, "Shawn, are you here?"

Silence came now.

Still frowning, he called out a second time and then a third, but no response came. Finally he pushed his hands deep into his pockets, took one last look around, and decided to leave it be for now.

"That's fine. You don't have to show yourself, but, if you want to talk to me, it could make things easier." And, with that, he slowly turned to walk back down the stairwell. As he reached the landing where he had seen Shawn before, he called out again, "Shawn, are you here?"

At that moment, several pieces of paper lifted up from the floor, as if by an unseen wind, and ghosted toward him. He froze, staring at the papers as they slid toward him. He grabbed them and asked, "Are these important?"

When no answer came, he held the papers tightly. In spite of himself, he took one last look around and left the building as quickly as he could. He could be just as affected by ghosts as anybody else—and, maybe considering his proclivity for his grandmother's world, even more so.

CHAPTER 17

O N THE BOAT, Kate couldn't turn off her busy mind, especially after Simon had found copies of the shell company created by Darrian Jackson for the Feldspar family. It was hard to just relax and to let everything fade away. She stretched out on the deck of the boat, on a cozy foldable chair, trying to let the day's events just drift away from her. It might help in solving some of her problems, but it sure as hell wasn't helping her relax enough to unwind and to enjoy being out here.

When Simon squatted beside her and handed her a glass of red wine, she looked at it and beamed. "That might help too."

He nodded. "It's obvious you're struggling. If I can do anything to help, let me know."

She grimaced and said, "This case is just confusing."

His lips quirked. "All of your cases tend to be confusing, and some of them are downright madness," he admitted, with a smile.

"Yeah, and this one's definitely not any different," she noted. "I just don't understand yet which way it goes and who's lying and who's not."

"Are we talking about the suicide that's not a suicide?"

She frowned at that and shrugged. "That's an entirely different case that's also very confusing," she agreed. "That one was already pissing me off, and then this other shit started," she muttered.

"That's just because you don't like Mulhouse's wife."

"Liking her or not has nothing to do with it," she stated, giving him a hard glance. "I truly believe she had something to do with the deaths of her other husbands, if not this one too."

Simon picked up his wine and stretched out on the deck, propped on one elbow so he could face her. "But you can't prove it?"

"No, I can't prove it," she admitted, with an audible sigh, "and that just pisses me off even more."

He smiled at that and nodded. "And nothing makes you quite so upset as thinking somebody has pulled one over on you." She glared at him again, and he smiled. "Hey, I don't blame you. Obviously you have somebody who knows what she's doing or is very capable of figuring out how to make the evidence look different from what you would expect it to be."

Kate frowned as she pondered that and as she thought about the notebook with the missing pages, the forensics, and how no GSR was on the victim's hands. She sat up with a jerk, as she got something different now. She snatched her phone and called Dr. Smidge's office. She was surprised to get him at the end of the day. "I didn't expect you to still be in the office." She was talking fast, as if excited.

"I didn't either, but something else occurred to me."

"With the suicide that's not a suicide?" she asked, all too happy now.

"Exactly." His tone was charged with suspicion. "What are you thinking?"

"I'm thinking that the wife was in there staging the scene

to make it look as if it *weren't* a suicide."

Silence came first on the other end. "Shit, you are nosy *and* creative, and that is one of the reasons I'm still here. We ran a few extra forensic tests, and we found threads on his hands, caught up in his nails."

"Threads?"

"Yes, threads from cloth gloves."

"Aha," she crowed, as she bolted to her feet and paced around the deck of the boat. "So he did commit suicide, yet wore gloves?"

"But," Simon interrupted, "why would he wear gloves to commit his own suicide?"

Kate quickly explained, "Sometimes they don't want to be ID'd for whatever reason *or* they themselves want to create suspicions around their own deaths, which is exactly what I think Robert Mulhouse was doing here. He was signaling for us to check out Amie further."

"But she removed the gloves?" Simon asked, frowning. "How odd."

"Maybe not so odd," she told Simon, then returned to her phone call. "So you found no GSR on his hands because Amie took off his gloves, then rearranged the scene to make it seem suspicious."

"Exactly," Smidge confirmed. "I presume she knew perfectly well that she wouldn't get any life insurance proceeds if his death was ruled a suicide. Thus, she muddied the waters," he suggested, with an amused tone, "but you'll still have to prove it."

"I know," she stated, "but, if you are changing your initial findings, from a murder back to a suicide," she took a moment to add dramatically, "that changes everything. We may have a way to flush her out all on her own."

"I'm not quite done," he forewarned her. "I'm not entirely happy with that explanation yet, and I want more of the forensics back. It would make a hell of a lot of difference if you could find the gloves."

"Yes," she agreed, calming down, her mind clicking away at max speed, as she thought about the implications. "That would be important," she muttered. "Even if we do find them, it'll make it seem that whoever wore the gloves is guilty or that the gloves were then used to murder him."

"Exactly," he replied, "so that'll be another bit of a challenge. However, if we found *only his* skin cells on the inside …"

"Yes," she said cheerfully. "If you think it's a suicide, and that becomes your official ruling, that's what the insurance company will go by."

He let out a bark of laughter at that. "You really don't like her, do you?"

She winced. "You know I'm not supposed to be emotional when it comes to this stuff."

"Bollocks. Just because we're not supposed to have feelings doesn't mean that we don't." He took a moment and added sarcastically, "We are human after all. Why don't you like her?"

"Because I'm pretty damn sure she had something to do with the deaths of her previous husbands. I think this one quite possibly killed himself, ahead of being murdered by her. He probably didn't figure he had a choice."

"That would suck, and it would also mean that he really didn't want to live, especially if that's what she was doing."

"Did you check to see if he had any life-altering disease or anything?"

"No," he replied, with a finality in his tone, "but you

could contact his doctor and see if anything was going on in that area.”

“I’ll do that in the morning,” she noted, with satisfaction in her tone. “Then you could confirm, correct?”

“Depending on what it was, yes,” he replied, frustrated, most likely because that again put it all on him and the forensics. “It’s not generally within the scope of an autopsy like this. I’m not looking for *any* cause of death.” He chuckled, as she sighed this time. “I’m looking to determine whether we’re dealing with a suicide versus a murder.”

“Got it.” She spoke with him for a few moments and then ended the call. She turned to Simon with a crow of satisfaction.

“Why are you so happy that this poor guy committed suicide?” he asked, looking at her oddly, and only then did she realize just how that probably looked.

She groaned. “It’s not that I’m happy he committed suicide,” she explained. “I’m happy he wasn’t murdered. And, of course, I’m not happy that the guy died at all. It seems it was his choice though, and obviously that’s important. I’m more concerned about the fact that his wife may have intentionally manipulated the crime scene so it would *look* like a murder. However, because it wasn’t a murder, there won’t be any evidence to find or any case to close. Still, she wanted a murder investigation, so the case would stay in limbo, trying to find some fictitious killer, all so she would hopefully get paid the life insurance proceeds.”

“Ah, now I’m getting there,” Simon said.

“Yeah. Once we find that it isn’t a murder but a suicide, plus potentially a tampered crime scene,” Kate explained, “that changes everything.”

“And you don’t want her to get the life insurance money, do you?"

She winced. "Again, that makes me out to be an absolute bitch, and I'm not. However, if I can't do anything about her previous husbands' deaths, at least I can try to keep her from benefitting from this guy's death."

"And you think that's why she's doing this?"

"I would bet my last dollar on it," Kate declared. "She has benefited each and every time in some way when her previous husbands wound up dead. I wonder whether husband number three had any idea that she was even contemplating his murder, or maybe he had just found out about her other husbands and what happened to them, or he might have just found out about her affair. Regardless of what Robert knew, it would only be natural that he would wonder when he would be next."

"Is that why you asked about any deadly illness?"

"Yes, but Smidge's right. I'll have to get Mulhouse's medical file."

"Smidge won't go take a look himself?"

"He could take a look, but, with budgets the way they are, and all the time and effort that kind of an autopsy would require, it is not ideal. If I could give him a place to start, or something he could confirm, it would help a lot. If it's obvious that Mulhouse is riddled with cancer, that's a different story, but Smidge wouldn't typically do a full autopsy on a case like this."

"And no need to either, right? I mean, the poor guy's dead, and it's just a kindness to close this chapter of his life."

"Yes, it's a kindness, and even better if Amie doesn't benefit from it."

"And you have no recourse on the other husbands?"

"This one's a suicide, and the previous one was a murder

in the Philippines. I would definitely have a hard time opening that case," she admitted. "The first husband was a suicide too. And she probably didn't gain from any life insurance benefit, yet got marital assets. I would probably leave that one alone, until I have a definitive answer as to something she gained from any possible murder there."

"So, you to think that she probably killed him?"

"Husband number one or husband number two? I think both, but I can't prove it," she said, raising her hands in frustration. "It's all conjecture and doesn't really give me the answers I need."

Simon smiled. "But you'll get them."

She looked over at him and grinned. "Absolutely I will."

"Tomorrow we leave, right?"

She sighed and then nodded. "Yes, tomorrow is soon enough to head back," she muttered, with a smile.

"Good. You do realize tomorrow is a Sunday though, right?"

She frowned at that and then shrugged. "Maybe that will impact things a little, but Monday will happen soon enough."

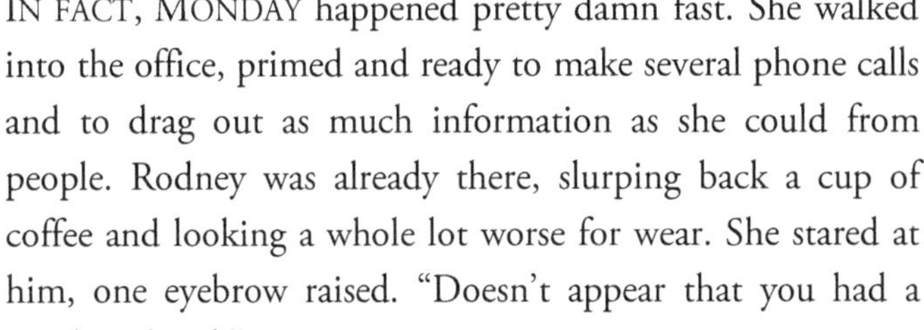

IN FACT, MONDAY happened pretty damn fast. She walked into the office, primed and ready to make several phone calls and to drag out as much information as she could from people. Rodney was already there, slurping back a cup of coffee and looking a whole lot worse for wear. She stared at him, one eyebrow raised. "Doesn't appear that you had a good weekend."

"Oh, I had a *great* weekend," he declared, with a grin, "but getting back to work? Now that's a bitch."

"Ah, yeah. I spent some of it out on the boat."

"Okay, that's enough of that," he declared, waving his hand. "Only so much us poor regular folk can handle."

She rolled her eyes at that. "Considering it's Simon's boat, not mine, that's really not the right thing to say to me."

"Considering it's Simon's boat," he repeated, with an eye roll, "let's not kid ourselves. You're enjoying it."

"I sure am," she admitted, with a laugh. "I didn't think I would. It's not something I've ever really wanted to do. I've lived in Vancouver all my life, sitting here, staring out at that world on the water, but never with any avarice or need to be out there sailing myself." She truly wanted Rodney to get it because she never wanted to have this conversation again, "I just never really thought that it could be something so nice. Or maybe it was so far out of reach that I just never considered it."

"And now that you know," he said, giving her a look, "I'm sure you'll want to go out all the time."

She nodded. "I would absolutely love to go out for a week," she shared, "but I don't know that either of us could ever make that happen. The next time I get a few days off, though, we'll sure try."

"I hope you do," Rodney said. "Meanwhile I went to a barbecue with some old school friends." He shook his head, smiling broadly. "Boy, am I feeling that today."

"Was it a barbecue, or some wrestling match?"

"You wish."

"You're not as young as you used to be," she noted cheerfully.

He glared at her, and she just chuckled. He asked, "Why are you in such a damn good mood? Oh, right, because you had a fun weekend out on the water."

"You had a fun weekend too," she pointed out, "just in a different way. Besides," she added, giving a dramatic pause, "I talked to Smidge, who surprised me by answering the phone Saturday night, but we potentially have a completely different scenario happening now with Amie and the *suicide*."

"Interesting," he replied. When she explained further, his eyebrows shot up. "So, you think it was a suicide after all, but she altered the evidence to make it look as if it wasn't?"

Kate nodded. "That would be my take on it, yes. Of course we need to find a few more things—the gloves, for example. That would help."

"But, if you found the gloves, couldn't it mean that she killed him herself?"

"In which case there will be GSR to be found on her, and, if it isn't a murder case, then as long as we find Robert's DNA inside the gloves, that should help." Then she stopped and shrugged. "Or it's left open, and we find the GSR and charge her with murder."

Rodney snorted.

Kate added, "I know it's not really a laughing matter, but, considering I sincerely don't believe she's innocent in the deaths of her other two husbands, that would definitely be something for me to take a look at."

He shook his head. "Why can't these cases be nice and simple?"

"Because people don't want to do the time for having done the crime," she pointed out, while quickly pouring herself a cup of coffee. Then she sat down at her desk, picked up the phone, and called the medical clinic, where Robert Mulhouse's medical records were on file. It took a bit until she could get through to the doctor. When she explained what had happened and what she was looking for, silence came on the other end.

Finally he spoke. "I'm not sure if I can say anything, not without a court order."

"You could wait for a court order," she noted, "and I can certainly get one, but all I'm asking you to do is confirm if Robert Mulhouse had any medical reasons for why he would contemplate suicide. That is not a violation of patient confidentiality, since you are bound to report suicidal tendencies anyway."

He groaned. "I did talk to him about getting some help because he was quite depressed."

"Was he only depressed about his medical diagnosis?"

"No, he'd been depressed for a while, even before he got engaged and married. I had hoped that finding love would help him. When he came in looking for antidepressants about two months ago, I went over his symptoms, which had gotten worse. So I didn't like a lot of what I heard. Thus I wanted to run a few tests. Those tests led me to a diagnosis of lung cancer."

"For somebody so young?" She gasped, legitimately shocked.

"Yes. When he got depressed, he smoked. He didn't tell me that he was smoking again, of course, not until I questioned him about it, along with the coughing he'd been experiencing. He finally admitted that he was smoking once more, and that was why he started coughing all of the sudden. Yet he didn't tell me when he started smoking again, which started at least ten years ago, after his father had died of lung cancer as well. He was a closet smoker, so he kept it from everybody."

"Oh goodness." Kate sighed.

"Yes, but I'm really sorry he chose the suicide route."

"Me too. Could I have something in writing regarding his condition, please?"

"Yes, I can do that."

"Do you know if he told his wife?"

"I'm not sure. All I can say is that … *she* was part of the reason he was so depressed," he stated in a hard tone. "I guess there is no point and no reason for not telling you that."

"Can you explain further?"

"He thought his wife was seeing somebody else, and he was quite perturbed over it all. He'd also found out something else that made him wonder if he knew her at all."

"Ah."

"He just mentioned that it was something about her previous relationships. Do you know what this is about?"

"Robert was her third husband, and her first two died while married to her," Kate shared.

"Good Lord." The doctor froze for a moment, then asked in a careful tone, as if not sure whether he should continue. "Nothing is suspicious about Robert's death, is there?"

"That's what we're still sorting through," she replied, "and another reason I needed something from you regarding an illness that could potentially make Robert suicidal. It panned out, I guess."

"He was suicidal, and I can say that with absolute clarity. We did talk about it, and I tried to get him to seek some help. When the lung cancer diagnosis was confirmed, I was quite concerned about what it would do to his mind-set. Yet he told me that he was fine and that he was figuring things out. I didn't expect him to be figuring it out this way though.”

“I’m sure you didn’t,” she said, “and it can’t be easy when patients face these situations.”

“Robert was my patient for many years,” the doctor shared, “a decade, more or less. You do get to know these people, and I was quite shocked that he didn’t seem to be too bothered to hear that he had cancer, which may have been part of the shock for me. He was just so laid-back about it and seemed as if he didn’t really care.”

“And that would go along with the depression then too, wouldn’t it?”

“Yes, to a degree, and that’s more or less when I realized just how significant his mood was. I just wish I could have done something about it sooner.”

“Understood. Send over whatever you’re comfortable with sharing from his file that I can put in mine, or at least give me a letter confirming the cancer diagnosis and what the prognosis would have been. And please mention that he was seeking antidepressants or that you put him on antidepressants and why.”

“Why don’t I just send over the file?” he suggested. “I don’t see that as a conflict at this point.”

“If you could send all your records, that would be the best,” she stated. “I can get a warrant if necessary to cover the release of the medical records. I’m just trying to get this wrapped up as soon as I can and not cause any more pain to a family who’s already lost somebody they care about.”

“Good point,” he replied. “Robert did mention he would contact his family and maybe even get another opinion, which I encouraged.”

“I didn’t realize that he had any family still.”

“Most of them are gone, but he has a sister, I believe.

Hang on a minute. Let me take a quick look in my files. … Yes, his sister lives in England." He gave Kate the number and added, "He intended to contact Hannah, but I don't know if he did."

"Okay, thanks very much." She rang off, then quickly checked the clock, shrugged, and dialed the number in England. When Hannah answered, Kate quickly explained who she was.

"Is this about my brother's death?" she asked.

Kate winced. "Yes, I presume you heard."

"Yes, Amie contacted me a little while ago," she stated curtly. "She told me that the police were considering that he'd been murdered." Yet Hannah seemed quite unsure of it.

"There is some confusion on that, and we're still waiting for the coroner to give us a final determination, but it's very possible that it was suicide."

"But that's not my brother."

Kate hesitated and then added, "I believe he phoned you not too long ago. Is that right?"

"Yes, yes, and he was quite upbeat and quite positive," Hannah replied in confusion. "Then to find this out?" She sighed. "It was just shocking."

"I'm sure it was. Did he tell you anything about his physical health?"

"No, not at all, but he sounded wonderful. Our conversation was just lovely, since we hadn't talked in a very long time," she murmured.

"That's one of the reasons why I was calling, to see if he shared something with you. I didn't know if he would have or not," Kate admitted.

Hannah asked, "Why?" The one word held an odd note of fear.

Kate wondered if the sister hadn't heard something herself. "I spoke with his doctor just now, and Robert had lung cancer."

"Oh, no," she gasped, and then she went really quiet. "Our father had lung cancer, and, by the end, it made for a pretty ugly death."

"Which just lends credence to the idea that Robert may have, indeed, committed suicide."

Hannah started to sob. "I didn't think I could be any more heartbroken," she cried out. "I don't know why he didn't contact me."

"Yet he did contact you, and I think that call was his attempt at saying, *Hi, I love you, and goodbye,* all at the same time," Kate suggested in a low tone. "Obviously saying goodbye is a hard thing to do, but I'm not sure that he had even figured out what he would do at that point."

With his sister sobbing noisily in the background, Kate rubbed her forehead and asked, "Robert was not the type to commit suicide, I presume?"

"He was quite depressed when he was younger," she murmured, "which had a lot to do with our father and his death because we were there the whole time, watching him die, and nothing is worse."

"I'm so sorry."

"Thank you. Although," she added, sobbing in between, "hearing that Robert committed suicide, I don't know that it makes it any better. I was honestly terrified to think that somebody had murdered him. Nobody could possibly hate my brother. You don't understand what Robert was like. He was such a sweetheart."

Kate listened as Robert's sister reminisced about him and gave glowing reports on her brother's personality.

Finally Hannah ran down. "Thank you," she muttered, "and thank you for letting me talk about him."

"That's fine. I'm sorry for giving you such rough news."

"No, in a way, this … is not good news, but I understand it."

"Good," Kate replied. "Don't say anything to anybody at this point, please."

"No, I won't. Does Amie know?"

"I don't know if she does or not, but I'll be talking to her soon, so I will break the news to her then."

"So, in other words, I shouldn't speak to her."

"No, please don't. That would just confuse the issues."

"Got it," Hannah said, and their call ended.

After that Kate wrote up her notes.

"So, is it a suicide now?" Rodney asked from behind her.

Without lifting her head from her notes, she replied, "Not officially, because Smidge wants more to go on, but I've got some medical documentation coming that should help. I think it was a suicide. I think Amie knew she wouldn't get any life insurance, so she altered the crime scene to make it look like a murder. That sounds most probable to me, but the jury is still out on that."

He looked over at her and nodded. "You don't even have to prove it, do you?"

She gave him a beaming smile. "Nope, because, as soon as that ruling of suicide comes down from Smidge, that's what it is."

"Amie can get a second opinion."

"She can sure try," Kate agreed, "but the coroner would still have to change his ruling for those life insurance policy benefits to come Amie's way."

"Got it. … You really don't like her, do you?"

She winced. "Jesus, people keep saying that, and I guess it's fair to suggest that I'm a little biased about this, but I'm trying to hold it in check. I'm much more concerned about the three dead men who came in contact with her and married her and then died before their time."

"Yeah," Rodney agreed, "that's a viable point. It doesn't seem as if anybody was looking after them, does it?"

"Exactly, and that's my point," she said in frustration. "Two of them had already passed on. Robert's the third, and I'm not sure anybody gave a crap."

"Or they gave a crap, but …"

Kate shrugged. When her phone buzzed a few minutes later, she checked to see it was Simon. "Good morning. Am I okay to enter the Paragon building?"

"Morning, and you're clear to go."

After that call ended, she sent a text, asking if he would purchase the property.

Still contemplating was his reply.

She snorted out loud at that. "Still contemplating, my ass," she muttered.

"Who's looking at your ass?" Owen asked sarcastically, as he walked up behind her.

She rolled her eyes at him. "No one," she declared, then blushed, remembering her weekend with Simon on the yacht. "The Paragon property, where the homeless guy was first found, still alive, Simon is considering buying it."

"Why would he want that run-down piece of crap?" he asked, with a laugh.

"Apparently it's one he's had on his wish list for a long time."

"Good God, the guy must be nuts to go after that dump," he muttered. "Who the hell would want anything to do with that building? It's a drop-down for sure."

"I'm pretty sure Simon would say it's the absolute opposite of a drop-down." When Owen looked at her in shock, she shrugged. "Hey, don't ask me to explain that mind-set. That's why I'm a cop, and I don't do real estate," she clarified, with a smile.

"Yeah, you're not kidding. Who would have thought that dump had any prospects?"

"You okay with your cases?" she asked him.

"I am. How are you doing on yours?"

"I'm okay."

"You haven't called Simon in to help on these last couple cases," he noted, with a teasing smile. "Is Simon slipping up, or is he too busy buying properties?"

"I have a hunch he'll always be too busy buying properties," she replied, with an eye roll. "But he certainly did connect with this one in a way because the dead homeless guy we found at the Feldspar house pretty much lived at the Paragon. Simon had spoken to him several times."

"So, why can't Simon just go into the building and say, *Hey, homeless dude, who killed you?* And get an answer?"

She wanted to shut him up, but instead she shared, "Jesus, Owen, you are too much. But, since you brought it up, Simon is a little concerned that the dead homeless guy *is* reaching out to talk to him." At that, everybody in the bullpen turned to look at her. She shrugged. "Don't ask me. Channeling or spirit-talking, or whatever the hell it is called, is not my deal."

"Well, shit," Owen muttered, looking a little bit pale and not laughing anymore.

At that, Rodney hesitated before suggesting, "You could ask him to try."

"I could ask him to try what?" she asked, narrowing her gaze as she spun in her chair to look at him. "To talk to a dead guy? Do you think that'll hold up in court?"

"No, it sure won't," Rodney agreed, "but it might give you something to go on." And he waggled his eyebrows at her.

She groaned. "No thanks. I would just as soon stick to the good old-fashioned police work."

"Yeah, until it doesn't work quite so easily," he muttered. When she glared at him, he just raised his hands in surrender. "Hey, it was just a suggestion. Don't mind me."

"Don't worry. I won't," she muttered, as she turned back to her desk. Yet it was hard *not* to think about it when so much craziness was going on. She just didn't want anybody to think that Simon owed them, or in any way should open himself up to the nightmare he had to live with. That woo-woo stuff was bad enough as it was for Simon, without her asking him to invite in *more* woo-woo stuff. She only had to deal with it peripherally during the nightmares he seemed to be forever plagued with, and that wasn't easy to watch. But her team didn't know about that, and it wasn't her business to tell them.

CHAPTER 18

S IMON WALKED INTO the Paragon building, once again caught up in the magic of being here with her. He gave a heavy groan and spoke to himself. "You might as well just accept it. You'll have to buy this one. If you lose it, you'll be crushed, and you know it," he muttered. When his words echoed in the big emptiness, he smiled, absolutely loving everything about it. As he stepped forward, going through the first floor, his mind was much clearer, much more analytical about what needed to be done and what the costs would be.

When his engineer called him and had a couple questions about another project, Simon asked Benjamin bluntly, "Where are you right now?"

"I'm downtown," Benjamin replied. "Why?"

"Just wondered if you could pop over and take a look at a building I'm considering. It would be great if you could do it now, since I'm here."

Benjamin laughed. "You don't have enough on your plate already?"

"Apparently not, and this one would be a huge project," he added. "So, I want to know whether I'll lose one shirt or two shirts."

Silence came on the other end, before the engineer groaned. "You do have the dandiest taste in buildings."

"Yeah, I do," he agreed in satisfaction, "but I've got to admit that I really love this one."

"Which one is it?" Benjamin asked, resigned to it now. "I'll see if I can swing around."

"The Paragon."

"Seriously?"

"Yeah, seriously."

"That's a hell of a building."

"I know it is, and I would absolutely love to have it."

"I didn't even realize it was up for sale," he muttered.

"Don't go thinking that you'll get it out from under me," Simon said, with a laugh.

"Oh, no way. I don't have the kind of money required to get that building on its feet," he shared. "Not even close. And honestly you need to seriously think about that one."

"That's one of the reasons why I'm busy looking at it again and called you just now. So I'll take your comments under consideration."

"And then you'll completely ignore them, I presume?"

"Ooh, ouch, do I have that kind of reputation?"

"Absolutely," he said, with a laugh, "and that can't come as any surprise. Anyway, give me … maybe twenty minutes, depending on traffic, and I'll be there."

"Good enough. I'll be inside, wandering around, taking a good look at it."

"Good, then take another—and another one after that," the engineer suggested in a sarcastic tone, "because you'll find that it needs way the hell more than you're expecting. That building has been around since forever."

"I know she has, but I also feel as if somebody needs to give her some love."

The engineer groaned. "Only you would say that. Dude,

you need to get a partner."

"Already got one," he declared in a cheerful voice.

"What does she think of all this?"

"Honestly, she's the one dealing with the dead body found there."

A shocked silence came on the other end. "I presume that means she's a cop—at least I hope she's a cop, although I guess she could be a coroner. I hope it wasn't a murder connected to that place."

"It was a murder, and it was one of two recent murders of homeless men connected to this place. However, it will not in any way impact how I feel about buying it."

"I guess it might make the price a little easier on you."

"It might at that," he replied, with a laugh, "but it's hardly enough of a reason to buy it or not."

"No, you've already got your thought process well into this one, so it doesn't matter what anybody says. I'll see you in twenty." And, with that, Benjamin disconnected.

Simon pocketed his phone and continued to walk around the property. He could see in his mind's eye what it would look like after his rehab, and that always meant he was on the right path.

With almost a childlike glee, he wandered through, seeing the entire property at its best, which put a huge smile on his face. When he got to the stairwell where he'd first seen Shawn, his smile fell away, and he groaned.

"Shawn, if you're around and if you want to tell me something, feel free," he offered. "I'm not very good at this, and I really don't know how to talk to ghosts and spirits, but, hey, if you want to tell me something about your death, I'll see if I can make somebody step up and take notice."

Suddenly a weird shimmer filled the air. Simon froze

and slowly turned to look up and down the stairs, expecting to see a spirit, but he didn't find anything of any form.

Out of the corner of his eye he caught a weird shimmer again, like a heat wave, but he wasn't quite sure what he saw or if he even saw anything. He wondered if it was just his imagination, which, in this case, it could very well be. Doing what he did, and having just enough talent to see things that probably weren't there, also gave Simon the ability to create them.

He groaned and called out, "Shawn, I'm not very good at this, so you might need to make it as definitive as possible." He waited a little bit more, and, when a door slammed upstairs, he frowned.

"Okay, that's pretty definitive." Moving quickly, he climbed up the stairs to the next floor. It wasn't that door that had slammed shut but one several more up. As he continued to climb, he looked around, wondering if somebody human was here. It was certainly possible. Why wouldn't there be? People were living in this place long before Simon ever took a look at buying it again recently, so it made sense that another homeless guy could be here.

As he walked up, he found the older homeless man he'd seen before and had talked to outside, the one who wore the cap. He was just sitting here, staring up at him. "Hey, are you okay?"

He shook his head. "Kind of lonely."

"I'm sorry, but you probably shouldn't be in here."

He nodded. "I know, but I thought maybe Shawn might be here. He was always going on about the ghosts. So I figured maybe he was one of them now."

"And the ghosts don't bother you?"

"*Nah*, they're dead," he said, with a shrug. "They can't

hurt me none."

Simon had to admit that was a refreshing attitude and one that he appreciated. "Did you ever think you saw Shawn's ghost here?"

The guy shrugged. "Maybe. I told him, if it was him, he should find a way to leave before getting stuck in limbo here. That would suck. After all, Shawn had found ghosts were here anyway."

"It did, indeed, suck, but hopefully he'll find some answers and get some peace somewhere. I'm sorry for your loss."

He looked over at Simon and nodded. "Yeah, the trouble is, most people don't give a shit about the homeless population. It's not as if we're thriving members of society."

"No, but you're entitled to live how you want, and, as long as you're not hurting anybody else, I'm happy for you to do you."

The older guy looked at him with a small smile. "But how do you know I'm not hurting anybody else?"

"I figure you're not. Regardless, it would be nice if you didn't," Simon said, with a nod, as he leaned against one of the walls.

"What are you doing back here anyway?" the homeless guy asked, eyeing him curiously.

"One, I feel bad about Shawn. And, two, I'm still looking at purchasing the property."

"But it's not even Shawn who they found here. It was Frankie."

"I know, but I didn't have the same connection with Frankie."

"Yeah, something was always a little off about him."

"Off in what way?"

"*Sly*," the homeless man said, with a shake of his head. "He was the one guy you probably shouldn't have left a backpack around because it would disappear before you had a chance to get your shit out of it," he muttered. "I know lots of guys on the street have a code, and they all talk about having groups and friends and sharing a creed on the streets, but Frankie was one who, if he could make a few bucks, he would make a few bucks."

"And yet is it fair to steal from the other homeless people? Aren't most of them hurting in the same way and in the same boat?"

He groaned. "Frankie didn't bother with street rules."

"*Huh*."

"Somebody asked him about Shawn."

"Somebody asked who?" Simon asked.

"Somebody asked Frankie about Shawn, and Frankie told me about it."

"What did Frankie say?"

The older guy shrugged. "He was a little excited about some money the guy promised him. Frankie told me that it was good money, but he was also kind of wary."

"He should have been. Seems the same guy could have killed both Shawn and Frankie. So did Frankie say anything about who and why?" Simon asked.

"No, just something about Shawn knowing somebody and getting into this black truck. Supposedly the same guy told Frankie that he would come back and take him out for a meal or two and they could have a talk, maybe even about getting him off the streets."

Simon nodded, as he listened. "But it didn't work out that way, did it?"

The old guy shook his head. "I'm assuming it didn't. …

I'm thinking it was probably the same guy too." He looked over at Simon. "It was, wasn't it?"

"I have no idea," he stated honestly, "but the cops are working on it."

The old man spat in the corner at that. "Damn cops."

"Not all of them are shit."

"No, not all of them," he agreed. "But the bottom line is, I don't trust them, and I can't talk to them. I did tell this to the one lady cop who was here earlier, but I'm not talking to them anymore."

Simon winced, and at the same time, wondered if he was referring to Kate. "I do know one cop who's worth talking to, if you've got anything to say."

"I got nothing," the older man said. "All I know is, Frankie talked to some guy, told him about seeing Shawn getting into a truck and talking to the driver. Haven't seen either again."

"Would Frankie have been smart enough to check out whether this guy was driving a rig that was the same color?"

The older guy stared at him and then slowly shook his head. "Honest to God, he probably wouldn't."

Simon nodded. "And that just brings up all kinds of nasty ideas."

"Ain't no such things as coincidence."

"Any idea why Shawn felt connected to this place?" Simon asked, as he turned and looked around at the huge building that looked so calm right now.

"He used to work here. At least that's what he told me."

At that, Simon stiffened and turned to look at him. "He worked here?"

"Yeah, I think that's what he said." He frowned. "Or maybe somebody he knew worked here, somebody who was big in his life."

"Ah, that's interesting. Maybe he thought the guy would still be here."

"Maybe, but I don't think his buddy died here or anything. I think he's just dead now."

"Interesting."

"Yeah, lots of people are interesting," the older guy said, followed by a hard sigh. He struggled to his feet, took a look around, then shook his head. "I won't be back. Hopefully Shawn's ghost can get the other ghosts to move on to where they are supposed to be." And, with that, he turned and walked out.

As he watched the older man leave, Simon turned and headed upstairs. He was going by sheer instincts, but the fact that Shawn spent time in this building because he had known somebody who worked here from years ago probably meant that he had known that somebody fairly well.

Considering that Shawn was also killed or at least found at the Feldspar house, it made sense that maybe that Feldspar connection stemmed from here at the Paragon as well. Shawn seemed to think so, even when he was alive. Yet Shawn never told Simon more about that, just wanting Simon to talk to the ghosts themselves. Simon snorted. As if that was going so well for him. Regardless he sent a message to Kate. **Shawn and Feldspar, it's probably connected to the Paragon.**

When she called him a few minutes later, she was fuming. "Are you in that damn building again?"

"I am. I'm waiting for my engineer to show up. But the homeless guy, the older one with the cap—"

"Yeah, what about him?" she muttered, her voice distant, as if he'd caught her in a bad time—but she'd been the one to call him.

"He said that Frankie talked to somebody about seeing Shawn get into the truck."

Silence came from her end for a moment. Then she spoke up. "Go on."

"Yeah, the old guy also told me that he thought Shawn had worked here in the Paragon, but then he thought maybe Shawn was close to somebody who worked here. It's confusing, but there it is."

"You would have to be pretty damn close to somebody if you kept visiting a building that was completely empty and gone in terms of what it used to be."

"I know," Simon agreed. "I just wondered, considering we're talking about Shawn ending up at the Feldspar house, if his death isn't connected somehow to the Feldspar business records you found here at the Paragon. Maybe Shawn had visited the Feldspar house before. Maybe Shawn is the one who found the business documents at the Feldspar house and brought them to the Paragon for some reason. I think even Shawn was known to sell information for a buck or two. Homeless guys are known for that."

"Well, crap. … I knew some of that, but it's good info, and the same old guy held it back from me. I'll follow up on that." And, with that, she was gone.

He stared down at the phone and sighed. "You're welcome, Kate."

Just then he heard a shout at the front door and grinned. That would be Benjamin, and now they could get down to business.

CHAPTER 19

KATE WAITED FOR the phone to be picked up. When Daisy finally answered, her voice slurred, as if tired and worn out, Kate apologized. "I'm sorry. Did I wake you from a nap?"

"Maybe," the older woman muttered, her voice slowly gaining in strength. "What can I do for you, Detective?"

"Did you or your husband have any dealings with a guy by the name of Shawn?"

"Shawn?" she repeated. "No last name, *huh*? I hope you're not asking about our client base because I couldn't possibly remember that many names."

"No, not particularly," Kate replied, now sighing. "It's a homeless person's case I'm dealing with right now," she clarified. "Apparently he hung around the Paragon offices because either he worked there with somebody in that building or he knew people who worked in the building that he was close to."

"That building was home to a lot of businesses over the years, particularly ones that came and went," she shared in astonishment. "What has that got to do with us?"

Kate hesitated and then added, "In this case, his body was found at the Feldspar house."

Daisy gasped. "Oh good Lord."

"Yes, so you can see why I'm asking if you know that

name."

"Know that name?" she repeated, sounding confused. "I mean, what was it again? Shawn? It's not ringing a bell, but I don't know. I can think about it some more and tell you later."

"That's fine, thank you. I just wanted to check. Maybe Shawn knew your husband, and maybe Jet helped out somehow. Apparently Shawn did military time, then came back with PTSD."

At that Daisy repeated the name a couple more times, then she gasped with shock. "Oh my, Jack Ludwig."

"Yes, I believe that was his legal name, although his friends on the streets called him Shawn."

"I don't know about Shawn," Daisy noted, "but Jack Ludwig, yes. He worked for my husband for a while. He was really good friends with … Oh my. Oh dear."

"What's *oh my*, and what's *oh dear*?" Kate asked.

"I do believe Jack knew the Feldspars, but I don't remember how they were connected."

"I don't really need you to tell me how they were connected, although it would certainly be helpful if you could tell me anything about Shawn. What he did with your company, and what the relationship was? That would be most helpful. Honestly anything at this point would help."

"Well, he was just … I really need a cup of tea and a moment to clear my head."

"How about I come visit?" Kate offered.

Daisy moaned. "I guess you won't let me off the hook on this, will you?"

"No, I'm sorry. I can't."

"Fine then," she said crossly. "Come over. I'll put on the teakettle."

With that, Kate once again bounded to her feet and raced to her vehicle. When she arrived at Daisy's house, she walked up to the front door, and Daisy opened it for her.

"I've been sitting here trying to think about Jack," she began, "and I don't have a ton of memories about him."

"I understand that," Kate replied, "and I get that it was probably a while ago."

She nodded and pointed to the tea service on her table. Both women sat down and Daisy poured tea for both of them. "I know that my husband was persuaded to hire him. Jack just did odd jobs—cleaning the office, filing, some hand-deliveries, things like that. But he did have a good head for numbers, and my husband enjoyed being around him. … I was going to say I don't know what happened and why he disappeared, but I think it all happened at the same time."

"You mean, the same time as the Feldspar murders?"

"Yes, I think so. … I seem to recall that … and I can only give you vague memories on this. Maybe Jack was profoundly affected by the Feldspar murders, and I seem to remember that he might have been good friends with somebody there."

"Like the son or the daughter?"

"I think it was the daughter, but, when the daughter was so badly injured … I don't know if he just couldn't handle it, or she couldn't handle it, or what. Honest to God, none of us could handle it," she admitted. "It was just such a horrific scenario, losing so many members of the same family at one time, and everybody was terribly affected by it."

Kate nodded. "Of course, and that makes total sense."

"It might make total sense now," Daisy pointed out, "but, back in the day, I think we were all just in shock mode and trying to function enough to get through the day. For me, the pain was much less because I wasn't as close to the family in the way my husband was. I didn't realize how close he was getting."

"You mean, with the niece?"

"Yes, exactly," she snapped, and then she groaned. "And you can see that all my attempts to stay calm and to be fair and balanced about the whole second-family thing go up in smoke."

"I am so sorry about that. It's not your fault, and you're still dealing with a very large betrayal."

"Yes, I am. Thank you for understanding that." She took a deep breath. "Maybe you'll want to go talk to them."

"I will," Kate noted. "I need to at least talk to both the sister and the niece."

"Good luck with that," Daisy replied. "First, the sister may be in a coma. She was that bad off. As for the niece, I know she's pretty bitter because she thought that my husband and I were divorced."

"And was there any talk of the two of you divorcing?"

"No, I didn't even know anything about it," Daisy snapped, as her shoulders slumped.

Daisy was tired, emotionally and physically. That made Kate sad to even bring up all this with her. "I'm sorry that this is all being dragged up again. It's hardly fair to you."

"It's not fair, but it is also the reality of life," Daisy stated. "As I have found, to my great chagrin, just because something isn't fair doesn't mean that it'll change and go your way. So, don't feel ashamed about having to ask me questions. I'll get through it the best I can."

"And that is much appreciated," Kate murmured.

"I also found another phone number for Rosemary—or maybe it's the same one as I thought was in the box, and I just wrote it down in two different places."

"Rosemary Feldspar? That's the niece, right?"

"Yes, the one my husband *married*," she said in a mocking tone.

"Ah, good, I'll contact her." And with that, she got the phone number from Daisy and wrote it down, aware that it seemed slightly familiar. As she pondered it, she muttered, "I almost feel as if I've seen it before."

Daisy shrugged. "I certainly hadn't seen it before she called me after the funeral, but who knows. My husband was definitely a con man when it came to keeping that side of his life separate from my side of his life. I had no idea," she muttered, with a sad sigh. "I think that's what made me the angriest because I considered myself an intelligent woman … somebody not easily duped." She shook her head, with sorrow written all over her expression. "He made me feel like a fool, and that, that's hard to forgive."

Kate understood that all too well. She got up after their tea and thanked the woman for her assistance. On her way out the door, she turned and added, "Just remember that what you're doing now goes a long way to standing up and facing what happened to you. You're nobody's fool, and anybody can get tricked by somebody they love. That's what love is about, totally trusting someone without a second thought. He broke that trust, but he didn't break you." With that parting wisdom shared, Kate turned and made her way to her car.

SIMON WALKED OUT the front door of the Paragon building, still energized from his discussion with Benjamin, who would send him a report, a general report based on what he'd found, and then they could go from there.

As he went to close the front door, he thought he heard a voice calling out to him. He turned to look, but nobody was there. Frowning, he stuck his head in the building and froze because he saw that same weird apparition, that shimmering form, now more of a defined shape. Simon stepped inside, keeping his gaze on the form, as he closed the door behind him.

"Shawn, is that you?"

The form shimmered a little brighter.

Simon wasn't sure if that was a yes or something else. "I don't think you're supposed to be here, buddy."

The form shimmered again ever-so-slightly.

"Did you call me?"

And again that weird echo came, half-yes, half-no.

He wasn't sure if that was an answer or if it was just some noise drifting through the building. He walked a little closer. "Is there something you need to tell me?" He could swear to God that the apparition spoke. He didn't see a mouth. He didn't clearly see anything, but he heard a noise, a word, and it was so clear and strong. Yet it made no sense because the word just hung there, alone.

"Feldspar."

"Yes, you were found in the Feldspar house," Simon confirmed, feeling the hairs on the back of his neck raise, even on his arms. All his hair stood up, and his instincts told him to run like hell. Yet, if he did run, how would that help whatever the hell this was? But, as soon as the ghost said *Feldspar*, the apparition slowly started to fade.

"Wait," Simon cried out. "What about Feldspar? What is it? What's wrong with it?"

Of course at the point of *maybe* getting some answers,

the apparition dissipated.

Simon groaned, as he stared around the space. He didn't know what the hell was going on, but definitely something was here. Just as he went to phone Kate, his phone rang, and he saw that it was her. "Hey, great minds and all that," he said lightly. "I was just about to call you."

"Are you okay?" she asked, her tone sharp. "I just got the sudden urge to call you."

He smiled. "I do like the idea of sudden urges to call me, but I'm fine."

"You're in that damn building, aren't you?"

He gave a small laugh. "Yes, and I think I just saw Shawn's ghost again. The only thing he would tell me, and, no, I don't know that the ghost was talking to me, so don't press me on this, but all I heard on the ethers—"

"Ethers?" she asked in a deliberately dubious and non-committal tone.

Simon let it go and came straight to the point. "All he said was *Feldspar*."

"Yeah, Feldspar is coming up, again and again," she noted.

"Did you ever look at all the old case files on Feldspar?"

"I've got them at my desk," she shared. "I've gone through them, but I haven't had a chance to completely analyze the data. It's also not a cold case that I'm really entitled to open, but I do want the details from it, which may be connected to the current cases I've got going now."

"You should bring some of the other guys in the office into the loop," Simon suggested. "It sounds as if you're getting somewhere."

"Am I?" she asked in a mocking tone. "I would have sworn I was nowhere at all."

"Oh, but I think you are," Simon declared, feeling a sharp pang of knowingness. "It definitely feels as if you are. Something that you just found out is putting you on the right track."

"That may or may not be," she muttered, "but you certainly couldn't prove it by me."

He laughed. "That's just because, once again, you are doubting everything in your world."

"Ha. I don't know about that, but I can tell you that Shawn spent a lot of time with the accounting firm in the Paragon building, and somebody in the Feldspar family or a friend of the Feldspars got Shawn the job there at the Paragon."

"Well, crap," Simon said in astonishment.

"Yeah, too bad Shawn didn't tell you about that."

"Too bad Shawn wasn't still around to tell me about anything," he stated firmly. "I wish he was."

"Yeah, me too, and I know that you have been quite affected by his death, and I'm sorry about that. … I would love to say that I'm almost there in solving Shawn's death because it feels as if I am, but I don't have anything clear and concrete to get there. Not yet anyway. This case is messing me up."

"You do realize that multiple people have been killed in order to keep quiet whatever happened," Simon pointed out, "and all your digging is petrifying me that you're coming up close against that killer and putting yourself in danger." Silence came on the other end of the phone, and he groaned. "*Right.* I don't get to say anything about that, do I?"

"It's not that you don't get to say anything," she countered gently, "but it's not as if I'll quit now, will I?"

He slowly let out his breath, aiming for control but

knowing that it would likely be a complete waste.

Then she came back with a retort. "And I'm not doing anything stupid. I'm definitely not trying to do anything more stupid than you would consider," she clarified, with a note of humor.

"I know, but bodies are dropping like flies around these two properties."

"Yeah, no kidding. I do understand that murders have been committed just to keep this all quiet," she conceded, "and that is definitely not something I'm terribly happy with. Shawn and Frankie deserved a better life than they had, even if it's one that they chose. However, the information I've just found out now is something that I need to double-check, and, for that, I need to get back to the office and make some phone calls."

"Or you can just come to my apartment and make some phone calls," he suggested.

"Too early yet," she muttered. "It's not even noon."

"I understand, but we haven't had a nooner yet," he suggested in a teasing tone. He heard her sucked-in breath, and he laughed. "Yeah, I shocked you."

"And yet I don't know why I should be shocked," she whispered, her voice thick. "Just hold that thought until I get home, will you?"

And, with that, she ended the call.

CHAPTER 20

B ACK IN THE office, Kate headed for her desk and plunked down just as Rodney came up to her.

"You're back already?" he asked.

"Yeah," she said, with business on her mind. "Had to go talk to Daisy in person. This whole nightmare has been pretty tough on her."

"Daisy who?" he asked.

"Mahoney. Surviving owner of the accounting company that was at the Paragon building and that did work for the Feldspar family."

"Ah, okay, and what did Daisy have to say?"

"Lots, and yet nothing concrete," Kate muttered, shuffling through the papers on her desk. "I'll have to go ruffle some more feathers."

"Oh, but that's the best part of the job," he declared, with a goofy smile.

"It would be if I knew exactly who and what," she shared. Finally she grabbed a physical file while double-checking the current file she had up on her computer because something was rattling around in her mind. "Now I get to go talk to some people about the Feldspar murders."

He bolted to his feet. "Can I come?"

She glared at him, as he was all excited.

Rodney added, "You probably shouldn't be alone, you

know? I should probably tell Colby that you're heading into dangerous territory and shouldn't be without backup."

She spun ever-so-slowly in her chair, her glare ready to drown him. Then she spotted the impudent grin on his face, and she sighed. "I was going to make a couple phone calls first and see what pops up."

"In what way?"

She went over the information she had just found out.

"So, hang on a second. This guy Shawn gets hired at this now-defunct accounting firm, and it was the Feldspar family from the Feldspar house that made his job happen, and now Shawn was on the streets and what? … He has PTSD? How did that happen?"

"He did a tour in the military, then came back after some pretty-ugly experiences and wasn't the same anymore. He apparently couldn't continue with the work he had done before the military at the accounting firm, but he hung around all the time. Eventually he got a little bit better and could do a little more but not enough for a full-time job, but they paid him anyway for his part-time work."

"Is there anything wrong about that?"

"No," she said, with a wave of her hand, "but it does explain why he was attached to the building, even though the company he worked for has been gone for over a decade. I don't know what sent him out onto the streets, but at least we've got a connection between him, the Paragon building, and the Feldspar family and their property."

"Sure," Rodney replied, "but it's pretty thin."

"Hey, I don't care because I found another connection to Feldspar, one that's pretty upsetting for Daisy."

"Oh, what's that?"

Then she explained about Daisy's husband, Jet Mahoney, the accountant, his dual life, and his second wife, who was the niece of the Feldspars, although she wasn't at their home during the notorious murders.

Rodney sat back and shook his head. "Wow."

"So now we have Jet Mahoney, a long-time friend to the Feldspars—but the Feldspars were *not* acquainted with his wife—and Jet is all concerned and upset over the murders ten years ago, helping out the Feldspar kids with a chunk of money from Jet and Daisy's joint savings account. Then, as time goes by and unbeknownst to Daisy, Jet hooks up with the Feldspar niece, Rosemary, telling her that he divorced his wife, and they end up married, having twins. Years pass, and then Jet dies. The second wife reads in the paper how he's been buried and is survived by his wife, *Daisy*. The niece phones Daisy, asking if she was really Jet's wife. Meanwhile the niece contacts a lawyer about Jet's estate after his funeral, and the lawyer thought everything had been settled, and Jet's wife was to receive everything. The niece pops up and declares, "*That's me.*" Then he tells her that Daisy was his legal wife, so Rosemary, this second wife of Jet's, had no standing. You can imagine how things went from there."

Rodney shook his head. "Jesus, people complicate their lives so much."

"Yeah, you're not kidding." Kate shook her head. "Of course, for Daisy, the only way she even found out about Jet's second family was that phone call after her husband's death. Otherwise she still may not have known."

"Which means that was a betrayal from the grave."

"Daisy could have gone happily on her way without ever finding out about that, but, of course, Rosemary Feldspar Mahoney had something to say."

"Yeah. Her husband's dead, and now look."

"Exactly." Kate slowly rolled her neck to release the tension there.

Rodney asked, "So what will you do now?"

"There is no shortage of confusion over the Feldspar murders. I thought everybody had been killed, *three generations' worth*," she noted, pulling up her file again. "But according to Daisy, and granted, she wasn't sure, but she thought a teenage daughter had survived, and a teenage son had survived too."

"I thought everybody got killed too," Rodney stated, frowning in her direction.

"The witness accounts in the file state that the daughter went missing and that the aunt was shot. According to Daisy, however, the daughter survived but has some major brain damage, in a coma even. And the daughter's aunt, the father's sister, has been missing since all the murders, with her body not found. She is presumed dead. So the witness statements contradict Daisy's recollection. Which means that now I have to track down the survivors and figure out what's what."

"Was the aunt living there or visiting the Feldspar home at the time of the murders?"

"I heard she lived nearby but was always at the Feldspar house. Regardless, per Daisy, the aunt appears to remain missing," Kate explained, rolling her eyes. "Apparently some of these files may be more confusing than the actual murders."

"Of course. It's possible the details may have been a little more confusing because people *intentionally* confused them," Rodney stated, nodding at her.

Kate shrugged. "Witnesses can be unreliable, as we all know. Still, a female was injured, resulting in a brain injury.

Per Daisy, it was the daughter, but Daisy did admit to being a little hazy on the details."

"And yet that's not in the file?"

"No, it's not, which leaves me to wonder why the hell not and how someone could have gotten the details so wrong."

Rodney raised his eyebrows. "I wonder if she's been stowed away in one of those places, like the case we had with the private mental hospital, where people were keeping brain-damaged family members under wraps."

"It's possible." Kate shook her head. "But, if it's true, I'll find her. What the file does give me, right here, if it works, is a phone number for the supposed sister." As she looked at it, she frowned. "Hang on a minute. This looks familiar. I had this phone number, supposedly for the son, and yet it's the same number Daisy gave me for Rosemary, the Feldspar niece, the second wife to Jet Mahoney."

Rodney frowned at her. "What?"

"Yeah, Jet's wife number two," she repeated. "The number is here on my phone but—" She held up the piece of paper that she had printed off with the phone number printed on the back. "Reese found this number and who it belonged to. It's the same one."

Just then Reese walked into the office and looked around. "Oh, there you are. I've been trying to catch up with you."

"Yeah, did you find anything on that phone number?"

"I did. Why?"

"You go first."

"It's registered to a Doug Feldspar."

At that, Kate nodded. "So, is he the surviving son?" At Reese's nod, Kate continued. "My next question is, why did

Doug Feldspar allow Rosemary, the second wife, to use his phone to contact Daisy, the first wife?"

Reese frowned. "Now, that's an interesting twist."

"And yet they're family. Doug and Rosemary both being Feldspars," Rodney pointed out, "so maybe her phone's broken or she can't afford to pay for it or something. So, it makes sense that she would use his phone. They're both Feldspars, after all. He might have just lent it to her for the moment."

"Maybe," Resse agreed, "and also, if you think about it, he might have lent it to her so Rosemary wouldn't have to deal with Daisy calling them back because any calls would have gone to Doug, and he would have made sure that that would have been the end of it."

"Let's find out, shall we?" Kate asked, with half a smile. She picked up her phone and quickly dialed the number.

SIMON WALKED UP the entranceway into his apartment building, and stopped to visit with Harry the doorman for a few minutes. Harry was a good guy, and Simon thoroughly enjoyed his company.

"So, what's this I hear about you buying another building?" Harry asked, staring at him in astonishment. "Man, you already seem to be worked off your feet as it is."

Simon laughed at that. "You do have a point there, yet that's how this business works. You've got to keep moving forward. Otherwise, you get stuck behind."

At that, Harry shook his head. "Seems to me that sometimes you need to just take a break and not get so involved, take a load off."

"Maybe," he admitted, "and you do have a point. On

the other hand, this is a building that's been on my wish list for a long time." When Harry studied him with a curious expression, Simon added, "It's the Paragon, downtown." It took a moment for the name of the building to settle into Harry's memory banks, and Simon could tell when he realized which building it was because his eyes lit up.

"Oh, man," Harry exclaimed, "that is one hell of a building."

"Right?" Simon said, with a grin. "Now you know why I'm excited and why I can't pass up this one."

Harry nodded. "Absolutely. That's quite a coup if you can get it," he replied enthusiastically, "but, man, she's an old one."

"She's old, and she's got a lot of rough history."

He nodded at that. "All kinds of people used to work in that place, not that I remember any of them now, but my father used somebody down there to do his bookkeeping. Yet he always thought something was really dodgy about him, and he didn't go back after the first time."

Simon laughed at that. "Yeah, I'm not at all surprised."

"So, do you do a full history on a building when you buy it?"

"I try to dig up some history," he replied, with a wave of his hand. "I can't do a full history just because it goes on forever. I continue to collect information because I think it's important, even after the purchase. Like a family genealogy, except for a building."

"Oh, it's absolutely important," Harry agreed. "It's pretty cool that you're doing that."

"Maybe," Simon hedged. "I haven't got it yet, still looking at it, still tossing it back and forth. And a homeless guy was found dead there recently, so that screws things up a little bit."

"Should make it easier for you to buy it though, right? A building like that needs some love, and not many people are willing to go that far."

He smiled at Harry and nodded. "Exactly. That's how I feel, but not everybody else does."

"*Nah*, they're just stuck on the bottom line," Harry stated, "and that's really not who you are."

"No, it sure isn't. I'm glad to see you picked up on that already."

Harry laughed. "As the doorman, I get to know people pretty well, you know? When you work in this place, it's hard not to. There are people who'll wait for you to open the door, and there are people who'll open the door for you, and there are people who'll make snide comments as they walk in. Anything from my weight, to my uniform, to the building," he shared, with a laugh.

"I guess that's about right."

"And then there are people who will see you're having a bad day and will stop by to make it better," he said, beaming at some internal thought. "I got your number," Harry added, bumping a fist with Simon's. "And that building? It's had some good times. It's had some bad times, but, if you can make it all good again, I'm right there with you."

"That's my plan, or at least that's my hope," Simon clarified, still with a smile. "I'm definitely not to that point though, and it could take more money than I'm really expecting it to, so there are all kinds of considerations."

"That may well be true," Harry stated, "but I don't think any of that will hold you back."

"I had my engineer over there today, taking a look," Simon shared, "and he'll send me a report on it."

"Doesn't he have to do a whole pile of tests?"

"He does. This is just a preliminary summary of what problems he can pinpoint at the outset. If I decide to go ahead with it, then there'll be more tests needed before I can do anything, and, of course, that starts the whole city permit process."

"Oh, boy," Harry muttered. "Anything to do with the city gives me the heebie-jeebies."

Simon laughed at that phrase. "Yeah, but more than that, right now we have to deal with the murders."

"Murders? As in more than one? That some serious stuff, *huh*?"

"Oddly enough, a homeless guy was murdered. I had first met him in the Paragon property, when I took a look at it, but he wasn't murdered there. ... Well, he might have been murdered there. We don't know yet. They haven't got the forensics back apparently, but he was dumped at the Feldspar house."

At that, Harry looked at him as if electrified. "The Feldspar house? You're kidding me. You probably don't know this, but my wife is one of those crime show fanatics, and, if I even *mentioned* the word *Feldspar*, she would be all over you for information. I won't tell her a thing," he vowed, with a laugh, "not without getting my ass kicked."

"Kate's right in the middle of it all."

Harry chuckled. "She'll get it all sorted out then."

"Oh, absolutely. And she's all about ethics, being the one who solves these cases," he stated proudly. "But now she's also got a connection with one of her recent murders to the Feldspar house, and that's opened a whole can of worms for her."

"Yeah, that mass murder of the Feldspars long ago was

quite the thing," Harry noted. "I think the daughter who survived is in a home not all that far from here. She's got one of those high-end places that looks out over the harbor," he said, turning to look out the window. "I can't remember which place it is though."

"Do you know what happened to her or why she's there?"

"Yeah, my cousin works at the home, so I can find out for you." He pulled out his phone, without Simon even asking him to, and quickly dialed. As they spoke, Simon listened to Harry's side of the conversation.

"Hey, Reenie. Do you know anything about the lady from the Feldspar house? I think you mentioned the daughter was somewhere close by. ... Yes, she is there, isn't she? ... I was just talking to one of my tenants here. He's looking at buying a building that's somehow connected to this mess. ... No, no, I'll tell him."

Harry ended the call and grinned at Simon. "I was right. She's just a few blocks from here, in one of those high-rise specialized care homes."

"Considering what happened to her, that makes sense."

"It does." Harry nodded. "That was quite the mess. People have talked about those murders forever ... and they still are," he added. "I mean, you think about the family members getting murdered like that, and all hell breaks loose, and people are panicking. Then it becomes something much bigger than you thought."

Simon nodded. "If you hear anything, let me know. It's a fascinating topic, but the case is Kate's," he said, with a warning. "So no asking her for information or even bringing it up because that'll just get me in hot water."

Harry laughed at that. "I won't make that mistake.

However, if she's on it, it may well get solved this time."

And with that vote of confidence Simon headed up to his apartment, hoping that Kate would make it over tonight.

CHAPTER 21

K ATE, SURROUNDED BY Owen, Rodney, and Lilliana, all listened as the phone just rang, rang, and rang. Just as she went to end the call, wondering why no answering machine was set up, a man answered.

He snapped, "What the hell do you want?"

She frowned, then quickly asked, "Is this Doug Feldspar?"

"Yes, it is. If you dialed this number, then that's who you were expecting. So what the hell do you want?" He was spitting venom. "Can't you tell I'm busy?"

"No, I couldn't have known that," she replied.

"Good, now get lost."

As he went to end the call, she added in a hurried tone, "I'm Detective Kate Morgan."

At that, his breath caught, and he started to swear. "What the hell do you want, Detective? I've had enough police for a lifetime."

"I'm sure you have," she agreed, "but that doesn't change the fact that I do need to ask you some questions."

"I'm not talking to you," he bellowed. "You can contact my lawyer."

"That's fine. Who is your lawyer? I can reach out, and we'll arrange for you to come down here for questioning."

Dead silence came on the other end, and she knew how

this would go.

"What's this about anyway?" Doug asked.

At least now, his tone showed a little more of a conciliatory attitude. "I have questions that relate to a series of murders that have happened recently."

He snorted at that. "They have nothing to do with me," he stated in disgust. "Murder is something I really try to stay away from, in case you don't know my history."

"I do know your history," she said calmly, "and it's one of the reasons I want to talk to you."

Silence came, and Lilliana's eyebrows shot up, as she mouthed to Kate, *Bring him in.*

"I suggest that—rather than doing this over the phone, and since you mentioned you would prefer to do that with your lawyer—you both appear here at the department at nine a.m. sharp, tomorrow morning." She quickly gave him the address and disconnected.

Looking over her team, she smiled. "That should be a really interesting interview."

Rodney nodded. "I want to join you too."

"You're welcome to," she said thoughtfully. "Definitely something is going on, and Doug's not happy about it."

"That doesn't mean he's involved," Owen noted from her side, "but it does make him look guilty as hell."

"The question is, what is he guilty of?" Kate asked.

"It could be anything from growing dope to stealing," Lilliana guessed. "Who knows. … I'm sure he's not thinking about his entire family line."

"No, of course not," Rodney agreed, "but now that you've told him that you know who he is and know about his history, and that's partly why you want to talk to him, you can bet that will all be on his mind."

"Yeah, probably so." Kate nodded. "I still need to question him."

"Absolutely," Rodney declared, "particularly given his attitude." He looked over at the wall clock and said, "Oh, jeez, I need to call it a day."

"Going somewhere?" Kate asked him innocently. When he glared at her, she smiled. "Go on and have fun."

"I will. At least that's the plan." And, with that, he was up and gone.

The others looked at her, and she shrugged. "All I know is that he was busy all weekend with a group of friends, and since then … he's been a little bit off."

"*Off*, as in *sneaky off?*" Lilliana asked, with a knowing smile.

Kate smiled. "*Off*, as in maybe somebody new is in his life."

"That should be interesting," Lilliana said, then groaned. "Seems it's been a long time since I was on a date. I guess now we have three out of five of us with a partner, which I think is just a pathetic score for our team." When Kate frowned at her, Lilliana shrugged. "I broke up with my ex a few months back. Not exactly something I publicize. You know the deal. This job's tough, and you can't really be there for people, and they tend to want more from you than you generally can give," she pointed out, looking over at Kate. "So, if you can make something work with Simon, go for it. … I'm not doing so well in that department." And, with that, she grabbed her purse and headed for the door.

Kate looked over at Owen, but he appeared to be on his phone. She knew that he'd been a happily married family man for years. She hoped that never changed for him.

She looked down at her phone and called Simon. "You

up for a visit tonight?" she asked.

"Absolutely," he replied in delight. "I was hoping you would come over, but then I feel like that all the time. So, whenever you can, it's great with me."

She winced at that because it sounded as if she never made time for him, and maybe that was true. Maybe Lilliana was right. This relationship stuff was tough, particularly when so much else was going on in Kate's world. But one thing was certain, whenever she wanted human contact, she would always reach out to Simon. "I'll be there in a little bit."

"Good, and I'll have food for you."

"Now that," she teased, "is guaranteed to get me there."

"Oh, I know. I figured that out a long time ago." And, on that note, he disconnected.

Laughing, she grabbed her keys, called out a goodbye to Owen, and quickly headed off, trying to let her mind sort out what tomorrow's interview would mean.

It would be interesting if Doug didn't show up because then she could send somebody around to pick him up and haul him in. She suspected he would show, but what she didn't know was whether he would show with a lawyer or alone.

CHAPTER 22

T HE NEXT MORNING, Kate walked into the office bright
and early. Rodney was there and already on the phone
talking to somebody, setting up something for the day. Kate
saw no sign of Lilliana, and she heard Owen in with Colby.
She sat down to go through the information that Simon had
given her the previous evening about the Feldspar sister in a
nearby home. She quickly located the facility's contact info,
and, with a short phone call, confirmed the sister was there.
Kate planned to meet her after Doug's interview this
morning. Then she made a list of questions she wanted to
ask.

When she got the phone call announcing that Doug
Feldspar had arrived, she asked for him to be taken into
Interview Room One. With that done she looked over to see
Rodney getting up. "You coming to join me?"

"Yeah, this is an interesting one."

"Yours isn't?"

"Mine is pretty simple, which is good," he said, with a
laugh. "Normally we work in teams, but when we can break
free and handle multiple cases at the same time, it's all good.
But this guy? I didn't like his attitude yesterday, so I'm
coming."

"Is that to give me support, or him?" she asked in a
mocking voice.

He flashed her a bright grin. "Oh, I know you can handle it yourself. That's not the issue. I just want to see what this guy thinks he's up to. I hate that there's no movement on Amie's case either."

"I'm still waiting for the file from Manila and more forensics. We move forward on the cases we can, while we wait on others."

And, with that, the two of them headed to the interview room. She walked in, noting Doug had an attorney with him, and she took a seat. When she turned on her recorder, she introduced herself and had the others identify themselves, along with the time and the date.

She then turned to Doug. "I have a few questions for you, Mr. Feldspar." She looked over at Doug's lawyer and then back at Doug. "Didn't want to come in without a lawyer, *huh*?" she asked, with a laugh.

"After your aggressiveness on the phone yesterday," he stated smoothly, "I decided I should have some legal representation."

"*My* aggressiveness on the phone?" she asked, still smiling. "I didn't even get a chance to introduce myself before you were ready to hang up, already so belligerent from the get-go."

He frowned at her. "You disturbed me."

"*Apparently*. ... So, you always yell at people who call you?"

"Most of the time, yeah. I don't like people and don't want anything to do with them."

"All people?"

"Everybody avoids some people," Doug declared.

"Fine. What is your relationship with Rosemary?"

He stared at her in shock, then sat back and frowned.

"What's this all about?"

Kate frowned at the lawyer, expecting an objection but getting none. So she turned to Doug and said, "Answer the question, please."

"No, I can't answer that question," Doug replied in a harsh tone, "not until you tell me what this is all about."

"You gave up your right to have a simple conversation over the phone yesterday," she explained in a smooth tone, "when you refused to answer a few basic questions. Now we're here with your lawyer—and on the record, I might add. So I want some answers, please."

The lawyer leaned over and whispered something in Doug's ear. Doug glared at her. "She's family."

"Close family?" she asked, writing down notes that she knew would make any suspect nervous, yet were just for her own purposes.

"Yeah, close family," he snapped.

"How would you categorize your relationship with Rosemary Mahoney?" As she looked up, she caught his facial muscles tensing. He seemed unwilling to divulge any details voluntarily. She raised an eyebrow. "Could you answer the question, please?"

"Close."

She nodded. "So, when you say *close*, you know about her marriage that's not a valid marriage then, right?"

"That fucking asshole," he roared.

"Why is that?" she asked, sitting back and staring at him.

Doug was fuming, and the tic in his jaw was more and more pronounced. "Because he fucking married her, saying that he was single and available."

"And yet, if you had even looked or contacted his first wife, Daisy would have clarified the matter. I am sure you must have known Daisy."

He stared at her. "So, hang on a minute. You're making this about me?"

"I'm not making this about anybody, but you're sitting here making accusations, and I would like some background for it."

"You already know an awful lot if that's why we're here. Rosemary is not at fault because she believed Jet was single. *He* was the bigamist. She was not."

"Neither was she legally married," Kate noted calmly.

"No, she wasn't," he agreed in disgust, "but she thought she was."

Kate shook her head. "I don't understand how the two wives did not run into each other, as everybody lived in town, right?"

Doug shook his head. "Vancouver is a big city, and Jet's first wife was a homebody. In fact, so was Rosemary, especially when the twins came along. They didn't run in the same circles."

Kate nodded at that. "I'm sure that was most difficult on Rosemary and Daisy to find out about Jet's deception."

"It was *very* difficult for Rosemary. Plus, she thought she would at least inherit something to live on, and instead it all went to Jet's first wife." Doug let out a snarl.

"Is that why you're so angry at life?"

"No, I was born this way," he declared sarcastically, glaring at her. "And, if you had any idea about my history, you would know perfectly well why I'm angry."

"I certainly know what happened to your parents and your sister and your grandmother."

"And my aunt," he snapped, "although everybody wants to forget about her."

"What happened to your aunt?"

"I don't know for sure, but she's gone, and nobody's seen her since my family died," he replied. "Not exactly a positive family memory."

"No, it was a very, very difficult situation, and I can understand that. How much do you have to do with your sister at this point?"

"Nobody can have very much to do with her," he snapped. "She's got a brain injury."

Kate nodded and continued to write simple notes for herself. She already knew about the brain injury and was planning to see the woman as soon as this interview concluded. "What is the extent of that brain injury?"

"What do you mean, the extent?" he asked in disgust. "She's not the same person anymore."

Kate looked up at him. "Do you see her?"

"No, I don't, and you better leave it at that. She's a reminder of something I don't want to be reminded of," he growled, "and, if that makes me a shitty person, whatever. Apparently I'm a shitty person."

She considered him. "You have a very interesting attitude about life."

"*Yeah*? I don't really give a shit."

She nodded. "What was your relationship with Rosemary's husband?"

"At the time it was fine."

"So, you had absolutely no idea?"

"No, I didn't. Jet and Rosemary were private people, happy to entertain at home. If I had found out earlier, I would have killed the bastard myself."

She nodded. "And yet you don't seem to think killing is problematic, do you?" she asked. "Or in any way wrong?"

"Certain things in life are right, and certain things in life are wrong."

"Murder is never right," Kate stated, "so, if you're involved in anybody's murder, I will nail your ass to the wall. Best to not make remarks like that."

He snorted at that. "You would have to catch me first."

And just something in his tone had her studying him carefully.

He glared at her. "No, I haven't fucking killed anyone, but my life was ruined because of somebody who killed my family."

She nodded. "What about Darrian?"

He looked at her in surprise. "Why are you asking me about Jet's former business partner? You've really done your homework, haven't you?"

"I'm asking the questions."

"Sure you are. You're digging for dirt, and there's no reason for it."

"Why is that?"

"Darrian's always been good to me."

"Is there any reason he shouldn't be?" she asked, eyeing him curiously.

He flushed. "No, he was always there after my parents were murdered. He did everything he could for me, and he's a good man."

"Is he helping you with your investments now?"

He nodded. "Yes, he handles quite a lot of it actually," he noted, his gaze narrowed. "He's ethical and honest."

She didn't say anything to that. "Do you know anything about the history between Darrian and your father?"

"Only that Darrian was Father's accountant, and then Darrian moved on to manage his own investments, and they became friends and business partners," Doug stated.

"So, Darrian and Jet used to work together and were business partners," Kate pointed out.

Doug sat up taller and growled. "If you're trying to dig up dirt on Darrian, you won't get any further answers from me."

"I'm not trying to dig up any dirt on anybody," she stated. "I want to make sense of what went wrong. From your remarks, I can see what you think of the police."

"The police couldn't solve the family murders," he snapped, glaring at her, "and I highly doubt you'll do anything about it either."

"It has been a while since those murders," she said, "and it's definitely much harder to get the information we need at this delayed point in time, but it is on my plate at the moment, and I will certainly do my best."

He sneered. "And you think you can do something about it when nobody else could?"

"I will do my best," she repeated. "Obviously that doesn't mean anything to you, and that's fine. I don't need your approval or your authorization."

He frowned at her, and she just ignored him. Doug continued. "I don't understand you people. What the hell would trigger any of this now? What has changed?"

"Obviously something has changed," she noted, facing him. "Are you aware that a body was found at the Feldspar house?"

He frowned at her. "A body?"

"Yes, a man was murdered, and his body was dumped there."

"Considering it's an abandoned building," Doug replied, "I highly doubt anybody gave a shit about the actual location, other than it was empty and probably convenient."

"Maybe, but the person murdered was somebody connected to Mr. Jet Mahoney."

"Rosemary's husband?" he asked.

"Yes."

Doug pondered that, as he stared out over her head. "That is interesting, but I still don't understand what any of it has to do with me. Are you asking these questions because I am a suspect in this recent death?"

"No, but, if you answer our questions, maybe we'll fill in some of the missing information and get some of this solved."

"I don't really care whether you solve anything or not," he declared, now slumping. "That part of my life was incredibly traumatic, and I have absolutely no wish to dredge it all back up."

"Even if it brings closure?" she asked.

"But will it?" he asked, glaring at her. "So far I'm just feeling the pain."

"So far, all you've done is fight me at every turn," she murmured. "A little cooperation might change how you feel about being a victim."

"I'm not a victim," he snapped, while she stared at him for a long moment. "I *was* a victim. I'm not anymore."

"If the murders still affect you to this extent," she pointed out, "then help me. Help me solve what happened back then, and maybe you can find some sense of closure and finally move on yourself."

"Meaning that you can't do it without my help." He sneered.

"That's an interesting judgment," she murmured. "If people have information on our cases and don't come forward with what they know, how do you expect the police to solve any crimes?"

"I don't know, and I don't care," he snapped. "You won't solve it either. I've heard so many cops tell me that, and it's ridiculous. *Oh, we'll get to it. We'll get it sorted, Doug,* and absolutely nothing happened. No one could ever tell me a damn thing about what happened or why."

She nodded. "I get that. For the fourteen-year-old boy who was in the family home at the time, it had to be incredibly traumatic."

"It was, and I believed the cops. More the fool, me."

"No, that's not it at all," she countered. "Everybody wants to believe there *is* an answer, but sometimes … it just takes a little longer to find."

He sneered at her again. "There's a *little longer*, and then there's impossibly long," he snapped. "I highly doubt that anything you could do will make a difference."

"What if I can?" she challenged. "Think about it. What if I can?"

He shrugged. "It doesn't matter anymore. My parents and grandmother are gone. My aunt is missing and presumed dead. Plus, my sister's brain dead, gone for all intents and purposes," he said, with a finger twirling around his ear, "and I'm still just as alone as I was back then."

"Is that why you're so close to Rosemary?"

He shrugged. "We both have plenty of reasons to feel as if the world has dumped on us."

"There was a big age difference between her and Mr. Mahoney, wasn't there?"

"Sure, there was, but she was also feeling a little on the lost side."

"And why is that?"

He stared at her and pursed his lips, then became calmer than she expected. "It's her story to tell. I'm not sharing anything about her business."

"That's fine. I'll be contacting her later today."

He stiffened at that and growled, "Leave her out of this."

She tilted her head, observing him and his anger. "Why? If she has information, even just a little bit, it can make a huge difference to a case. You don't always know when something might be important," she added, stressing her point, "and that's the problem. Too many people think they don't know anything important. Yet they do, and it's very important that I have this information for my investigation. I'm the one holding all the pieces, big and small. Until I can get enough pieces to start putting them together, we're stuck."

"Maybe *you're* stuck," Doug muttered, "but that's your problem, not mine."

"So you won't help?"

"No, I won't," he declared in a deadly tone, glaring at her, "and you better leave Rosemary alone."

"No can do. I'm conducting an investigation into several murders of your family members. It's my job to ask questions of her and you and any other related parties."

Doug looked over at his lawyer. "I want to leave now."

The lawyer turned to Kate, who just nodded. "That's fine, just don't leave town." Doug glared at her, and she shrugged. "Hey, for all I know, you murdered your parents in order to get the inheritance." Without warning, he lunged across the table at her, slamming her backward onto the ground. Both the lawyer and Rodney pulled Doug off Kate. She got up, dusted herself off, then looked over at the lawyer. "He's no longer leaving. Now I've got every right to hold him."

And, with that, she called for a guard, turned, and walked out. She got back to her desk and just sat here for a long moment, letting her breathing return to normal.

When Rodney joined her, concern was etched on his face, "Are you okay?"

"Yeah, I'm fine." She smiled. "He needs to be in court-ordered anger management classes. He's definitely a spitfire, isn't he?"

"Yeah. Jesus, if any of these murders were crimes of passion," Rodney noted, "I would definitely be looking at him. But I don't think any of them are, are they?"

"It's hard to say. He's also very easy to manipulate."

Rodney nodded. "Can't disagree with you on that one ... but it definitely brings up some interesting points, doesn't it?"

"It absolutely does." Kate stared down the hall, watching a uniformed cop transporting Doug to jail. Her phone rang just then.

"Now you've got him for forty-eight hours," Colby greeted her. "Make the most of it."

"Oh, I will. I'm heading out to visit the sister right now, then Jet's second wife." She had just disconnected, when her phone rang again. Dr. Smidge.

"We found the gloves."

Typical of him to not issue a greeting either. Then it hit her. "Seriously?"

"Yes, I sent a team back in the house to look for them. They were in Amie's bottom dresser drawer. Yes, they have blood on them and GSR. They also have his DNA inside."

"So it's suicide?"

"It's suicide. No insurance payout for her." He gave a

blunt laugh. "I'll send over the paperwork today. I wouldn't mind if you found evidence that points to her involvement with either of her first two husbands."

"I haven't given up on that yet. Waiting to hear back from Manila on the second husband. I also sent you the case file on her first husband. Any luck there with his suicide?"

"No. It was a bullet to the head, and he too wore gloves, and they were found on him. So that case was closed quickly as a suicide. Little more is in the file for me to go on."

"Then maybe Amie got no payout on that first suicide. Hence her attempt to interfere this time."

"I wouldn't doubt it. Hopefully Manila has answers for you."

EARLY THE NEXT morning found Simon on the steps of the Paragon building once again. He had a hot cup of coffee in his hand, and he sipped it. He turned and looked around, getting a feel for the neighborhood, for what would be good for it, what potentially could work really well for this property and this location. Of course hotels were always an option, but usually among the last options for him. He wasn't such a big proponent of tourists as much as he was about the residents who made Vancouver itself so special.

As he stood here, his phone rang, and he looked down to see it was Ariel, the nagging realtor. He shook his head.

Then she called out from beside him, "No point in not answering that."

"Now why is that, I wonder?" he asked, without turning around, hearing her advance on his position. "Why bother calling me if you're here anyway?"

She laughed. "Maybe I wanted to see if you would answer."

"I didn't, so what does that tell you?"

"It tells me that I can't trust you when you're not answering."

"It could just mean that I'm busy and don't want to be interrupted by a call," he noted, trying to hold back his irritation at the intrusion. "What are you doing here anyway?"

"I'm waiting for a client," she replied smugly.

"Good."

Her frown fell away. "You almost said that as if you believe it."

"I do. This building needs the right person."

"Oh, and you're not the right person now, is that it?" she asked in a half-mocking tone. When he just gave her a flat gaze, she frowned. "Fine, that wasn't exactly called for."

"Considering somebody has just been murdered in this building," Simon reminded Ariel, "surely a little more respect is in order."

She glared at him. "Oh, no you don't. You won't turn that all on me," she muttered. "I get that somebody was murdered, but that has nothing to do with me."

"If you say so." He watched as two businessmen approached. He nodded, as they frowned at him. He just waved them inside. "Don't mind me. I'm considering the property, but, out of respect for the person who was just murdered here," he added in a dry tone, "I'm waiting to get the go-ahead from the police."

At that, the men stopped, and he heard the realtor hiss. He looked back at her and asked, "You did phone the police, didn't you?"

Recovering her composure, she pointed. "All the tape is

gone now."

He quickly pulled out his phone and sent Kate a text. **Good morning. I love you.** When he got a heart emoji back, he smiled. Looking up from his phone, he announced, "You're clear to go." He stepped out of the way, then watched as the two men frowned at each other, then headed in. Ariel glared at him, and he stated in a clear tone, "You really don't want to start crossing the police on this."

Uncertain, she gave him an odd look, then quickly raced inside behind her clients.

He smiled in spite of himself. It was a little bit of a dirty trick, but, hey, if the prospective buyers didn't know that a murder had just happened here, he definitely didn't trust Ariel to fill out the paperwork to say that a body had been discovered on the premises, which should always be disclosed. Now at least, if they put in an offer, they would take that into account.

He laughed at that and decided to leave for now. Just as he turned to head out, he heard a voice calling to him. Simon figured he was the only one to hear the spirit speak. He slowly turned, hoping he was the only one outside at the moment, and, sure enough, that same white shimmering vision appeared in front of him yet again. He shifted so he could look at it with his peripheral vision, hoping it would be clearer and a little stronger. Instead it was still just more of the same hazy illusion. He also figured he was the only one to *see* the spirit too.

He frowned and replied softly, "Yes, I'm here." Nothing came for a long moment.

Then that voice once again said, "Feldspar."

"I get it. Feldspar is a big part of this." Then he stopped and asked in a shaken tone, "Did you have something to do with the Feldspar murders?" Horror slammed into him, making him wonder why it had never occurred to him before. Yet a case could be made for it. Still he didn't know, and he highly doubted that Kate had considered such a thing. He waited, hoping the spirit would say something more, but again nothing came.

Deciding that the rest of his day's activities could wait, Simon shared, "Fine, I'll head to the Feldspar house." He hesitated and then added in an uncertain tone, "However, you're connected to this place, aren't you?"

He wasn't so sure what was going on, but it was obvious he needed to go. Instead of taking a cab to the Feldspar house and back again, he made his way back to his apartment, picked up his wheels, and drove across town to the Feldspar property. He got there, then realized he needed to ask Kate if he could go in. He hesitated, sitting in his vehicle, then called Kate.

"What's the matter?" she asked, which meant she was caught up in something else.

"I'm at the Feldspar house."

"Why the hell is that?" she asked.

"Can I go in?" He sensed her shock, then pondered her question.

"Why are you even there? Maybe you should tell me that first."

"Because I was back at the Paragon just a bit ago, and I swear Shawn told me once again about Feldspar house."

"*Hmm.* That's interesting. I just released Doug Feldspar, who attacked me yesterday," she muttered. "He's out on bail and promised to behave."

"And what difference does that make as to whether I go into the property or not?" he asked, genuinely curious.

"I wouldn't be at all surprised if Doug heads over there."

Simon frowned at that.

"I'll head over there myself," she stated, and Simon heard her moving about. "Can you wait twenty minutes?" she asked him.

"Absolutely. I'll pick up a coffee and come back."

"You do that, but grab me one too." And, with a laugh, she disconnected.

He sat here and waited, not bothering to leave to pick up coffee because, out of the corner of his eye, he saw several ghostly figures moving through the place. The sight unnerved him, and he felt sick.

He shook his head. "Gran, you never once warned me about this," he muttered out loud, as he looked again, their shimmering forms lit up the place.

"Are these spirits of the Feldspar family members who had been murdered, or is this something else entirely?" He had to wonder, but he didn't know. If these were the ghosts of the dead Feldspar family, then who were the ghosts at the Paragon building, besides Shawn now? Was there even a connection? Didn't ghosts haunt a particular place, not two different ones? For all Simon's gifts, they sure brought on more unanswered questions. Plus, ghosts had no timeframe. They could have been in that particular location for well over a century in which case there would be no answers. Not only that, but Simon was starting to get a really weird feeling about the whole thing, and none of it was any good.

CHAPTER 23

KATE CROWED AS she read the email that just came in from Manila. Now that was news. Kate got up from her desk to find Rodney standing right in front of her. She stepped back, and he was all over her.

"Why did you release Doug?"

"I want to see what he does," she replied, "and this is not the time to discuss it. Call Amie in for an interview for tomorrow, will you? Looks as if we have something to discuss. But I can't do it today. I'm heading up to the Feldspar property."

"Why?" Rodney asked, his eyebrows shooting up. "I'll come with you."

"Don't need to," she murmured. "Simon is apparently already there."

"Ah, in that case, at least you won't be walking into a bombing or whatever. Did he ever figure out any more to explain his initial warning?"

"No, not yet," she replied, "but he's asked to go into the house now, so it must be safe enough."

Rodney nodded. "You be careful."

"I will." She smiled. "I'm not sure what's going on, but it does feel as if maybe I'm getting somewhere. I just have no idea where that is, though."

"If you're stirring up a lot of ghosts, people won't be

happy. Somebody's gotten away with murder for a very long time, and they won't take kindly to that changing now."

"I know," she murmured, "yet, just because they got away with it for all this time, doesn't mean they will again and again." And, with that, she dashed out to her car. As she got in and turned on the engine, she got a text. It was Rodney again.

Please just be careful.

She sent back a quick message. **I will.**

As she drove up to the house in question, she wondered about so many things in play here, but absolutely nothing would break apart unless people started talking. Yet quite likely the Feldspars had their own secrets for a long time, and, when there were secrets, people tended to keep those to themselves.

But she had to wonder about Doug. He was such an angry man, as in angry like the whole world was out to get him. She wondered where all that came from. Obviously he had had a tough time with the violent loss of his parents and his grandmother, his missing aunt, and even his sister had been taken from him, with her serious brain injury. Kate certainly understood the pain, the trauma, and the tremendous adjustments Doug had to make after that loss. However, he was still so incredibly angry all these years later.

She pondered that, as she pulled up in front of the abandoned home and parked beside Simon's car. Normally it was unusual to see him out in his vehicle, as he generally preferred to walk around town on his own if he could. Yet this was an unusual circumstance, she was sure.

As she walked up to the front door, she still saw no sign of him. She'd asked him to wait, and it was unusual for him to not pay attention to that. As she stood here studying the exterior, wondering where he was, she heard a voice behind her. She turned, and Simon approached her, with a cup of coffee in each hand.

She smiled, reached out to take a cup, and muttered, "I was afraid you'd gone in."

"No, you told me to wait, so I was just walking the neighborhood. Outside of this property, it's a pretty incredible place."

"Yeah, so you want to buy this one too?" she asked in a joking manner.

"Possibly, although I don't know what I would do with it," he admitted, "and it's not in my preferred location."

"It might not be your location," she noted, "but I highly doubt that would stop you from turning a profit."

He gave her a curious look. "And yet turning a profit isn't particularly of interest to me."

She smiled and nodded. "I know that, but I doubt too many others do."

"I don't really care about everybody else," he said, with a wave of his hand. "As long as the people in my world know, then it's fine by me."

She nodded and walked into the house. "Have you seen anybody around here since you drove in?"

"Should I?"

"I half expect Doug Feldspar to show up here." He stopped and frowned at her. She nodded. "Not that I'm setting you up or anything."

"Are you sure about that?" he asked, with a wry look on his face. "Because telling me that now makes me feel that way."

"No, not at all," she replied. "I told you that on the phone already—but you were distracted, I guess."

Simon admitted, "As a matter of fact, I was distracted."

Kate added, "It is a bit of a concern in the sense that he's looking for information himself. He's not had an easy time of it, and I think he's just as cracked up and upset over it all as anybody."

"Of course," Simon agreed. "He did have his entire family murdered."

"Not quite all," she clarified, with a headshake.

"Weren't you supposed to go check on the sister yesterday?"

"I was, and then I got called away on something else, so I'll fit that in later today."

"Or maybe you don't need to go there."

"Yeah, I do," she confirmed, as she faced him. "Even if it's just to confirm that she can offer nothing for information."

"Ah, I guess it's all about getting that final bit of info, isn't it?"

"You never know what you don't know until it appears," she shared, with a smile. Inside the building she stopped and looked around. "This would have been quite an incredible building in its day too," she murmured.

"Yeah, it sure would, but it doesn't have the same feel to it as the Paragon."

"What feeling is that?"

"Cozy. Elegance, warmth," he replied. "Yet here?" He shuddered at something inwardly. "It feels cold, as if it was a possession, a status symbol," he explained, as he wandered around the place. "It doesn't feel as if it was somebody's heart and soul."

"And yet the Paragon does?"

"Yes," he declared, "I can even remember the feel of it.

People in that building absolutely thrived and loved being there, loved that part of their lives and everything about it."

She just frowned at him and then shrugged. "If you say so."

"I do." He laughed.

"Why are you here now?" she murmured, studying his face as he wandered the house. "I mean, yes, the crime scene has been released, and, yes, I'm here with you, but did you have a specific reason today?"

"Only Shawn," he replied.

"Only Shawn, *huh*? This place has been vandalized, has been broken into multiple times, and the family has pretty-well taken what they wanted out of it," Kate reported. "And it's just been left to rot for the rest of the time. I highly doubt anything could be found here, except for a place to stay overnight."

"For the humans maybe. I saw some ghosts in here while I was waiting for you."

Kate raised her eyebrows, not surprised though to hear Simon say that.

Simon added, "I needed to come anyway."

She could respect that, though she didn't understand it. But she didn't have to understand everything in Simon's life in order to know that his gift worked. She just followed Simon's lead as he walked around the property. When she heard a noise outside, she looked out one of the windows, and, sure enough, there was Doug. She smiled. "Exactly what I thought he would do," she murmured.

"And yet you wanted him to, didn't you?"

"Yeah, the only way you'll get answers in a cold case like this," she murmured in a low tone, "is to get people upset and make them say things and think things that they hadn't thought before, you know? To make them reconsider life from a different viewpoint." When Simon studied her curiously, she shrugged. "I'm no shrink," she muttered, "but Doug Feldspar has some serious issues to sort out."

"I don't know that you're *not* a shrink," Simon pointed out, "because, damn it, you come up with things that make me stop and wonder."

She laughed. "Not really. It's just a simple case of understanding humanity and what humanity needs out there."

She walked to the entrance to meet Doug. When she opened the door to him, he immediately glared and snapped at her.

"What are you doing here?"

"I'm here on police business," she stated, "and I could ask you the same. What are you doing here?"

"This is my home."

She cocked her head to the side. "Yet it's currently registered to a holding company."

"Which is mine."

"It's a numbered account," she added, staring at him.

"Yeah, that's mine too."

"Yours and Darrian Jackson's?"

"Yes." Doug glared at her, almost getting in her face. "After all this, I think I want to sell the place. … It won't increase in value, and it won't offer any solutions to anything, so I might as well just move it on." He stared gloomily around the front hall and muttered, "Darrian's been good for me, helping me to handle everything."

She nodded. "I don't suppose he's the beneficiary, is he?"

He frowned at her. "Don't even start talking shit about him. You don't know anything."

She smiled cheerfully. "If he is, maybe you should think

about changing that."

He shook his head. "See? You're just trying to cause trouble." Then he gave a menacing laugh. "All you cops are fucking insane."

"I'm just giving you a warning about life and con artists."

"This isn't about *life*," he clarified. "I never lived a life as it was. You're just starting trouble."

She shrugged. "It's the cop in me."

"Yeah, that's all you do. You start trouble and hope that people react in a way that gives you something."

"Wouldn't that be nice," she said, with a smile.

Just then his gaze widened, almost in horror, as he looked behind her.

She didn't need to turn around to imagine he had seen one of the ghosts Simon noted were in this house. She was surprised that Doug could see them, when she had not seen them. Frowning, she asked Doug, "Are you okay?"

"What the hell is that thing?" he cried out.

She turned but didn't see anything. "What thing?" she asked cautiously. He pointed, but she shrugged. "Look. I don't know what you're seeing, but I'm not seeing anything."

He turned to her, looked back at the room behind her, then calmed down somewhat. "I don't know what I saw there for a moment," he muttered.

"Could be ghosts," she replied. "Shawn, who was found dead here, was very much of the opinion that this place was haunted."

"Shawn was homeless," Doug stated, "and, anybody with half a brain wouldn't be homeless, so you can't believe him."

She sighed. "Yet you seem to have seen a ghost. Regardless, maybe if you had gone through the military trauma Shawn experienced, you would understand," she shared calmly. "I would have thought that being through trauma yourself, you, of all people, would understand."

He stared at her for a moment. "I don't give a fuck," he snapped and turned to leave.

She asked him, "Were you this angry before you lost your family?"

He turned and glared at her, then shook his head. "No, of course not. Their murders are what's made me so angry."

"Maybe." She studied him intently. "But you have an awful lot of anger, especially after all this time."

"Oh sorry," he bellowed, "sorry if I didn't get over it as fast as you think I should have." He sneered at her. "But that's so typical of a cop, isn't it? You know it all and expect everybody else to listen to your BS."

"Seems as if you're spouting your own BS."

He glowered at her, as he backed up. "You don't know what the hell you're saying. This is private property, and you need to get the hell out of here."

"It's part of an official police investigation into a current murder," she reminded him. "So I'm not leaving until I'm done. In fact, I could kick you out for disturbing my crime scene. However, if you've got a legitimate reason to be here yourself, that's fine. You can stand around and watch me, while I go through everything in this house, looking for clues."

"Clues to what?" He shook his head. "My parents were murdered a decade ago. So no way anything is left around now."

"Yet there absolutely is," she countered, looking at him.

"I guess you don't really understand forensics, do you?" And, with that, she gave him a superior look, then turned and headed deeper into the house.

He followed her cautiously, looking around uneasily.

"You're really spooked by ghosts, *huh?*" she asked him.

"If there's such a thing as ghosts," he replied, "which I'm sure as hell not saying there is. However, the only ghosts that I figure are here would be my family. Yet I can't say that makes me feel any better."

"There's always Shawn," she noted. "What about his ghost? His body was dumped here at least."

"So what? That doesn't mean jack shit."

"No, it sure doesn't. I'm glad to see you understand that much about the system."

He stared at her. "You're not like other cops."

She shrugged. "I'll take that as a compliment."

"It's *not* a compliment," he snapped, that same tic in his jaw active again. "Jesus, you don't even know when you're being insulted."

She laughed. "That could be true. I'm only interested in the facts. So, if you've got something to say, why don't you just come out with it?"

"I don't like you in my house," he snapped.

"I don't think you like being in this house either, so I'm not sure what difference it makes."

He frowned at her and asked, "What do you mean?"

"It gives you the heebie-jeebies to even be here. Just the thought of ghosts around this place is setting you off. That's what you were thinking, and that's what you were seeing earlier."

"You don't know anything," he snapped.

She shrugged. "For all I know you actually saw something from way back when."

He stared at her in shock. "What?"

"You heard me," she said, staring at him. "Don't act as if you didn't." With that, he started to visibly shake. She nodded. "See?"

"You can't know that," he said. "You can't."

"You might be surprised at what I know," she declared, ruthlessly digging into Doug's phobias. "The only way to free yourself from all that is to talk to me."

"No, no, no," he argued, backing up. "Talking to you is not smart. I know what cops do. They twist words around and make it so that you don't know what end is up."

"If you're telling the truth, what difference could it make?"

"The thing is … the truth isn't always the truth."

She sighed loudly, staring at him. "That's a very interesting statement. Are you sure you don't want to tell me about the night your family died?"

"There's nothing to say." He shook his head. "I was in my room. I came down and found blood everywhere." He shuddered again, this time as if to shake something off. "That's what happened. And, ever since then, I keep waiting for you guys to solve this, and you never do."

She frowned at him for a long moment. Something about his short summary didn't ring true. "Where was your sister?"

"Upstairs in her room too."

"Did she go downstairs with you?"

"No, she didn't."

"So, when did she get the brain injury?"

He glared at her and then shrugged. "I don't remember how or what, but she got shot. I think during the robbery."

"But you said she was up in her room."

"Yeah, she was, but I don't know when she went downstairs," he shared. "It's been one of the mysteries."

"What if she wasn't up there in her room at all? What if she was downstairs the whole time?"

"I don't know," he cried out. "You think I haven't thought about that a time or two?" He shook his head. "Do you think I've just been sitting here, doing nothing the whole time? You people think you're so smart and think it's all about you, and that's bullshit too."

"I'm glad to hear that you're still considering what happened to your family, to your sister," she replied, giving him a little bit of space. "It can't be easy to have horrific memories that don't fade."

"No, it isn't, and you start thinking that maybe you didn't understand what happened at all."

"Your sister is older than you, isn't she?"

"Yeah, she is."

"How was her relationship with your parents?"

He hesitated, then shrugged. "Difficult."

"Any idea why?"

"Yeah, but we can't talk to her about it, and I don't know for sure, so I don't want to say anything."

"What don't you know for sure?"

He went silent for a moment, then he spoke again. "I think she was being abused."

"What?"

"I think my father was abusing her, but I don't know that for sure," he snapped.

"You heard her say something about it or what? You heard somebody say something?"

"Darrian mentioned it," Doug replied, as he seemed to

be pulling on some memory for that.

"Did Darrian come over that night?"

"Yeah, I called him, and he came over right away."

"Before the cops?" she asked, her eyes widening at the thought.

He glared at her. "Yeah, *before* the cops."

His answer confirmed the fear that she felt in the pit of her stomach. She let out her breath. "Did you consider that maybe that wasn't the best thing to do?"

"No, I didn't," he declared. "I just reacted. I needed a friend. I needed somebody to come help. Darrian came and he helped."

She nodded. "Of course he did."

"Look. He's not a bad guy in any way, and he's not guilty of any damn crime. I just needed somebody to help."

She didn't say anything because Doug's version of Darrian compared to Daisy's version was something completely different. "How much do you deal with him now?"

"He handles all the family trust investments, so I don't have to deal with anything."

Kate felt less and less comfortable with each passing second.

"Mostly I just roam around the world, pissed off," he shared, glaring at her.

"You might want to work on that."

"It would be nice if you actually worked on giving me some closure then."

"I am," she stated. "Not everybody in this world is out to get you, you know?"

"Sure seems like it," he barked, as he glanced around this house. "Look at this place. … Look what happened to my world."

She nodded. "I get that, yet other people have experienced pretty traumatic events in their lives too."

"Oh, *right*," he muttered, "so I'm supposed to feel better because other people have it shittier?"

"No, not at all. You're supposed to take heart that there can be life, even after this," she suggested. He stiffened and then relaxed, and she realized that was probably Simon's influence coming through. She turned, looked at him, then nodded her silent thanks.

Simon walked out the front door and headed out into the yard.

"What the hell is he doing here?" Doug asked in confusion.

"Just part of the whole murder mess that we have to deal with."

Doug shook his head. "Christ, I don't understand any of this."

"I don't either," she confirmed, with a shrug. "So, if I asked you to show me some of the paperwork you have from Darrian, would you?"

"Sure, it's not as if I ever open that shit."

"How come?" she asked, curious.

"Because I don't understand any of it," he admitted. "It's pretty technical stuff."

"Good. I really want to see it then."

He glared at her. "You're just trying to cause trouble for Darrian."

"I want to confirm that everything's on the up-and-up for you and your sister. I'll also go see your sister. I wanted to do that yesterday but couldn't make it. I'm heading there this afternoon."

"If you *say* so, but it won't do you any good."

"Why is that?"

"Because she can't talk anymore. She can't do anything anymore, and, if my father was responsible for that, I wish I would have killed him myself."

She contemplated that for a long moment. "What if … and just bear with me please. What if your sister went down and shot your family?" He stared at her in shock. "Don't tell me that you haven't contemplated such an option."

"Not for any length of time, no," he declared. "That's not who Alison was."

"Unless she *was* being abused, in which case there's always a breaking point."

He nodded. "I did consider it, but she wouldn't have killed my mother or my grandmother. No way. They were close."

Kate nodded. "I noticed there's no security camera footage from inside or outside for that entire time the murders occurred."

"No, the burglars took the tapes with them."

She nodded at that too. "Very convenient."

He shrugged. "I assumed that's what burglars do."

"They probably do."

He stared at her. "You sure say some weird shit."

She snorted. "I'll come to your place after I'm done here and get the paperwork."

"I can email it to you." He pulled out his phone, clicked on a few things, asked for her email address, and then looked up at her. "There, that's some of the latest documents."

"Good enough. Thanks." She smiled at him.

He shook his head. "I don't understand."

"I know. If I find anything, I'll let you know."

He looked a little relieved at that but added, "You won't

find anything."

"Good. Where was your bedroom in this house?"

He stared at her and then shook his head. "The front bedroom on the second floor."

She looked up, frowning. "So, if you had burglars, you didn't hear any activity on the first floor?"

He shook his head. "No, honest to God, I didn't hear anything. I had my headset on. I was playing video games."

"Okay, I can see that, and then what did you do?"

"I came racing downstairs and saw the carnage."

"Why did you race downstairs? What was the trigger? Can you remember that?"

He pondered that for a moment. "I took off my headset, and I called out to my mom. I thought I heard somebody downstairs, but my parents weren't supposed to be here. They were out for the evening. It was pretty early for them to return. So I called out, and, when no answer came, I bolted downstairs."

"Yet, from the time you called out to not hearing anything and coming downstairs, did you hear anybody run away?" Kate asked.

He shook his head. "No, I didn't."

"So, you didn't hear shots fired? You didn't hear anything?"

"No, I didn't," he repeated in frustration.

She envisioned that scenario from his perspective. "That's just made your life that much harder, hasn't it?"

"How would you feel?" he snapped. "I mean, you're here at the time, and you don't even know. You just come downstairs and *boom*. ... They're dead."

"Your sister, where was she?"

He walked toward the living room and stood on a spot

in the hallway. "She was right here … at the bottom of the stairs."

"Interesting. And she was bleeding from the head wound?"

"Yes. It was gross."

She took a deep breath and nodded. "I don't suppose you took any pictures, did you?"

"You've got the crime scene photos," he said, looking up at her in astonishment.

Something rose inside her. Again that same pull was building up to this point. "You did take some, didn't you?"

He flushed. "Yeah, Darrian had already talked about how the police couldn't be trusted and how there would likely be all kinds of cover-ups, making my dad look like he was some sort of a cheat," Doug snapped. "And, sure enough, that's what lots of people were doing. Trying to say that he was in these bad deals, and that's exactly what ended up happening."

"I want your pictures," she stated calmly.

"What will you do with them?" He frowned at her.

"Compare them to the crime scene photos."

He stared at her in shock. "Seriously?"

"Yes, seriously," she repeated, "and, if anything's been doctored or changed, then I can tell. I really need to see those photos."

He shrugged. "Whatever." He pulled out his phone. "I only took a couple."

He quickly forwarded them to her, and she nodded. "Good enough. Now I can bring up the crime scene photos back at the office and compare them."

"But even if something has been retouched," Doug noted, "how will you know if it was me, the cops, the coroner, or Darrian for that matter?"

"I won't, but it'll be a place to start."

And, with that, his shoulders sagged. "Yeah, okay. Thanks. … Look. I am sorry for being a jerk. Please just solve this." And, with that, he turned and raced to his car.

She could almost see his shoulders relaxing for the first time, and she realized how deeply he was still affected by all this one decade later.

For a moment there, she wondered if an angry fourteen-year-old would have been angry enough to have wiped out his family, and it certainly happens. It's definitely happened in the past, and she didn't want it to be the case here. Now, for the first time, she realized it probably wasn't him.

SIMON WAITED FOR Kate to find him, and it didn't take long after the young man left. He looked over at her, smiled, and asked, "Was that Doug?"

"Yeah."

"He didn't seem ready to punch you this time."

"No, I think being here made him more of an emotional wreck than anything."

"Did it help at all?"

"Maybe," she murmured. "He apparently took a couple photos of the crime scene from back then. So, we will see where that goes."

He slowly nodded. "I can't say I'm terribly surprised, although I would be surprised that it was on his phone. Wouldn't the cops have checked?"

"They might have but may not have realized that it meant anything," she said, with a nod. "Doug was quite a mess at the time, and they may not have taken his phone. He was just a kid and may not have looked as if he would be a decent suspect or witness. In a crazy highly charged scene like that, the cops do the best they can and hope they covered all the angles. But Doug did send me the photos, so, when I get back to the office, I'll take a look. I also need to stop in at the facility where his sister is. Plus, I need to sort out a few other things, like this Darrian guy."

Simon stared at her, clearly surprised. "Darrian? Darrian Jackson?"

"Yes, why?"

"You want to stay away from that guy."

She stiffened. "What do you mean?"

"He's a crook, very slimy. He deals in offshore accounts, funneling money outside the country, tax evasion, and, if you want somebody to give you a hand in doing something shady, he's the guy to do it. If there's ever a chance of somebody getting in trouble, you can bet it won't be him."

"Yeah, now that's a problem. The accounting firm in Paragon had Darrian Jackson as a partner, before he got too slimy. Then Darrian was a friend and maybe a partner of the Feldspar family. Doug back then was a fourteen-year-old kid who called Darrian before he called the police."

Simon whistled at that. "Jesus, really?"

"Yeah, which is part of my concern right now. I have the crime scene photos that Doug just sent me, but who's to say that Darrian himself or this kid didn't do something to change the crime scene?"

"I wouldn't trust them at all," Simon stated.

"I also got Doug to send me some of his financial information, since this Darrian character has been handling the family trust for him."

"Do you have somebody to go over it?"

"I hope so. I'm not stupid, but this stuff isn't really my forte."

Simon suggested, "If you want, I can take a quick look whenever."

"Maybe," she murmured.

"Are we done here?" he asked.

She turned to him and asked, "Did you find out whatever you needed to find out?"

He shrugged. "I'm not really seeing anything, which is kind of a problem because it did feel as if I needed to be here. I did see what I thought were at least two ghosts earlier, but I am not sure I really saw that either."

"While I was talking to Doug, he saw something behind me that shook him, and he's quite worried about ghosts."

"Of course he is," Simon noted. "Think about it. You've got a traumatized kid with all kinds of memories from here, all kinds of shit coming down. If you have anything to do with it or if you're in any way attached, any ghosts could easily be his family members."

"Did you see any family members?" she challenged.

He smiled. "Definitely some shit is going on here."

"When you take a moment, I already know you're holding something back." She paused herself then added, "Did you find anything useful?"

"No."

But you could have.

He turned and looked at her, puzzled. "How could I have?"

"I didn't say anything."

He stared at her for a moment. "You didn't say, *But I could have?*"

"No, I didn't." She frowned at him. "What are you hearing?"

He slowly turned and looked around the house. "Somebody said, *But you could have*, which means I need to take another look."

And, with that, he headed back into the house, determined once and for all that he would figure out what the hell was pissing him off here. He walked through the house, using his senses more than anything. When he got to the rear kitchen and stepped into the massive backyard, he kept on walking and walking and walking. When he got to one spot, he turned and looked back at her, yet stood here for a long minute.

"Simon?" she called out, and he just remained there. Taking a deep breath, she walked up to him.

"I know this is a big ask," he began, "but …"

She frowned at him, looking around, shaking her head. "Don't tell me a body is here."

He winced. "I can't tell you that. All I can tell you is that I'm being directed here."

It was a serene spot and had the potential of revealing something important, but no way could she get budget money allocated for this, and yet Simon wouldn't back down. "I would need a cadaver dog in order to even contemplate it," she explained, "and, besides, what's it got to do with this case?"

"I don't know," Simon snapped back in frustration. "All I can tell you is that it's got something to do with this property. Did anybody here go missing?"

"Doug's aunt."

Simon looked at the ground below his feet and then back at Kate. "Guess what?"

Kate shook her head, and then her shoulders slumped.

Simon nodded. "I think we found her."

CHAPTER 24

K ATE KNEW WHAT to expect from her request.

"There's no budget money for that," Colby declared, staring at Kate. "If we have a really good reason for bringing in the dogs, that's one thing, but you know how hard it'll be to convince anybody, especially when we're basing it on Simon's words alone."

She winced. "Nobody's found the Feldspar aunt's body. If the dogs find something, then it's a whole different ball game."

"What possible reason would there be to bury the aunt on the property, when three other dead bodies and a wounded sister were left inside the home?" Colby asked, trying to keep the snap out of his voice, though that wasn't working either.

"Convenience, as far as I can tell. That's about the only thing."

"That's a stretch, at best."

"The aunt went missing at the same time most of the family died, or maybe she was part of the murders and disappeared. I don't know," Kate admitted. "But, from what Simon and Doug told me today, the Feldspars have a fairly messed up family dynamic."

Colby waved his hand at that. "That applies to families all over the world. ... Let me see if I can get any support for this concept. In the meantime, dredge up something to back me up, so I have a tangible reason for this."

She nodded, then escaped quickly.

Lilliana asked Kate, as she returned to the bullpen, "Any luck?"

"Not really. He'll see if he can get a cadaver dog, but we don't have anything besides Simon's words, Simon's feelings."

"Yeah, that'll be a problem," Rodney added, as he walked into the room with some coffee. "Psychics being what they are."

"I know," Kate snapped. "So it's up to me to figure out if I have any reason why the aunt would be buried there."

"What have you got so far?" Rodney asked.

"Somebody didn't want her to survive, for one thing."

"Maybe," he conceded. "The question is, survive what and why?"

She sat down at her computer and opened her email, her attention immediately drawn to those that Doug had sent her. She stared at his crime scene pictures, then brought them up on the big screen and compared his set to the official crime scene photos.

Lilliana walked up beside Kate and asked, "What is this?"

"Doug Feldspar took these two pictures of the crime scene, while he waited for Darrian to show up and to help him out, which is something that just blows me away. More than that, Doug waited until Darrian showed up, and *then* they called the cops. Doug said he was so shocked that he didn't know what to do and that Darrian was a really good friend of the family, so he called him for help."

Lilliana shook her head. "That's all kind of dodgy in the

first place."

"Exactly. I know that, and you know that. Yet Doug swears that absolutely no way would Darrian be involved in anything negative."

"Do you believe that?"

"Not necessarily, especially if I consider Daisy's stories regarding Darrian. According to Daisy, her husband and Darrian were initially business partners, but Darrian was inclined to use more *creative* business practices that were marginal at best, and so their accounting partnership split up because of that. As a result, Mr. Mahoney used to refer clients who wanted that sort of shady service over to Darrian. So, they maintained an association the entire time, and Darrian is the one who handled certain accounting and income tax returns and eventually became a partner in multiple deals with Doug Feldspar, after he inherited all the investments of his parents, who were murdered in the Feldspar house."

"*Doug* inherited the Feldspar family trust?"

"I'm not sure what, if anything, the brain-damaged sister got out of it, other than maybe paying for her medical care and for her rent at the facility. Otherwise it seems Doug inherited it all. Yes."

"Does he still have the family trust?"

"It is currently owned by a holding company that supposedly Darrian Jackson set up for Doug."

"I've started looking at that," Reese joined in, coming from behind her. "The paperwork is legit, except for one thing. The only person listed as a beneficiary to that entire family trust is Darrian Jackson."

Kate nodded. "I did warn Doug today that he should look into this, in case anything happened to him, and he got quite angry at me," she shared, with an eye roll. "I mean, it's just good business sense, but coming from a cop was apparently insulting. Doug also sent me the latest statements he had received from Darrian on his holdings."

"If you give them to me," Reese suggested, "I can check into the history on the company registration and that sort of thing."

Kate immediately forwarded the emails to Reese, then asked her team in general, "What is our current situation with anybody who can analyze these things and make sense of them?"

Lilliana replied, "Forensic accounting, but I've heard they're pretty backed up at the moment."

Kate shared, "Simon offered to take a look at them, but I wasn't exactly sure that would be seen as legit."

"Probably not," Lilliana guessed, "unless you can get it cleared." When she nodded toward Colby's office, Kate winced.

"Maybe I'll check out the forensic accounting situation first." She quickly picked up the phone and explained her issue.

The tech replied, "I can't do a full-blown analysis, but, if you just want a quick overview to get a sense of things, I can take a look. Probably nothing's irregular, but it could certainly happen."

"It's related to the Feldspar murders from a decade ago, brought up after we've had two homeless guys murdered recently, and now may have found the potential dead body of the Feldspar aunt."

"Send it over," the tech guy replied, sounding much more intrigued. "Who knows what we'll find."

With that she sent over the financial records and sat

back down to look at the crime scene images she was trying to compare. Just as she sipped her coffee, her gaze caught on one thing. She leaned forward and then looked back and forth from one set of photos to the other, then announced to the room in general, "Can somebody come here and confirm what I may or may not be seeing?"

Lilliana walked over briskly and asked, "What's up?"

"Look. Do you see anything irregular … here and here?"

Lilliana looked at it for a moment, then frowned. "This one shows the feet of a second body, and this one taken from a slightly different angle *doesn't*."

"And yet," Kate asked, "how much of a difference in angle is there?"

"What are you saying?"

"We should have three dead bodies, the parents and the grandmother."

At that, Rodney came over and took a look. "Yeah, I get what you're saying." He peered closer at the pictures. "Here we've got the feet of another body, and over here … we don't."

She nodded as she switched out the photos. "So, now considering that this is the other body …"

"Shit … and that's a different room," Lilliana pointed out.

"Exactly, but we have the feet of another body in this room, so how does any of that play out?"

"Are you suggesting there's a fourth dead body?"

"Clearly something isn't adding up." They were still standing here, huddled together, studying the big screen, when Colby came out of his office and came closer. "What's the matter?"

Kate pointed at the screen. "We may have a fourth dead

body in this crime scene."

"Or it could have been the sister presumably on the floor, not dead but injured by a gunshot," he pointed out. "So that could be the sister's shoes."

"Maybe," Kate said in a noncommittal voice.

"What possible reason could there be for hiding the sister's photo, if she didn't die?" Lilliana asked.

"I don't know," Kate muttered. "I really don't know at the moment. I'm just saying that something is off, and there are no more photos to explain this."

Colby nodded. "Apparently you or Simon have friends in high places. I got an okay for a cadaver dog. But just one, and use it covertly please."

She couldn't believe her luck, then nodded and made the phone call. "As soon as you can would be great, and, given the notoriety of the original case, we don't want to start some media shit show. Therefore, do this very discreetly." She disconnected, then announced, "I'm heading over there now."

"They're going now?" Lilliana asked.

"Yep," Kate confirmed, with delight in her gaze. "The sooner we sort this out, the better."

Colby still stood in front of the pictures, frowning. "Why the hell didn't the kid turn these over way back when?"

Kate had no good idea herself. "He was fourteen, a mess at the time, and maybe the cops back then didn't particularly worry that he might have taken pictures, not the way we do now."

"Better go ahead and talk to whoever was assigned to the case," Colby noted.

"We can't," Reese replied, from across the room. "He

and his partner are both deceased."

At that, Colby stiffened, then turned to her. "That was Foster and Brooks, wasn't it?" Everybody was looking at him for more details. "They were killed in a car accident, out of the blue. We very suddenly lost two men."

"Jesus, Sergeant," Kate muttered, looking through the related case file that Reese had just handed to her. "They were assigned to this case, and, although things have been looked at since, a lot of it more or less died with them."

Colby stared at Kate. "You're not thinking what I think you're thinking."

"Oh, I probably am. I just don't have evidence yet that people were killed when they knew too much, either the two detectives back then or the two homeless guys this week. Or worse, that two detectives were involved in the initial cover-up." She turned her attention back to the crime scene photos. "If that's not the injured sister on the floor, it could be the missing aunt."

"And yet why hide *her* body? What possible reason would there be for secreting away just one of four dead bodies?"

"I don't know, not yet. However, this is not the sister with the brain injury because," she explained, as she clicked on the photos, "that's her there at the bottom of the stairs. So, by my thinking, this extra dead body could be the missing aunt, Albert Feldspar's sister."

Rodney tried to wrap his head around what Kate had just shared.

Kate explained, "The file is confusing, and the media reports have been confusing, and the information from people I've interviewed is also confusing and does not add up. We have Doug and Darrian messing with the crime scene. Then add to the mix that the two detectives with the most firsthand intel on the case wound up dead, and it's even more confusing." As far as she was concerned, this investigation had gotten even broader.

"Hells bells," Rodney muttered, "maybe this was all a smokescreen, right from the start."

Kate nodded. "I'm heading up to the Feldspar house now to meet with the cadaver dog team."

"I'm coming with you," Rodney declared.

When Kate started to protest, Colby spoke to her sternly. "No," he stated with finality. "From now on you guys travel in pairs on this. I don't know for sure what happened to Foster and Brooks, but I can tell you that I knew both of them, and they were … Let me just say that rumor had it that internal affairs was looking at them."

"Ah, shit. What for?" Kate asked.

"Bribes," Colby muttered.

"So maybe that accident wasn't so accidental," she mumbled, turning to look at the crime scene pictures. "All the more reason to sort this out."

Sergeant Colby nodded. "So, bring back some proof, and then we'll have something to go on."

"Yeah," Kate agreed. "So far, whoever has been cleaning this up is doing one hell of a job." And, with that, she turned and left.

SIMON PICKED UP a coffee and sat outside his favorite coffee shop. He looked around, wondering at such a world where his instincts, or whatever he should call it, were telling him where a body was buried. It was not exactly what his grandmother had told him would happen, but she had warned him that just when he thought he understood what his gifts were and what he was capable of doing with them, they would change, and he wouldn't know anything at all.

When he got a text from Kate, saying the cadaver dog was on, he winced because that was money, that was people working to see if Simon was right. As much as he wanted to be correct, that also meant some poor soul had been secretly buried in the ground, and he didn't want to be correct about that at all.

Just then his doorman, Harry, walked over, grabbed a coffee, and greeted him. "Man, you cover a lot of ground," he teased.

"I know." Simon raised a hand.

"Any news on that Feldspar thing?"

"Maybe. Do you know very much about the family?"

"*Nah*, just that part about the sister being in a home."

"What kind of condition is she in?"

"Not great. I don't know if she's even verbal, you know? She's been through a lot."

"Any idea just what all happened to her?" Simon asked.

"No, I sure don't, but Kate should be able to tell you that."

"Yeah, she could, but I don't really want to push it."

"I get it," Harry said, "but, hey, my cousin's full of gossip, so let's talk to her some more." He pulled out his phone, called her, and asked, "That patient I was asking you about the other day? What kind of condition is she actually in? I know you mentioned full care, but what exactly does that mean?" Harry frowned as he listened to his cousin Reenie. He put the call on Speakerphone, turning down the volume, glad they were outside and away from other patrons.

His cousin replied, "She's basically a vegetable. She gets

full care, feeding tubes, the whole works."

"She hasn't woken up?" Harry asked.

"No, I don't think she *can* wake up at this point. Though I could be wrong, I guess."

"But she's not been kept in a drugged state or anything like that?" Harry asked.

"I don't think so, but it's one of those ritzy private sanitariums. If people wanted to keep her out and away from life, that would be one way to do it."

"Which would be pretty disgusting," Harry muttered.

"Yes, but it happens," she confirmed. "I heard about a case not too long ago."

"I know. I heard about that one also," Harry noted, knowing perfectly well that Kate had been involved in that case too. "Have you ever thought that something like that might be going on with her?"

Harry's cousin said, "I wouldn't want to lose my job over this."

Reenie didn't realize that Simon was listening in, but she had his attention.

She added, "It's a pretty decent job."

Harry asked, "How would you feel about it being a decent job if you knew people were being kept against their will?"

"I have no reason to think that they are, but it would be pretty shitty if that was the case."

"Yeah, it would."

"Are you saying that's going on here?" she asked in alarm.

"I'm not saying anything," Harry clarified. "I'm just curious about the Feldspar sister's update."

"Well, if you think something like that's going on, you

should do something about it because she probably was a really nice little lady."

"Did you know who she was before, or can you talk to her now?" Harry asked.

"No, no … she can't talk. … I don't have any reason for even saying that. … Listen to me talking about her as if she's got a chance at waking up, but I don't know that she does."

"If so, it would be nice for her to get that opportunity," Harry noted.

"You're not kidding, but that's not my decision or even my business. I've got to go." And, with that, Reenie was gone.

Simon looked over at Harry and noted, "Interesting philosophy."

"So many people are that way today," Harry said. "They're almost untouched by everything going on around them, so focused on getting by in their own world that they can't see past it."

Simon nodded. "I think a lot of that is age-related too," he murmured. "The older you get, the more of life you have to deal with, so you realize how quickly it helps to change who you are."

Harry nodded. "Yeah, like some other tenants in the building, who have no respect for anybody else."

Simon smiled. "Of course not."

"Don't worry about me," Harry replied. "I just get frustrated with it every once in a while."

"I get it. Who wouldn't?"

They both laughed, but then Harry added, "I don't know about you, but I'm getting a really ugly feeling about that poor woman in that facility."

"I don't know if it's possible to even do anything for her

at this stage," Simon shared, "but I'm tempted to go over there and see if they are taking *new patients*."

"Oh, you should do that," Harry agreed, with a smile. "At least then maybe we'll get some answers. While you're doing that, I've got to go get ready for my shift," he muttered. "I can't just sit around chatting over coffee all day." And, with a laugh, he got up and left.

Simon smiled, hopped to his feet, and decided there was absolutely no point in waiting. He might as well go check out the facility. As he walked toward the high-rise a few blocks away, right where Harry had said it was, he heard that damn voice again, and this time it was much stronger.

Feldspar.

"I know," he muttered, "I found something at the Feldspar home, or maybe I found someone. Anyway Kate's gone to check it out. So give me a break, will you?" As he got up to the facility's address, he looked at the business directory found on the first floor and froze. Located on the twelfth floor of this building was a medical facility called Felden Spark House.

He let out his breath, took a picture of the directory, and sent it to Kate. Felden Spark and Feldspar were way too close for comfort. Stepping off the elevator on the twelfth floor, he walked into the reception area, where a woman looked up at him and smiled.

"May I help you?"

"Yes, I'm looking for a decent place for a family member."

Her smile grew compassionate, and she nodded. "Of course. You're lucky, as we do have one bed available."

He looked around and nodded serenely. "Can you show me?"

CHAPTER 25

KATE FROWNED AT the text, not able to leave right now anyway, as she sat on the steps of the deck in the backyard of the Feldspar house, watching as the handler took the cadaver dog and swept through the property. They'd come close to the area Simon had indicated, and the dog had tugged in the right direction, but the handler wouldn't let him go there yet, as they were doing a systematic grid system, which Kate didn't really understand. Why not just let the dog run directly to the spot and see if he reacted? Of course, it wasn't her dog or her area of expertise, so it really wasn't up to her to make that decision.

But, sure enough, as soon as the dog got closer again, he immediately sat down. The handler looked back at Kate and waved her over.

She got up and walked over to exactly where Simon had stood. "What does that mean?" she asked.

"A body is here," the handler confirmed.

"And we know that it's human?"

"This cadaver dog is only trained for human remains," he explained. "Even if pets are buried all over the yard, we only search for people."

And, with that, Kate picked up the phone and called Colby. It would likely take about an hour for forensics and a digging team to get here, but, once they had the area cordoned off, Kate would just sit back down and wait. Shortly they arrived and got set up and started digging. It didn't take too long before they found remains. She got up and walked closer but couldn't tell what she was looking at, except white bones. Smidge walked past her and glared, as had become a custom greeting for the two of them, and she glared right back.

"This better put an end to it," he grumbled.

"I sure hope so," Kate muttered, "because things are definitely breaking apart right now."

"Yeah, well, remember that you're pissing in somebody's backyard." Laughing at his own joke, he replied, "Quite literally, I might add."

She rolled her eyes at his attempt at humor. "Yeah, *backyard*, got it. Yet somebody won't be a happy camper about this, so keep an eye out."

"Are we in danger here?" he asked.

He had mentioned it so casually that she wasn't sure he even gave a damn if they were or not. "No clue," she said, showing her palms. "I'll be back in a little bit. Let me know what else you find." But he had already bent down to the work at hand. She got in her vehicle and headed straight to the Felden Spark House. As she got up to the proper floor, she looked at the photo on her phone, shook her head, and stepped inside.

A woman looked up and gave her a professional-looking smile.

Kate held up her badge and immediately the receptionist's smile fell away.

"May I help you?" She looked alarmed.

Kate nodded. "Yes, I'm looking for Alison Feldspar."

"She's one of our favorite patients here," she replied,

with a smile.

"May I see her?"

"Not without family permission," she noted in a quick and fast tone. "I'm sorry. We can't have strangers coming in off the streets."

"Even a stranger with a badge?" Kate asked caustically.

"Yes, even a stranger with a badge. Just a moment while I get the director."

Kate waited, and, moments later, an officious-looking man raced toward her.

"Yes, Detective. What can I do for you?"

"I want to see for myself that Alison Feldspar is here."

"Of course she is." He frowned. "Why wouldn't she be?"

"It's just a detail I need to verify," she replied, with a casual tone.

"She did go through a rather horrific experience."

"I know that, sir." Kate motioned at him. "Please take me to her."

He hesitated, and she just stood here and waited.

"I can't let you enter her room, but I can take you to the door, where you can look in through the window."

She nodded. "That's a start, but, if I need to get a court order, I will."

His face turned white with alarm. "What could possibly be the problem?" he asked, as he hurried down the hallway, with Kate in tow.

"Hopefully nothing. I understand that she had a very difficult head injury?"

"Yes, yes, she did," he confirmed, "and she won't recover from it."

"Ever?"

"No, not ever," he declared, with an overly sorrowful

tone.

Kate sighed. Given that he was dealing with the families of these patients all the time, she doubted that his sorrow could possibly be sincere. When they neared the room in question, he pointed out, "It's this next one up here."

As Kate reached the door, she stared in through the window but couldn't see anything. "I need to see her face," she stated, turning to look at the director. When he frowned, she added, "I won't say anything, and I won't touch her. I just need to look at her face." When he still hesitated, that did not sit well with her. "Or I can get that court order, and then I can come back in with a whole team, and we will see *all* the patients and *all* your records while we're at it."

"Whoa, whoa, I can assure you that won't be necessary," he replied hastily. "We aren't doing anything illegal here. We just take care of some of the most vulnerable members of society."

"That's why I'm here as well. Consider it a courtesy call. I'm trying to confirm that the vulnerable members of society are being taken care of."

Confused, he opened the door and stepped inside the private room with Kate. She walked toward the bed and stared down at the woman. "So, this is Alison Feldspar?"

"Yes, she's been here since almost the beginning of her injury," he replied, with a nod.

"Of course, and let me see. … Is somebody named Darrian Jackson a major contributor to your place?"

He looked at her in shock and then nodded slowly. "I really don't like what you're implying."

"I'm not implying anything yet," she stated, as she continued to stare down at the woman in the bed. "So, now I have another request."

"I'm afraid I can't help you any further."

"Oh, I think you will because I'll need a DNA swab on this woman."

"Oh my." He stared from the woman in the bed to Kate and back again. He didn't appear to know what to say.

"Surely that's not an invasive act," Kate noted. "We can just take a swab from her mouth."

"Yes, yes, that. I must contact the family."

"Feel free. I'll be standing right here, waiting."

"Oh dear."

"I spoke to her brother Doug just this morning."

"Right, yes, I could call Mr. Feldspar. Excuse me." He hurried outside, then quickly disappeared down the hallway, almost running.

Kate stared down at the woman who was way too old to be Doug's sister. After all, Kate had just met the man two days ago. Something was seriously off.

SIMON WALKED BACK to the main part of the reception area, and, when he heard what he thought was Kate's voice, he turned to see her down a hallway, standing outside of a door while on her phone. He wasn't at all sure what was going on, but she turned in his direction and then frowned and narrowed her gaze.

He smiled, looked down at the receptionist, and, appearing grateful, said, "Thank you very much for your time."

"No problem," she murmured in obvious delight.

"Do you have a rate sheet or something?"

"No, sir, I'm sorry. It will all depend entirely on the needs of the patient," she murmured. "We can certainly set you up with a consultation though."

He nodded. "Okay, let me consider my options, and I'll get back to you." She gave him a beaming smile and he headed out to his car. As soon as he got there, he sent Kate a text. **What's up?** But he didn't wait long before she came out of the building and down the front steps and headed right for him.

"Why are you here?" she asked him.

Such an ominous tone filled her words that he shook his head, then smiled. "After talking to Harry and his cousin Reenie, who works here, I decided to check it out. Alison has been here as long as Harry's cousin has worked here, and she didn't think there was any chance of Alison's improvement or recovery."

Kate nodded. "According to the medical records, that's quite true."

"I just didn't want it to be another case of someone being drugged and held against their will."

"I'm not even sure it's a case of that," she muttered. "It may well be far more sinister."

He frowned at her. "What is more sinister than not letting the sister ever wake up again?"

She sighed. "In this case, I don't think the patient here is Alison Feldspar, the sister."

AFTER SPEAKING TO Simon, Kate headed back inside the facility and sat in the reception area, when Doug bolted in.

When he sat down beside her, his chest heaved badly. "What the hell is going on?"

"Try to calm down. I just want to do a DNA test," she whispered.

"Why do you need that? It's my sister," he declared, staring down the long hall.

"How often have you visited her?"

"Never. I haven't. I just couldn't."

"Okay, so come with me then." Kate stood. "Come tell me that your sister is the patient here."

He bounded to his feet and stared nervously down the hall. "I haven't seen her since … you know."

"And yet she's your sister."

He glared at her. "Don't judge me."

"Then let me have a DNA sample from her—and from you, for that matter." He looked at her in astonishment. She shrugged. "Is that so hard to understand?"

He frowned, then nodded. "Let's go."

And, with that, she led him down the hallway. As she opened the door to go inside, Doug stopped her.

"Wait, I'm really nervous."

"Why?"

"I haven't seen her in so long."

"Come on, You can see her now," she suggested encouragingly.

He sighed, stepped inside, and looked at the patient in the bed. "This is the wrong room."

"Is it?" she asked. "This is who they say is your sister."

He looked again at the woman in the bed and shook his head. "No way. This cannot be. My sister is way younger than that."

"Exactly," Kate murmured. "This is why I need this woman's DNA. And yours."

He stared at her in shock. "But then where's my sister?"

"I don't know," Kate replied. Yet the nagging in the back of her mind said that Kate should have a good idea where Alison Feldspar was.

***

BACK IN HER office, after delivering two DNA swabs to forensics, Kate was sitting at her desk when Dr. Smidge called her.

"It's a young woman, about eighteen years of age at the time of her death. I'll have more for you when I get her on my table."

"A couple more things before you go," she added. "What caused her death, and how long has she been in the ground?"

"I'll say close to a decade in the ground, but you'll have to wait for a definite answer on that. Cause of death? Yeah, a gunshot to the head." And, with that, he disconnected.

She sat down and got out her notes, then put up a big whiteboard and methodically placed evidence there just to clear her mind. When Lilliana, Rodney, and Owen joined her, she was still zoned out from the events of the day so far. When Lilliana called her name, Kate snapped out of it.

"I got DNA from the patient in the care facility just a few blocks from Simon's place. That's supposed to be Doug's brain-damaged sister, Alison Feldspar, but no way in hell it's his sister, she's too old. Doug agreed. Now Smidge has confirmed the dead body in the Feldspar backyard is most likely the sister, age eighteen, buried ten years ago."

"Did Doug explain why he never went to see her?"

"Yeah, he hasn't seen her since the murders went down. He's got this phobia about hospitals, and she was a vegetable anyway, and visiting her would just be a constant reminder of what happened."

"He sounds like a real piece of work," Owen muttered in disgust.

"He's still a very traumatized young man," she murmured. "That's what I see. As much as I wanted to think that he might have done all this, I don't see it now."

"So, we have a case of mistaken identity," Lilliana noted, "but, so far, we don't have more than that."

"I presume the comatose woman in the facility is the missing aunt, who was obviously much older than Alison."

"What possible reason would there be for switching the sister with the aunt?" Lilliana asked, looking at Kate in confusion.

"That's the question of the day," Kate said, "and I'm waiting for more data."

Reese came in just then. "I did a review on the Feldspar trust and the company in charge of it and got the formal partnership filing and board of directors' information."

"And?" Kate asked, turning to look at her.

Reese smiled and asked, "You already know, don't you?"

"I have a pretty good idea. I just don't know how we're supposed to prove any of it. That's where you come in."

"DNA should prove something," Rodney added, now at her side, as he looked at Reese. "Kate seems to have figured out some of this mess, but we haven't. So you want to fill us in?"

Reese laughed. "It would appear that whoever survives this gets to keep everything in the estate."

"Of course, and that much all of us can guess," Kate said. "Come on. … Give it to me straight."

"What you don't know is there is a court order where Darrian Jackson has full guardianship and power of attorney over the entire family."

"Interesting. With most of the family dead, including the sister, or so we think now," Kate pointed out, with half a smile, "that leaves surviving brother Doug and the no-longer-missing aunt, now comatose in a facility downtown?"

"Yes, those two."

"Interesting, but who is the ultimate beneficiary?" Lilliana asked.

"My money is on Darrian," Kate spoke up. "To further complicate things, I think the DNA swabs will confirm Doug's birth father is actually Darrian, and Doug's supposed aunt, who's the brain-dead one in the facility, may actually be Doug's birth mother."

"Whoa, whoa, whoa. Hang on a minute. How does that work?" Lilliana asked.

"The aunt and the sister both had very similar features, and the aunt took a shotgun blast to the face. It's amazing that she didn't die, and everybody identified her as Doug's sister, Alison, ten years ago. However, today Alison has been potentially ID'd and found buried in the Felspar backyard."

"In other words, it's all conjecture until we get the DNA."

"Yes, but that still doesn't make any sense," Lilliana complained, hopping to her feet, as she started pacing. "So, we have a couple, who have a daughter and a son, but the son doesn't belong to them. He really belongs to the aunt and Darrian?"

"Yes," Kate stated. "There was a formal adoption of Doug by the Feldspar parents, and, because it was an adoption, everything Feldspar had was left to him and his sister. Since Alison died, Doug was the only heir remaining. All the shares, the companies, the assets, all of the Feldspar earnings, everything was given to Doug, but biologically he is Darrian's son. Now, whether Doug knows that or not is a different story."

"Right," Rodney agreed, "but that doesn't mean that Darrian killed anybody. He's an accountant, potentially just looking after his client's assets, which happens to be his son in this case."

"Exactly," Kate noted. "So the question is, why all the cover-ups? Why the swap of the sister with the aunt? Why is the Feldspar aunt in a hospital bed under Alison Feldspar's name, and why did they then bury the Feldspar daughter in the backyard? The Feldspar murders were originally reported to be three dead; the parents and a grandmother."

"Have you seen the full face on this woman in the facility?" Lilliana asked Kate.

"Yes, but half her face is completely twisted, from the original gunshot wound, and maybe cosmetic procedures to fix them. So I really couldn't tell how old she was for certain. Plus, patients in comas age very quickly in some cases, so age is not always that easy to estimate."

"Right, so either way, we have a mess. Does Doug know he was adopted, and does it matter? And who the hell would have killed the entire family?"

Kate stared off into the distance. "Only one person would have been in the middle of all this, and that's Darrian." She turned to Rodney. "We need to bring him in for a talk."

He nodded, as he headed toward his desk to make some calls and to get Darrian picked up.

Meanwhile her phone rang, and she picked it up.

"What did you say to him?" Doug cried out, "What did you say to him? I told you that he had nothing to do with this!"

"Whoa, whoa, whoa, Doug, hang on a minute. What are you talking about?"

"Darrian, I'm talking about Darrian! He told me that he's leaving the country and that he won't be back. The cops are on his case, and no way you'll set him up for any of this."

"I haven't even talked to him," she stated in astonishment, even as she motioned to Lilliana, mouthing to her, *Call the airports.*

Racing to her desk, Lilliana made those calls.

"Listen, Doug. I haven't even talked to Darrian. I haven't contacted him in any way, so whatever he's telling you, he's getting his information from somewhere else, potentially from a long time ago."

Silence came from the other end. "He said you tried to make it look as if he was involved."

"First of all, are you aware that Darrian is your birth father?"

A shocked gasp came on the other end. "What?"

"Yes, you are adopted, and your birth mother was also

not who you thought she was. Your birth mother was your aunt, Albert Feldspar's sister. Your aunt and Darrian had an affair, and you were the result, and the Feldspars adopted you. So they had one boy and one girl. Of course you were already family, so that was good. Your biological mother, the woman you were raised to believe was your aunt, could never have any more children, so it appears she stuck close to the family because that was the only way she could stay close to you."

"No, no, no."

Kate continued. "As you know, we're in the process of doing a DNA test run on the woman in the hospital bed. I believe we will find she is your aunt, your birth mother."

"Well, she sure as hell isn't my sister."

Kate took a deep breath. "We also found a body buried in the back of the Feldspar property. We think it may be Alison."

He started to cry. "What are you doing? Why are you saying all this?"

"Because it's true, but we haven't positively identified the body yet," she clarified. "All I can tell you is that it'll take a little bit for us to sort through all this."

"Jesus," he muttered. "So you're saying Darrian is my father, and my sister was murdered a decade ago, and my biological mother is in that hospital bed? How is that even a thing?"

"I'm not yet certain which one of the women—your adopted mother or your biological mother—is in that hospital bed, but it's not your sister."

"But she's also not my sister," he wailed.

"She's your adopted sister. Biologically speaking, she would have been your cousin too."

"Christ," he said in a gutted tone. "What does any of this have to do with anything? It's too much," he muttered, "and it doesn't make any sense."

"No, it doesn't make any sense," Kate agreed, "but, if you had looked at any of the financial documents you've been getting quarterly, maybe some of it would have."

"All of this has now been revealed because some homeless guy died?"

"Because a homeless guy who was always at the Paragon building and had either stolen documents from your house or been given documents from the Feldspar house … or something," she shared. "Those papers led us back to this cold case of the Feldspar murders. Plus, the papers you sent me confirmed that you have a family trust that Darrian runs. If anything happens to you or the woman in the facility, Darrian gets everything. Regardless he has full control over everything in your world."

"Jesus Christ." Doug started to bawl.

"I'll come over and talk to you."

"No, no, don't. … I need some time."

"Okay," Kate relented, "but don't do anything bad."

"No, no, not at all," he whispered, "but you just dropped a ton of bombs on me."

"I know … but you wanted answers, and I'm just doing my job. What about your other cousin? Rosemary? The one who had the twins with Ted Mahoney?"

"What about her? Or is she not my cousin either?"

"I don't know, but it would be interesting to get her DNA tested."

"Why? Is she part of this?"

"I don't know. How has Darrian treated her?"

He hesitated. "Honestly? Like shit."

"Then chances are she's not anybody's family member and has no money?"

"No, Rosemary definitely had no money, and honestly I think she really liked the old guy, Mahoney. I think she really cared for him."

Kate agreed. "From what I've learned, Rosemary had a shitty life, I think, until she hooked up with old man Mahoney."

"She spent a lot of time with my father—my adopted father."

"The same way your sister Alison spent time with Albert?"

"Yeah," Doug muttered.

Kate shook her head. "Rosemary was pretty damn young, so that sounds like grooming to me. ... You might want a talk with her about that because, if you were right about your sister being abused, it could explain why Alison is dead. Maybe somebody killed her to keep her quiet. I still don't know why your adoptive parents were killed."

"I don't know either," Doug muttered, "but none of this makes any sense."

"It will," Kate noted. "It will eventually, but I need to talk to Darrian."

Doug gave a broken laugh. "Absolutely no way he'll talk to you now."

"Yeah? Let's hope you're wrong about that."

"Why?" he cried out. "Isn't it bad enough that you've absolutely destroyed my life?"

"I'm trying to help you put it back together again," she declared, her voice firm. "You can't make any headway here if it's all built on lies, so you need the truth. All of it."

"The truth as you say it," he snapped. "I lost my adoptive parents, and now I won't even have my own parents anymore."

"Your birth mother, your aunt, may need to be reevaluated, so don't give up hope for her. And Darrian remains your biological father, a living family member, whether he lives here or not," Kate pointed out. "How come that doesn't fill you with joy?"

He hesitated.

She took a deep breath and forged ahead. "It doesn't fill you with joy because, in your heart of hearts, you never really trusted Darrian. Yet do you realize how much you have left in his care? The whole Feldspar family trust is in his hands."

"I didn't care about the money," Doug muttered.

"I know that, but remember my suggestion about looking after yourself and these assets in case something might happen? You have more reasons than ever to do that right now."

"He won't do anything to me," Doug snapped. "I'm his son, remember? And my mother, the one he had an affair with, he's been paying for her care at the facility. So what's the problem?"

"Yeah, but you didn't know all this before, and maybe he didn't want you to know. Maybe he's happy *not* telling you."

"That would imply that he knew about all this."

"Don't you think he did?" Kate asked. "Who do you think arranged for your adoption?"

"Ah, shit. So he didn't want me either."

"Or he wanted you taken care of in a way that didn't require him to put in too much effort," she suggested. "Either way, let's get to the bottom of it, once and for all."

Just then in the background she heard another voice on

Doug's end of the call.

Doug replied, "What are you doing here? I thought you were heading to the airport?"

Kate frantically yelled, "Doug, get out of there. Get out of there now!"

"What are you talking about?"

Then she heard a loud *bang*.

SIMON WALKED AROUND downtown, heading from one rehab project to the next. He was a little confused over what was going on at the facility he had recently visited, but he knew that he wouldn't see Kate until she got to the crux of the matter. In his mind, he kept going over why they would try to pass off one patient as another, and it always came back to money. As he headed toward another rehab project he had going on, he felt something weird cross his shoulders. He looked around but saw nothing. He also had a weird sensation of being followed. So he stepped into an alleyway and waited. When he thought that maybe the timing would be right, he stepped out, only to again find nothing there.

Swearing, he called out, "If any ghosts are here, damn it, leave me alone." At that, he heard a laugh behind him, and, sure enough, he saw the older homeless guy, always wearing the same cap.

"Yeah," he replied, still chuckling. "Ghosts are here all right, and they've been haunting me forever."

"You mean, since your two friends died this week?"

He nodded. "Yeah, since then."

"That's because you didn't tell the cops everything."

He glared at him. "What the hell am I supposed to do?" he muttered and then looked as if he were about to cry.

"They're cops. We don't talk to cops."

"No, but you talked to the wrong guy too, didn't you? *Darrian.*"

He nodded. "Yeah, everybody talked to Darrian."

"Why is that?"

He shrugged. "He used to pay us for information on the streets. So, we would listen in on deals, listen to conversations in coffee shops, street corners, wherever," he explained. "If we came up with something good, he would pay us for it. But Frankie was getting a little too snippy about how Darrian didn't pay for every tip, but still Darrian paid for the best stuff. Every once in a while, if you had something you knew was golden, Darrian would still be good for it. But it wasn't the same as before, and we had to prove we had something of value in order to be of interest to him," the older guy explained.

Simon nodded. "I need you to come down to the police station and tell all that to the cops."

"*Nah,* I don't feel like telling them nothing."

"How about the fact that Darrian is behind a lot of these murders, including the deaths of your two friends?"

He swallowed. "Now that I believe," he moaned.

"Yet, if you don't tell the cops, you'll always be looking behind you for Darrian because you can't stop him. You can't take the chance of letting down your guard because Darrian could end your life. Guaranteed."

"If you put him behind bars, then I won't have to worry about it, will I?"

"That's why I need you to come back with me and talk to the cops."

"Nope, not unless you get him locked up first," he argued, stepping back from Simon. "You get him locked up so he'll never get out, then maybe I talk to the cops. In the meantime, no way in hell."

Simon glared at him, shaking his head. "What about your friends? Don't they deserve anything?"

"They were stupid. I told Shawn not to talk to Darrian, to just leave him alone, that he was bad. Darrian hadn't been the same since he got all *bigwiggy*."

"You mean, he hadn't been the same since the Feldspar murders?"

He nodded. "I always wondered if he had something to do with that. I still do, but I have no reason for it though."

"Oh, there's a reason for it, probably all about greed. We'll find out even more soon," Simon shared.

At that, the older man whispered, "Probably about the young girl."

"What young girl?" Simon worried this old man knew way more than he was saying.

"The one he was abusing."

"Darrian? I thought Albert Feldspar was the abuser?"

"Maybe." He shook his head. "Darrian likes them young, probably was abusing both cousins. It doesn't matter to him, he just likes them. It was Darrian's idea that Mahoney married Feldspar's niece and had the whole second marriage."

"You knew about that?"

"Sure, we knew about it. We were always listening for gossipy tidbits. That's the thing with guys like Darrian. He wants to hear the word on the street, and then we get some that is all about him. Seems Darrian was a blood relation to Albert."

Simon frowned at that, thinking of all the tangled webs in that disturbed family. He had to tell Kate, but he didn't want to interrupt this guy, not while he was in a sharing mode. Simon nodded.

The older guy continued. "Shawn told him way back when about the second marriage."

"Hang on a minute, Shawn told Darrian?"

"Yeah, Shawn told Darrian that Jet and Daisy were still married. Shawn had seen them together at work, and that's when Darrian went to Mahoney's second wife and told her."

"And you know this for sure?"

He shrugged. "Shawn told me, starting to wonder what was going on. That was a while ago. But I think he put a little bit too much together eventually, and that killed him."

"So, how did he end up at Feldspar's house?"

"Probably looking for justice. He wanted to go there anyway, and he might have been looking for some evidence. You know there's a secret room in that house, right?"

When Simon just stared at him, the older guy nodded. "Will probably take a builder to find it."

"Or maybe not," Simon muttered. "Maybe I'll find it. Any idea what floor it's on?"

"No clue, but, if you find it, you put away that asshole Darrian. You do that, and I'll come give a statement because that Darrian guy is bad news." And, with that, he turned and walked away.

Simon picked up the phone, calling Kate. When he got no answer, he raced up to the Feldspar house himself. He got into the empty house and gave it a serious analysis, then headed up to the second floor and smiled. Off the master suite was an extra six feet that wasn't accounted for.

He quickly picked up his phone and took several photos of it, and then seeing a rip in the dry wall on one spot, he punched his fist through it and started ripping out some of the wall. Sure enough, he found a small room. A sickening little room with all kinds of sex toys. But it was also a room that seemingly nobody could get in or out of. As he stood here staring in shock, his phone rang.

"You called? What's up?" Kate asked.

"You need to come to the Feldspar house."

"I can't. Darrian is on the run. I've got everybody out looking for him. He shot Doug."

"Ah, hell, I'm fucking too late again."

"That depends on what you've got."

"I've got a secret room in the Feldspar house, full of what seems to be a little torture chamber."

"Yeah, probably made by Albert especially for Alison, his daughter," she shared in disgust.

"I think there may be two victims because the niece, Rosemary Feldspar, was also abused. And maybe both girls were abused by both Albert and Darrian."

"I'm on my way to go talk to Rosemary then," Kate replied in exasperation. "If you can take some photos and send them to me, I'll turn them over to a forensic team."

"One more thing. Darrian and Albert seem to be related, may be brothers." He ended the call and promptly took several photos, then sent those to Kate. Meanwhile Simon waited until the forensic team showed up. It only took a few minutes, as a team was still working in the backyard. He pointed them to the secret room, and they stood there staring.

"Christ, sometimes I hate my job," Smidge muttered.

"If no blood is in there, what are the chances it was consensual?" Simon asked, hoping against hope.

The forensic guys looked at him and shook their heads. "It would be nice to think that we could find a situation like that once, but it's the exact opposite. Nobody gets to say yes or no in a deal like this. It's always all about satisfying the addictions of the men."

"I suspect that's what we'll find in this case too," Smidge added.

Simon shook his head. "I'll leave it to you." And with that, he turned away.

Feeling a certain disbelief and edginess, probably brought on by his own history, he turned and escaped that house of horrors. It might be a good property for somebody, but it sure as hell wouldn't be for him.

CHAPTER 27

K ATE STOOD IN front of the room of horrors, shaking her head, when her phone rang.

"We got him," Rodney crowed. "Darrian was already at the boarding area for the plane."

"As long as you got him, that is awesome. Bring him on down to the station. We need to have a little talk with this asshole."

"Where are you?"

"I'm heading over to speak with wife number two, after seeing this little chamber of horrors."

"Is it really all about sex abuse?"

"It was for somebody anyway. I'm not sure who though. Could be both Albert and Darrian as abusers of both Alison and Rosemary. Regardless it'll still be about money too," she noted.

"Christ, those guys are sick."

"I'll see you at the station." When he ended the call, she got back into her vehicle, tired beyond belief, and drove to see the cousin. As Kate walked up to the front door, Rosemary opened the door, her shoulders slumped.

"What do you want?" she muttered.

"First off, Doug is in the hospital. Darrian shot him."

The woman's jaw dropped.

"Doug's injured but should be okay. Darrian has been

picked up, trying to leave the country, and is now on his way to my station, so I can interview him before jailing him."

At that, she burst into tears. "Please tell me that you're not lying."

"I'm not lying. I'm telling the truth as I know it."

"He's really been picked up?"

"Yes, he won't hurt you or Doug again."

Rosemary started to sob. "It wasn't him, as much as it was Albert Feldspar," she murmured. "I mean, it was Darrian for a while, but I just wasn't enough to be of interest. But Albert? … It just got ugly."

"Is that why you married Daisy's husband?"

She nodded. "Darrian told me that Jet wasn't married, but I knew he was," she whispered. "I was just trying to get away."

"How old are you?"

"I'm thirty. I married Jet when I was what? Seventeen?"

"Just to escape Albert?"

"Yes, and I couldn't have cared less who it was, but, as it turned out, Jet was a good man to me."

She nodded. "I'll need a statement from you too."

"Yeah, I understand, but I need you to wait so I can get a babysitter arranged."

"That's fine."

Rosemary quickly arranged with a neighbor to come over. While getting into the car with Kate, Rosemary asked, "Does Daisy hate us?"

"I think she feels betrayed at the utmost level, but she's also old and dying and very sad. She doesn't know who to blame, more or less."

Rosemary nodded. "When I realized Jet had died and knew he really was married, I felt so guilty, like I was the bad person," she shared, "and it just brought everything back."

"Do you know what happened ten years ago at the Feldspar house?"

She nodded.

"I need that statement from you too, and then I need to go see Doug," Kate murmured.

"He's alive, right? He's a good guy, but he's just so messed up."

"I know," Kate agreed. "We weren't exactly sure who was involved in this mess, but Doug is probably in the clear."

"No *probably* about it," Rosemary declared, "he is."

"Did you also know he's adopted?"

She stared at her in shock. "No, I didn't know that at all."

"He's Darrian's biological son."

Rosemary slapped her hand over her mouth in horror. "Who's the mother?"

"His aunt is his biological mother."

"Oh my God. Jesus Christ." She said, staring at Kate in horror.

"What is your biological connection to them?"

She shook her head. "None that I know of. I was adopted too. I wound up living with the Feldspars for quite a few years because my birth parents were killed in a car accident."

"The good news is," Kate noted, "you should be no blood relative to Doug then."

Rosemary looked over at Kate, and a slow smile started in her gaze. "How did you know?"

"Because he's very protective of you, and you're very protective of him," Kate explained. "Maybe now you both can get past all this bullshit and heal and maybe have a real life, full of love and fun and happiness."

"Only if you put Darrian away."

"That's why I need your statement, about the sexual abuse at the very minimum."

Rosemary started to sob.

Kate added, "We found the secret room."

"Oh, God, that room. The first time I woke up in there … I had been drugged and was inside that room. I can remember everything when I woke up … my hands secured with handcuffs on the wall," she whispered, and then she started to cry, completely past the point of being able to talk.

Kate nodded. "It was also happening to Alison, Albert's own daughter, wasn't it?"

"Yes, both of us, yet we never said a word to each other. And then that night that Albert and Mandy were supposed to go out, but Albert came home early, without Mandy. Alison was there. Albert went to take her into the secret room, but she fought and fought and fought. It got ugly, very ugly, and honestly I don't even know who shot who," Rosemary admitted. "The next thing I know … everybody's supposedly dead. I left the house, screaming. I felt terrible forever afterward because Alison died that night. I was outside hiding in the trees, just so Albert wouldn't find me. But I could hear them. God, I could hear them."

Kate listened, knowing some of it was being filled in by poor memories, and some of it was being filled in by images and sounds seared into Rosemary's mind. Yet the bottom line was that they were finally getting to the bottom of it. "And Darrian? When did he show up?"

"He showed up immediately because he was already there," she declared. "I don't even know if Doug knew that, but Darrian had been in the backyard on the phone at the time, though I don't know for how long."

"Did you hear the gunshots?"

"Not really, no," she replied, shaking her head. "I was crying in the backyard because of Albert coming home early. It got so ugly, and I took off," she murmured.

"They told the cops that an intruder broke in."

"No, I'm pretty sure the intruder was either Darrian or Alison fighting back." Rosemary looked at Kate hopefully. "Maybe that all escalated when Mandy Feldspar came home looking for Albert. I don't know. … Yet I would be totally okay if Alison fought back," Rosemary whispered. "We had a shitty life there."

"I get that," Kate agreed, "but I highly suspect Darrian was the shooter."

"I always wondered, since he was just a little too conveniently there. Yet we were so shocked and so upset that we didn't know who, what, or anything. And then it wasn't that long before the cops handling the case were killed too. That was terrible, and we didn't know what happened, yet we were scared that we *did* know. It seemed anybody who was involved could be killed. So everything just went away. Nobody had answers, and we didn't ask for any or offer any. As long as you didn't open that door, the boogeyman can't come in, right?"

"That's exactly what the problem is," Kate muttered. "I'm pretty sure it's the boogeyman you both knew."

Rosemary sobbed, wiping her eyes. "I'll make a statement."

"Good, and what will that statement say?"

"That Darrian sexually abused me for years, both Albert and Darrian did. That night of the murders, Albert Feldspar went after Alison, and her mom was gone somewhere. I think Mandy came home, maybe suspicious because her husband came home at an odd time. I don't know," Rosemary said. "It's just bits and pieces I figured out over the years. Mandy probably found out what Albert was doing."

"So, who shot who then?"

"I don't know," she whispered. "I really don't know."

But Kate was pretty darn sure she knew. She headed down to the station and got Lilliana to take the statement from Rosemary. As she walked into the interview room, Darrian sat there in his expensive suit, cleaning imaginary lint off his sleeve.

Sitting down, she smiled and pressed Record and began, "Everything is about to come crashing down on you. I am not sorry for you at all."

He stiffened, glared at her, and stated, "My lawyer is on the way."

"Good," she said. "You'll definitely need him. We have first degree murder, four counts. Plus, we have the sexual assault of two minors, which abuse continued for years. Let's see now. What else? We also have fraud and illegal adoptions and what we'll call kidnapping for now." She flipped through the pages of notes she had written down.

"What the hell?" He stared at her in shock. "What are you talking about?"

"Did you really not think anybody would ever find out about all that? We have proof that Doug is your biological son and that Alison is buried in the backyard of the Feldspar property and that you shot Doug's biological mother in the face and, when she didn't die outright, you drugged her for a decade."

The color drained from his face.

Kate continued. "I presume that the only reason you buried Alison in the backyard was so you could continue to control the trust fund." Darrian opened his jaw, then closed it, and she nodded. "Yeah, we've got it all, including statements from Doug and Rosemary, how the only reason Rosemary married Jet Mahoney was to get away from you and Albert."

He flushed bright red now.

"Right?" Kate asked but didn't expect an answer. "Why did you kill Albert and Mandy Feldspar? I would like to think that you killed them out of some altruistic ideal, but I highly suspect you had a more sinister motive."

"He was abusing that poor girl," he stated stiffly, "I would have done anything to protect her."

"That poor girl?" she repeated, looking at him "What do you mean, *that poor girl?* Alison, the same poor girl who you were abusing? You were abusing both Alison and Rosemary, weren't you?" He flushed. "Wow, are you and Albert brothers?" His eyes widened, and she nodded. "That even makes more sense now, and that's why you spent so much time over there. That's how come you were as busy with him as you were. Did Albert even know?"

Darrian shook his head. "He didn't know. We were adopted at birth by separate families. We found each other quite a bit later."

"So, you're both just the same kind of people? You both liked to abuse young girls."

"That's not fair. I absolutely loved that little girl."

"Your niece, Rosemary, or Albert's daughter, Alison?"

"Yes, I loved them both," he stated. "However, I think a certain part of my brother started to hate Rosemary because he felt as if he couldn't ever cut his ties to her, and he constantly wanted her."

"And what about Alison?"

"Her too. It was a pretty-ugly scenario there for a while."

"And Doug?"

"He didn't know about any of it. I suppose you'll tell him now."

"Oh, he already knows about Alison being abused by Albert. However, Doug doesn't know about you abusing Rosemary and Alison, or the fact that you killed Alison."

"I didn't kill her," he said in a monotone. "Her father was doing a hell of a good job of that. By the time his wife got home, screaming and yelling at him, Alison was already dying on the floor in front of them both. Mandy ran to get the gun from the safe and came back down to shoot her husband. When I took it from her it went off accidentally, and there was nothing I could do. Mandy died right in front of me. Then I turned, and, using her hand, pulled the trigger and killed Albert, the piece of shit that he was."

"You mean that piece of shit who was your brother?"

"Yeah, the one who was so busy damaging these girls so much that he actually killed one."

"Whereas, you just loved them."

He looked at her and nodded. "Yes, I wasn't going to abuse them any longer," he shared, staring off in the distance. "I don't expect you to understand."

"I don't," Kate declared. "It's hard for me to believe that you had sex with these young girls and were ever planning on stopping it."

"I *was* planning on stopping it," he said softly, "but it was really hard to do."

"So, you never quite succeeded."

"I let Rosemary get married off, didn't I? That was her way of getting out of it, and I respected that and let her go. Didn't she get out and get married?"

"So, if that is true, which woman is comatose in the facility?"

He flushed. "Don't bother making it sound as if it's Alison because we know that it's not." He nodded. "Alison had her own trust funds from her grandmother. It was a huge amount of money, but it was left without a will because she died so young. Her father, Albert, being the idiot that he was, hadn't set it up to go to anybody other than himself, and I couldn't take the chance of losing it. So, considering that his sister and, therefore, my sister, is unconscious in that hospital bed, it just seemed to be a prudent idea to keep the money flowing until I could move it all."

"And did you?"

"Oh, yes, I sure did." He shrugged. "Honestly, the family is beyond wealthy, a stupid amount of money, and why should they have it all?"

"And the incest continued, as you obviously had sex with your own sister, who later gave birth to Doug?" Kate felt the bile rising in her throat.

"I don't suppose you will keep that from Doug either?" he asked, maybe feeling some shame at this point.

Kate shook her head in disbelief. "What baffles me is how you don't question all this abhorrent selfish behavior—until you are found out. Disgusting." His only response was to remain silent. "So, of course, with you in their lives, your own son and niece and sister remain desperately in need of financial, medical, and emotional help, yet not getting the benefit of what is rightly theirs."

"They aren't *desperately in need*," Darrian argued. "Yet you'll make sure I don't get anything now, right?"

"You'll be in prison. You will never get free. You won't see the light of day again from your cell," she stated, with a nod in his direction. "So I don't really think that your lack of money will be a problem."

He glared at her. "You don't understand."

"But you'll tell me, won't you?"

"Why should I?" he asked, crossing his arms.

But she sensed the wariness in him. "Because you're done, and you're tired. I don't know if you've got a disease or something, but when you ran to the airport to get out of the country, you couldn't quite do it, could you? You came back and shot Doug, and I think that finished something inside you."

He stared at her, that tic in his jaw working away.

That tic must be a genetic thing. "You really cared about Doug. He's your own blood. You knew that, right?"

He nodded slowly. "I did know. Is he dead?"

"No, and hopefully he'll survive."

He closed his eyes and nodded. "Thank God for that."

"So was it all just about the money?"

"No," he replied rather forcefully. "It was about love and money. … I know it may sound stupid to you," he began, with a shrug, "but we were two rich old men, having whatever we wanted. Only when I realized what Albert was doing to his own daughter did I also realize how perverted and how wrong my own addiction was." He swore under his breath. "Yet there was no way to fix what I'd already done."

"Did you abuse Rosemary after she married Jet?"

He shook his head. "No, I even got her into therapy, but it won't ever be enough to make up for what I did, for what Albert did. I know that."

"No, it sure won't," Kate agreed. "That one night alone had a hell of a lot going on there."

"Maybe, but shooting Mandy was an accident. Shooting

my brother? That was deliberate. ... He had killed his own daughter," Darrian shared, with a sad sigh. "Then of course, today I shot my own son." He looked off in the distance. "I don't know what's wrong with me. I don't know what's wrong with any of us." He dropped his head. "Somewhere along the line, all that money, all that ability to have and to do whatever we wanted, it corrupts you."

With that, Kate stood, sick to her stomach. "You'll have the rest of your life to contemplate it."

And she turned and walked out.

⸻❧⸻

"I DON'T UNDERSTAND why I had to come in," Amie snapped, glaring at Kate resentfully. "You could have told me over the phone."

"We're waiting for the Crown prosecutor as to whether he wants to press Obstruction of Justice charges against you for trying to make your husband's suicide look like murder."

Amie's gaze widened, and she looked at Rodney for sympathy, but he wasn't having any of it. He shook his head at her. "The Crown prosecutor will make that call."

Amie glared at him. "So I can leave now?"

"No," Kate stated cheerfully. She placed a copy of the email and the documents she'd received from the Manila police department in front of Amie.

"What's this?" Amie asked.

"A written confession from a murder-for-hire killer out of Manila."

She paled, her skin flashing white, before it flushed in a deep and dark ugly red. She didn't look at the paperwork but instead glared into Kate's eyes. "You hate me so much that you would dig that deep?"

"I didn't have to," Kate said serenely. "This killer friend of yours was caught in reference to a *different* case, but, while he was ratting out the rest of those he knew on other cases, he ratted you out too. He grew up with you, and, when you were desperate to get rid of your husband, he dropped the price to something you could afford, as he was happy to help you out, for old time's sake."

She sucked in her breath and forgot to breathe.

Kate wondered if she would have to call in help, until Amie's breath finally gusted out.

"I didn't kill him."

"Correct," Kate agreed. "You paid your childhood friend to do the job for you. And, of course, Manila wants you back to serve time over there. Apparently you're still a citizen, and the murder was committed in their city. They are not happy."

"I can't go back," she cried out. "I'll never get a fair trial. You don't know what it's like over there. Everyone is a criminal. The place is a fucking nightmare."

Rodney stood and added, "Sounds as if you'll fit right in."

"Wait. There must be something I can do to not go back," she cried out in a panic. "Surely there's something? Anything?"

Rodney eyed Kate. Kate glanced at Rodney, then back at Amie. "With all this uncovered, now there are questions regarding your first husband's death. If you're in jail here, you can't be extradited."

It took Aimie seconds to make that decision, and she nodded. "I killed him. I made it look like a suicide. I didn't know I wouldn't get the life insurance. Which is how I knew I couldn't let my last husband go out the same way, or I would get nothing," she snapped bitterly. "It's all wrong. All of it."

"It so is," Kate agreed smoothly, as she slid a pad of paper across the table, along with a pen. "A full confession on murdering your first husband now."

Amie's face pinched, but then she picked up her pen and started writing. When done, she was escorted away.

Rodney looked at Kate. "Will you tell her that Manila can ask for her to be deported *after* she's served her time here?"

Kate gave him a fat smile. "Absolutely ... *not*."

CHAPTER 28

KATE STARED UP at the blue sky. The sun was hot, but it was December, where it could be chilly at night, especially when out on Simon's boat on the water. She had on a hoodie, atop her long-sleeved T-shirt and jeans, and she was stretched out on the deck, with a tumbler of coffee beside her.

Simon was stretched out beside her, her back to his chest, as they gently floated in the ocean. "Are you okay?" he asked.

"I'm okay, just a very strange case."

"Power and money corrupt. We know that."

"People who can have whatever they want?" She gave a headshake. "They just feel as if they're entitled, even when they're hurting other people."

He nodded. "That's quite true. There is that sense of entitlement always."

"It's sad and it sucks," she muttered.

"I can't argue with you on that," he said. "I just want to ensure that, at the end of the day, you can walk away from it and know that you did a good job."

"I did do a good job, and hopefully now maybe the survivors will have a chance to settle into something better," she suggested, "but it'll be a pretty long haul to get the Feldspar case to trial."

"Do you think Darrian will plead guilty?"

"At this point in time, I think he will, unless his attorney talks him out of it. Darrian seems pretty disgusted with life at the moment."

"What about Doug and Rosemary?"

"Honestly, I think together they may begin to heal and to be a lot better for it. What would also be good is if Daisy could meet them and could find some peace for herself too."

"Daisy Mahoney, the first wife of Jet, right? So, what about Doug's biological mother?"

"Now that she has legit medical care, the best money can buy, she has hopefully more possibilities available to her. ... It's a beautiful day out here, warmer than I expected."

"It is," he replied.

She sat up, took off her hoodie, and stripped off her T-shirt. In seconds she was down to the buff.

He gasped, sat up, looked around for nearby boats, and whispered, "I didn't think it was *that* warm."

"Oh, the cold is not so bad," she shared with a knowing look. "I figured I can warm you up, at the same time I warm myself up." And she started stripping him down, while he laughed—not exactly fighting her off but definitely making her work for it. By the time she rolled down onto the cool deck beside him, he was more than ready for her. He pulled her arms up over her head, slid down her body, showering her with deep, passionate kisses. Then he murmured, "If this is makeup sex after closing a case, I'm all for it."

She pulled him down and whispered, "Less talk, more action." That was the last coherent word she managed to get out, as they made love outside in the sunlight.

When he finally collapsed beside her, she groaned and whispered, "And, no, it's definitely not makeup sex. ... It's

I'm so happy to be alive sex."

He rolled over, kissed her gently, pulled her up against his chest, and whispered, "That's okay too."

She smiled. "I'm glad to hear it."

"You cold? Do I need to grab a blanket?" With her nod, Simon stood and grabbed a couple blankets off the nearby deck chairs. He quickly covered her, then spooned with her, covering them both with the second blanket. "Now what is on your plate?"

"I get a couple days off to relax, and then you know what will happen. It'll be back to work on the next case. That's just how the system works."

He laughed. "With time off to sail and to have *happy to be alive* sex, you seem to handle things just fine."

This concludes Book 9 of Kate Morgan: Simon Says... Die.
Read about Kate Morgan: Simon Says... Think, Book 10

Simon Says... Think: Kate Morgan (Book #10)

Vancouver Detective Kate Morgan has had bad days before, but getting a message about her long-lost brother hit her hard. She couldn't trust some anonymous source, yet neither could she let any tip slide. What if it was the one tidbit that gave her information as to what happened to Timothy, now missing some twenty-six years and counting? She would do anything for those answers.

Simon St. Laurant, the reluctant psychic and her steadfast boyfriend, knows Kate is hurting on a level he has never seen before. He understands and would do everything possible to help her, even if it pushes him out of his comfort zone with his *gift*. When a little boy contacts Simon from the other side, he's trying to be hopeful …

However, as the case unravels, it doesn't go in the direction either of them thought—or had hoped it would.

Find Book 10 here!
To find out more visit Dale Mayer's website.
https://geni.us/DMSSSThink

Sneak Peek from
Simon Says... Think

Mid-December

SEVERAL DAYS LATER Kate Morgan walked into the office at ten o'clock in the morning.

Rodney looked up and smiled. "Wow, a late start for the day, *huh*?"

She groaned. "I had to stop in and see the dentist this morning." She tapped her mouth. "When Doug tackled me in the interview room, I took a blow on this side and had some cyst form," she muttered, as she headed straight for the coffee machine.

"That sounds disgusting."

"Yeah, right?" She gingerly sipped her hot coffee and winced as it washed over her mouth. "Anyway, it's all fine now." She sat down at her desk, sighed loudly, let her eyelids drop, and just relaxed. "Besides, I needed a couple days off." She'd spent it with Simon celebrating the purchase of the Paragon. Not that she understood his satisfaction with that building. Still, he was thrilled.

"You sure did." Rodney chuckled. "The good news is, we finished the rest of the open cases. Of course the bad news is that we have more new ones to take their place."

She nodded. "There is always another case." She sighed and asked, "Anything important?"

"They're all important."

"Don't give me that," she said. "Anything major, anything different, anything unique?"

At that, Reese walked in and put a parcel on Kate's desk. "This just came in for you."

Kate frowned at it, then opened it up. It seemed to be a wooden puzzle box. She shook her head. "I don't know why I have this."

"I don't know either," Reese confirmed, "but it's obviously addressed to you."

She frowned at the intricate box. "I hate these damn things. I hate anything that makes me feel stupid, and puzzle boxes always make me feel stupid."

"Why?" Rodney asked, as he walked over, looking at her gift. "Who's it from? How come nothing identifies the sender?"

She frowned, picked up the packaging, and nodded. "Good point."

Rodney added, "We should also have some system in place where we don't let people open parcels like these, unless we know for sure it's safe."

"I don't know that it *is* safe," she murmured, "but it's, for sure, a wooden puzzle box."

Rodney nodded, examining the gift. "I think you take out one of those pieces, and the whole thing comes apart somehow."

"You think so?" she asked. She frowned at it and tugged on one random piece. Sure enough, it came right out, and the whole thing fell apart. Inside was a small piece of paper. She picked it up, thinking it must have been some note from Simon. As she read the words, she froze. "*Uh-oh.*"

"What's the matter, Kate?" Rodney asked.

She looked over at him, the color draining from her face as she tried to speak.

He came around and snatched the note from her hand and read it. "What the hell?"

She looked at it again and frowned at Rodney.

Lilliana came over and asked, "What's going on, you two?"

"Look at the message that was inside the puzzle box." Rodney pointed at it.

"Read it," Kate muttered. "Read it out loud." Kate waited, squeezing her eyelids closed, waiting to hear the words that were now indelibly burned into her brain.

Lilliana read it out loud, as requested. "*Kate, if you want to see your brother again, time to start looking. You know what happened. You just have to think. Or maybe get Simon to help.*"

Kate swore, as her thoughts mixed and churned in her head. She stared up at the two of them. "Oh my God."

"Easy, Kate," Rodney told her. "You don't know that your brother's alive. You don't know that this isn't just some sick joke."

She stared up at him, tears in the back of her eyes, and she nodded. "I know that. … I know all of that, and yet it doesn't make a damn bit of difference. If there's any chance that my brother is alive—"

"I know. We understand," Rodney stated firmly. "We'll get to the bottom of this, honest."

She swallowed hard, even now as tears welled up in her eyes, and nodded. "Maybe, but who the hell would even know I was back to work today? Who the hell would know that my brother had gone missing all those years ago? Who the hell knows about Simon?"

Rodney and Lilliana shared a glance, then faced Kate.

Lilliana said, with no mercy in her tone, "Those are questions we'll have to ask you."

Find Book 10 here!

To find out more visit Dale Mayer's website.

https://geni.us/DMSSSThink

Author's Note

Thank you for reading Simon Says… Die: Kate Morgan, Book 9! If you enjoyed the book, please take a moment and leave a short review.

Dear reader,

I love to hear from readers, and you can contact me at my website: www.dalemayer.com or at my Facebook author page. To be informed of new releases and special offers, sign up for my newsletter or follow me on BookBub. And if you are interested in joining Dale Mayer's Reader Group, here is the Facebook sign up page.
http://geni.us/DaleMayerFBGroup

Cheers,
Dale Mayer

About the Author

Dale Mayer is a *USA Today* best-selling author, best known for her SEALs military romances, her Psychic Visions series, and her Lovely Lethal Garden cozy series. Her contemporary romances are raw and full of passion and emotion (Broken But … Mending, Hathaway House series). Her thrillers will keep you guessing (Kate Morgan, By Death series), and her romantic comedies will keep you giggling (*It's a Dog's Life*, a stand-alone novella; and the Broken Protocols series, starring Charming Marvin, the cat).

Dale honors the stories that come to her—and some of them are crazy, break all the rules and cross multiple genres!

To go with her fiction, she also writes nonfiction in many different fields, with books available on résumé writing, companion gardening, and the US mortgage system. All her books are available in print and ebook format.

Connect with Dale Mayer Online

Dale's Website – www.dalemayer.com
Twitter – @DaleMayer
Facebook Page – geni.us/DaleMayerFBFanPage
Facebook Group – geni.us/DaleMayerFBGroup
BookBub – geni.us/DaleMayerBookbub
Instagram – geni.us/DaleMayerInstagram
Goodreads – geni.us/DaleMayerGoodreads
Newsletter – geni.us/DaleNews